UNFORGIVABLE

THE COMPLETE SERIES

ELLA MILES

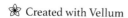 Created with Vellum

HEART OF A THIEF

BOOK ONE

I'm the villain in most romances.
I'm a thief that steals happily ever afters.
Except unlike most romances, love doesn't conquer me, I conquer it.
I've stolen countless women from unsuspecting men.
Gotten my one night with them.
And then watched the heartbreak that occurs in my wake.
Love doesn't survive once I enter the picture, if it ever existed at all.
Although, stealing Sloane might be my greatest challenge of all.

Asher is a villain trying to a put a horrible life behind him by doing
the only two things he knows to do: surf and steal. Sloane is an angel
that runs a charity helping children needing a fresh start. Asher will
do anything to have her. There is just one problem...she's about to
marry another man.

1

ASHER

I GRAB a beer out of the mini fridge while I wait to see if Danielle is coming up or not. I pop the cap off against the counter in my hotel room and then bring the cold liquid to my lips as I stare at the door.

I met Danielle three weeks ago. It was a lucky happenstance really. Well, lucky for me, not so lucky for her. I met her like I meet most of my targets—in a bar. She was with her fiancé, minding her own business, just having a drink at the bar, when he was called away for work. That was when I stepped in and gave her the attention that she was so desperate for.

That's all it took. One night of being nice to her, and I knew I could steal her from her fiancé. I knew it wouldn't take long. I probably could have had her that night if I really wanted. But that's not my game. Cheating isn't enough. Many a men take back fiancées or wives who have cheated on them. No, I don't entice the women so that they will cheat on their husbands. I hit on the women to steal them and make them mine—at least, until I get bored with them.

I'm not looking for anything long-term. I've never dated a woman for longer than a few weeks after claiming her as mine. Others, I get bored with much faster. I'm not really after the women. I'm after the chase that comes with stealing them away, and that satisfies the rush I used to get when I stole objects instead of people.

I don't know which makes me a worse person. Stealing things like cars, money, or jewelry. Or stealing women and their hearts. But, this way, at least I don't have to worry about going to jail.

I sit on the edge of the bed as I take another sip of my beer. I thought tonight was the night I would claim her. I thought tonight was the night I would steal her away. But, as every second passes, I become less sure of myself.

Maybe Danielle loves her fiancé, Wade, more than I thought she did.

I hear a soft knock on my door. Once, twice, and then a pause before the third knock. I grin before I down the rest of my beer and toss it into the trash can as I walk to the door. I open it and widen my eyes when I see Danielle standing outside my door, like I'm surprised that she is standing here even though I'm not the least bit surprised.

"What are you doing here, Danielle? Shouldn't you be in bed, dreaming about that fiancé you are going to marry tomorrow?" I ask.

I haven't stolen her yet. Not fully. I don't win until she's broken up with him, and I've had her in my bed.

Danielle wraps her arms across her chest, covering her cleavage that was sticking out from beneath her sparkly white dress that she wore to the rehearsal tonight.

I didn't have to do much to get Danielle here. At least, not tonight. All I did was show up at the rehearsal. I made an appearance in the background, and it was enough to convince Danielle that she might be making a huge mistake.

"I'm not getting married tomorrow," Danielle says.

"Oh," I say, my voice dripping with sadness that isn't the least bit real. "Would you like to come in?"

She nods, and I hold the door open for her. She walks over to the edge of my bed and sits down. I walk over to the mini fridge and pull two beers out. I open the caps on both and then hand one to her. She takes it, loosely holding it in her hand. She stares at it for a while, not able to look at me.

I keep my distance until she is ready to talk. Leaning against the counter next to the mini fridge, I sip on my beer.

"I broke up with Wade tonight," Danielle finally says.

"I gathered that. Why though?"

She looks up at me with puppy-dog eyes. "Because I don't love Wade anymore. I love you."

I look at her seriously and say, "I want you."

She hears *I love you* though. It's clear from the goofy smile and blushed cheeks.

But that's the one thing I won't ever do. I won't lie to these women. I can't help it if they hear what they want to hear.

I put my beer down and walk over to her until I'm standing between her legs. I take the beer out of her hand and place it on the counter. Her eyes follow me.

I push her back on the bed, and then I take the off the T-shirt I'm wearing... She bites her lip as she stares at my abs that have formed from surfing every day.

"Tell me you want me to fuck you," I say.

Danielle sits up and unzips the back of her dress, letting it fall to her waist, revealing her white lacy bra that holds her perky breasts in, away from me.

"Fuck me, Asher."

I grin as I grab ahold of her dress and roughly pull it off her body. She lets out a gasp.

She grabs at my neck, trying to pull me in so that she can kiss me. I let her pull me into her. I let her kiss me, and then I turn the kiss into rough kisses that show her what I really want.

"You like it rough," she says.

"Don't you?" I ask.

"I like anything with you."

I flip her over on the bed, and she lets out another surprised gasp.

I slap her ass. "I'm going to fuck this later, but first, I have to claim your pussy."

"God, just fuck me already. I can't wait," she cries into the pillow that she is now face down on.

I sigh. "They never have patience," I mutter to myself, annoyed that I can't take my time to properly enjoy her body.

"What?" she asks.

"Nothing," I say, hitting her hard on the ass, causing her to cry out.

I shove my shorts and briefs down and pull out a condom from the nightstand. I quickly slip it on before she finds a way to get herself off without me.

"Ready?" I ask, pulling her panties down and positioning myself at her entrance.

"Just fuck me already."

I do. I push inside her tight pussy that I know is anything but ready for me. I've barely spent any time turning her on, but if this is what she wants, I won't object.

She moans loudly and then quickly starts screaming, "Yes...yes," over and over.

I keep thrusting until I come, not concerned at all if she comes or not. I'm an asshole after all. Although most have called me worse than that.

She must have come because she screams loudly, followed by nothing.

I pull out of her and go to the bathroom to clean myself off. When I'm done, I stay in the bathroom with my hands clenching either side of the sink as I look at myself in the mirror. I can't handle this woman much longer. It was hard enough to pretend to like her to get her to want me, but now that I've had her once, I don't think I can keep up the act to fuck her more than that. I'm ready for the implosion to happen.

I walk back out and dig through my suitcase to find a fresh pair of briefs to put on. After I do, I glance over at Danielle, who is now under the covers of the bed. Her cheeks are flushed, her brown eyes heavy, and her long brown hair is a mess on top of her head.

"That was amazing," she says.

I nod and force my lips to curl up into something that resembles a smile.

"I'm ready to go again if you are. Or if you want to sleep some first..."

I take a deep breath, ready to tell her that I'm through with her, that she can't stay here, when I hear a loud pounding at my door.

I hold up a finger and then walk to the door in just my briefs, not caring who is on the other side. I throw the door open, and before I can register who is standing there, a fist flies at my face and hits me square in the nose. My body jolts backward with the hit, and I put my hands up to my nose as another hit rains down on my face, followed by another. My nose is pouring blood now, and I'm sure it's broken. My eyesight is blurry, but I think I make Wade out through the haze. Or, at least, my prior experiences with ex-fiancés verify that he is most likely on the other end of the fist that keeps coming at my face.

"Wade, stop!" Danielle screams, running to my aide.

I hear Wade breathing heavily.

"I'm done. I'm done with both of you. You're a rotten scumbag who deserves to be locked up in prison. And you're a lying, cheating slut. I'm done with both of you."

The blurriness finally leaves my eyes long enough for me to see Wade stumbling out of my room, clearly drunk. It's a wonder he was even able to aim for my face. The door slams shut, and then I see Danielle standing naked in front of me.

"I'm sorry about Wade. He's just upset that I broke off the wedding, that I no longer love him. He'll get over it."

I walk into the bathroom without saying a word and see that I was right about my nose. It's most definitely broken as blood pours down my face. I grab one of the towels and hold it up to my nose to try and stop the bleeding, but I know it is going to take a while to stop.

"Here," Danielle says, holding up a bag of ice.

I take the bag from her and hold it up to my face.

"It stings," I say, wanting to pull it away from my face.

She laughs. "It will help with the swelling and stop the bleeding."

I keep it on my face and walk back to the bedroom. Danielle follows me.

"I think you should go," I say.

7

"What? Why?"

"I don't want to worry about Wade coming back and beating me up."

"He won't."

"And I don't think you and I are going to work out. You're not worth my trouble."

Danielle's jaw drops. "I broke up with Wade for you though. I called off my wedding tomorrow for you. I want to be with you. I'll do whatever it takes."

"You made a mistake then. You should have stayed with Wade, or you should find someone else. I'm not the man for you, Danielle."

"He's not going to take me back now," she says, her voice shaking.

I smirk. "No, I don't think he will take you back."

"You fucking bastard! You asshole!" Danielle shouts, raising her hand to no doubt slap or punch me.

At least, this time, I'm ready for the attack. I grab her wrist midair, stopping her from hitting me.

"You are an evil, vile person," she says through tears.

I nod. "I am."

She jerks her hand out of my grasp. "Why would you do this?"

I open my mouth to speak, and she holds a hand up to stop me.

"Never mind. I don't want to know. I don't want to spend another second listening to this crap." She grabs her crumpled dress from the floor and quickly puts it back on, not bothering with her underwear. She cries the whole time.

Occasionally, the women recover after this. They are able to convince their fiancés to take them back. But I don't think Danielle will. And I'm not sure she is strong enough to fully recover from it either.

She hesitates a second, like she is trying to decide if she should say anything or if I'm going to. When I don't, she storms out the door without another word.

I take a deep breath as I go over to the bed and lie down, ensuring the ice pack is still on my face.

Shit, I curse to myself when the ice stings my face again.

If I'm going to keep this up, I need to be better prepared. I can't keep getting hit like this. Next time, I might get a concussion, and then I won't be able to surf. I won't let that happen. Next time, I'll be ready for a hit.

Maybe I should take some boxing classes or something.

I grin. Despite the pain I'm feeling now, I'll sleep like a baby for the first time in weeks. I stole her heart and then tore it to pieces. It feels good.

2

ASHER

ONE YEAR Later

I see the towering wave in front of me. It's huge and getting bigger by the second. It doesn't stop me. Instead, I push my board to move faster as I surf into the wave. My heart pounds fast and hard in my chest as the wave surrounds me, forming a tunnel that can collapse at any second. If it does, I'm going to have to fight like hell to get back to the surface to be able to breathe. I've been crushed by waves like this before and ended up with a couple of cracked ribs that hurt like a bitch and take forever to heal.

I'm not going to let that happen to me again. But remembering that pain doesn't stop me from attacking this wave either. Most wouldn't bother. Not when it isn't a competition. Not when I don't have anyone out here to rescue me if things take a turn for the worse. It's just me and the wave. That's how I like it.

I love the thrill. I love knowing that one wrong move could fuck everything up, even my life. I could die if I don't do everything perfectly.

This is what I live for though. I don't live to win competitions even though I win a lot and the money is nice. I live for this feeling right now—the feeling that, at any point, the ocean could steal my life from me or I could conquer it and live for another day. There is no other feeling like it in the world.

I surf the wave and come out the other end of the tunnel, unscathed. I win—for now. I step off the board and let the cool, salty water refresh me before I begin heading back to the beach. It's starting to get dark, and as much as I would love to stay out here all night, I'm hungry, and I have other cravings I need to satisfy.

Because I lied when I said that there was no feeling like surfing a wave that could destroy you. There is one feeling that is better—the feeling of stealing someone's happily ever after. The thrill of chasing a woman already claimed by another man just does something to me that nothing else can. It twists my soul and makes me want more of the drug that pulses through my veins every time I finally make the woman mine instead of his. It's a drug that pulls me in over and over again, a thrill I can't resist.

But why would I want to?

I'm a thief and a surfer. Both things keep me completely satisfied. And neither makes me feel guilty. I don't feel bad for the women or the men I hurt. I'm doing them a favor really. They believe in true love and happily ever after. They believe in the fairy tales they have been fed their whole lives. I just teach them how wrong they really are. In the real world, love doesn't exist.

"That was some wave, Asher," Luca, my only friend in the world, says.

"What are you doing here? I thought you were supposed to be home, resting, after your concussion. Or are you finally taking my advice over the doctor's and getting your ass back out here?" I ask with a grin before walking over to where my towel is slung over the back of my pickup truck. I toss my surfboard in the back before I take the towel and begin drying my shoulder-length dark hair.

Luca laughs. "Nope, just wanted to see if you wanted to grab a drink and a bite with me."

I stop drying myself off and grab a T-shirt to throw on. "Is that new girlfriend of yours coming?"

Luca frowns. "Hell no. She's back on the mainland, visiting her family. But, even if she wasn't, I wouldn't let you anywhere near her."

I walk to the driver's side of my truck and open the door. Luca is already climbing into the passenger seat without waiting for me to say that I want to hang out tonight. He already knows my answer is yes.

"Why not? I should meet her if you guys are getting serious, shouldn't I?"

I climb in and start up my truck, waiting for the purr of the engine before it fully starts. It doesn't start up right away. I get out and give the hood a love tap with my fist before I jump back in and turn the key over again to get it to start.

"You should really get a new truck, Asher. This thing is a piece of junk, and you can afford a lot better."

I narrow my eyes at him. "Why would I want anything better? The truck still runs, and all I use it for is to get me from my place to the beach. Why would I want to get a new truck? It would be a waste of money. After one drive, it would be full of sand and look just as bad as this old thing. How would I know if the new truck could handle the sand as well as this old thing anyway?"

Luca nods to the truck. "This old thing can barely handle the sand. They do make trucks designed specifically for handling sand and rough terrain nowadays, you know?"

"When this one dies, I'll think about it."

I don't have to tell him the real reason I don't have nice things. People would assume I stole the new car instead of buying it. I've learned it's actually better to live without the finer things in life.

I reach my hand out the window as I drive back to my house—if you can call my place a house. It's more like a shack on the beach. But it has the most amazing view. I love feeling the warm, salty air as I drive the couple of miles back. Luca does the same. You can't help but do that here.

"So, back to your girlfriend," I say.

Luca frowns and grabs ahold of the frame of the truck as we

bounce along the dirt road that leads back to my house. "You don't get to meet her—ever."

"What? What about if you decide to marry this one? You've been with her for, what? A month? That's a new record for you. She might be the one. I need to vet her first. And I'll have to meet her at your wedding anyway when I'm your best man."

Luca shakes his head. "Not happening. You are never going to meet her. You don't even get to know her name. You don't even get to meet her at my wedding or even after we get married."

"You do know, it's not possible to hide her from me forever? Hawaii is a small island. I will figure out who she is."

"Not if we move far away."

I chuckle. "Not going to happen, dude. Once here, no one moves away from Hawaii. They move *to* Hawaii."

Luca shakes his head. He's not going to tell me right now. And I don't blame him for not telling me. He knows that I have been looking for a bigger challenge, a harder chase. Most of the girls around here have been too easy to steal from their unsuspecting fiancés or husbands. That's the nice thing about living in Hawaii though. Everyone comes here to get married. So, I always have an endless supply of women to hit on and steal. But, lately, it's been too easy and the damage I have done has been minimal at best. If Luca really is in love with his girlfriend like I think he is, if he can see himself proposing to her in the future, then they could be my biggest challenge yet.

But I need to make sure they are really in love first, that they want to get married. Then, I can plan my move. So, for now, I'll wait. I'll wait for my best friend to fall in love, and then I'll destroy him. It might destroy our relationship, but I doubt it. Most of the men blame their cheating girlfriends, not the guy their girlfriends fell in love with. Well, on second thought, they do blame me, but after a good square punch to my jaw, their anger at me usually dissipates. Occasionally, it lasts a bit longer, but then I've never been friends with any of the men whose girlfriends I have stolen. Luca might hate me after this, but it is a chance I'm willing to take.

I park the truck outside my shack of a house and climb out. "Give me two minutes, and I'll be ready to head out," I shout to Luca.

I run up to the door of my house. Luca doesn't answer me, but I hear my truck door slam behind me, indicating that he climbed out of the truck. I push my unlocked door open; I never bother locking it. There isn't anything in here that is worth stealing anyway. I don't even own a TV. The most expensive items I have are my surfboards. Nobody wants to steal mine when they have their own. And, even if they did, my sponsors would just supply new ones.

That's the key to life—not having anything worth stealing. That's why I don't own anything worthwhile. That's why I don't fall in love.

I walk toward the back of my shack. It's just one room with a fridge and small stove that I rarely use for cooking, a bed, and a dresser. I don't even have a bathroom inside. I have an outdoor shower and toilet. But it satisfies all my needs and ensures that any woman who gets close to me isn't going to stick around for long. No woman wants to live in a shack on the beach, no matter how beautiful the sunsets are.

I reach my dresser and pull out a fresh pair of swim trunks and a new T-shirt. I only own one pair of clothing that isn't swim trunks, and I'm not going to bother wearing it tonight. I prefer to live my life in swim trunks. For one, women find them sexy as hell. They know right off that I'm a surfer without me having to say a word, which makes my job easier. Two, they are way comfier than any other clothing around. And, three, I never know when I'm going to want to go for a swim or go surfing. It's better to always be prepared.

I grab the fresh clothes and lay them on my bed before stripping and heading out into my shower. I rinse the salt water out of my brown hair that is far too long before drying off and heading back in to put on compression shorts, my new trunks, and T-shirt.

I walk outside and see Luca standing with his hands in his pockets, staring out at the sea.

I know he's still nervous about getting back out there again. He took quite a hit the last time he was out there. It was a life-changing, almost life-ending, event. I know he still doesn't know what he's going to do now. He was never the best surfer out there. I've always been better. Always gotten more sponsors. Won more championships. I'm not bragging; it's just the truth.

But a surfer doesn't know how to do anything else. He doesn't know how to live a different life. I know his comment about wanting to move somewhere else to keep his girlfriend away from me was just as much about him. If he stays here and decides he can't surf anymore, he is going to have to face his decision every day for the rest of his life. If he moves where there isn't an ocean staring back at him everywhere he goes, then maybe he can move on.

I get it. I just don't know how he could ever give this life up, no matter how dangerous it is. Life isn't worth living if you aren't doing what you love.

"Ready to go?" I ask.

Luca nods and turns toward me, and then he laughs. "Why did you even bother changing if you were just going to put trunks back on?"

I shrug. "At least they are clean."

"It's no wonder that you don't have a girlfriend."

I grin. He's right about that. I don't have a girlfriend or a fiancée or a wife. I never have and never will. The swim trunks help ensure that. I'm a fling that women think they can fall in love with, but when they realize they can't change me, they move on and deal with the heart-break they caused when they left the men who actually loved them. While I get freedom. And that's how I like it.

3

ASHER

"You're going to give yourself a heart attack with the way you eat, man," Luca says, staring down in disbelief, as I scarf down my second double cheeseburger.

I shrug and then shove a couple of fries into my mouth. "At least I'll go out doing what I love and not eating that healthy crap you eat."

"It's called fish and vegetables. You should try it sometime. You might actually find that you like it, and you will feel better when you're working out and surfing."

"Nah, I'm good." I drink down my beer. "So, when do you think you and that girlfriend of yours are going to be moving to the mainland? I need to know when I need to get a new wingman."

"I'm not talking about her. I already told you that."

I sigh. I'm frustrated and bored. And it's been weeks since the last woman. Tara was it? Sara? Cara? I can't remember.

"Fine, then help me pick out my next prey," I say.

Luca laughs. "Not going to happen, bro."

I frown. "You used to help me."

"That was when I was evil and didn't have a heart, like you. I've since grown up."

I shake my head. "You haven't grown up one bit. Just help me find someone who is an actual challenge this time. Sara wasn't enough of a challenge. I was able to get her to sleep with me and break up with her fiancé in less than a week. It was pathetic really."

"First of all, her name was Nicole, not Sara. And, second, you really need to stop. If you don't, you are going to fuck up someone's life so bad that it is going to rebound and hurt you, too."

I laugh. "Not likely."

Luca shakes his head as he drinks his beer. He reclines in his chair, lifting the front two legs off the ground. "Don't say I didn't warn you. It's going to happen. One of these times, a woman is going to hurt you as bad as you hurt them, and I'm going to be there, laughing in your face while eating popcorn. It's going to happen, bro. It's called Karma."

I take a swig of my beer and then grin. "I would love for a woman to try and hurt me as badly as I hurt them. I would love to see one try because it's impossible. I don't have a heart for them to destroy. Remember? I'm the devil."

"You've got that right. But even devils can get hurt. And I can't wait for it to happen to you."

"Whatever. It's not going to happen."

"Because you've been so right about everything before." Luca snickers.

I frown. "I'm right about this," I say sternly, challenging Luca to question me again.

He doesn't. Instead, a slow smile forms on his face, but he doesn't say anything. He doesn't say that I'm completely wrong about this even though I know I'm not. He doesn't say I'm as wrong about this as I was about encouraging him to go surfing with me the day of the accident that almost killed him. He should rub that shit in my face forever. Blame me for his accident. He doesn't though. He doesn't blame me. He has always said that it was just an accident. Completely unpreventable. That it was fate. I don't believe in fate. I believe in taking the world into your own hands and making yourself happy because no one else is ever going to.

"Look, a bachelorette party. Isn't that right up your alley?" Luca says.

I grin and turn in the direction that Luca is looking. About ten women are all scantily dressed in skirts and tight dresses. Glitter and stickers cover most of their bodies along with sashes saying what their role in the wedding is, like *Bride's Main Bitch* or *Bride's Bitch.* They don't understand how easy they make it for a guy like me.

I scan the group of women until I lock in on my target. The bride. She's easy to spot because she is the only one wearing white. She has a sash that says *Sexiest Bride-to-Be* and a crown that has a veil coming off of it.

She's a blonde, which makes me feel torn. I haven't had a blonde in a while, but then again, they are often the easiest to steal. But I'm ready for a challenge, not an easy lay. To my surprise though, she seems like a local girl. You can always tell by the tan or lack thereof or sunburn. She is nicely tanned, obviously used to the strong summer sun here. At least half of her bridesmaids are a weird shade of orange from the tanner they have been using. The other half are burned to a crisp.

The bride though is gorgeous. Her white dress shows the perfect amount of cleavage and is short enough to make her legs look long and toned. Legs that I desperately want wrapped around my body. And, if I play my cards right, that could happen by the end of the night. She doesn't look that in love. She looks like she is desperate for a way out of the situation she is in.

I watch as the group makes their way over to a corner of the bar where the bartender pulls together three couches for them to all sit on around a couple of low tables. The bride-to-be, of course, is given a couch all to herself since this is her special day, when it's supposed to be all about her.

She doesn't know how lucky she is. Today isn't going to be her special day. Today is going to be her lucky day.

"Definitely. I knew you'd still make a good wingman even if you gave up your old ways. You'll always be a monster to me."

Luca frowns. "Just don't forget to leave cash to pay for your half of the bill. I'm not paying for all the shit you ordered. I'm unemployed, remember?"

I roll my eyes. "Stop being dramatic. You weren't going to do another competition for another month anyway. You have exactly the same amount of money you would have had whether you had the accident or not. But"—I pull out my wallet and throw enough money down to cover both of our meals—"since you pointed out my next target and are going to help me convince them that we are cool guys and to not have us thrown out on our asses, I'll pay your bill."

"Not going to happen, bro."

I grin. "Are you sticking around to watch or going home?"

"I'll stick around until you start taking your shirt off, and then I'm out of here. But I'm still betting those women are going to get you thrown out of here."

I roll my eyes. "Always the pessimist." I pick up my beer and head over to the women, putting Luca out of my head.

"Hello, ladies. You all look beautiful tonight. Can I—"

"No, you can't join us," the bride-to-be says.

"Even if I buy you all a round or two of drinks and find the hottest guy in town to strip for you?"

I grin slyly and watch everyone's eyes soaking me in. Even if the bride doesn't want me to stay, her bridesmaids do. They *need* me to stay. Because, unlike the bride, they don't feel special tonight. And they all think I'm the guy who will make tonight a little easier by making them forget that they aren't the ones getting married and most likely aren't even close to getting married.

"Yes!" one of the bridesmaids sitting next to the bride says, taking her life in her own hands instead of waiting for the bride-to-be to answer.

She just doesn't know that I'm not here to have a one-night stand with one of the hot bridesmaids. Although I might regret that because several of the bridesmaids are easily in the top ten hottest women I have ever seen. One is wearing such a short dress that I can already glimpse her perfectly shaved and pierced pussy from where I'm standing.

I force my eyes to turn away from the piercing that I desperately want to see in action. I'm not really sure how it could make sex any better, but I'm sure that it could.

When I look back to the bride-to-be, she is glaring at me.

"So, when's the wedding?" I ask the bride-to-be.

"Sloane is getting married next month," the same loudmouthed bridesmaid from earlier answers.

I grin. It's a perfect timetable. I don't have a competition for about five weeks. I can seduce this woman, make her fall for me, and get it out of my system before I have to get serious when competition season starts next month.

"What can I get y'all to drink?" Paige asks. She's the bar's new waitress from Georgia, and she has that Southern accent to go with her adorably naive smile.

The women start shouting out drink and shot orders. But I'm not really interested in what any of them are ordering. I'm interested in what Sloane wants to order.

Paige looks to Sloane, and Sloane leans back in her chair.

"I'll have a whiskey." She pulls something out of her purse. "Do you mind if I smoke this in here?"

I know the bar has a no-smoking policy, just like every other bar in the city.

"I won't tell," Paige says, winking.

I raise one eyebrow at Paige. I'm surprised by both women—Paige, for having the guts to say that Sloane can smoke in here when she can't, and Sloane, for holding a cigar in her hand.

Paige leaves to go get everyone's drinks while I take a seat next to Sloane.

"Have you ever smoked a cigar before?" I ask.

I doubt that she has. Someone must have bought her a cigar to celebrate her engagement. That's all this is.

Sloane laughs. "Why? Are you going to show me how to smoke a cigar?" Her voice teases me, but her eyes travel up and down my body, drinking me in.

She might be laughing now, but I'll have the last laugh.

"No. I'm just don't want you spending your night coughing and sick after one inhale. I don't want you to miss the show I'm going to put on later," I say with a wink.

She lights the cigar, takes one puff, and then slowly releases the smoke from her mouth. My eyes fixate on her mouth because it is the goddamn sexiest thing I have ever seen.

"First of all, you don't inhale a cigar. You would know that if you had ever smoked a cigar before. And, two, thinking that I have never smoked a cigar because I'm a woman is the most sexist thing I've heard in a while. And I run my own company, so I hear sexist things all the time. And, three, I would rather spend my evening in the restroom, puking my guts out, than watch whatever show you will be putting on."

I grin the whole time as I stare intently at Sloane's mouth, waiting for more of the sexy smoke to escape her lips. I love how fierce and take-no-crap she is. Women like this are always the hardest to crack, always the hardest challenge. But it will only be a challenge if she is really in love with her fiancé. If she just sees her arrangement with him as a business deal, which I imagine is how she looks at much of life, then it won't be that difficult to get her to cheat on her fiancé. It won't be that difficult to convince her that she could fall in love with me.

"So, did your fiancé get you into smoking cigars?"

She frowns and then puffs on the cigar again before slowly letting the smoke out. "No, I got him into it."

I smile because I don't believe her. There is no way a beautiful woman like her would take up such a nasty habit without a man convincing her to try it. At least, I've never met a woman yet that would smoke a cigar because she wanted to and not to impress a man.

"So, when did you start smoking cigars?" I ask as I casually put my arm around the back of the couch and behind her back. I'm not touching her, but I can tell it makes her uncomfortable because she leans slightly forward.

"College."

I smile. "What brand did you smoke that first time?"

She frowns. "Why do you care what brand I smoked?"

I shrug. "Maybe I want to take it up, and I want to know what brand I should start with."

"Alec Bradley Prensado."

"Who were you with when you smoked?"

"Jessie, Wes, Kirsty…"

I turn to the loudmouthed bridesmaid who has been eavesdropping on our conversation. "Who is the lucky guy that is marrying our Sloane here?"

"Wes Finnigan."

I smile. "So, Wes was there the night you smoked your first cigar, but he wasn't the one who convinced you to try your first cigar?"

Sloane's cheeks turn a nice shade of pink, but I don't think her cheeks are pink due to embarrassment. No, it seems like anger is the cause.

"Fine, Wes was the one who got me started smoking cigars. You happy now?"

"Not particularly." I lean in so that I can whisper into her ear without her nosy bridesmaids hearing me. "I won't be happy until I have you in my bed. And it's going to happen, Sloane. Whether that's tonight or a month from now. You need to have one last fling before you marry the wrong guy or preferably kick him to the curb and replace him with me."

I stand up before she can get a slap or punch in. I've said a very similar line to too many women before. Sloane is the kind of women who will slap first and ask questions later. She's tough, strong. And probably too uptight for her own good. But I'm not sure how in love with Wes she really is. I'll have to wait and see if this is going to be too easy or one of the hardest steals of my life.

Paige is back with the drinks, and I help her pass them out before letting her know to put all the drinks on my tab. When I hand Sloane her whiskey, she is fuming so much that I'm afraid she is going to throw the drink in my face.

She doesn't, but I can tell that it crosses her mind.

"So, who's ready to see the hottest man on this island strip for you?" I ask.

I am answered by an array of hoots and hollers.

I grin and then pull out my phone to start up some music. I start dancing to the music in the center of the group of sofas and tables that all the women are sitting around. Immediately, the women start digging into their purses to start pulling out dollar bills, twenties, or anything to tuck it into the waistband of my swim trunks.

I know my end target is Sloane. But, first, I give everyone else my attention. Sloane needs to see how the rest of her friends feel about me. She needs to see how desperate they are to just touch me, how they scream when I remove my shirt and reveal my rock-hard abs and strong chest. She needs to see what she would be missing if she said no instead of yes.

I strip down until I'm in nothing but my compression shorts that I wear under my swim trunks. All of the women's eyes in the room are filled with lust and desire. Including Paige, who has been coming and checking on everyone's drinks way more often than she should be. But she does nothing to stop me from stripping in a bar. I think because it has increased the number of drinks the rest of the women in the bar are ordering as they try to sneakily take a picture of me.

I have been ignoring Sloane the entire time I have been stripping. She thinks I'm doing this to hook up with a bridesmaid of my choosing. That, after this show, I will have my pick. She thinks she's safe. She is anything but safe.

"And, now, a special dance for the bride-to-be," I say.

Everyone hoots and hollers their agreement, and as I turn my attention to Sloane, it takes her a minute to realize that I'm talking about her. But, despite how she tries to hide it beneath a glare, I can see the lust and sin in her eyes. I can see the hint of temptation to do something that she knows she shouldn't do, that she would never forgive herself for. Still, it's there.

I grab Sloane's hand and drag her to the center of the circle. I have her take a seat on the edge of the low table in the center and then continue to dance around her and up against her. I give her an up close and personal view of my body, letting her get used to my body being close to her. When the music changes, I step it up a notch. I dance closer to her and eventually push her until she is lying on her back on the table.

I climb on top of the table and pretend to hump her without touching her, and when I hear the screams of the women around us, I know that I'm giving a good show.

I can see Sloane's anger growing right along with the lust. But I'm slightly disappointed in her. She's making this too easy for me. I want her to be in love with Wes. I want her to imagine herself with only him. When she falls in love with me and realizes that I can never love her in return, I want to know that it will ruin her. I want her to feel the kind of pain and devastation that she will never be able to return from. If I don't get that, then going after her now isn't going to be enough for me. Because I live for the devastation that I cause.

So, I up the ante when the music stops. I go in for a kiss because, if she isn't that in love with Wes anyway, she isn't going to be the woman I steal, and I might as well leave with a kiss.

But my lips barely brush hers before I feel the sting of a slap across my cheek, followed by a hard kick to the nuts. I roll off the table and crumple to the floor in unbearable pain as Sloane frowns over me along with all of her friends. Every one of their faces has turned from drunk happiness to anger. A few still have the lingering lust in their eyes, but most long pushed that thought out of their heads as soon as I went into the kiss.

"I'm marrying Wes. I love Wes. And any guy who thinks he can come in here and threaten my relationship with Wes deserves what's coming to him. Because Wes and I have been through too much to let some asshole like you who thinks he's God's gift to women to destroy that. It's not going to happen. And, if you do anything again, I'll make sure that your most prized possession is no longer attached to your body. Understand?"

I grin at Sloane. I can't help it. She loves him. It's music to my ears.

Sloane doesn't take my grin as a compliment though. She takes it as a grin from an arrogant asshole who is still going to try and get his way. And she's right.

Sloane grabs what is left of her whiskey and dumps it on my head before I can react. I abruptly stand up and watch Sloane begin to walk out of the bar. But, before I can say anything else or run after her, another drink is thrown in my face. Followed by another and another until all of the women have thrown their drinks in my face. One woman kisses me on the lips before throwing her drink in my face and then slaps me after.

These women are crazy. But it's exactly what I want. Crazy, in-love women. I smile like a madman.

Luca walks over, laughing in my face.

"I thought you'd left," I say.

"I said I would leave after I watched you get thrown out. So, now, I can leave," he says.

"I didn't get thrown out."

He laughs again. "You're right. You just got a dozen drinks thrown in your face. That was much better than getting thrown out. I'm glad I stuck around to watch it happen. But what I don't understand is why you are grinning like an evil bastard. You do realize that you just got rejected by a dozen women, right?"

I nod. "I did." My grin curls up wider as I wipe my face off with my T-shirt, and then I put my swim trunks back on.

"Then, why are you still grinning? They won, and you lost. You look like a complete idiot."

"Because she loves him."

"Huh?"

"Sloane, the bride-to-be, loves her fiancé. That is going to make this so much sweeter when I finally steal her away."

Luca's smile drops.

I begin walking out of the bar, and Luca follows.

"I'm smiling because I think I just found my greatest challenge yet. Sloane."

4

ASHER

THE SUN BEGINS to rise over the ocean as I sit in my hammock outside my shack on the beach. The bright yellow color that the sun brings is what I live for. Usually, before the sun starts to rise in the morning, I am already on the beach with my surfboard in hand. Early morning is the best time to catch some waves because very few people get up this early in the morning. The beach is empty as well as the ocean.

But today is the first time in years that I haven't woken before the sun with a surfboard in hand. The last time I remember missing a morning surf session was when I was sick with the flu. And, even then, I tried to get out of bed. I planned to go surfing that morning. My stomach just didn't agree with me, so I never left the bathroom that day.

I even go out surfing when the weather is less than perfect, which is rare for Hawaii, but still. I've surfed with the rain pouring down and lightning and thunder overhead.

Today though is the first day that I've chosen to do something else. I open my old laptop that I rarely, if ever, use and I type *Sloane* and *Hawaii* into the search bar. I don't have her last name, and I know it's a complete long shot, but maybe I'll get lucky. If not, I'm going to have to go back to the bar where I met her last night and convince Paige, the waitress, to tell me her last name.

It takes a minute for my Wi-Fi to connect and for the page to come up. But, finally, it does. I click on the first link and see Sloane's pretty, green eyes, luscious red lips, and shoulder-length blonde hair pop up on the screen.

I grin. This is too easy.

Her name is Sloane Hart. She runs a nonprofit called Kindness First with her grandmother. Actually, it's one of the biggest employers on the island and also has satellite locations around the world. I'm surprised I've never heard of her. But it's not like we run in the same circles. She's the complete opposite of me in fact.

I'm the devil. I destroy people's lives. She's an angel. She gives children food and a chance at life.

I pause for a second. I shouldn't do this. I shouldn't destroy a woman's life when she does so much good for the world.

What if, after I rip her heart out, she doesn't have the strength to continue her nonprofit work? What if she never leaves her house again? Becomes a hermit?

I would have not only destroyed her life, but also thousands of kids around the world. This is on a whole different level, even for me.

I stare back at the woman on the screen who looks so similar to so many local girls. In the picture, she is wearing a simple T-shirt with her company's logo and jeans. She's surrounded by kids that I'm sure she has been feeding. But, if you put her in a bikini, she would look just like every other girl on this island.

Except for one thing.

The twinkle in her eyes. It's different than anything I have ever seen before. It could just be this picture. The photographer could have just caught her eyes at just the right moment to catch the sunlight that caused her eyes to sparkle.

Or it could be her. I choose to believe it's Sloane causing the twinkle. The rest of her body language indicates as much.

And her smart mouth from last night tells me that she is used to being in control and is good at it. She's strong and kind. She'll survive. I might destroy her, but I have no doubt that she will keep the nonprofit going. And, if she doesn't, well, it's not my fault if thousands of children go hungry. I'm sure her job isn't that important anyway. Another organization would just take over caring for her kids.

I start reading article after article, trying to find out everything I can about Sloane Hart. She went to Harvard and majored in business. She graduated at the top of her class in fact. She grew up on the East Coast but would visit her grandmother here in Hawaii every summer. She moved here after graduation and has been working alongside her grandmother ever since. She met Wes at some point in college, but that is about all the articles say about Wes. He went to Harvard as well, so he can't be that stupid, but none of the articles talk about him running his own company or having any involvement in her company. They all just talk about their upcoming wedding. That's it.

I sigh when I finish reading the last article about Sloane that said much of the same as every other article about her. She's smart, loving, strong. The best person in the world to run a nonprofit organization. They all believe that, in the next five years, her nonprofit could become the largest in the world. She's that good at what she does. I've studied everything I can about her on paper, and I haven't found a weakness. Not a single one.

As far as I can tell, she doesn't have one. I grin, but this is exactly what I wanted. A challenge. And Sloane is not disappointing me there. This is exactly what I want.

I crack my neck from side to side as I begin to think of all my options to get into her life.

Apply for a job at her company? I shake my head. I don't have time for that, and as soon as she found out I was working for her, she would fire me.

Stalk her? Wouldn't work with Sloane. She'd call the police on me the second she spotted me.

Randomly run into her? She'd think I was stalking her.

My phone buzzes, interrupting my thoughts. I frown when I see the name on the screen. I answer though because I know, if I don't, she'll just keep calling me back.

"What?" I answer the phone.

"Well, hello to you, too. Why aren't you at the beach?" Shauna, my agent and basically my boss for all intents and purposes, asks.

I frown. "How do you know I'm not at the beach this morning? Are you spying on me? I'm allowed to take a break from surfing every once in a while."

She laughs. "I don't give a shit if you practice every day or not. All I care about is that you look good in your swim trunks and show up to the appearances and bookings we have given you. That's it."

"What are you talking about? I don't have an appearance or shoot today."

I can practically feel Shauna frowning on the other end of the line. That's how annoyed she is.

"I knew we shouldn't have hired a surfer. We pay you millions a year, and you can't even remember to show up when you're told. Even our basketball stars know how to show up even if they are still hungover from the night before. But, no, we decided to go with a surfer. Surfers are cool, are in right now. A surfer will help our brand. Right now, all I think is, we are paying you too goddamn much to not show up when you're told."

"Shauna, I'm sorry you're having a shitty day or PMSing or what-ever is going on with you. But I was never told about an appearance for today." I check my calendar and email quickly to make sure, but there is nothing there.

I grin because I'm right, and Shauna is wrong.

"Shit, you're right. Why the fuck do you have to be right?"

"Because I'm the devil."

She sighs. "That, you are. Regardless of whose fault it is, I need you on the beach in ten minutes, or the cushiony paycheck we pay you every month will go away."

I laugh. "No, it won't. This is your fault. You screwed up, not me. And, if you think I care about the money, you are wrong."

"Goddamn it, Asher! Just get your ass down to the beach now. It's not like you have anything better to do. You surf; that's it. That's your entire life. So, just do it."

"And what will you do for me?"

"I won't kill you. Now, go! You need this job anyway. Even though you still win plenty of events, you are getting less sponsorships because of your reputation with women, which we need to discuss later. You aren't a great image for many people's brands. So, just be happy that you are getting any work."

I frown and then hear her mumble something about surfers and how she'll never work with a surfer again before she realizes she never ended the call. When I hear the beeping sound, indicating that she did hang up, I get up out of my hammock and return my laptop to my shack. The laptop was secondhand and cost less than a hundred dollars, so it's not like anyone is going to come in and steal it.

Shauna forgets that I don't care about money, or maybe she just doesn't remember. As long as I can buy beer and food, I'm good. I could easily make money by flipping burgers for a few hours each day and still have plenty of time to spend most of my day surfing.

I change into swim trunks and then climb into my truck that already has my surfboard in the back.

I begin driving toward the best surfing spot on the island. Shauna never said where I was supposed to go or what the appearance was. But I know where she is talking about. And, no matter what the appearance is, I'll need to be in swim trunks, or they will tell me what they want me to wear.

And maybe a distraction away from Sloane for a couple of hours isn't such a bad idea. It will help me to get my thoughts in order so that I can form a plan of attack for later.

I pull up to the spot on the beach ten minutes later. And I jump out of my truck and find Shauna looking as sassy as ever in her heels and dress. She starts walking toward me, and I laugh as her heels sink in the sand.

"Are you ever going to learn to dress appropriately for the beach?" I ask her as I cock my head to one side.

She frowns. "I don't have time for your crap today, Asher."

"Honestly, I think you are the only person in the world who hates the beach. Most people would love to have your job and be able to hang out in Hawaii all day."

She rolls her eyes. "Today, you are giving surf lessons."

I frown. "Surf lessons? Really? That's the big money-making opportunity that I was going to cost us if I didn't show up today?"

Shauna motions to the camera crew behind her. "We are filming it for a couple of ads, and the guys are paying big bucks to have you teach them."

I groan. "You couldn't have at least found a group of women who needed surf lessons?"

"That's not what we are going for. We want you to show that surfing can make any guy look cool."

"You know women with boobs sell a lot better."

She laughs. "It sells better to *guys*. But we aren't trying to sell to guys. We are trying to sell to *women*. And what better way to sell to women than with a bunch of hot guys who are single?"

"Don't you think we will come across as gay?"

She shrugs. "Maybe, but women also like knowing they can turn a hot gay guy straight. Or at least fantasize about it. It doesn't matter. Just be hot and teach these guys how to surf. They agreed to let us film them, and they all happen to be hot as well, so lucky us."

I frown. "I should have stayed home."

"Then, you wouldn't have gotten paid. Now, go teach those guys how to surf."

She swats my ass as I walk by.

"I don't care about the money, and I'm pretty sure that was sexual harassment!" I yell back as I jog toward the group of guys awkwardly holding surfboards at the edge of the water.

"Then, sue me!" she shouts back.

I smile.

I turn my attention to the idiots standing on the beach. "I'm Asher. I guess I'll be teaching you how to surf today."

A blonde guy with a short haircut and, I hate to say, a fit body sticks out his hand. "I'm Wes."

My lips curl up just a little at the mention of his name. "Nice to meet you, Wes."

"And these are my cousins and groomsmen, Elijah and Cody."

I shake each of their hands.

"I'm his best man," Elijah says.

"Don't let him fool you. I'm his best man," Cody says.

Wes rolls his eyes. "The best man spot is still up for grabs."

"And the spot of the bride?" I ask.

"That's taken by Sloane Hart. You might have heard of her. She runs Kindness First, a nonprofit whose headquarters are located here on the island."

I shake my head. "Never heard of her. But you sound like a lucky man."

"I am," Wes says, smiling like an idiot.

That's when I realize what Sloane's weakness is. Wes. Wes is her weakness. It's clear he doesn't have a lot of guy friends if he brought only his cousins, and he doesn't clearly have a best man. That means, there is a spot open for me. I can become his friend. His best man even. That will ensure I get to spend plenty of time with Sloane. And Sloane won't be able to turn me away because I'll be Wes's best friend. That's my way in. Through Wes.

"So, have any of you surfed before?"

All three shake their heads.

I put on a fake smile. "Well, let's see what you've got."

"You aren't going to teach us how to stand on the board on the ground first?" Elijah asks.

I raise an eyebrow. "Do you really want to spend all day jumping up on a surfboard on the sand, or do you want to learn how to surf?"

"Well...I-I..." Elijah stutters.

I roll my eyes. "If you were looking for a babysitter to teach you, then you came to the wrong place. I believe in learning from doing, not pretending. I'm the best surfer in the world, currently ranked number one. If you want to learn from the best, then you don't get to question my methods. If you aren't willing to take my terms, then stop wasting my time."

Wes smiles. "Teach us your ways, oh great one."

I nod. "Good. I'll get my board and meet you out there. Lie on your board and swim as far out into the ocean as you can."

"Shouldn't we wait for you?" Cody asks.

"Don't worry; I'll catch up."

I jog back to my truck to grab my board, happy that this has taken such a good turn. The only thing better would have been if Sloane herself were asking for lessons, but something tells me that, even if Sloane didn't know how to surf, she wouldn't be the type to ask for lessons. She would be the type to learn how to surf and be great at it the first time out. She wouldn't need an instructor.

I grab my board and then begin jogging back to the beach. I see the cameraman aiming his camera at me as I jog. I can't imagine how they are going to turn this into a commercial, but if I can buddy up to Wes while getting paid to do it, then I'm not going to complain.

As I jog back down the beach with my board in hand, I glance out at them floundering in the ocean, seemingly barely moving at all, as wave after wave crashes down on them. I wouldn't have brought first-time surfers to this beach, but I know why my sponsors chose this spot. It has the best waves and lighting. They'll just be lucky to get a shot of any of them up on a surfboard. Although maybe they just want an ad of a bunch of hot guys hanging out and looking stupid while I surf.

Wes is the only one who is making any progress at all, though he isn't that far ahead of the rest of them.

I run into the water with my surfboard and then dive under the first wave. I swim hard, kicking my feet to propel me forward, and then finally come up for air several feet in front of Wes.

"Dive under the next wave!" I shout to Wes.

I sit on top of the waves for the next one so that I can see how he does. He tries but ends up coming up, quickly coughing up the salty water.

I chuckle. "Try again. Blow out through your nose this time as you dive, so you don't get a nose full of water."

Wes tries again, and this time, he makes it to me before he comes back up.

"Not bad," I say as he breathes heavily next to me.

"Yeah, I'm awesome. I can dive underwater and hold my breath for five seconds. I was born to surf," Wes says sarcastically.

I laugh. "Well, you are doing better than Tweedle Dee and Tweedle Dum back there."

Wes laughs as we both stare back at his cousins, who have barely moved from the edge of the beach.

"I guess we should wait for them," I say.

"Nah, I need a break from them."

I nod. "All right, so one more dive, and you should be in position. This time, dive down and kick hard until you can't hold your breath anymore. That should get you on the other side of the swell. Then, we'll have you up and surfing."

He laughs.

"And dive," I say.

We both dive down into the water. When I come up for air, I see that Wes has, too, but he's going to have to take one or two more dives down to get to where I am. I wait patiently as he does. When he finally reaches me, he is breathing heavily. He's in decent shape, but the ocean definitely takes a different toll on the body if you aren't used to it.

"So, why do you want to learn how to surf anyway?" I ask.

"My fiancée. She's spent many summers here, and if we are going to live here full-time after we get married, I figured I'd better learn how to surf. I know she loves it even if she rarely makes time to surf anymore. I want to be able to do something with her that she enjoys and not look like a total imbecile."

I nod. "I think you are going to need more than one lesson today to accomplish that."

"Yeah, well, I was told you'd only do the one."

"I think I could fit you into my schedule for the next couple of weeks."

"That would be great."

I look back to the camera crew, who is growing impatient. "I need to get up on the board to ensure I get paid. After I go, give it your best shot. You're going to fall if you even get up, but I think that is what they are wanting."

Wes nods. "Yeah, I figured."

"But don't worry; I'll have you surfing. Just give me a week or two."

I see the next wave coming. It's not perfect, but then nothing ever is. I wink at Wes, and I take off with the wave.

I don't have to think as I surf; I just do. I've done this so many times before, and this wave is nothing compared to the larger waves that I often surf. Still, I respect the wave, the ocean. I know that, every time I come out here, I'm putting my life at risk. That this could all be over if I'm not careful. So, I try to keep my thoughts on what I'm doing and not on Sloane. Not on the plan that has practically fallen into my lap.

I reach the shore and jump off the board before I remember that I'm being filmed. I make sure to smile as I kick the board up with my foot and then carry it all the way up the beach. I turn my attention back to Wes, who is sitting on his board, looking completely clueless and completely terrified.

I watch the next wave come, but it is going to be much too strong for him. "Hold off till the next one!" I shout.

He nods and tries to maintain his position as the next wave comes. It really doesn't matter which wave he tries. I doubt he even manages to stand on the board his first time out.

I watch as another wave begins. "This one, Wes! Start paddling and then try to stand!" I shout.

Wes begins paddling and then starts trying to climb up onto the board. His timing is off, but somehow, he muscles his way up until he is somewhat upright. Then, he immediately falls over as a wave crashes down on him.

He comes up for air a couple of seconds later, looking a bit dazed but otherwise fine. He slowly makes his way back to the beach and then falls to the ground.

"I don't know how you are able to make that look so easy. I don't think I'll ever be able to stand up on the board," Wes says, panting hard.

"Well, you won't ever be able to do what I just did unless you plan on devoting your next twenty years to surfing. But I can at least get you upright your next time out."

I extend my hand to him, and he takes it and stands up.

"Same place tomorrow?" Wes asks.

I glance over at the police cruiser that is creeping by far too slowly, staring at us.

I laugh. "No. We are going to try a much tamer beach next time."

5

ASHER

It's taken me three weeks to get Wes to stand on a board and do anything that resembles surfing. It has been much longer of an investment than I initially planned. I thought one week, maybe two, and then I'd not only have him surfing, but he would also have made me his best man. Apparently, I'm better at making friends with women than with men.

"I told you I would have you surfing," I say to Wes as he trudges up to his car.

"Woohoo! That was awesome! I can't wait to show Sloane on our honeymoon."

I place my surfboard into the back of my truck. "Where are you going on your honeymoon?"

"Australia and then New Zealand. Sloane has always wanted to go. She's the adventurous type. She wants to surf, scuba dive the Great Barrier Reef, hike in the forests. I, on the other hand, just want to avoid being eaten by anything and kick back and enjoy the food. She'll be impressed though that I took surfing lessons and can sort of surf now."

I smile every time Wes talks about Sloane. I can't help it. I've learned a lot about her from my time with him. And everything that I have learned makes me want to claim her more. Makes me want her more. And this new fact is not any different.

"I think, with a little more practice, you are definitely going to impress her."

Wes opens the door to his car. "Hey, you want to come out with us tonight?"

I raise an eyebrow. "I don't want to be a third wheel."

Wes laughs. "I didn't mean, me and Sloane. I meant, me and the guys. They are kind of throwing me an informal bachelor party tonight. You should come."

"I don't want to intrude."

"Oh, come on. Don't leave me alone with my cousins. They are the absolute worst. I need at least one normal guy who is on my side tonight."

"All right, fine. I'll come hit the bars with you tonight. But you owe me for putting up with your cousins."

"First round is on me."

I nod. "Done."

———

I get to the saddest-looking bar on the island, where Wes texted me to meet them. I frown as I stand outside the building that looks like it could collapse at any minute. I'm not one to judge a book by its cover. After all, I'm nothing like what I appear on the outside. But this is absolutely ridiculous. If they weren't going to pick a strip club, they could have at least picked a clean bar that had average-looking waitresses who were scantily clad.

I shake my head. If I convince them to go to any other bar tonight, I'll be considered a savior after Wes tries one drink in this place. Tonight, I need him to start thinking of me as one of his best friends. I need to start finding a way to connect with Sloane. I need to start sneaking into her life. And, if Wes isn't that way, then I will need to find another.

I walk into the bar, still dressed in swim trunks, a T-shirt, and sandals. I don't have to look long to find them. The three of them are sitting at the edge of the bar, all looking sad. They are the only ones in here besides an older gentleman who is behind the bar, fixing them drinks.

"Cheer up, guys. The party is here," I say, heading over to them.

Wes smiles when he sees me, but Elijah and Cody both give me a glare that is a mix between anger and annoyance.

I don't bother to pull up a chair because we definitely aren't staying here.

"Close out your tabs, boys, and let me show you how a local parties in Hawaii."

Wes immediately jumps up, but Cody and Elijah both continue to frown.

"We are in charge of the bachelor party, not you. We will decide when and if we want to go elsewhere," Cody says.

I raise an eyebrow. "Well, you've chosen one of the worst dumps on the island. But, if you want to stay, be my guest. Or we could go to a bar that actually has decent drinks and chicks, most scantily clad and likely ready for a good time."

"Aw, come on, guys. It's my night. I appreciate you guys trying your best, but Asher knows the island better than any of us. Let's give him a try."

"Fine," Cody says.

I pull out my wallet and throw some cash down so that they might like me a little better. Although I think it does the opposite of helping. I don't really care if they like me though. I just need to convince Wes, which is easy since he's comparing me to them.

I throw my arm over Wes's shoulder. "Come on, let's go get you drunk and see some naked chicks."

———

Three hours later, and I have succeeded in getting everyone drunk, and we have had a string of naked women coming all night. I might have succeeded in my mission.

Cody is passed out at the bar, clueless to the fact that he is lying in spilled beer. Elijah has spent the last half hour in the restroom, most likely vomiting. And Wes is a stumbling mess, no longer speaking in coherent sentences.

I sigh. Why the hell I thought I wanted to spend an evening with just the guys is beyond me. I don't even like spending time with Luca, and he's about the only person on earth who can stand me.

Unfortunately, there aren't many cab options on the island this late in the evening, so it is up to me to either get them home or leave them here. I should leave their asses here. They are all grown men who can take care of themselves. But I keep picturing Sloane.

I smile, thinking of her. There is one benefit to everyone being drunk out of their minds.

"Come on, Wes. It's time to let your best man take you home," I say, putting his arm around my shoulders and helping him to stand up.

Wes smiles as I guide him outside to my truck. I knew well enough not to get drunk tonight.

I throw Wes in the truck before I decide I'd better go get Elijah and Cody.

"Don't tell Elijah and Cody that you're my best man. They'll be mad," Wes says, slurring every other word out of his mouth.

"Don't worry. It will be our secret," I say before slamming the door shut.

Finally, I think as I go back to get the other two drunk assholes.

I can't put up with these guys any longer without at least getting a glimpse of Sloane.

Phase one is complete. Now, it's on to the more fun phase. Enticing Sloane.

6

ASHER

It FEELS strange to wake up and not be teaching Wes for once. But it's also incredibly fucking nice. I jump out of bed and glance out my window. The sun is just starting to rise over the ocean, and it looks like it is going to be the best goddamn day.

Wes already gave me a schedule of events I need to be at as his best man over the next month. I don't have any events that I need to be at for my sponsors.

Today, I'm a free man. I can just surf.

I slip into my swim trunks and don't bother to throw on a shirt. Then, I run out the door and get in my truck to head to my favorite spot on the beach.

When I get there, I jump out of the truck and grab my surfboard before running toward the ocean.

"Hey, man!"

I freeze and do my best not to groan.

I turn and face Wes. "Hey, what are you doing here? I thought we were done with lessons."

"We are. Just wanted to show my fiancée what I'd learned."

I see it in her eyes the second she spots me. Immediate recognition, regret, and anger. She recovers quickly and tucks a loose strand of her blonde hair behind her ear as Wes turns to grab her hand.

"This is my fiancée, Sloane Hart. Sloane, this is Asher Calder," Wes says.

Sloane holds out her hand to me, and I shake it with a mischievous grin on my face—or at least, that's how I imagine she views my grin.

Sloane smiles politely and shakes my hand. "I've tried teaching Wes how to surf many times, so I'm still not convinced that he has learned how to actually surf, even by someone as experienced with surfing as you are," she says as she retracts her hand.

Wes laughs.

I cock my head to one side as I study Sloane. She looked up who I was, or she'd already known who I was. That has me even more intrigued with her.

"Are you underestimating my surfing skills?" I instinctively move toward her, unable to resist closing the distance between us.

Sloane holds tight to Wes, like he is going to be able to stop me.

"No, just your teaching skills and Wes's lack of coordination."

Wes and Sloane laugh together, like most couples do. Like they share a secret no one else knows. Seeing them happy together just makes me want to rip them apart even more.

"Well, Wes, you'd better go out there and prove her wrong for both of our sakes. I wouldn't want her to find either of us lacking."

Sloane frowns every time I speak, but the second Wes looks at her, a fake smile appears on her lips. It's entertaining really, watching her.

Wes kisses her on the lips, and I study them both. When Wes kisses, he closes his eyes and lets her into his soul. When Sloane kisses, it's clear that she isn't fully in the moment. Her eyes don't close all the way, and her lips don't part all the way to let him in or so that he can fully claim her mouth with his.

Sloane gently pushes Wes away. She tries to hide it. She tries to make it seem like she wants nothing more than to be kissed by Wes all day. It's clear that me being here makes her uncomfortable.

Wes smiles at Sloane, so oblivious and in love that he can't even tell that she had issues with his kiss. He grabs his surfboard and then begins walking toward the water.

He pauses just before going in. "You coming, Asher?"

"Nope, this is all you."

Wes runs into the water with his surfboard in hand and begins paddling out.

Sloane folds her arms across her chest and watches Wes with laser focus. So much focus that I am able to move until I'm standing right next to her.

"He's good, isn't he?" I say into her ear.

She jumps.

I lean back, away from her ear, as she turns to me.

"What are you doing? Why did you give Wes surf lessons?"

"Are you accusing me of setting this all up so that I could see you again?"

"Yes, that is exactly what I'm accusing you of."

I fold my arms across my chest and watch her eyes linger on my abs for a second before looking me in the eye again.

I laugh. "As luck would have it, fate stepped in. My sponsors arranged the lessons, not me. It would seem the world thinks we should be together."

"You're an asshole, a douche bag, a bastard, a—"

I laugh. "Is that the best you've got?"

She narrows her eyes. "I'm engaged! What kind of man thinks I'd be willing to have a one-night stand with him, a complete stranger, on a normal night, much less when I'm about to be married? There isn't a name so bad to describe what you are."

I shrug. "At least none that you can call me from your pretty, little mouth."

She glares at me, and I know she means it as a warning that I have no doubt she would follow through on if I tried anything, but all I can think is that I want to see that same passion in her eyes when I kiss her. I want to see how angry she would be if I kissed her right now. I want to feel that anger with just the tiniest hint of desire. Because I know that, once she got a taste of me, no matter how much she loved Wes, she would keep coming back for more.

"You'd better turn your attention to your fiancé. You wouldn't want him to see that you couldn't take your eyes off me when you were supposed to be watching him."

Sloane huffs but doesn't say another word as she turns her attention to Wes, who is now sitting on his surfboard, waiting for a wave. I, however, don't take my eyes off of her. And, even though she tries her best to fix her gaze on Wes, she still looks at me out of the corner of her eye.

"Oh my God...he's..." Sloane says.

I reluctantly tear my eyes from Sloane to look out at Wes. He's now standing on a surfboard. He's a little shaky but standing fairly well as he glides down toward us.

"How did you do it?" Sloane looks at me with wide eyes.

"I'm a good teacher, and your fiancé isn't that bad of a learner."

Sloane turns back to Wes, who is still up on the surfboard. "He's a terrible learner. He has no coordination and no athletic ability really. He occasionally runs and lifts weights, but beyond that, nothing. I've been trying to get him up on a surfboard for years. How did you do it?"

"Like I told you, I'm a pro. I'm very good at what I do. I never lose. I always get what I want. If I want to get someone up on a surfboard, I will. And, if I want to get you in my bed, I will."

"I'm thankful to you for helping Wes, but I'm very happy that I will be the first time you lose. You will never find me in your bed. In fact, you will never see either of us again. It's clear that Wes doesn't need your services any longer, and we still haven't decided where we will be making our permanent home after we are married, but I can assure you, it won't be anywhere near you."

I lean in close to her ear and smell the flowery perfume she is wearing. "Actually, you'll be seeing a lot of me."

Wes falls off the board, and Sloane's mouth falls open as she watches him hit the rough water.

"What do you mean?"

"Just that, since I'm Wes's best man, I expect that you will be seeing a lot of me. So, make sure you are strong enough to resist my charm if you are going to make promises about being the first time I lose."

Wes runs toward us, carrying his surfboard. "What do you think?" he asks.

"You were incredible. I can't believe you were able to do that," Sloane answers. She kisses him on the lips, but it's a chaste kiss.

"I'm ready to go again. Want to join me?" Wes asks Sloane.

Sloane looks over at me and then back to Wes. "No, I'm not feeling the best. I'd rather just sit here and watch you."

That's when I notice the strings of Sloane's bikini sticking out from the neck of her T-shirt. I'd love to see her in nothing but a bikini.

"You going to join me and make me look like a fool?" Wes asks.

I laugh. "Well, I did come here to train, but you don't need me to make you look like a fool. You already do that by yourself."

Wes laughs and starts heading back out into the water. I turn back to my truck and grab my own surfboard.

I walk slowly past Sloane, knowing full well that the only reason she didn't take Wes up on his offer to go out surfing with him is because she wanted to stay back and have it out with me. I raise an eyebrow as I walk, daring her to talk to me.

"You can't be Wes's best man," she hisses.

"And why not?"

"Because you are a horrible person who is just doing this to try and sleep with me."

I grin. "That's exactly why I'm doing this. But it's also exactly why you can't do a damn thing about it. You love Wes, and Wes chose me as his best man. And, if you really think you can resist me, there is no harm in giving Wes what he wants."

Her mouth drops open, but no words come out. I take off toward the ocean, knowing that her eyes are on me. She can't help but watch.

And, when she sees how awesome I am at surfing, how I glide over the water like it's in my control, she will want me to control her in the same way.

7

ASHER

I STEP foot inside the building that Wes texted me in order to get fitted for my tux or whatever he, his cousins, and I are wearing at the wedding. It's a small building jam-packed with tuxes and men's formal attire.

I spot Wes in the back, standing alone, talking to one of the salespeople.

I grin. "Thank God it's just us. I wasn't sure if I could deal with your cousins today," I say, bumping fists with Wes.

"If you want to avoid them, then you'd better try on your tux quickly. They'll be here any minute."

I frown. "Let's get this started then."

"This is my best man, Asher," Wes says to the salesperson.

"I'm Luther. I just need to take a few measurements, and I'll have you try on a couple of jackets and pants. Then, I'll get you out of here," Luther says.

"Excellent," I say.

Luther begins measuring every inch of me. Well, every inch, except for the one part of my body where size really matters—at least, I think so. When he's done, he thinks for a moment and then grabs a couple of jackets and pants.

He carries them into a dressing room. "Try them on. I might have to make some adjustments with the jacket. You will have to go up a size or two to fit your biceps, but then we will need to take it in at the waist to fit everywhere else."

I head into the dressing room and begin trying on the first pair of pants. It feels strange to wear anything this formal. I haven't worn anything this formal since—

I stop thinking. I will not let my mind go there. Not today.

I try the jacket on over my T-shirt. It's a bit snug, so I try the larger size and then step out of the dressing room.

"Just as I suspected. To fit you in the arms and chest, you need the bigger jacket, but we are going to have to take it in to make it fit your waist."

Luther starts messing with the jacket, trying to ensure it will fit, while I stand there, sweating in the thick material.

"Did you say where you are getting married, Wes?" I ask.

"The beach," he answers.

It's like I suspected.

"Are you sure you are going to want to wear tuxes on the beach in summertime in Hawaii? You do know it gets hot here, right?"

Wes frowns. "I didn't really think about it, but now that you mention it—"

"I already told you that the tuxes were stupid. You should just wear khakis and a dress shirt," Sloane says, seemingly appearing from nowhere.

I smile when I see her. I didn't realize that she would be here, but it makes my day so much better.

"Khakis and a dress shirt, I could get behind as well," I say.

I wink at Sloane. She just rolls her eyes and focuses her attention on Wes.

"I need to think about it. I'm not sure khakis are formal enough."

Sloane throws her hands up in defeat. "You don't have time to decide. You have to decide today."

"Then, tuxes. This is going to be in every newspaper in the country. It will be going in countless magazines. I want to look like I'm getting married, not like I'm a bum hanging out at the beach one day."

"We are going to be sweating like pigs in these, man. Just think about that," I say.

"I don't care. It's just for a couple of hours. It won't be that bad," Wes says.

"Don't say I didn't tell you so," Sloane says.

"What do you think of the fit, Ms. Hart?" Luther asks.

Sloane walks over to me and pretends to care about how my jacket and pants are fitting. "Seems to fit fine, but I'm guessing he'll want it a bit looser with all the sweating he will be doing."

I laugh.

Wes frowns.

"Oh, come on. I'm only kidding," Sloane says.

Wes takes Sloane in his arms. "I just want everything to be perfect for you, baby. I don't care about a little sweat."

I can't help but laugh to myself when Wes calls Sloane baby. She seems like anything but a baby to me.

Wes's phone rings, and he steps away to answer it.

"We need to talk," Sloane says, hissing through her teeth in a similar way that she did two days ago when she spoke to me on the beach.

"Then, talk," I say, adjusting the jacket, and looking at myself in the mirror. I look strange in a tux and not just because I'm wearing a T-shirt under the jacket, but also because it is the complete opposite of who I am. I hate fancy things.

I see Sloane staring at me in the mirror, and then her eyes dart to Luther and back to me. I smile. She wants to talk to me alone.

"I don't have lunch plans. Would you and Wes like to join me for lunch?" I ask.

Wes walks back over. "What is this about lunch?"

"I thought we should all go have lunch together, so I can get to know your fiancée a little better."

"I wish I could join you, but that was Elijah. His car broke down. He needs me to pick him and Cody up and bring them to the tux fitting. But you two should go. It would make things easier if you two got along," Wes says.

"I'll just get changed, and then we can go. I'll let you pick the place," I say before heading into the dressing room to change.

I put my swim trunks, T-shirt, and sandals back on while I listen to Wes and Sloane whisper to each other. I can't make out what they are saying, but it doesn't sound like happy whispering.

When I open the curtain separating me from them, they stop and both put fake smiles on their faces.

"Ready to go?" I ask Sloane.

She nods.

———

I sit down at the booth across from Sloane in the swanky restaurant she chose to have lunch at. I don't have to open the menu to know that the prices are outrageous. Most places on the island are expensive. This is just over the top.

I'm not opposed to having a good meal or even going to a swanky place on occasion but not for lunch, especially when I doubt we are even going to be able to make it through this meal.

Sloane is wearing a pale yellow dress and heels today. She looks hot as hell, and it makes me want to take her into the restroom and rip the dress off of her. I won't. That's not my game. But I can still imagine it.

"What are you grinning about?" she asks.

"You don't want to know."

"I do. Otherwise, I wouldn't have asked."

"You, naked."

She rolls her eyes. "You really are a one-track-mind kind of man, aren't you?"

I shrug. "So, what did you want to say?"

"I want you to leave me alone."

I smile and lean back in the booth, extending my arm on the back of the cushion. A nicely dressed woman at the table over gives me a disgusted stare.

"Now, who has a one-track mind?"

"Can I get you anything to drink?"

"White wine," Sloane says, clearly needing a drink to get through this meal.

"Water," I say.

"That's all you want? I'm buying," she says.

I laugh. "You think I can't afford to buy myself a drink? Really?" I shake my head. If I hadn't already decided to go after her, this would have been a major turn-off—her thinking she was better than me because she dressed better. "I'll have water," I say again to the waiter. "I have a training session after I leave here."

Sloane doesn't blush in embarrassment, like I expected. She just sits there, unfazed by me calling her out. She just went up a few notches in my opinion.

"Are you ready to order lunch?" the waiter asks.

I raise my eyebrows at Sloane. "Do you think you can make it through a whole meal with me?"

"I'll have the grilled chicken salad," she says.

Of course she orders a salad, like any other thin girl on the planet would when eating with a man she secretly wanted to bang. If she truly wasn't interested in me, she would have ordered the burger or pizza or anything that had carbs.

"Pepperoni pizza," I say.

The waiter leaves, and then it's just Sloane and me.

Another woman passing by the table stares at me, and at first, she seems disgusted that they would let someone wearing swim trunks into the restaurant. But then, when she looks up further and sees my body and my crooked grin that I know turns her on, she doesn't seem to mind so much.

"Do you always wear swim trunks everywhere you go?"

"Yes. Why wouldn't I? I live in Hawaii, and I'm a surfer."

Her eyes study me, and I know she's wishing that I wasn't wearing anything either. That she would love to see what was beneath the swim trunks.

"You can't be in the wedding. You can't be Wes's best man."

"Sure I can. I have the date cleared and everything. I don't have any competitions or any events I have to attend for my sponsors, and I don't have any women to pick up that day. So, I will definitely be making your wedding."

The waiter brings our drinks. I expect Sloane to slug down her wine, needing liquid courage or strength to deal with me. She doesn't. She sips it coolly, like she deals with propositions from men every day and she just has to come to the right terms to get me to say I'm not coming to her wedding. If that's the way she wants to play, then fine, I'll play along.

"What do you want? Really? You can't think that I'm going to sleep with you. It's just a fun game for you to try. You could probably have dozens of women in the amount of time it would take you to chase me. Is that what you like? The chase. Chasing women you can't have? Is that what turns you on?"

I cock my head to the side. "Something like that."

"What do I need to do to get you to go away? How much money?"

I laugh. "I don't want money. I have too much as it is."

"Then, what do you want?"

"Go out with me."

"What?" she asks, her eyes growing wide.

"Go. Out. On. A. Date. With. Me."

She slowly shakes her head. "I'm married, remember?"

I cock my head and smile. "I thought you were just engaged. Did you two secretly get married, or do you already feel like an old married couple?"

She frowns. "You know what I meant. I'm about to be married. Almost-married women don't go out on dates."

"But you aren't most married women. One date, and I'll leave you alone. One date, and if after the date you still want me to leave, I will. I'll tell Wes that I can't be in the wedding. Something came up, like a surf competition or event that I couldn't get out of. Just one date."

"No."

"Think about it before you say no."

"No."

I laugh. "If you don't go out with me, I'm going to drive you crazy. I'll be at every wedding event that you have. The rehearsal, the wedding, the reception. I'll be there, haunting you. And don't think you'll get rid of me after the wedding. I'll still be there. I'm Wes's best friend after all. I'll be at every family event. I'll start a double-date night with you and Wes. I'll be there every week. I'll be there after the birth of your first child and every birthday afterward. I'll hit on you every time."

"No." She narrows her eyes in defiance this time before taking a sip of her wine, like she thinks she is going to be the one to win this.

She won't. She forgets, I never lose. Ever.

"You'll always wonder if you don't go on a date with me. I'll haunt your dreams. You'll always wonder, *What if?* What if you were wrong about Wes and I was the guy for you?"

"No."

"If you go out with me, you can confirm to yourself that I'm the asshole you think I am. You'll never have to wonder."

"I don't wonder."

"Yes, you do. If you didn't have the tiniest hint of wonder about me, you wouldn't even be bothering with me. You wouldn't be here."

"No."

"My body will haunt you. You'll always wonder about my body, my abs, and other things," I say winking.

"No. Wes has great abs," she says. But there is a hint of seduction in her voice. A hint that she knows what I'm saying is true. That she wants me.

"Not like mine. He's nothing like me."

"No, because you are the devil."

I nod. "True. But, if you truly loved Wes, you'd have nothing to lose by going out with me. In fact, you would be saving Wes from a monster like me."

Sloane takes another sip of wine and clears her throat. "Okay."

I smile smugly. "That didn't sound like a yes to me. Will you go out on a date with me?"

"Let's get one thing straight. I'm going out with you to get rid of you. And the second the date is over and I tell you I'm done is the second you leave my life forever. Got it? I don't play games."

"So, is that a yes?"

She crosses her arms.

"I need to hear you say it, or the deal is void. I need to hear you say that you will go out on a date with me. A real date."

She rolls her arms. "Yes, I will go out on a date with you."

I grin. "Good."

The waiter brings us our lunch, which is good because I am starving and really do need to go to training after we get finished here. I dig into the pizza that is in front of me, eating quickly. After my second slice, I look up and see Sloane staring at me.

"What?"

"You're a pig."

I shrug. "I'm hungry. I assume you are planning on leaving now that you got what you wanted, and I have places to be. So, what if I eat a little fast? We aren't on a date right now, so what does it matter?"

She rolls her eyes for the millionth time it seems since we sat down at this table.

"You should eat, too. You'll need your strength for our date this weekend."

She huffs. "I'll have days to gather my strength to deal with you on our date."

"You should eat anyway."

She starts eating her salad while I finish off my pizza. And then I chuckle to myself.

"Now what?"

I shake my head. "I just can't believe you said yes."

8

ASHER

I ENTER the lobby of the fancy condo building that Sloane lives in. I stare up at the large ceiling that goes up in the center to what must be the top floor with all the other entrances to the rooms surrounding the center. The whole building seems extravagant. Everything is wrapped in gold or silver. Flowers decorate the main floor lobby, but there isn't a dead flower in sight, making it clear that the flowers are pruned and replaced on a regular basis. There is a lot of wealth in this place.

Too much wealth if you ask me.

I walk to the elevator and am stopped by a nicely dressed man in a suit.

"Who are you here to see, sir?" the man asks politely, blocking me from entering the elevator without telling him first.

I look down at my khaki shorts and button-down shirt that is open at the collar. I thought I would dress up a bit for our date tonight, but looking at myself now and where I am, I should have dressed up more because Sloane is a princess who no doubt lives on the top floor of her castle. Despite working for a nonprofit she inherited, she makes plenty of money and expects to live with the finer things in life.

"I'm here to see Sloane Hart," I answer.

"And your name is?"

"Asher Calder."

I expect him to request to see my ID before he will let me up. But, to my surprise, he pushes the button for the elevator, and he steps aside to let me in as the doors open. He steps inside and presses the button for floor number ten.

"Ms. Hart's place is the first door on your left when you exit the elevator. Have a good day, Mr. Calder," he says before leaving the elevator.

I run my hand through my hair as the elevator makes its way up. I can't believe people live like this. I know he is here mostly for security purposes, but it still seems ridiculous that she lives in a place where somebody stands at the elevator and pushes a button for her whenever she wants to go up. As if she is incapable of pressing a button. It's a good thing I don't want her forever because we don't belong together. She wants a fancy life, full of finer things, while I want to live with as few things as possible.

I shake my head at the thought of ever imagining myself with anyone for more than a couple of months. That's not my style. I don't do the boyfriend or girlfriend thing, and I don't imagine ever getting married.

The doors open, and I step off and knock on her door. I wait longer than I expected. She doesn't answer right away even though, if anything, I'm a few minutes late. I pull out my phone, ready to text her with the number that Wes gave me, to see if she is still coming or if she changed her mind, when she opens the door.

She's wearing a beautiful pale blue sundress that, to my surprise, has more cleavage than I would have thought she would wear for a date that isn't really a date. Her blonde hair is curled, but it's her eyes that have my complete attention.

It's clear that she has been crying. Despite trying to dry her eyes, her eyeliner and mascara are smudged, and her eyes are still a bit swollen and red.

"So, where are we going?" Sloane asks, plastering a fake smile on her face.

I frown. "What's wrong?"

Her smile falters. "Oh, nothing. Just allergies."

"Don't lie to me."

"You're one to talk. You lie all the time."

"No, I don't. I have made my intentions very clear to you. I want you. In my bed. As soon as possible. Now, what is wrong?"

"My grandmother died."

I feel her pain immediately. It's clear that she was close to her grandmother.

"I'm so sorry."

I see the tears forming in her eyes again, but she holds them back, not letting me fully see her pain.

"You should be with Wes tonight. We can reschedule, or I can..." I can't quite convince myself to say that I'd leave her alone. Because I can't promise it. I want this too much. I want to steal her heart and know it's mine and not his. I want to be the cause of her pain. But I'm not devil enough to do it when her grandmother just died.

"Wes is gone," she says.

"Gone?"

"He's in LA on business."

"Does he know?"

"Yes," she whispers.

"Are you going to be able to forgive him for not being here?"

"I have to."

"No, you don't."

She shakes her head, and I drop the subject.

"Come out with me," I say without thinking.

She wraps her arms around her shoulders, and I'm afraid that she won't be able to stand on her own two feet much longer, much less come out on a date with me.

"I don't mean as a date. Just that you shouldn't be alone. I can be good, I promise."

She looks down, obviously thinking about it but not yet convinced.

"Just let me feed you and distract you for a few hours. You can talk to me about your grandmother or not. Or you can yell at me and call me names if it will make you feel better. Whatever you need. Today, I'll just be a friend."

"And tomorrow?"

"Tomorrow, I'll go back to being the monster you think I am."

At that comment, I get the tiniest smile out of her.

"I know you are."

I nod.

"I'll come as long as I can leave when I want."

"I'll bring you back whenever you want."

"Yes then."

We both smile when she says yes instead of her giving a less convincing answer.

"Let me just grab my purse."

"No. Change into something comfortable and at least bring your swimsuit."

She frowns. "Why?"

"Because the ocean can be an incredibly healing thing whether I'm there to enjoy it with you or not." I take a breath. "And, if nothing else, I'll get to see you in a bikini."

I wink, and to my surprise, she chuckles. It's not a full-body laugh, but it's enough for now.

"Fine. I'll wear my bikini underneath something more comfortable." She starts walking to her bedroom. "I'll be right back. Make yourself comfortable."

She closes the door to her bedroom and leaves me in her living room. I walk around, staring at all the things in her living room that are varying shades of white. I'm surprised that I don't find many photos in her living room. I don't see any of Wes. The only one I see is a picture of Sloane with who I assume is her grandmother.

I pick the picture up and study it a moment. Sloane is a little younger-looking in the picture but not much younger. She has her arm wrapped around her grandmother's shoulders while her grand-mother blows out the candles on her birthday cake. It's a sweet picture. Full of love. It's obvious that Sloane loved her grandmother.

I place the frame back on the end table where I found it, and a familiar feeling washes over me. I shake it off because the feeling makes no sense. I haven't been in this building before and certainly not in Sloane's place.

I walk over to the kitchen counter and see a pile of pictures and papers piled up. I don't think anything of it at first until I spot a surf-board that is very familiar, sticking out from beneath one of the papers. I pull it out and see a picture of myself staring back at me.

What the fuck?

Why does Sloane have a picture of me?

I rifle through more of the pictures. They're all of me. Then, I realize what the pictures are when I spot Wes in the background. Sloane is the one who hired me to take the ad photos and video. That just leaves me even more confused. I know Sloane works for a nonprofit, so why would she want to have photos of a surfer for advertising? It doesn't make sense to me.

"I didn't realize it was you that I had booked; otherwise, I wouldn't have booked you," Sloane says from behind me.

I turn and look at her, and I completely forget about the photographs. "You're beautiful."

She shakes her head and blushes a little, which makes her all the more enduring. She doesn't blush when she should be embarrassed, but one tiny compliment, and she's a blushing fool.

Sloane runs her hand through her hair, shaking out the curls that were there before. "No, I'm not. I'm in a T-shirt and shorts. I don't have an ounce of makeup on, and I'm blotchy from crying. It's not possible to look beautiful at the moment."

I frown, trying to come up with the words that will make her see what I see. I doubt I can convince her of anything in the moment. "It doesn't matter if you believe me or not. You're the most fucking beau-tiful woman I've ever seen. And, right now, you are more beautiful than I have ever seen you," I say, meaning every fucking word, my eyes glued to hers.

She stares back at me until she is finally convinced that I am telling the truth. I don't know when she'll realize that I never lie. Never. I don't lie to women to get them to leave their husbands. I want an honest fight. I just usually win, which must mean that the women don't really want to get married. Marriage is a ridiculous concept anyway. No one should be with just one person for the rest of their life. People are constantly changing and not always in the same way.

Why would you stay with the same person when you no longer fit together anymore?

I try to search her eyes to see if she is just like the rest of the women, who were looking for an escape from a marriage that they thought would be everything they'd ever dreamed up but realized too late that it was going to be a nightmare that there was no way out of. But whatever she feels, she hides it well. She might just be the exception. She might really love Wes and want to marry him. I just can't see how a woman like her, who seems to have such ambition and is constantly changing and wanting more out of life, would be happy with settling down with one man for the rest of her life.

"The video and pictures we took are for an ad my new head of marketing came up with. I don't love the idea, but she is insistent that, since I spend so much time in Hawaii and many of our donors live or at least vacation here, we need to add more inspiring images of what our children and families could eventually achieve with the money they are given instead of just images of hungry children."

"Why don't you use images of people who have gone through your program and made something of their lives?"

"We did."

"I didn't do any ads with children that have gone through your program.

She shakes her head. "You did."

I pause for a second. "Wes? Really? But he always seems like—" I stop myself from saying how I really feel about Wes.

Sloane smiles though. "Like a spoiled rich kid."

I nod.

"He thinks he needs to act that way to fit in with me and my family."

I glance around her expensive apartment and raise an eyebrow. "I can understand why."

She lets out a huff of air. "I guess so."

I don't want to spend the rest of the evening talking about Wes. My job today is to cheer her up and be her friend. I made a promise, and I won't go back on my promise.

I hold out my arm to her, like the gentleman that I am. "Hungry, or should I take you to the beach first?"

Sloane walks toward me. Her hips sway as she does, and I have never wished I were standing behind a woman like I do right now.

I think she is going to take my arm, but she stops short.

"Beach. I don't have an appetite for food."

She walks past me and toward the door, and I finally get the view that I was desperate for a second earlier. Her tight ass moves from side to side, just barely covered in her tiny shorts, making the fact that she isn't holding on to my arm so that I could feel her skin worth it.

"You coming, or do I have to go myself?"

I grin. "Definitely coming."

9

ASHER

SLOANE IS BEYOND INDEPENDENT. She doesn't let me do anything for her as we make our way out of her condo building. I don't get to open a door or press an elevator button or rest my hand on the small of her back to guide her. She avoids me at every turn.

Her surfboard is waiting for her in the lobby when we get down. How they managed to get it so quickly, I have no idea since she just texted them that she needed it when we got into the elevator. But, somehow, they managed or knew that she would need it. Because here it sits.

I run forward to take it off their hands before Sloane is able to.

"Relax, Asher. I appreciate the help, but I can carry my own surfboard."

I hold it up high over my head, so she can't reach it. "I don't care if you can. You shouldn't have to."

She frowns and crosses her arms. "I don't need a man to take care of me. If you think that's why I'm marrying Wes, you're wrong."

"I realize you don't need a man or anyone else to do anything for you. But that doesn't mean you should stop every man from doing something nice for you."

She rolls her eyes and then begins walking toward the parking lot.

I can't tear my eyes away from her ass as she walks. I'm too focused on Sloane to notice another woman in the room, one that I should have been paying attention to.

I feel the slap before I notice the girl. I grab my stinging cheek as I look at the woman who just slapped me.

"You're an asshole! I can't believe you had the nerve to come back here. Leave me the fuck alone!" she screams at me before turning and walking out of the condo.

I glance up at Sloane, who has her head cocked to one side, her arms folded across her chest, and the cutest grin ever on her face.

"Who was that?"

"Nicole," I say, realizing why I had a familiar feeling while I was in Sloane's condo. I've been here before—with Nicole.

"And why did she slap you?"

"Because I'm an asshole."

Sloane laughs.

"Did you bring your surfboard? If so, we can just surf right out here. It's a private beach."

"No, I didn't bring it." I think that is the first time I have ever spoken such a sentence. I always bring my surfboard. This is exactly why I always bring my surfboard and swim trunks with me.

"My car is just over this way. I can drive you to wherever you want to grab yours."

I smile when she mentions her car. Of course she wants to drive. She wants to do everything herself. And, since I'm trying to appease her and make her forget about how sad she really is, I'm not going to argue, no matter how much I want to show her how well I could take care of her if she let me.

I follow her to her pristine white Jeep that doesn't look like it has ever been driven.

"Is there something wrong?" Sloane asks when I stop and stare at it.

This woman is the epitome of contradiction. She works for a nonprofit, giving money to those who need it most, but also has more money and spends it like she enjoys showing off the money she has.

She likes surfing and adventure but dresses like she never leaves the business room. I can't understand her.

"Nothing," I say.

I place her surfboard on top of her Jeep, quickly strapping it in, before climbing into the passenger side. Sloane is already on the driver's side and begins backing out as soon as I get in.

We drive in silence. It's clear that Sloane is lost in thoughts of her grandmother, bringing back the feelings of sadness and pain that I can't stand to watch. It's not hot in her Jeep. The AC works almost too well, which is strange for me since I can't recall my truck's AC ever working.

I roll my window down and stick my hand out into the warm breeze, like you should in Hawaii.

"What are you doing?" she asks sternly.

"Enjoying Hawaii."

Her hair blows as the breeze gets stronger inside the car. She runs her hand through her hair, trying to keep the wind from further tangling it.

"But it's too warm outside, and the AC is working fine. Why would I open the window?"

I laugh and shake my head. "Do you really never drive around with the windows open?"

"No. It's much too warm here."

"Turn the AC off, and open your window."

"No."

"Stop being stubborn, and just do it."

She looks at me like I'm mad but finally concedes. Her hair becomes even more tangled, blowing in front of her face as she drives. She seems agitated and annoyed, which is the opposite of what I'm going for.

"Now, relax, and stick your hand out the window."

She raises an eyebrow at me.

I laugh, my whole body shaking. I can't help it.

"Are you sure you grew up here? You are acting like you grew up in outer space."

She frowns, clearly not amused.

"Like this," I say, sticking my hand out the window.

She does the same, and it only takes seconds for her to relax. To breathe and become one with the wind, letting go of some of the sadness was overtaking her. But there is too much sadness and pain in her for a simple car ride with the wind blowing around us to fix. Not that anything is going to fix the pain or sadness. I know that as well as anyone. I've experienced it myself and caused it in others. I've watched them all handle the pain in different ways. Some handle it better than others, but then some weren't really in love.

Sloane loved her grandmother. So, the pain will never go away. But she does need to learn to live with it, and the sooner she does, the better. If only for my selfish reasons. Because, the sooner she heals, the sooner I can rip her heart out.

"Pull over," I say.

"Why?" Sloane asks but doesn't pull over.

"For once, can you just do what I tell you without asking why?"

She frowns. "No. We haven't known each other long enough for me to do that."

I laugh. "Do you do what Wes tells you without asking why?"

She scrunches her nose. "No."

"Exactly. It doesn't matter who is asking. You always have to be in control. For once in your life, let someone else have control. Don't think. Just do."

I reach over and touch her hand that has a firm hold on the steering wheel. She doesn't flinch even though that was what I expected. She doesn't glance down either. She acts like I'm not even touching her.

She's a much better actor than I am. I can feel my heart pounding in my chest at the touch of her soft skin. I have to be good today. I'm used to practicing self-control. But Sloane makes that incredibly hard to do.

"Pull over," I say calmly.

Sloane takes a deep breath. I watch her chest rise and fall and wish she weren't wearing the T-shirt covering the bikini underneath. Better yet, I wish she were wearing nothing.

Sloane pulls the car over onto the side of the road.

"Now, put the car in park."

She does without hesitation.

"Turn the car off."

She slowly reaches up, and I reluctantly move my hand away from hers as she turns the car off.

"Take a deep breath, and then get out of the car."

I watch her chest rise and fall again, and then she gets out of the car. I do the same and pull her surfboard off the top of the car. I begin carrying it to the beach.

"What are we doing? You don't have your surfboard or swim trunks, and this is one of the worst places for surf on the island. There isn't even anyone here."

I shake my head from side to side. "No questions. You have to trust me. This is what you need."

She frowns, but I keep walking toward the edge of the water with her surfboard in tow, not giving her another choice.

She walks behind me.

When I get to the water, I stop and wait for her to catch up. I hand her back her surfboard.

"Now, surf, and don't think. About me or Wes or your grand-mother. Or anything else. Just surf. Go through the motions."

She opens her mouth to say something, but I put a finger up to her lips to stop her. Her lips are as soft as I imagined. She bites her lip, and I pull my hand away.

"Don't say anything. Now, go." I point toward the ocean.

She grins. "I was only going to say, can I take my T-shirt and shorts off first?"

I want to say no because it doesn't matter. She's thinking too much, and she needs to just get in the water. But I'm desperate to see her in nothing but her bikini. I can just imagine her walking back toward me after surfing, beads of water dripping down her breasts. I need to see her body like that. Although a white T-shirt drenched in water might be equally as awesome.

"It was implied," I say.

"Sure it was."

She shimmies out of her shorts first, but her T-shirt is long enough that it covers her ass, revealing nothing new to me. But then she removes her shirt, revealing the toned body that she was hiding beneath her T-shirt.

Damn. I don't know what I was expecting, but I wasn't expecting this.

She's toned and fit beneath her tiny black bikini. I can see the muscles rippling in her stomach, arms, and legs. But she also has the perfect amount of curves outlining her muscles. Her breasts have me aching to touch them. Her hips are curvy, making me want to grab her and have her right here in the sand. Even though I've done that before and as much as I like the beach and ocean, fucking a woman on it is much worse than the fantasy.

She doesn't smile as she begins walking into the ocean. Instead, she seems determined. She walks in a ways before she gets on the board and starts paddling out. The waves are pretty tame here, and there isn't anyone out here that she has to pay attention to. No, this is the perfect spot for her to clear her head and get used to the pain she is feeling.

I just wish I had my own board, so I could join her.

It doesn't take her long to paddle out until I can barely make out the curves in her body from where I stand.

She takes her time in choosing a wave. And then she is up on her board, surfing with obvious experience. She doesn't do anything fancy. But the way she moves over the ocean is beautiful. She glides easily, like she has been doing it her whole life. I could watch her for hours.

The wave suddenly changes and causes Sloane to lose her balance and prematurely fall off the board. The wave crashes down on top of her with a lot of force. I know it's not enough to keep her down for long. I know the wave wasn't that bad. But, still, I can't help but throw off my shirt, jump into the water, and swim out to her to ensure that she makes it out of the water. To air. To safety.

I swim as fast and as hard as I can to reach her. I try to calm my beating heart and nerves that are shooting through my body. I don't understand the feeling. I don't understand why I care so much if she is alive or dead. In pain or not. She is nothing to me.

Still, I swim hard, not thinking about why my heart is beating hard in my chest. Or why I care if something happens to her. I dive under the water, swimming faster until I see her body right in front of me. I grab hold of her and look up to see the wave has stopped pounding down on top of us. And then I kick hard over and over until we reach the top.

We each take a breath of air at the same time when our heads hit the surface. Sloane flips her head back to get her hair out of her face, and she scowls at me. Her eyes look unforgiving, a deep V has formed between her eyes, and her mouth turns down into more than a frown.

"What are you doing?"

"Saving you. You went down and didn't come back up for air for quite a while. I wanted to make sure you didn't die."

She shakes her head as she wades in the water and rests her arms on her surfboard. "I don't need saving or rescuing. I have surfed before even if I am a bit rusty."

"I know."

"Then, why are you here?"

"Because I can't help but be near you."

"I thought you weren't going to hit on me today."

"I'm not. I'm just telling you the truth since you are so insistent on asking a million questions, needing to know everything."

She doesn't say anything else, but I can tell she is deep in thought again, no longer here with me.

"Swim back out, and go again," I say.

She turns to do just that. At least, now, she is listening to me instead of questioning. She pauses though after swimming a foot or so and faces me.

"What are you going to do?"

"Join you."

"How? You don't have your surfboard."

I grin. "Sure I do."

I start swimming out while she paddles on her surfboard. When she stops, I swim up behind her, guiding her toward the front of the surfboard while I climb on behind her. Neither of us says anything, and I have honestly never surfed with someone else on the same board before. But it can't be that hard. She's more than capable on a surfboard, and I'll figure out the rest, no problem.

We wait through the first wave, agreeing it's not the right one without having to say anything to each other.

When the next wave comes, I say, "Start paddling."

We both do.

"Stand up," I say after a few seconds of paddling.

Sloane does, and I do a second later. Then, we are both up on the board at the same time. I take a step forward and place my hands on her hips as I begin maneuvering the board through the wave. She moves with me as I move us as one. It feels different, maneuvering while having to think about someone else on the board. I can't just do what I want. I have to ensure that she wants to go the same way as me. I have to think about her, too.

I want to show her what a surfboard can really do though, so I grip her hips harder and begin moving us higher onto the wave. She doesn't question me. She goes with me. We surf until the wave takes us close to shore. We step off at the same time, both speechless.

Our eyes lock after such an intimate moment together. I don't know what I see in her eyes. I'm used to being able to read people, but I can't read her. She doesn't give anything away with her eyes. I just know what I hope I'm seeing there. I hope it's the same thing that I'm feeling.

I reach my hand up to her cheek. "I want to kiss you," I say.

I wait for her to slap me. A slap always follows when I say something so bold. I brace for it. But it never comes. Instead, she leans in closer to me, like she is considering it. Like she is desperate for it. I feel her warm breath against my lips. I have to ball my hands into fists to keep from closing in the last few inches and kissing her.

I won't kiss her though. If she cheats on Wes, it has to be her choice. That's the only way to steal her heart, to ensure she's mine, and then I'll toss her aside when I'm through with her. She has to be the one who does the betrayal.

When she realizes that no temptation is going to get me to be the one to make the first move, she steps back and turns to look out over the ocean at the sun that is just now beginning to set over the ocean.

"We should go sit on the beach and watch the sunset, so we can try to dry off before getting back into my car. We forgot to bring towels," Sloane says so matter-of-factly. Like the almost kiss didn't happen. Like I haven't affected her at all.

My eyes widen as I stare at her walking back toward the shore. I begin to follow her. I walk until I'm standing right next to her on the beach. She's staring at the sunset while I'm gaping at her.

"What are you doing?" she asks, still staring straight ahead at the sunset, while she wrings out her wet hair.

"Gaping at how you never cease to surprise me."

"Why is that?"

"You never behave in the way that I think you will."

She nods. "Would it surprise you to hear that you aren't the first person to make that observation?"

I laugh. "No, I guess it wouldn't."

She looks at me. "I get it from my grandmother. My unpredictability."

I walk over and find my T-shirt that I threw on the beach before I jumped into the water. I pick it up and carry it over to where Sloane is standing on the beach, trying to dry off. I lay it on the ground.

"Here, sit on the T-shirt, so you don't get sand all over you."

She sits on my T-shirt, and I sit on the sand next to her.

Sloane laughs at me.

I rub my neck as I listen to her beautiful laugh that I didn't think I would get to hear today. "You're going to have to tell me what is so funny."

She keeps laughing though until her whole body is rocking back and forth from the force of her laughter. "I'm sorry," she says in between laughs. "It's really not funny. I don't understand why I'm laughing at all. It's just that you thought I should sit on your T-shirt to avoid getting sand on me, but then you sat down on the sand. And, unless you are walking home, you are going to get sand in my car."

I stare at her, taking in her laugh again that continues to force itself out of her. But she has a point. So, I get up and rinse myself off in the water. And then I march back to her.

"What are you doing?" she asks, still laughing.

I don't respond to her basically never-ending question. I guess I should dictate everything that I am doing, as I'm doing it to satisfy her. She really is a control freak.

I plop down behind her so that I can sit on the tiny bit of remaining T-shirt that she is not sitting on. She squeals and laughs, like she probably would if Wes had sat down behind her.

"You're getting me all wet," she squeals as the water drips off my chest and onto her back.

"Damn it! I promised I wouldn't hit on you; otherwise, I would have a great line about getting you wet."

This causes her to laugh hysterically all over again. She throws her head back, hitting me square in the jaw.

"Oh my God! I'm sorry," she says, still laughing.

I laugh now. "I don't think you are the least bit sorry. You probably think I deserved it."

"You're right. I'm not sorry at all. You deserved that and more."

Sloane continues to laugh until her laugh turns into hiccups. I rub her back under the guise of trying to calm her down and make the hiccups go away, but I also can't stand to be this close to her and not touch any part of her body, except for our legs that are barely touching. Her skin is soft and warm.

"The sunset is beautiful," she says as she leans back a little but not enough so that she is leaning against my chest, like I want.

"You're beautiful," I say automatically.

"That sounds like you are hitting on me."

"Nope. Just stating a fact."

She takes a deep breath. I can tell from watching her rib cage rising and falling.

"Thank you for this," she says.

I don't say anything because the hesitation in her voice tells me she needs to say more.

"I needed this. I don't know how you knew this was what I'd need, but I did. I wouldn't have survived being alone tonight."

I think she's crying, but I can't be sure. But, from the sniffling sound in her voice, I can guess.

I don't comfort her though. She doesn't need that. She needs to find her way on her own.

"I don't know why I feel her loss so much. She hasn't been in my life in the last five years. Not really. She had Alzheimer's, and she lived in a nursing home. I tried to visit as often as I could, but she didn't know who I was. She's been gone for the last five years. I thought I'd come to terms with the fact that the woman who had raised me was gone."

She turns and faces me, and I see the full tears coming down her face.

"She's really gone now though. Body and mind. She was the only person who ever really made me feel loved." Her voice is shaky.

I know that there are no words to make it better for her. I can't help her through this. She has to deal with this pain, this sadness, this new reality. All I can do is wrap my arms around her and let her know that she isn't alone.

So, that is exactly what I do.

She resists me at first, pushing my arms away, but I hold on tighter. Not because I'm hitting on her or because I need to feel her close to me. But because I know she needs the connection to another human being right now.

She finally relaxes against my chest, as I continue to hold her in my arms. She continues to cry as we both look out over the ocean as the sun sets. We don't say anything else. Sloane can't get any other words out between her tears anyway. And I can't say anything that will make her stop crying. So, we just sit until the warmth of the sun is long gone, and there is nothing but the noise of the highway behind us and the ocean waves in front of us.

"Do you want me to take you home now?" I whisper in her ear.

She doesn't answer. I move my head forward, so it is closer to her face that is lying against my chest, and I listen to her calm breathing. She's asleep.

I'll have to find a way to get her back to her condo at some point. But, for now, I just want to sit here, in one of my favorite places, holding a beautiful woman who I don't think, no matter how hard I try, I will fully understand.

I think about the last words she said to me.

"She was the only person who ever really made me feel loved."

I don't know if her words were true or if she was just upset and said it because she was missing Wes and not feeling loved. But I have to find out. Because I can't really steal her from Wes if he's never really loved her.

10

ASHER

I CARRIED Sloane back to her car that night. She didn't wake up. She didn't stir. She was too exhausted from dealing with her grief to wake up.

I drove her back to my place after I realized I would never get her back into her place without waking her. I figured, after she slept for an hour or so, she would wake up, and then she could drive herself back home in her car.

She never woke up though.

I placed her in my bed and fell asleep on the couch, waiting for her to wake up.

The next morning, she was gone without a word, which didn't surprise me. What did was how early in the morning she'd left. I'm always awake before the sun. She woke up and left before I did.

I haven't spoken to or seen her in almost two months. The wedding was postponed after her grandmother's death to give her time to mourn, to heal. I've been busy with winning a couple of surfing competitions. There haven't been any wedding-related events that I've had to attend. But that's not why I have stayed away. I've stayed away because I'm torn.

Sloane doesn't make anything clear. I can't read if she really loves

Wes or not. And, since I can't tell how she feels, I don't know how I want to pursue her or if I want to pursue her at all. Not because I've had a change of heart. I still want to destroy her. I still want to steal her heart. I just need to give her time to realign her loyalty to Wes because, after that night, I know I could have had her in my bed. I laugh because I did have her in my bed. But she would have fucked me that morning if she had stayed. That is why I suspect she left before I woke up.

I also know the longer that I stay away, the more she will think about me. The more she will build up that night in her head as being either one of the most meaningful moments in her life or something that makes her hate me even more. Either way, when I walk into the church and see her again, her emotions will be amplified, which will make them much easier for me to read. The only problem with my plan is that my ability to control myself is dwindling. I want Sloane more than ever, and even if it's not the right time to steal her heart, I'm not sure I'm going to be able to resist her.

I get out of my pickup truck and walk toward the beautiful stone cathedral where the rehearsal dinner is to be held, and the rehearsal is to take place on the beach just outside the building. It's a beautiful building, but it is nothing compared to the beach.

If I were getting married, I would do it on the beach with as few people as possible. I laugh. Not that I would ever get married. But, from the number of cars parked in the parking lot just for the rehearsal, I know that this wedding is going to be a big affair.

I enter the church and immediately feel everyone's eyes turn to me. I look down at how I'm dressed in the same shorts and button-down shirt that I wore the last time I saw Sloane. I thought I was dressed up enough for a rehearsal. I was wrong.

I glance around the room at the suits and formal dresses that everyone else is wearing. But I don't apologize for wearing something casual. I'm not going to bother spending money on something that I'd wear once and then never wear again.

"You made it," Wes says to me, holding out his fist that I bump against mine.

"Of course, man. This seems like quite the ordeal here," I say.

Wes smiles. "Yep. This is heaven to me. Everyone that I care about is here, and tomorrow, I'll get to marry this amazing woman," Wes says while wrapping his arm around Sloane's waist.

She smiles at me while holding on to him. I hate watching her with him. I hate it. But, other than picking her up, carrying her over my shoulder, and literally kidnapping her, I don't really have a choice at the moment.

"It's good to see you again, Sloane. Excited to get married tomorrow?" I ask.

She stands in front of Wes, and he possessively puts his arms around her, which seems strange for her to allow when she is such an independent person.

"Of course she's excited. Aren't you, honey?" Wes asks.

Sloane nods, her smile never faltering. She looks like a happy bride on the brink of marital bliss as she stands in the arms of her fiancé in a white lace dress that makes her boobs look amazing and her legs long and lean. But she's not happy. I know her well enough to know that, no matter how much she loves Wes, she's not happy with him, and she won't be happy marrying him.

She's made my decision for me. I must steal her before she gets married tomorrow. I'll actually be doing her a service. She'll have to deal with the pain for a couple of days to avoid a lifetime of unhappiness.

"I'm sure she is," I say, sticking my hands in my pockets to keep myself from ripping Sloane out of Wes's arms.

The minister begins waving Sloane and Wes toward the front of the church.

"I guess that's our cue to go," Wes says, grabbing hold of Sloane's hand and leading her to the front of the church where the minister stands.

I follow slowly behind, keeping my hands in my pockets and staying on the outskirts of the crowd that is gathering around the couple.

"I'm Dean, the minister who will be conducting the ceremony

tomorrow. Tonight, we are just going to run through the rehearsal, so everyone knows what they will be doing tomorrow. Then, you will be able to enjoy the dinner that the bride and groom are providing you.

"There has been a change of plans due to the weather tomorrow. Due to the extreme heat, we will be having the ceremony as well as the reception inside the church."

My eyes go to Sloane. She doesn't give away any hint of sadness. Or at least she doesn't think she is giving away any hint that she doesn't want to get married inside this damn church instead of out on the beach. But the people who know her well or take the time to know her at all can tell. I can tell even if there wasn't the tiniest bit of welling in her eyes. I can tell that this isn't what she wants.

The minister continues to talk about how the rehearsal is going to happen and what everybody needs to be doing, but I don't listen. All I can see is Sloane. How she kisses Wes. How she mirrors his movements. How she is anything but independent when he's around. It's bizarre—her behavior.

People start moving into positions, and I follow Wes to the side of the church. Wes says something to me and his other two groomsmen standing behind me. I nod automatically and then follow Wes when he walks out into position. I stand next to him with the other groomsmen standing behind me. We all know where to stand, despite none of us listening.

Music starts up, and the bridesmaids begin walking toward us. It seems to take forever to get them down the aisle even though there are only three of them. Then, they stand opposite us. All beautiful, of course, but none beautiful enough to make me give up my plan to steal Sloane. She is my only focus.

The music changes, and Sloane finally starts walking down the aisle. She's beautiful, of course, as she walks down the aisle by herself. Her blonde hair seems to blow, as if a fan were directed on her the whole time she walks. Her skin seems to glow. Her eyes though are what interest me the most. Everyone else who sees her walking down the aisle assumes she is looking at Wes, holding his gaze.

She isn't though. Her gaze is on me.

Sloane looks at me the whole time she walks down the aisle, and her eyes tell me everything. That she wants me to rescue her. To save her from this. I grin because that is exactly what I'm going to do.

Sloane makes it down the aisle and goes through the motions of the ceremony as the minister explains everything that is going to happen. And then he calls for everyone to do everything again. Everyone sighs and moans quietly to themselves. With large fake smiles on our faces, we all go through the motions again while being completely bored out of our minds.

The only positive thing I get out of it is being able to study Sloane as she walks. Every curve of her gorgeous tan skin. Every curl of her blonde hair. The green color of her eyes. The confidence in which she walks or does anything.

The minister finally dismisses us, saying that we can all head into the dining hall where we can enjoy a dinner on the bride and groom. I head into the dining hall with the other groomsmen. I take a seat at the same table as they do even though I know they all want to punch me in the face. I've learned though not to take it personally. It is just the reaction I provoke in people.

Waiters start bringing out the first course of soup and salad. But the happy couple still hasn't made their appearance. I pick at the salad. I've never been one for eating anything remotely healthy.

The waiters take the first course away and start serving the main course of chicken and vegetables. I scan the room but still don't see where the bride- and groom-to-be are. A few other people have noticed, too. I can see the worry and anxiety on some of their faces.

I get up from the table and hear a woman say to her husband, "It's strange that the bride and groom haven't made it to the rehearsal dinner yet."

The husband laughs. "They are probably just doing it in a back room somewhere."

I feel a tightness in my chest as I think about that possibility. It's never bothered me before when the women I was trying to steal slept with their fiancés. But knowing that is what Sloane could be doing drives me crazy. I don't want Wes touching her or kissing her or fucking her. I don't want him anywhere near her. She's mine.

I start walking back to the chapel where the rehearsals took place, as it was the last place that I saw either of them. The second I enter the chapel, I hear their voices ringing throughout the room. I'm surprised that we couldn't hear them arguing from the dining room just down the hallway from here.

"No, we aren't postponing until the weather cooperates so that we can get married outside!" Wes shouts.

"But it's important to me!" Sloane shouts back.

"Isn't being married more important than where we get married?" Wes shouts.

"Of course, but this is the one thing I care about. The beach reminds me of my grandmother, which is why I want to get married there instead of in this church."

I slowly walk up, trying not to be noticed, but they both seem so entranced in their arguing that I don't think they would notice me, no matter how loud I was being. They start walking, and I keep following. Sloane starts running out of the church, visibly upset and shaking with anger.

"I'm so tired of hearing about your grandmother. We postponed the wedding in the first place because of your grandmother's death. I don't think we have to do everything because of your goddamn grandmother."

Tears well in Sloane's eyes, and I can't stand it any longer.

I start to move forward when Sloane says, "I can't breathe."

"Sure you can. You just don't want to admit that you're wrong, and I'm right."

But Sloane truly can't breathe. Her face is turning bright red, and she falls back to the ground. I run forward at the same time that Wes does. Her face has started to swell.

"Sloane, what's wrong?" I ask.

But she can't answer me. I can tell she is running out of oxygen fast. I pinch her nose and lower my mouth to hers, breathing a breath into her, but the air barely seems to make a difference.

I feel something sharp hit my neck, followed by a buzzing sound. Bees. She must be allergic. I grab her purse that is lying next to her.

"Call 911, Wes," I say as I dig through it and find the EpiPen that is inside.

I quickly read through the instructions, but I know I'm running out of time. So, I remove the cap and then jab it into her thigh, like the instructions say.

"Come on, Sloane, breathe. You're going to be fine. Just relax, and try to breathe."

She slowly takes a breath and starts to sit up. My heart slows when I see that she is going to make it.

"Thank you," she whispers.

I nod, but saving her did nothing to stop my own anger. If anything, it just made me angrier. I help Sloane to her feet and then over to a bench outside the church where she can wait for the ambulance to come and check her over. And then I turn toward Wes, who is standing next to the bench, and I punch him square in the face. He completely falls back, startled by my punch.

"You don't deserve a woman like Sloane," I say, staring at Wes now lying on the floor, still in complete shock.

I turn to face Sloane as the ambulance pulls up. "Don't marry him. Not because I want you and am desperate to claim you, to fuck you, but because you deserve better than an asshole dick of a man who doesn't understand how important your grandmother is to you. You don't have to choose me, but don't choose him either. You deserve love, not years of unhappiness."

11

ASHER

I GRAB the six-pack of beer and take it out to the beach. I considered just going home after I punched Wes. I left the rehearsal before Wes came to his senses and decided to start a fight. But I stuck around in the parking lot long enough to see that Sloane didn't even have to go to the hospital. They checked her over and determined that the EpiPen was enough. That she was going to be okay. She went back into the rehearsal, and I left. I couldn't bear to stay and watch her prepare to marry him.

My surfboard is in the back of my truck. I consider bringing it down to the beach with me, but I don't really feel like surfing. Instead, I plop down on the sand with my beer.

I'll drink for a while, maybe take a dip in the ocean, and then sleep off the alcohol in the back of my truck or here on the beach. I open the first beer, trying to do anything but think about Wes and Sloane. I've never punched anyone before. I know that punching someone accomplishes nothing but making the puncher feel a bit better—at least, for a moment. But, now that I have, I want to go back and beat the shit out of Wes for treating Sloane so poorly.

And Sloane...I have no idea what she is going to do. Marry him most likely. I don't see her canceling the wedding the night before.

She's different than all the other women I've seduced. She is stronger and no-nonsense, all business. I'm not even sure that she is marrying Wes because she loves him. There has to be another reason that I am overlooking. Something that makes her feel like she has to go through with it—not because she loves him, but because that is what is best for her future.

Maybe her company's future? I have no idea.

But Sloane was right about one thing. I was going to lose this game. I was never going to claim her. Even if she decides not to marry Wes, she will never be mine. She is too intelligent, too independent, too rational to let her heart go to a man like me.

I sip on my beer, trying to forget about all of it. I stare out at the ocean. I should take a trip somewhere. Get away from my normal life for a week or two. I've always wanted to travel overseas. But it would have to be somewhere without a beach because, after our time together on the beach, in the ocean, I can't be out here without thinking of her.

It was a mistake, coming here now. I should have just gone back to my shack. Maybe then I can forget about her. I glance down at the six-pack on my left. Maybe, after drinking all of them, I will forget about her.

"Can I join you?" a soft voice says behind me.

I freeze, not sure if she is really here or if I am imagining her.

She doesn't wait for me to answer. Sloane just sits down in the sand next to me, not caring that her white dress is going to be covered in sand. She takes a beer and opens the cap with the bottom of her shoe. She didn't bother asking if she could have one. She isn't that kind of girl. She doesn't ask permission for anything; she just does.

"Thank you," she says after a long pause.

I stare at her with wide eyes. I'm not sure if anyone has ever thanked me before, for anything. And I never expected to get multiple thank-yous from her, of all people.

"You really need to stop thanking me. For however bad Wes treats you, I'm worse."

She sips her beer. I watch her mouth close around it, and I can't help but imagine her lips wrapped around my cock. Although I don't see that happening—ever.

"I'm not getting married tomorrow," she says.

I nod. "I guessed that. I'm not sorry. I don't think he's good enough for you."

She finishes her beer. "I'm not sorry either. Not really."

She takes another beer out, which makes me smile at her.

I finish my own beer and start on a second. "So, what now?"

"First, I'm going to finish the rest of these beers with you."

I grin. "Of course. And then?"

"And then you are going to fuck me and make me forget about Wes."

I spew the beer out of my mouth. She looks at me straight-faced though, and I know she is dead serious.

"You surprise the hell out of me, Sloane."

She drinks down half of her second beer. "You don't surprise me at all."

"I'm not sure if that was meant as a compliment or a dis, but I'll take it if it means I get to fuck you."

"I don't like surprises."

"I love surprises if they come from you."

Her lips crash with mine, surprising the hell out of me again. Her kiss is hungry, like she is desperate for more and more and more. And I'm more than happy to give her everything she wants and more.

I kiss her back, equally as hungry. My tongue slides into her mouth, and to my surprise, she lets me. Each step I take with her is going to surprise me because I thought she hated me. She has every reason to. I broke up her wedding. I ruined her life.

But she is kissing me like I'm the only man she has ever wanted. My hand tangles in her hair, pulling her closer to me, and at the same time, she pushes herself on top of me. We fall back and break our kiss.

Sloane lies on top of me, breathing heavily from our quick make-out session. We stare at each other for a moment, deciding if we want this to go any further.

"We can stop. No one has to know that you kissed me. You could still go back to Wes. But, if you do this, he will never take you back," I warn.

I've seen it before, and as much as I thought I wanted to destroy her, I was wrong. I don't want to hurt her. I care too much about her, which is strange, especially since I have never slept with her.

"Don't ever stop. I need this. I don't want Wes. I want you even if only for one night."

I pull her bottom lip into my mouth, bringing her lips back to mine. Her hands go back around my neck, and my hands rub against her bare back, running over her smooth skin, as we kiss. Each kiss, our tongues dive deeper into each other's mouth, showing how desperate we are for each other.

Without thinking, I begin to undo the zipper that starts around her waist. I slowly unzip it until my hand can slip beneath the lace fabric. My hand slides over her ass, and I find the same lace material covering it.

Sloane starts tugging at my shirt, running her hand over my abs and up my chest. I love the feel of her soft hands so firm against me, demanding what she wants. I've never had a woman so clearly tell me what she wants without even saying a word.

She wants me to take her here, on the beach.

The wind picks up, and salt water and sand brush over us. And I'm reminded why I never fuck women on the beach.

"My car is"—I kiss her soft, luscious lips—"just"—she kisses me, stopping me from speaking—"over—"

Sloane shuts me up again with her kisses. I don't give a fuck that rough seashells are poking into my ass as she rides me. I don't care that we are going to get salt water in our eyes as I fuck her. I won't be able to close my eyes for a second because I would hate to miss even a moment with her. I don't give a shit that I'm going to find sand for days to come in places that I don't even want to think about.

I'm going to fuck her here, on the beach, where anyone could see us, because I can't help but give her everything she wants and give myself exactly what I want as well. Because I've never wanted anything more than this completely unpredictable, self-sufficient, beautiful woman.

"I want to strip you naked, but I couldn't stand it if anyone else got to see you naked on the beach," I say.

She lifts up the hem of her dress and jerks it over her head, revealing her black lace bra and underwear that she somehow hid under the white material of her dress, like the devil she hides underneath her angel facade. My eyes widen from the shock of what she just did and how perfect her body is. How her breasts overflow from her bra, begging me to touch them.

"No one comes to this beach. And it doesn't matter if anyone does. I'm not going to last long enough for them to get much of a show anyway."

She kisses me again, and I forget that we are on a public beach and that anyone could see her. I no longer fucking care.

"Plus, I'm not ashamed of my body. I know I look hot, naked or not."

I bite her bottom lip again. "I couldn't agree more."

She grabs my dick from beneath my shorts and underwear, and I cry out like a fucking girl. I didn't even realize she had found a way through the fabric of my shorts. Her kisses and body are so fucking fantastic that I can't even realize anything else that is going on in the world. I blame it on the fact that all my blood is now pooled in my dick instead of my brain.

Still, I can't have her completely exposed if someone decides to come looking. So, I roll us over in the sand until she's on the bottom, and I'm on top.

"Can't handle a woman in control?" she asks, her eyes full of lust and her lips plump from all the kissing.

I chuckle. "Oh, I would love to see you take control and ride me. I don't think there is anything I want more. But there is no way I'm letting anyone have a chance at seeing you naked. I want to be the only one. I'm too controlling about things that are *mine*."

"I don't like to be claimed. I'm not anyone's."

I roughly kiss her until she is purring a little bit in her throat.

And, when I stop, she has a blank look on her face, which makes my grin wider.

"Well, I'm very much up to the challenge of making you mine."

I kiss her again as she pushes down my shorts when I realize...

"Shit."

"What?" She curiously looks at me and then around the beach, assuming I spotted someone looking at us.

As I look at her, I scowl at my unpreparedness. "I don't have a condom."

She grins and then lets out a small chuckle before reaching into her bra and pulling out a gold little square that contains a condom.

"Thank God," I say, grabbing it from her and ripping it open.

I don't waste time in thinking about why she had a condom in her bra, if she was planning on using it with Wes. I roll it on my dick before sliding my fingers under her panties. I feel the moisture, that I caused, immediately cover my fingers as I find her entrance and slip them between her folds. She moans, and it is a beautiful sound that I never thought I would hear.

I spread the liquid up over her clit, and she bites my lip to keep from screaming. As it is, her screams are loud enough that I'm sure everyone within a square mile can hear her.

"Fuck me, Asher. Make me belong to you."

I slip inside her, and it's heaven.

"I'm never leaving again," I groan as I move inside her.

"Fuck, I don't want you to stop—ever."

I fuck her against the sand as the waves crash against us. I thought I was in love with the ocean and beach before, but now, I know I will never get enough of it. Not after I've had her here.

I thrust and move and build us both until neither of us can hold out any longer, no matter how desperate we are to make this moment last forever.

"Jesus Christ, Asher!" Sloane cries as she comes.

And I come right along with her.

I collapse on top of Sloane, feeling every inch of our bodies pressed together. "You're mine now," I say. I don't add forever. Despite how much I want this to be forever.

Jesus Christ! What the hell is wrong with me? I can't want her forever.

We both hear the sirens in the distance at the same time. I jump off of her and grab her hand, pulling her up and holding her close to me, like I'm going to be able to protect her against the police.

Not likely.

I scoop up her dress off the sand and hand it to her. I pull up my pants and grab my shirt and beer, and then we both start running toward the parking lot.

I don't know why we are both running like the police are going to come arrest us. From a distance, we look plenty clothed for the beach. She's wearing her bra and panties that could easily be mistaken for a bikini, and I'm wearing shorts. But, still, we run like we are running for our lives.

When we get to the parking lot, I don't give her the chance to go back to her car. Actually, I don't even see her car in the parking lot. Instead, I pull her straight to my truck. I open the passenger door and help her inside before running around to the driver's side and jumping in. I turn the key to start the truck up, but of course, it doesn't start.

"Shit," I curse.

I jump out of the car and bang the top of the hood. It still doesn't start.

"Shit, shit, shit."

Sloane rolls down the window. "It sounds like a problem with the starter. Have you checked the wires?"

I don't question how she knows so much about cars. Of course I've tried it before. I've had plenty of experience with getting cars to start. But I humor her and try it anyway. To my surprise, it starts right up.

I jump back into the truck and peel out of the parking lot. I start heading back toward my shack on the beach just as the sirens begin to get loud enough that I'm sure they are right on top of us. I glance in the rearview mirror and see the police heading into the parking lot we just vacated.

Sloane laughs and exhales at the same time. It's a nervous laugh, more like a release after the tense moment we just had. She begins to put her dress back on and then buckles her seat belt as I drive.

"I'm sure the police weren't after us," she says.

"Maybe," I say, trying not to lie. I'm sure they were after us. Or at least *me*.

"Still, it was exciting nonetheless." She dusts off sand from her body. "I'm going to be getting sand out of places for weeks."

I laugh and relax a little, watching her try to dust off sand out of her hair and body but to no avail.

"It's not funny," she says with a smile. "You should look at yourself. It's going to take you at least as long to get rid of all the sand."

"What makes you think I want to get rid of the sand? I live at the beach, and every time the sand rubs against my skin, I'll have a reminder of how I made you mine, if only for a few minutes on the beach."

She blushes a little, and it's the most adorable thing in the world. I take her hand and hold it, like we have been together forever. Like it's the most normal thing in the world to do. And, to my surprise, she seems to relax.

"Where did you park your car? I can take you back to it if you want or take you home or..."

"I want to stay at your place tonight. I can't face my family at my condo. Or Wes. I think you owe me enough to let me spend one night with you."

I grin. "You're welcome to stay at my place for as long as you like."

What the hell has happened to me? I don't say things like that. I don't let women stay for as long as they want. I call the shots.

"Just remember that my place doesn't have as nice of amenities as you are used to."

She cocks her head to one side. "The shack I stayed in is your only place?"

I nod.

She smiles. "Really? It's your only place? You make who knows how much money with your sponsorships and championship winnings, and you don't have a nicer place than that shack and this beat-up truck that doesn't even run properly."

"Yep."

"Why?"

"Because I have realized that possessions don't make me happy. Even when..."

"Even when what?"

"Nothing. It doesn't matter. I just realized that I was happier in a shack on the beach with awesome sunsets than a large mansion with lots of rooms."

She smiles. "I prefer the mansions."

I laugh. "Well, good thing we aren't getting married then or doing anything beyond tonight. We would make a terrible couple. We have nothing in common."

"You're right. We would be miserable together."

"Yep. Miserable."

I turn left onto the gravel road leading toward my shack. "Last chance. I can always take you to a hotel to stay at tonight if you prefer." Although that is the last fucking thing I want. I want her in my bed, shower, couch. I want to claim her in every inch of my shack if this is our last night together.

"I think I can handle the shack for one night."

I exhale deeply as I relax, knowing that I get to have her at least one more time. Or a dozen times if I get my way tonight.

I pull up next to my shack of a house and turn off the engine. Then, I hop down out of my truck and run over to Sloane's side of the car to open the door, like the gentleman that I am. I hold my hand out to her to help her down. Her dress is still undone, barely hanging on to her body, as she begins walking toward the front door.

"The door is unlocked, so just go on in. I need to get my surfboard out of the truck."

"You don't keep your front door locked?"

"No. Why would I?"

She smiles and then walks into my home. I hurriedly take my surfboard out of the truck and rest it on the rack to keep it out of the elements in case it rains, as it does so often here in the early summer. And then I run inside to find Sloane.

I open the door and find Sloane already completely naked, standing in my living room/bedroom—depending on how you look at it since I really only have one large room that is everything.

She turns and grins at me before she nibbles on her finger. "Your mouth is hanging open," she says, her smile widening.

I instantly close my mouth. "I'm sorry. You are just so incredible."

My eyes go up and down her body, drinking in every drop of her that I felt beneath me earlier but never got to fully appreciate.

"I was going to shower to get cleaned up, but you don't seem to have a shower or bathroom of any type."

I laugh. "I have a shower and bathroom. It's just outside. But I might demand payment in order for you to use it." I take a step forward.

She grins widely and cocks her head to one side. "And if I don't want to give you payment?"

"Then, I guess you are going to have to stay dirty."

She bites her lip as I walk closer, wishing that lip were in my mouth.

"What kind of payment do you have in mind? Because I do like things dirty," she says with a twinkle in her eye.

"Dirty, it is then," I say.

I slip out of my shorts, and I walk over to my dresser where I keep a stash of condoms. I grab one and then walk straight to Sloane before throwing her over my shoulder. Then, I head out to the outdoor shower. I don't put her down until we are both in the shower, and then I flick the water on, drenching us both with cold water that I know better than anyone is going to take at least ten minutes before it resembles anything close to lukewarm.

I'm used to it, but Sloane screams as the cold water rains down on us. I kiss her, knowing that is the best way to warm her up. We both forget about the cold water as my hands are finally able to grab her bare breasts. As we are finally together, completely naked, skin on skin. If the beach was perfection, being with her now in the water is magical.

"I need you inside me—now. I know I just had you, but now that I've had a taste of you, I want you more than I did before," she says.

I grin. "But I haven't had a taste of you yet."

I lift her up and press her back against the wall so that I can bury my head in her pussy. She grabs hold of my head, encouraging me to keep at it. To fuck her with my mouth, my tongue. To make her scream, to make her come. She comes quickly with the flick of my tongue and the cold water pounding down on top of her.

I lower her and then flip her around so that her back is to me before I enter her.

"Yes, Asher!"

I don't last long inside her. And, somehow, she manages to come again and again as I thrust inside her. When we have both come and there is nothing left but the water pouring down over us, I reach for the soap to attempt to get the sand properly off of us. I know, realistically, it is going to take days to get it off, and if she decides to spend her next few days mostly at the beach, like I do, she is never going to be able to fully get rid of the sand.

I take the bar of soap and start slowly moving it over her body, washing her. Getting to know every inch of her skin, the smell of her hair, the curves of her body. She doesn't say a word as I do so. She just lets me take care of her, and it seems more intimate than any other time we have had together.

When I have touched every part of her body with the bar of soap, she takes it from my hand and does the same to me. Our eyes are locked. When she finishes, she shivers.

"Does the water ever warm up?" she asks to give a reason for her shiver.

I know her shiver has more to do with our intimate moment than with the cold water.

"Not really," I say.

She nods and then swallows hard so that I can see her throat moving. I imagine my cock down her throat, and my dick instantly becomes hard.

When my eyes go back to hers, I see something different there. More serious than before.

"Marry me," she says.

My whole world stops. I can't breathe, and I'm afraid my heart has stopped.

"Marry me."

Two words that I never thought I would hear or ever say to any woman.

But this woman is different. Sloane is different, so I know, when she says those two words, there is more to this story than I understand. She didn't preface it by saying she loved me, which there is no way for her to have fallen in love with me so quickly. She's not like the other girls. That isn't what she wants. She has a reason for asking me that she just hasn't told me yet.

I surprise myself by even considering saying yes, but it could get me more sex and a chance to really destroy her later if I decide I want to.

She thinks I'm predictable. She hates surprises, or so she says, but that just makes me want to surprise her even more.

So, I say the one word that I know will shock her the most, "Yes."

12

SLOANE

He said yes.

I don't think I can believe that word. He just said it to shock me. I know him well enough to know that. I know he doesn't want to get married—ever. I just asked him because I couldn't hold it in any longer. I needed to ask. I need him to know the truth.

"Yes? That's your answer? Just like that? You don't even want to have a discussion about it or ask why I am proposing marriage when, only hours ago, I was engaged and going to get married to another man the next day."

He grins.

Damn it, I hate his grin. It makes me do things I never thought I would. It makes me feel things I shouldn't. Asher is a dick, an asshole. I have to remember that above everything else. I have to stay strong and not let him influence me. This is just an arrangement to solve my problem, nothing more. That's what I have to convince him of anyway. Even if my heart flutters much too fast anytime I am around him.

"I'm sure I'll figure out why you want me to marry you soon enough. I know enough about you to know that there is a very clear reason why. And I know that reason has nothing to do with love. But

97

at least it gives me another shot at fucking you in the shower, on the beach, and on every inch of this place and yours before we are through."

Damn it.

He grins again, and all I can think about is how much I want him to fuck me in his bed, my bed, and every other surface that we can come across. And I hate him for making me want him when I should still be in love with Wes.

He turns off the water that never really got warm and then hands me a towel from the rack that is just outside the shower. Our fingers brush against each other. And I can see in his eyes how much he wants to dry me off but doesn't want to overstep his bounds. He thinks he's pushed his luck already by washing me. And he's probably right. I need to dry myself off and gain some control over my life again. Especially if we are going to have any sort of serious conversation instead of jumping each other again for the third time in an hour.

I take the towel and quickly dry off before wrapping it around my body. Asher does the same, and then we head back inside his home. I'm still not sure I believe him when he says this is his only place. It can't be. He says he doesn't lie, but I don't imagine he stays here year-round. He uses this place when he is surfing and wants to be near the beach. Or when he's trying to get rid of his latest one-night stand. But this can't be where he spends most of his time. There simply isn't enough room.

I take a seat on what he calls a couch. Although I don't think it can be considered a couch. It's barely held together. There are no longer any legs on the bottom, the stuffing has settled so that there is a hole in the middle, and the fabric covering it is worn and contains mostly holes.

Asher goes over to his dresser and pulls out a pair of boxer shorts and a T-shirt. He tosses them both to me and then pulls out another pair of boxer shorts. He drops his towel like I'm not even here and begins to put the boxer shorts on.

I look down at the clothes he just tossed to me. They would be much more comfortable to wear than my dress I came here in, and I can't stay in this towel forever. But it just seems too intimate to be wearing his clothing.

"What? Don't tell me you're getting shy on me now," Asher says, raising an eyebrow.

I stand and drop my towel to the ground, showing my naked body to him. I'm not the least bit concerned with what he thinks of me or my body. And then I put the clothes on that he tossed to me. I try not to smell his scent on them. I try not to seem affected.

Asher comes over and takes a seat next to me, not seeming the least bit concerned about why I asked him to marry him. Or what our future holds. He slings his arm over the back of the couch.

I smile. I can't help it when his hand grazes the back of my neck.

"So, let's hear it. I know you are dying to tell me and to get everything straightened out. I can see it in your eyes. You want to talk about us getting married," he says.

I take a deep breath. "I do."

We chuckle, both a bit nervous.

"Well?" he asks.

"I have to get married," I say.

He chuckles. "I doubt that. You seem more than independent enough, and I know you don't need a man to keep you company. And you are more than capable of making enough money on your own; therefore, you don't need a man to take care of you either. And I know calling off the wedding must be embarrassing, but your family and friends will get over it soon enough. So, why in the world would you have to get married?"

I frown. "Fine. I don't have to get married. But I have a proposition for you. Marry me for one year. It will help me ease the embarrassment of turning down Wes. I could say we used to date years ago and rekindled our love when I found out Wes was really an ass. The company and I could really use some good press. We've been struggling to get new donors, and as sexist as it is, the company will get more donations if I have a man by my side. The press thinks I'm going to die alone. They are already comparing me to my grandmother, who spent most of her life living with just her cats."

Asher laughs. "You're serious."

I nod.

"You want me to marry you to save face?"

"Yes."

"And what do I get out of all of this?"

I think for a moment. "A chance to become a better person instead of a thief who tries to steal women who are already taken."

He frowns, and I can see that it's not enough.

"And you can teach me how to live again. How to enjoy life and be a bit of a wild child again instead of the uptight snob I currently am."

Asher chuckles again. "You, a wild child? I don't believe it's possible for you to have been anything but the perfect child growing up."

I shake my head. "Well then, you'd be wrong. I was a complete wild child, always getting into trouble. Trust me."

"I doubt you were a true wild child. I imagine your parents thought that because you wouldn't eat your vegetables or something silly like that."

"No, it was much worse than that. Anyway, my grandmother was the one who convinced me that I shouldn't continue my wild ways into adulthood. She gave me a job at the company, and I finally realized my purpose. I worked my way up the company, almost the same as anyone else. Although I know I was given an easier time than most since I was related to my grandmother."

"Why would I want to help you? I still don't see anything in this for me."

"Money then. I'll pay you. You could actually live in a nice place on the beach."

He grins. "Sweetheart, you forget that I make plenty of money. And I prefer living this way."

"That's not what I've heard. I've heard that your sponsors are starting to drop out because of a certain reputation you have with the ladies. They think it's inappropriate to work with someone like you.

So, being married might help your reputation and help you make more money."

He shakes his head. "Again, like I said, I don't need any more money."

But I can see that he is at least thinking about what I said. I've struck a nerve, but it's still not enough.

I look around the room he calls home. I doubt he's telling me the full story about this. But I can see I'm getting nowhere.

His eyes drop to my chest to see my nipples harden as a cold draft slips through. Now, it's my turn to grin because I know the way to get what I want.

"Sex. You can have all the dirty, filthy sex with me you want."

His eyes perk up as he listens. And I can see the bulge in his boxers grow.

"Did you ever love Wes?"

His question surprises me.

"*Love* is a strange word. I loved him, sure. But was I in love with him? No, I don't think so. I would have ended it much sooner if I wasn't so much of a planner that I wanted to be married by twenty-five and have two kids by the time I was thirty."

He frowns.

"I don't want to have kids with you. I just don't want to feel like a complete failure when I do turn twenty-five next month. I want to be married and have that experience. If, after you, I still don't find my happily ever after with a man, then I'll be fine with adopting or getting artificial insemination."

Asher frowns, thinking.

"I know that we are the absolute worst match for each other and that this is going to be mostly about sex, but I need that right now. I need to be married. I need to not be shamed by my family. I need sex."

I fidget with the hem of the shirt I'm wearing, where it is already starting to unravel. It's obviously a shirt that he wears often.

"So, what do you say? Can we come to an agreement? Will you

marry me?" I don't add that it's the least he can do after he broke up my wedding, but I'm not afraid to sound desperate.

Asher chuckles. "I already said yes. But I will say it again if the first time didn't do enough to convince you. Yes, I'll marry you. I'll give you whatever you want. Just..." He pauses, trying to think of the right words.

"Just don't expect you to stick around forever?"

He nods.

"Fine. I'll have my lawyer draw up a prenup to protect us both, and then we can get married anytime after that. I don't want a big affair. I just want the legal marriage so that I can face the world again. But you will have to stay loyal to me. I don't do cheating even if this is a temporary arrangement. It won't last forever anyway. I expect, after a year, we can quietly divorce, and I can marry someone else and have a kid or two."

"I would never cheat on you."

I raise an eyebrow. "That's not what I've heard. I've heard you have cheated on plenty of women."

He scoots closer to me on the couch. "I. Don't. Cheat. On. Anyone. And. Especially. Not. You. Occasionally, women I have been with cheat on their husbands or fiancés with me, but I never do the cheating."

"I didn't cheat on Wes, if that is what you are implying. I broke up with him first."

He smiles. "I'm not calling you a cheater either."

"Have you ever been in a committed relationship with a woman before?" I ask.

He laughs. "Of course I have. What do you think I've been doing these last few weeks? I've been committed to you."

"To breaking me and Wes up."

He nods and leans back a little, like he's preparing for me to slap him. And, although I've had the urge to do just that many times in the past, I don't have the urge at the moment.

Maybe it's because he just gave me two of the best orgasms of my life.

Maybe it's because, when this conversation is over, I want to see if he has anything else up his sleeve.

Whatever the reason, I no longer feel like slapping him, but I don't want to let him know that. I like that he feels like he should always be on alert when he's around me. I like having that control.

"Do you have anything planned for tomorrow?" I ask.

"Other than having you tied up in my bed all day, I don't have anything on the agenda."

I smile. "Good. You can do that—after we get married."

He grins and then leans forward and kisses me, letting me know he's ready for another round if I am.

But all I can think is, *I can't believe my crazy plan is working. Now, the only thing I need to do to keep this plan working is to not fall in love with him. That should be easy, right?*

13

SLOANE

I LOOK in the mirror at myself in my wedding dress. I'm not the type of woman who dreamed of what my wedding day would look like. What I would wear or even whom I would marry. But, if I had imagined what I would wear, this is what I would have imagined.

A simple, light white dress with a little bit of lace but not enough to overpower the dress. It's long but doesn't have a train, so it will be easy to wear on the beach. I'm not wearing shoes, which is how I prefer it so that I can walk barefoot on the beach. And, other than a couple of witnesses the minister is bringing, no one will be there to watch us get married.

The man, on the other hand, is nothing like I would have imagined ever marrying. I figured the only way I would ever marry was if the man had really convinced me of his love and if I thought that love would last. I never thought I would get married out of lust or a need to fix things.

I hear a rattling on my door, and I walk over to it and open it to find my lawyer standing there.

"You look beautiful," Chance says, looking me up and down in my dress.

"Thank you. Were you able to get the prenup written up?"

"Of course. I wouldn't be here if I hadn't finished it. It's just as we discussed. But I know you will want a chance to read it over all the same."

"Thank you. I trust you, but I could never sign something I didn't read over with my own eyes."

"That's why I enjoy working with you so much. You take your business and life into your own hands."

Chance hands me the papers, and I take them over to my table and begin reading through everything. It takes me a good half hour to thoroughly read over everything. Chance waits in the living room while I read in my office. I make one small change, but otherwise, everything looks to be exactly as I wanted.

I hear another knock at my door, and I glance at the clock in my bedroom. It's a good thing I was ready prior to my lawyer coming over.

I glance in the mirror one last time. I left my hair down in loose curls and kept my makeup natural-looking. Everything is still in place, so I walk quickly to the door and open it to see Asher standing in the doorway.

His jaw drops open, and his eyes widen when he sees me in my dress. "There are not enough words to describe how beautiful you look right now."

"You look very nice as well," I say, staring at the muscles of his chest.

There's just enough manly hair peeking out from beneath his nicely pressed dress shirt that he's kept unbuttoned at the top. He rolled up the sleeves and is wearing khaki pants and sandals.

He raises an eyebrow, as he always does when he is about to say something snarky. "Nice? I look better than nice. I look hot, and you know you want to jump my bones before you even marry me."

I shake my head. "Business first."

He pouts. "Not even—"

I swat his hand away that reached out to try and grab my ass.

"First, we sign the prenup and then get married. If I still like you, you can fuck me."

"I'd better hurry and make sure all the legal parts are covered then. I don't want to get in the way of the fucking," Chance says, smiling.

I frown even though I've been friends with Chance forever, and he works for me on many occasions. I still don't like him joking about me and Asher fucking.

Chance and Asher exchange knowing glances before I head to my office to grab the prenup papers. When I come back, I get straight down to business, not wanting to wait any longer to get this part over with.

I place the papers on my dining table, and Chance takes them.

"It's a standard prenup that basically says that when—"

I glare at Chance. I haven't told anyone of my plan, and even though I know that our marriage is going to end in divorce, I don't like others implying it already. Even Chance.

"I mean, *if* you two decide to dissolve the marriage, it basically states that you will each keep your own property and money that you earned before the marriage and during. Sloane has already read it over, but if you'd like to have a quick read through it," Chance says, sliding the papers over to where Asher is standing.

"Do you have a pen?" Asher asks.

Chance smiles as he looks at me, like he knows I'm marrying an idiot who doesn't even read a contract before he signs it. But then Asher comes from a different world. Other than whatever contract he signed with his agent, I doubt he has ever signed anything of importance.

Chance hands Asher a pen, and then he points to the first spot that Asher needs to sign. "You need to sign here and then initial every page. Then, sign again at the end."

Asher does so without reading a single word on any page and then hands the pen to me. "There is no backing out after this. I guess we will just have to learn to trust each other."

I take the pen and quickly sign everywhere that I'm supposed to.

Chance takes the papers and scans them, making sure everything is in order. "So, when's the wedding?" he asks.

I cock my head to the side as I look at Chance.

"I'm kidding. Go get married, you two crazy lovebirds. I know that I'm not invited, but I'm sure I'll see you again soon," Chance says as he begins heading toward the door.

"That's because no one is invited. It's more romantic that way," I say.

"I'm sure it is," Chance answers before letting himself out of my apartment.

"Was that a stab at me, saying that our marriage won't last?" Asher asks.

"Yes. I didn't tell him the truth. He just has his suspicions. Why, do you think this marriage is going to last?" I ask.

Asher hesitantly touches my arm, running his fingers slowly up my arm, like he's trying to decide if I'm real. If what we are about to do is really happening. And then he firmly grabs my arm, pulling me to him until our lips clash together and then kiss. My tongue slips into his mouth almost automatically, like I've been kissing him for years instead of only hours.

He smells of cologne, which I find strange but also so enticing on him. When I had him yesterday, he smelled of salt and ocean. Now, he smells like a man who spends his days in an office instead of out on the beach. I don't know which I like more—this cleaned up version or the dressed down version on the beach. No, I prefer the naked version who likes to take control in bed.

The part that made me want to marry him in the first place was knowing that I would get to fuck him every night while we were together. That's what makes this all worthwhile for me.

We stop kissing.

"It won't last, but I am going to more than enjoy it while it does."

I blush. "Come on. The minister is waiting." I start walking toward the door. "Unless you want to back out?" I ask, turning back to see Asher still standing, looking at me with his hands in his pockets.

"Not backing out. Just admiring your ass in that dress and all the different ways I plan on bending you over and taking you."

———

In complete silence, we walk down to the beach where we are to be married. I'm still not sure he is going to actually go through with this. He's known to be one to try and break women's hearts. And I suspect he thinks, if he marries me and then breaks up with me later, it will make my pain that much worse. But he can't hurt me if I don't let him. He can't break my heart if I don't let myself love him.

As we walk though, I have a strange feeling that this is the worst idea I've had in a long time. I've never felt that marriage is important. My parents got divorced when I was young. Most of my friends' parents are divorced. I'm not sure we are really supposed to be with one person all our lives. But, walking down to the beach with Asher, who will be my husband in a matter of minutes, makes me doubt everything I've thought before.

Asher grabs hold of my hand as we get closer to the minister, who is standing at the edge of the water with folded arms over a Bible. I suck in a breath when he grabs hold of my hand. I don't know why his touch affects me, calms me, but it does.

Asher is the devil. I know that. But, somehow, the devil is what I need in a moment like this. Knowing who my enemy is and not being surprised by it, I guess, comforts me.

We reach the minister, but neither of us lets go of each other's hand.

"Are you both ready?" he asks us.

Asher turns to face me with a large grin on his face that makes me grin as well.

"Yes," we say in unison.

The minister starts talking, but the butterflies in my stomach prevent me from hearing anything he says.

Asher leans down to my ear and whispers, "Just look at the ocean. The waves. It will help calm you."

I smile. I don't think anything can calm me. But I look out at the ocean and watch the waves roll in, and then I immediately feel calm. It feels nice to know that, that is one thing we share. We both love the ocean.

And to fuck, the dirty side of me thinks.

"Do you, Sloane Hart, take Asher Calder to be your husband in sickness and health as long as you both shall live?"

I look into Asher's eyes and see the waves reflected in them. "I do," I say.

His eyes seem to twinkle just a little bit. Like he's happy to hear it. I push the butterflies down. The look doesn't mean anything. He is just doing this for the sex and to try and hurt me. That's all this is.

"I do," Asher says with a grin so wide that I'm afraid his mouth is going to be stuck permanently like that.

I feel my heartbeat race much too fast in my chest as Asher kisses me, holding me in his arms as he dips me backward, sucking all of my breath away. He slowly lets me back up.

"We're married," I whisper.

"We are, Mrs. Calder. Or are you not planning on taking my name?" he says with a wink.

I bite my lip and blush a little. "I think I'll be keeping my name."

Asher lifts me up, and I let out a high-pitched gasp.

It's a wonder I can breathe at all after the ceremony. Thank God it was fast, or I'm sure that I would have passed out from the mix of the sun bearing down on me and my inability to breathe.

It's too late to back out now though. I'm married. I just hope I made my life easier instead of harder.

Asher twirls me around, and for the first time since I was a kid, I feel like a princess. It's not a feeling I ever thought I would want to experience. Not at my age. But I love the freeing feeling it gives me until I realize what Asher is doing.

"No!" I scream, grabbing hold of his neck and shoulders.

But it's no use. He drops us both into the water. We go under, all the way until the water is covering our heads. When we come back up, I know my dress and makeup are ruined, but I can't help but laugh when I see Asher's goofy face.

"That was way too serious. I thought we needed to chill out and laugh before we left," Asher says, still holding me in his arms.

I throw my arms and head back, floating on top of the water. "We don't need to leave yet. You'll have plenty of time to fuck me later. Now that you have gotten me into the water, I don't want to leave," I say, relaxing on top of the water.

"Well, I hate to tell you, but you don't have much time to relax. But you'll have plenty of time to relax and fuck later," he says.

I stand up and look at him. "I have no idea what you are talking about, Asher. The only thing on either of our agendas today was to get married. Now that, that is done, we can relax." I pause. "Actually, the last thing we need to do is tell our families that we eloped."

"Already done," Asher says.

I frown. "How is it already done? I haven't spoken to my family today. Did you already talk to your family?"

"I don't have any family. I only have one friend. I texted him, but I don't think he believed me. I let my agent know so that she would be prepared to deal with the publicity."

I sigh. "I still need to tell my family."

"No, you don't."

I laugh. "I think they deserve to know if I got married or not."

Asher shakes his head. "I just meant that I already told them."

"What do you mean?" I ask, my eyes wide with worry.

"I called and spoke to your father to ask for his permission to marry you. Well, more his blessing than permission. I think asking for permission is a bit archaic."

"And?" I ask, cocking my head to one side, not believing that he spoke to my father.

"And he seemed pleased that you had found someone to marry. Even a scoundrel like me."

I smile.

"I spoke to your mother as well. She seemed more than pleased that she could tell all of your family that you got married to a longtime friend you had known since you were young. A love that rekindled after Wes treated you so badly. She also said it would be announced in the papers tomorrow to combat any bad press about you leaving Wes the night before you were supposed to marry him."

I study Asher, who seems so at peace in the ocean. He seems so right here, in the water, and it's why he sometimes seems so out of place on land. I know that he's a scoundrel, just like my father called him, but honestly, I've seen too much of his nicer side to think of him solely as a scoundrel.

"Thank you," I say.

He softly kisses me on the lips, clearly not wanting to start something here. And, looking around at the beach that is beginning to swarm with people, I agree.

"You really need to stop saying thank you."

"Then, you need to stop being so nice to me."

Asher glances up at something on the beach. I turn to look but have no idea what he is looking at.

"We need to head back in now," Asher says.

"Why?"

"I'm not telling you. But, now that you are my wife, you have to do what you are told. It's in the vows or something, right?"

I laugh. "No way in hell am I obeying you. And it wasn't in the vows." *Was it?*

He laughs. "You have no idea what that minister guy said anyway, do you?"

"No, I don't."

"So, are you going to come with me without asking questions or not?"

I frown, not liking where this is going at all.

"I thought you wanted me to bring out that wild child inside of you again, the one looking for excitement and adventure?"

I frown. "I don't like surprises."

"I know." He lifts me in his arms again and begins carrying me out of the water. I fight to get down at first, but I know it's no use. So, I surrender to Asher carrying me up to the beach like a caveman.

When he reaches dry land, I say, "You can put me down now."

"Not going to happen."

I sigh and try to enjoy being in his strong arms. I try to relax and just give up control. But I struggle to let go of the control even though I know he isn't really in control. I was the one who orchestrated this. I'm the one in control. I suck in a breath, but he is the one that smells so amazing.

He carries me back up to my condo before he puts me down. "You have five minutes to get changed into something dry and comfortable."

I frown. "I need longer than five minutes. I'm a mess. My makeup is smeared, and my hair is a mess from the salt water. And, if you tell me what we are doing, then I can be better dressed for the occasion."

He shakes his head. "Five minutes. Wipe the makeup off your face. Your hair is perfect the way it is. And wear something comfortable, like jeans and a T-shirt."

I don't know why I agree to what he said, but I do. I strip out of my wet wedding dress, leaving it crumpled on the floor. I long for a warm shower to wash off the salt water, but I know I don't have time. If I shower, I'll be in there for much longer than five minutes, and as much as I don't want to admit it, I want to find out what Asher has planned. And, if I'm not ready in five minutes, then I'm not sure I'll get to find out the surprise.

So, instead, I throw on a pair of jeans and a light blouse instead of a T-shirt because, honestly, I feel more comfortable a bit dressed up. I feel strange even wearing jeans. I only own two pair anyway. And then I head to the bathroom to try my best to get rid of the makeup and fix my hair.

I scrub at my face with makeup remover until it is clean again. And then I run a brush through my wet hair before scrunching it to give it a little bit of a natural curl as it dries. I pinch my cheeks to ensure some color and apply a little lip gloss. But that is all I have time for as much as I want to do more.

I head out of my bedroom and find Asher standing in my living room. He's now in khaki shorts, a T-shirt, and flip-flops, looking much more like himself.

He shakes his head. "You had to defy me just a little bit, didn't you?"

"I did exactly what you said. I got ready in five minutes, despite wanting to take a nice long bath to rinse off."

"I said, a T-shirt."

I smile. "Well, you need to get used to me not listening to everything you say. Now that we are married and all."

He walks toward me, his eyes challenging me. I stand my ground until he is inches from my face.

"I wish I had time to punish you."

I grin. "That isn't going to get me to obey you in the future."

He slightly shakes his head. "I know. But I would enjoy punishing you all the same." He grabs my hand. "Come on, or we will miss our flight."

I step back. "What do you mean, flight? I don't have any luggage. I haven't let the company know that I'll be gone. How long will we be gone? Where are we going? You can't just spring shit like this on me..."

Asher just stands stoically with a large grin on his face and an eyebrow raised as he waits for me to stop talking. When I let my questions trail off, he says, "Are you finished?"

"Yes," I say, nodding.

"We are going on a honeymoon, as is expected. I have handled everything. This is me holding up my end of the deal to help you find the part of you that likes adventure and needs to let go more."

I frown. I didn't expect him to move so quickly on holding up his end of the bargain. I know that this is what I need.

"So, are you coming with me or not?"

"I'm coming," I answer as confidently as I can muster.

I don't trust at all that he has gotten everything figured out. But I can call from the plane and have someone at work handle all the business things that need handling this week or for however long we are staying. This week, I just need to enjoy myself.

I step into the elevator, still holding on to Asher's hand. He presses the button for the ground floor, and the doors close, locking us inside. I feel trapped, like there is no escaping now. I need to stop worrying about it now though. Now, I just have to enjoy the ride and try not to fall in love with the handsome stranger whose hand I'm holding.

14

SLOANE

"Venice. Is that really where we are going, or is it one stop on many?" I ask as I take my seat next to Asher on the flight to Venice.

He sighs. "I can see that you are going to drive me crazy with questions from now until the trip ends."

"Yep," I reply.

Asher rolls his eyes. "Fine. We are starting in Venice because I heard it's beautiful and romantic, and I figured that is what is needed for our first night as a married couple."

My heart is racing in my chest as I think about what Venice is going to be like. I live in one of the most beautiful places on the planet and have traveled extensively on business, usually to the poorest places in the world. But, now, I get to go experience the beauty of another place.

"And then?" I ask because it seems like there is more up his sleeve than just going to Venice.

"And then we are going to backpack across Europe. Stay wherever we can find a place to stay or sleep in a tent. It will be a great adventure, waking up every night in a new place, not knowing where or what we are going to be doing the next day."

I smile, but it doesn't sound at all exciting. It sounds terrifying. I like control too much to be okay with his plan. Maybe once we get to Venice, we will love it so much that we just stay there. Or maybe I can arrange for us to visit several places in Europe while we are there.

Asher grabs my hand and kisses me on the lips. My eyes close when his lips touch mine, and I feel the softness of his lips before his tongue moves with mine.

When he leans back, he grins. "Are you relaxed now?"

"Mmhmm," I say with a goofy smile on my face.

He quickly kisses me on the forehead. "Stop worrying. Stop trying to control everything. Just relax."

I lean my head back in my chair and close my eyes, trying to do just that. When I open them again, I see Asher staring at me. Happy to be doing nothing more than just watching me, it seems.

He slowly puts his arm around me, and I settle in against his chest and close my eyes.

"Just sleep. When you wake up, we will be in a whole new world."

I smile and take a deep breath as I close my eyes. Immediately, I feel sleep coming for me. I didn't realize how tiring it was to plan two weddings this week. But, for now, I get to sleep.

———

It's early morning by the time we land in Venice. I slept almost the whole flight, only waking when they served us breakfast before we landed. I have no idea how Asher managed the flight. I slept against his hard chest, and somehow, he must have slept, too, because he seems to be just as rested as I am when we depart the plane.

As we leave the cab that brought us to our hotel in the heart of the city, I don't get to focus on how beautiful the city is. Instead, all I can think and worry about is how there is no way he brought everything that I'd need in the single backpack that he has slung over his back. No way.

Asher rolls his eyes at me and takes my hand, like I'm a five-year-old child he has to corral. He leads me into the lobby of the hotel and over to the front desk.

"Are you checking in?" the man behind the desk asks in English with a sharp Italian accent.

He can already tell that we are American tourists, just from looking at us.

"Yes. I'm Asher Calder."

"Ah, the honeymooners!" the man says.

He grabs a key that looks to be an actual key, not a card, and that's when I realize this isn't a hotel. At least not what I think of when I think of hotels.

The man starts scurrying us along as he starts speaking in Italian, much too fast for either of us to understand. But we follow until we get to a room at the top of the stairs. The man opens the door for us with a large smile on his face. He hands Asher the key and then says something else I can't make out before leaving us here.

Asher sets the backpack down on a chair as we both look around the room. It's beautiful. Smaller than I'm used to but definitely full of beauty and charm. It feels as if we stepped into a different time though. The bed looks to be an antique although the bedspread is a beautiful material of red and gold. The nightstands also look to be solid wood with deep carvings on them, nothing like the stark cold-ness of hotel rooms back home.

I see a door to what I assume is the bathroom, but I don't look inside. Instead, I follow Asher out onto the balcony that is attached to our room, and my jaw drops. The balcony is small. Just big enough for both of us to be out here with a tiny table and set of chairs, perfect for two people to sit on.

But, my God, the view.

"It's like nothing I've ever seen before," I say as I place my hand on the edge of the balcony and look down at the river below.

Asher's fingers brush against mine, and then I feel his eyes on me. "Like nothing I have ever seen before either."

I suck in a breath, but I love hearing his words all the same even if they are a lie. I want to feel loved even if I can't fall in love back. And lines like that show that Asher is one step closer to falling in love with me.

I grab Asher's neck at the same time as he grabs my hips, and we press our lips together in a passionate kiss, agreeing that we need this more than exploring Venice. We need it as much or more than the air we breathe. We need sex. We need that connection that we haven't had since yesterday evening before we were married.

His tongue slips into my mouth, and he has me moaning and wet with just his tongue in my mouth and not yet on other places. I cry silently to myself, thanking God that I get to have this man completely to myself. I don't think about the fact that this is a temporary arrangement. That he isn't really mine forever. He's mine for now, and that's enough.

Although I could kiss him for hours, I need more. Now. I need his tongue all over my body. I need to see his muscles flexing as he moves inside me. I need to feel his hard dick pressing into my soul. I've been with plenty of men before, but for some reason, I think Asher could show me things that none of the others ever have before. He's made me come more in one day than Wes did in a year. Although I'd never admit it to Asher. His ego is already too large.

I grab hold of his shirt and begin pulling it up, loving how my fingers ripple over the ridges of his abs as I move the shirt higher and higher. Wes was in shape. But nothing like Asher is. I pull the shirt off and stop kissing him long enough to properly admire him. Now that we are married, I can gawk at him without feeling ashamed.

I suck in a breath as my eyes soak in every bit of his body.

"Strip naked, so I can get a better look at you, and then fuck me," I say.

He chuckles. "You dirty girl."

He doesn't do what I asked though. Instead, he lifts me, carrying me in his arms back inside. "I'll fuck you anyplace, anywhere. But I'm not going to fuck you on a hard balcony where anyone could glimpse your body. Not when we have a nice soft bed just inside."

I'm surprised at how gently he is carrying me. It's almost romantic. Not that I think this man has a romantic bone in his body. But, still, it's a nice feeling.

Asher gently tosses me on the bed. "Strip."

I smile. I hate admitting that, as much as I want to be in control in almost everything in my life, I love having Asher boss me around.

"No," I say because I want to hear him order me around again.

His eyes darken just a little as he glares at me. "Strip, or I won't make you come."

I frown. "You play dirty."

"I thought you liked it dirty," he says, winking.

I suck in a breath and then take off my shirt.

He grins when I finally give in. I quickly take off my bra and start moving to my jeans when Asher starts stripping as well. And, suddenly, I move much slower with my own clothes because my eyes are too transfixed on him instead of the task at hand.

"Strip," Asher says again more firmly.

I move quicker until I'm completely naked and lying on the bed. Asher grabs a bottle of champagne that I didn't see chilling when we first came into the room. He moves to the backpack on the floor and pulls out a condom. He picks up his T-shirt for some reason before he walks toward me.

As he walks, my eyes drink in every bit of his hard body. His cock is already hard, waiting for me. He sets the condom and bottle down on the end table next to the bed. He takes his T-shirt in his hand as he straddles me, his cock pressing into my stomach.

He takes the T-shirt and moves it over my eyes.

I frown. "I want to see you."

"You will. Just not with your eyes."

He ties the T-shirt over my eyes, and other than another pout, I don't protest. I let him cover my eyes. I let him be in control.

I feel his lips on mine, rewarding me for letting him put the blindfold on. His lips move to my neck, and the feeling is more intense than anything I have ever felt before.

I bite my lip to keep from moaning too loudly. I'm not sure how insulated the walls are, but I don't want our neighbors to hear me.

Suddenly, I feel cold liquid trailing over my breasts, followed by his lips warming the liquid as it moves over my breasts. The difference between the hot and cold sends shivers down my spine.

"I want to properly enjoy every bit of your body, Sloane. I didn't get the chance to earlier."

I take a deep breath in and out. "I don't know if I can wait until you have properly enjoyed every bit of my body."

I feel his grin against the peak of one of my nipples as I squirm beneath his touch. I grab hold of the nape of his neck, trying to push his head down to fully take my nipple in his mouth instead of teasing me like he is. He does relent though, and I squirm as his tongue expertly glides over my nipple that is covered in the cool liquid.

"Fuck, Asher," I say, my toes curling, as he moves to the other hard peak.

I feel more of the cold liquid over my smooth stomach, going down my body with his warm lips moving it around, igniting every nerve in my body. The liquid moves down one leg, and his lips trace the liquid down, making me come unglued at his touch.

"Don't move," he says.

His lips start moving down my inner thigh, and I can't help but squirm.

"I. Can't. Help. It. I need—"

But Asher already knows where I'm going with my moans. His tongue and lips encase my pussy as I moan and pray for him to never stop what he is doing. Never. Because I've never had a man move his tongue over my clit like this man is doing now.

I thought sex with him was good before, but now that I've had his lips on my pussy, I can't imagine that my days of feeling like this are numbered. That I won't get to experience this every day for forever.

I shake the thought away though as his tongue moves faster over my clit just as he slips a finger inside me.

"My God, Asher," I say, barely able to get the words out.

"Don't come. Not yet, sweetheart."

My whole body tenses, trying to do as he asked. To not come until he tells me to come. But, every second, I inch closer to coming and not caring about disobeying him.

He must sense how close I am because he stops. And, suddenly, his body isn't touching me anywhere. I take a deep breath in and out, in and out, trying to slow my beating heart, as I wait for Asher to touch me.

He doesn't. He takes his damn time because he has more patience than anyone on the planet. He must have patience to have me naked, lying in front of him, and not fucking me immediately. I know he wants to fuck me just as badly as I want to fuck him.

I reach up, trying to touch him.

"Stop," he says as soon as I move.

I do.

"Patience," he says. "Trust me," he whispers in my ear.

I nod a little, letting him know that I do, despite everything I know about him. Knowing how horrible of a person he really is, I do trust him. At least I do with my body. He has more than proven he is capable of handling that.

So, I try to be patient. I try to think about what adventures we are going to have in Venice. But, for the life of me, I can't remember what Venice is famous for or even what country I am in at the moment.

All I can think about is Asher. His grin. His abs. His cock. And how much I want—no, *need* him to fuck me right now. Every nerve in my body is alive and on fire. Every part of me aches to be his. Every part of me is begging for him to do more. Touch me. Kiss me. Fuck me.

Anything. Just do anything.

I hear him move. Barely, but I hear it. I hear him opening the condom wrapper, and I assume—no, *hope* that he is rolling it onto his cock.

He moves. He's in control. He didn't tie me up. I can move if I want to, but somehow, he controls me all the same. I don't move because he told me not to.

I feel him climb back on top of me. I feel his cock settle in between my legs. I feel his breath on my neck. And I know, if he so much as whispered the word *come*, I would in a second without him even touching me.

"Take me," he says as he finally pushes inside me. His lips kiss my neck as he fills me.

I try to stifle my cries and moans.

"Scream, Sloane. Tell me how much you want this."

I let out a cry of pure ecstasy that I'm sure is much too loud, but I don't care because Asher told me to.

"Not yet," he says as he thrusts inside me.

I stop screaming and go back to biting my lip and curling my toes to keep from coming. I've never been blindfolded before, but now that I am, I'm not sure I want to go back to seeing. Because losing my sight has made everything that much better. I can see with my whole body.

He moves again, and I suck in a breath, but I know I can't keep from coming any longer.

"Come, Sloane."

I do as he screams, "Fuck, baby!"

We both come, and then he collapses on top of me. He removes the blindfold as we catch our breaths, and we stare into each other's eyes.

"I don't think I'm ever going to get enough of fucking you, Sloane."

I grin and bite my lip because I don't think I'm ever going to get enough of him either. And, as much as we are compatible when it comes to sex, we aren't one in any other way. I can't fall in love, or even lust, with him because this isn't going to last.

———

We can't keep our hands off of each other as we walk down the street to the closest café. One fuck isn't enough to satisfy either of us.

"If your stomach hadn't growled three times while I was fucking you, I would still have you in my bed right now, finding every possible way to keep fucking you," Asher whispers into my ear.

I grin. "Then, we must eat quickly."

Asher shakes his head as he drinks in my body again. I'm wearing a simple sundress that Asher packed for me. He brought one dress, one pair of jeans, one pair of shorts, a few pairs of underwear, and my toothbrush. Everything else, he said we could buy or make do without. And it seems that we are going to be spending most of our time naked anyway. So, I guess it doesn't matter.

We are seated at a small table and have to break apart in order to sit down. But, as soon as the waitress leaves, Asher scoots his chair over so that he is sitting right next to me. He puts his arm around my shoulders as we both stare down at the menu that is in Italian.

"Do you have any idea what any of these things are or how to pronounce them?" I ask.

He shrugs. "Does it matter? We are in Italy. I'm sure whatever we order is going to be amazing."

"I don't think I care as long as I can fill my stomach and then get back to our hotel room," I say, winking.

He laughs. "I am not letting us go back to our hotel room until we have at least had a chance to explore more of Venice first."

I frown. "Then, you are going to have to fuck me in an alleyway because I'm not waiting past lunch to have you again."

Asher's eyes dart playfully from mine up to where our waiter is standing, looking at us with a bit of a shocked expression on his face. We might not understand Italian, but it is clear that he understands English.

"What can I get for you two lovebirds?" he asks, finally smiling at us after the initial shock of hearing me swear in front of him.

"Um..." I look down at the menu, not having a clue. I'm not the most adventurous person with my food.

Asher notices my expression. "We will each have a glass of wine. Whatever red you recommend for me and..." Asher looks at me, waiting for me to answer.

"White," I say.

"White for her. And we will have whatever you recommend for our meals. Something with a bit of variety would be good. We would love to try as much as we can."

"Excellent, sir. I'll have the chef prepare a sampler platter for you."

"Thank you," Asher and I say at the same time.

The waiter leaves and returns in seconds with a bottle of red and white wine that he pours for each of us. He leaves us again, and I open my mouth to say something when a basket of bread suddenly appears at our table.

Asher smiles at me and moves to hold my hand, but then he grabs for the bread instead. I laugh at his antics and then grab a piece of bread for myself.

"Oh God. This is the best damn thing I think I've ever tasted. Sorry, sweetheart, but this bread tastes better than you," Asher says.

I laugh again and take a bite of the bread, and I immediately fall in love. "I think I've just fallen in love with a piece of bread," I say with a mouthful of bread.

Asher laughs but shovels in more bread. I do the same.

The waiter comes back a few minutes later with two giant plates of all sorts of different foods. My eyes grow wide as I look at all the food we're expected to eat.

"Bon appétit!" the waiter says before leaving us to eat our enormous meal.

We dig into the food. Neither of us speaks. We just eat. And eat and eat.

But, eventually, my stomach starts to grow full, and my hunger turns back to other needs. Asher is still shoveling in food, but I know he can't keep eating for much longer. He must be close to as full as I am at this point.

And I don't want him thinking that we are ready to go exploring just yet. I need to explore more of him before I spend any time exploring the town. I need a lot more of him. Like at least the rest of today, tonight, and part of tomorrow before I'm satiated enough to be able to focus on exploring the rest of the town. I just need to figure out how to get him on board with my plan.

We are seated outside on the patio of the restaurant. There are a couple of other couples here, but none seem to be paying us any attention. I know Paris is considered the place to go for love, but it looks to me like Venice might give Paris a run for its money.

I don't think anyone is going to be able to see me or even care if they do realize what I am doing. So, I take a chance. I slide as close as I can to Asher and slide my hand under the napkin in his lap. He doesn't look up from his plate. He just keeps shoveling in food until I slip my hand into the waistband of his pants. I find his cock, and within seconds, it starts to grow hard within my grasp as I massage him.

He cocks his head to one side and looks at me with a grin on his face. "Is that the way you are going to try and gain control back?"

I smile. "Is it working?"

He sucks in a sharp breath when I tighten my grip on his throbbing cock again.

"It depends on what you think a win is for you."

"Getting you to spend the rest of the day fucking me in our hotel room is a win. So, have I won yet? Or do I need to work *harder*?" I say, winking.

Asher adjusts his chair, forcing me to let him go. I frown as I watch him reach into his pocket and pull out some money. He waves our waiter down and hands him money, asking if it's enough. When the waiter nods, Asher grabs my hand, pulling me from my chair.

I grin as he does. I won. I knew I would. No man can resist, not once they are turned on, no matter how much they want to win.

We exit the restaurant and start walking the couple of blocks back to our hotel room when Asher pulls me abruptly into an alleyway. He pushes me up against the brick wall and kisses me harder than he ever has before. I can't breathe while he kisses me. It's too much and not enough all at the same time.

"What are you doing?" I ask when I can breathe again.

"I'm winning by fucking you here instead of in the hotel room."

I grin. "I don't care as long as you fuck me."

15

SLOANE

OUR PLANE LANDS back in Hawaii, and our fake honeymoon ends. Although we are back in paradise, we are back in the real world. Back to work where we can't just have sex every day and pretend like the real world doesn't exist. We have to get back to work, and I have to continue on with...

I don't even want to think about it.

All I want to think about is all the sex. Sex in our hotel room. Sex in the alleyway. Sex in the restroom of every restaurant we ate at. Sex on the balcony. We had more sex than I think I've ever had in a week's time.

And, even though we were in Italy and Asher planned on having us travel across Europe, I guess that is going to have to wait for another time, I think, smiling.

Because I wouldn't change our honeymoon for anything. I wouldn't have given up the sex for seeing all of Europe. Ever. Because sex with Asher is better than anything I ever imagined. I've never felt so in touch with my body. I've never ached to feel someone else's touch so much that I'm in a constant state of pain because I can't have him.

"So, what happens now?" Asher asks as we climb into a taxicab.

I give the cab driver my address.

"What do you mean?"

"I mean, I'm sure you have our whole lives planned out. So, let's hear it. What is your plan?"

I frown. I hate that he thinks I have everything planned out because, honestly, I don't. I know what I want the end result to be. I know what I want from this arrangement. But that's it. I don't know how to get there. I'm just making it up as I go along.

"Well...you move in with me, and we continue on with our married life. We go to work. We make occasional appearances together as a couple. We have sex."

"And how do we decide when this ends?"

I sigh. "When we have had enough."

He nods but doesn't say anything else until we get to my condo. We get out of the taxi.

"I don't know when you need to get back to work or training or whatever you usually do with your time. But I would love for you to go to work with me today or tomorrow to meet everyone. And I can have a moving truck at your place to move whatever you want over to my place today or tomorrow or whenever you would like."

He frowns. "Why are we moving into your place? Why not my place?"

"Because my place is..." I trail off, not wanting to finish that sentence the way I intended.

"Better," he finishes for me.

I nod and blush a little. But I'm not going to apologize because it's the honest truth.

"My place is better than your place. It's bigger. It's more secure. It has furniture that isn't falling apart. It—"

"My place has the beach. It has everything I could ever want," Asher says.

I frown. "My place has a shower that actually shoots out warm water."

"Mine does, too. You just have to wait a little longer for it to warm up."

I throw up my hands. "There is no arguing with you, is there?"

"For however long this arrangement lasts, I just don't want to have to deal with your snobby attitude, thinking you are better than me. Because you're not."

I raise an eyebrow. "I'm not saying that. At least not because I have nicer things and you don't. But I definitely have different morals than you. You think it's okay to steal and cheat while I don't."

"Yes, you're a saint, and I'm the devil. We've already established that." He paces back and forth. "You know what? This isn't worth it. Just file for divorce or an annulment or whatever you need to do to get me out of this mess." Asher starts walking back to the cab.

"Wait," I say, grabbing hold of his arm.

He stops.

"I'm sorry. You're right. I am asking a lot from you to do this. And I appreciate you doing it. How about we come to an arrangement?"

He frowns. "Another arrangement?"

"A deal then? You stay here for a week. Then, I'll stay at your place for a week. Then, we can decide what is best."

He sighs. "Fine, but I expect plenty of sex, no matter which place we stay at."

He walks over and kisses me on the lips, letting enough tongue in to let me know he is ready for sex right now if I'm up for it.

"Oh, I think I can arrange that. But, right now, I need to get changed and ready to go into the office for today. You want to come with me?"

"Sure. If it would help."

I smile. "It would. Come on, let's go get showered and changed, and then I can show you my life."

———

I run a brush through my hair again and then head out of my bathroom in my khaki dress pants and pink blouse. I stop in my tracks when I see Asher in his swim trunks and T-shirt.

"Is that what you are wearing?" I ask.

"Yes. You have a problem with that?"

I shake my head. "Nope." I grab my purse and then head to my door. "Let's go."

Asher grabs hold of my hand. This time, it feels more like he's trying to reassure me that he's with me, which I desperately need because, unlike the honeymoon, as soon as we step foot inside my office building, we are going to be swarmed with questions.

And, sure enough, the second I pull up to the building, we are swarmed with photographers and reporters. I guess it is a big deal when the local girl who runs a large nonprofit almost dies, calls off her wedding, and then marries someone else all in a matter of two days.

I climb out of the driver's seat of my car without even thinking about Asher. I'm sure he's dealt with his fair share of press before. I smile and wave as lights flash all around me. I walk toward the back of my car and wait for Asher to join me. He looks a little shell-shocked, but when he makes it to the back of my car and I grab his hand, his smile lifts.

"You didn't tell me there would be so many people excited to see us, sweetheart," he whispers into my ear.

I laugh. "Just smile and wave until we make it inside where we will get a whole new group of people attacking us."

I start leading him toward my office building as dozens of reporters yell out questions to us.

"When did you get married?"

"Where did you get married?"

"How long have you two known each other?"

"How are you doing after your near-death experience?"

The questions keep coming and coming.

I see Marissa, a reporter who I actually respect, standing near the entrance to the building. She smiles at me and then leans into my ear as I open the door.

"Give me an exclusive, and it will get this mob of people to leave you alone."

I look at her, giving her an I'll-think-about-it look.

She smiles brightly because she thinks I'm going to take her up on her offer. And maybe I will if it will get all the photographers outside to leave us alone.

I take a deep breath once inside. Even though I can already feel the stares on me when we enter the two-story building, I don't care. This is my home. This is where I flourish.

I start walking toward the stairs that lead up to my office, but Asher freezes, holding my hand. I turn and look at him with a fake smile on my face. I shake my head sideways, trying to get him to come on.

He leans down and whispers in my ear, "I've never felt like I should have worn something nicer so much in my life."

I laugh and look at him. He looks like a wrinkled mess. I doubt he even owns an iron. Other than the stubble that covers his face and the tiny lines around his eyes, giving his true age away, he looks like he's eighteen.

"You're fine. Now, come on, or we are never going to make it to my office, and I have work to do." I let go of his hand and start walking toward the stairs.

"Hello, Miss Hart—I mean, Mrs. Calder," my receptionist says from behind her desk.

"It's still Ms. Hart. I'm going to keep my name," I say.

"Of course, Ms. Hart." But Bonnie's eyes don't stay on mine long. Instead, they are eating up Asher.

He must have gotten his confidence back because he is strutting behind me as all the women ogle his body that I know they wish were more visible than what his clothes allow.

I sigh and walk back the five feet to where Asher is now getting swarmed with people asking for his autograph.

"Asher needs to come with me now. But I'll make sure you all have plenty of time later to talk to him and get his autograph," I say a little too sternly.

I grab hold of his hand again, feeling like a mother corralling a two-year-old, which, at the moment, makes me never want kids if it is anything like having to deal with Asher. We make it to the stairs, and I start taking them two at a time, despite my heels.

Even though I live in heels, my work requires me to be quick on my feet. I'm always putting out one fire or another. And I like interacting with the kids who live next door. They've been trying to better their lives after the abuse, neglect, and trouble they got into prevented them from reaching their full potential. I love seeing how resilient the kids are and how they are able to turn their lives around.

"I don't know how you do that in your heels," Asher says when we make it up the stairs.

I smile at him. "Years of practice. I wasn't always so good in heels. I know you won't believe me, but for much of my childhood, I lived in tennis shoes and T-shirts. It wasn't until my early twenties that I started wearing heels and dresses."

"I would have never guessed, but then I've learned to never guess with you."

I keep walking until I get to my office at the back of the building. It's a small room. Not anywhere close to the largest office in the building. But I like it this way. I like having a small office that is just mine. It keeps other people from feeling like they can hang out when I have work to do. Plus, we have plenty of conference rooms that I can go to if I need to meet with more than one person. But there is one awesome benefit to my office that none of the other offices have.

"Holy shit! I thought your condo had a nice view, but this..." Asher says when he walks into my small office.

I take a deep breath, looking at the view. "It was the main reason I chose this building to house our offices."

Asher walks over to the large window that my desk faces. It makes more sense for my desk to face away from the window, but there is no way I could have given up the view.

I take a seat at my desk and fire up my computer. I wait for the endless amount of emails that I get to start pouring in.

"So, what do you want me to do? Besides stare at this incredible view all day," he says.

When I look up, he isn't looking out at the ocean anymore. He is looking at me. I'm the incredible view he is talking about. I blush slightly but am not really that embarrassed.

I glance at my clock. "My mom is going to be here in half an hour. She's excited to meet you. So, it would be great if you could take her to the café downstairs and just get a coffee or something with her."

"Without you?"

I nod. "Most likely. I have a shit-ton of emails I need to answer. And then I need to go over and talk with some of the kids today. I've heard there are a couple who are struggling with the program, and I want to go see to them personally."

His eyes are wide as he looks at me.

"You'll be fine."

"I don't do parents."

I laugh. "Well, my mother isn't really a parent. Technically, I lived with her when I was growing up, but I wouldn't call her a parent. I usually refer to her as Catherine anyway instead of Mother. Especially when I'm at work. So, I really don't care if you impress her or not. Just keep her out of my hair and keep her from drinking anything alcoholic—at least until after lunch."

He sighs. "Fine. But you owe me the dirtiest sex ever on your desk or pressed up against this window after this."

"Well, at least wait until I'm gone for that. Although I would be happy to take you up on that offer if my daughter doesn't," Catherine, my mother, says.

I frown and take a deep breath, trying to calm myself before I get up.

Asher, on the other hand, doesn't bother to apologize for his words, which is one of the things I like about him. He doesn't apologize unless he feels he is actually in the wrong, and it turns out, that isn't very often.

I give my mother a quick hug, like I actually love her and am happy that she is here.

"This is Asher, my husband," I say.

Asher finally stands and extends his hand. "It's nice to meet you,

Catherine. I haven't heard much about you, but I'd love it if you would catch me up over some coffee."

Catherine lights up. "I would love to."

I wink at Asher and say a silent, *Thank you.*

He smiles back, conveying that I owe him.

I nod and grin because I actually think he is going to be good at talking with my mother. All he has to do is flash some muscles, and he'll be good.

As they leave, I realize I need one more thing from him.

"What's your schedule for the week, Asher? Do you have any competitions or training that I need to work around?"

"I usually train for at least three hours every morning. After that, I can do whatever for you, sweetheart."

I smile.

Then, my mother grabs hold of his arm, and I know he isn't going to get another word in for the next hour. I turn back to my computer. But at least I can get some work in instead of focusing on my husband who isn't really my husband. I feel myself caring a little too much about him at the moment, but it's nothing a long morning of work can't fix.

———

After working for almost three hours and getting through most of the urgent emails, all I can think about is Asher.

Shit.

I shouldn't want him. I just had him last night. And, on the plane, we did hand stuff under a blanket. I've gone weeks, months, without sex in the past. *Why am I this needy now?*

Because I never had sex with Asher before. Because I never knew what I was missing before him.

I get up from my desk, stretching. I'm surprised that Asher hasn't texted me that he can't take my mother any longer and I need to come rescue him or that he's calling the whole thing off and asking for a divorce. That's what I would have done if I were him.

Nothing is worth having to deal with my mother—or father, for that matter—for this long. It makes me wonder who has murdered whom.

I slip my heels back on that I kicked off while working, and I make my way down to the café where I told Asher to take my mother. I search for five minutes, but I don't see signs of either of them. I walk over to the barista behind the counter.

"Have you seen my husband or mother?" I ask, hoping that she knows who the hell I am. "My husband is a surfer who would be hard to miss, and my mother is dressed like she is going to a ball later today."

The barista smiles. "They were here earlier. Your mother left in a car about an hour ago. And your husband asked for something more fun to do. I sent him across the street to talk with the kids."

I nod. "Thank you."

I run outside into the warm air. I immediately feel drenched in sweat every time I step outside. It makes me wonder why I even bother to wear nice clothes. Maybe Asher has it right. It does make sense to always be wearing swim-type clothing while in Hawaii.

I make it into the building across the street, and thank God for the air conditioner. I'm actually surprised that I didn't see any press waiting for us outside.

But, after I emailed Marissa, she must have kept to her promise to help get rid of the press. I don't know how she managed it. Maybe she allowed them to pick up the piece as well. I don't know.

I run my hand through my hair as I search the home that holds somewhere around a hundred kids on any given day. The age range of the kids varies. But all of the kids here are in need of a fresh start. It's expensive to fly them to Hawaii. But we have found that most of the kids thrive after they come here because it is so different from the environment they were in before. They can actually see a future after coming here. They see the beauty in the world again. So, the money is well worth it.

They come here and heal while we work to find them new homes. And, with the older ones, we work to get them jobs, college scholarships, or anything else that they need to make it in the real world once they graduate high school. We become their substitute family.

I start walking down the hallway, looking for Asher. I don't have a lot of time to look for him. I need to find the couple of kids on my list and spend the afternoon with them, so I can figure out how to help them. I stop dead in my tracks when I see Asher sitting with one of the teenage boys, playing a basketball video game on the TV. I stand in the doorway and watch them.

"You're kicking my ass, Jordan," Asher says.

"Fuck yeah, I am," Jordan says back.

"Do you cuss like that in front of the ladies?"

Jordan thinks for a minute. "Yeah. But they love it."

"Do they? Then, the chicks must have changed a lot since I was your age. Because most of the women I know don't love it when I cuss. Not the ones I hope to spend more than an afternoon with anyway. If you want a woman you can take out on a date more than once, you are going to have to reduce the amount of cussing. You feel me?" Asher asks.

Jordan nods slowly. "Yeah, I feel you, man. Thanks."

"Now, if you really want to impress a girl, then you should take her surfing."

"But I've never surfed before in my life. I would look like an idiot."

"Well, I can help you with that. An athletic guy like you, I could have you up on a surfboard in no time."

"Really?"

"Absolutely. What does your school schedule look like?"

"I have classes until three and then free time after that."

"I'll come by around three then, and I'll teach you how to surf and how to get that girl to go out with you. But you have to go to classes, or the deal is off. Understand?"

"But why do I need school? I want to play professional baseball. I want to be an athlete. Look at you. You are a surfer. What do you need school for?"

"You don't think I needed an education to do what I do?"

"No, all you do is surf all day and get paid for it."

Asher laughs. "No. It isn't that simple. I don't make a lot of money off of my competition wins. I make most of my money off of sponsors and advertising, which means I have an agent. I spend a lot of my day signing contracts. I have to read contracts and understand them. Otherwise, I'd get screwed out of money that I deserve. I have to be able to protect myself. If not, I don't get to be a surfer anymore," Asher says, looking up at me. Like he knows how stupid it was for him to sign a prenup without actually reading it. But it also says that, above everything else, he trusts me.

"And what is your genius plan if you get injured in your first year? You will need a degree so that you could work as an agent or do something else related to baseball, if that is your passion. But you need education."

Jordan nods and is seriously thinking about everything that Asher said.

"So, do we have a deal? No more skipping classes."

Jordan takes his time but holds out his hand to Asher. "Deal."

Asher shakes it. "Good. Now, get your ass to class."

Jordan smiles, gets up, and then walks past where I'm standing with my arms crossed, leaning against the doorway.

"You married an awesome guy, Mrs. Calder," Jordan says.

"Thank you, Jordan." I consider correcting him, but it seems that everyone is going to start calling me by Asher's last name.

Once Jordan is gone, I walk over to where Asher is sitting on the couch and take a seat next to him.

"How did you just do that?"

"Do what?"

"Jordan is one of our most troubled kids here. I was actually coming over here to talk to him. How did you not only pick him out of all the kids here, but also get him back on track?"

"I don't know if he is back on track or not. It's up to him to decide if he really wants and is ready to be back on the right track. But, hopefully, I gave him a good push."

Asher grabs my legs and drapes them across his body. "And, as far as how I picked him out of all the kids here, I guess I could see a little bit of myself in him."

I cock my head to the side as his lips softly kiss me. Far too soft for what I want. I want passion, the kind where he is going to carry me to the restroom and fuck me.

"What do you mean, you see a little bit of yourself in him?" I ask, genuinely curious now about his childhood. I honestly don't know much about him.

He shakes his head. "I'm not going to spill my guts until you tell me more about you. Because, after spending two hours with your mother, I have a better understanding of how you turned into a wild child. So, tell me a story, and maybe I'll tell you one from my childhood."

I frown. I don't like sharing anything about myself. But I guess it's only fair.

"My parents were never there for me, growing up. They basically left me, and...I mean, they left me to my own devices. They didn't even bother to hire a nanny or cook. I was just on my own. That's why they sent me to Hawaii to live with my grandmother every summer. They didn't want to deal with me, and my grandmother was the one who actually straightened me out. Anyway, my parents would have all of these parties where their fancy friends came over with their fancy jewelry and money. I kind of got good at pickpocketing."

He raises an eyebrow at me.

"I know. I would pickpocket them and take any cash they had. They usually had a couple hundred dollars. But I never spent the money on myself. I would always donate the money or give it to friends who had less money than I did."

"So, you were kind of like Robin Hood? Stole from the rich to give to the poor."

I laugh. "I guess you could say that. I think running this nonprofit kind of became my penance. My parents gave me plenty of inheritance. Enough to comfortably live off of without working another day in my life. So, I live off of that money and don't take a salary from the nonprofit."

He nods.

"Your turn," I say.

"My story isn't really that exciting."

"I don't care. I want to hear it anyway."

He sighs. "Fine. I never knew my mother. She left me when I was still a baby. My father raised me. And, honestly, much of my childhood was amazing. My father was the best. We didn't have a lot of money, but it didn't matter because we loved each other, and we were all either of us needed. But then he died."

"How old?" I ask when Asher stops talking.

"Eleven."

"I'm so sorry."

He shakes his head. "It's okay. It happened a long time ago."

I hold his hand and kiss him on the cheek, hoping that I can somehow take his pain away even though I know I can't.

"I moved from California to Hawaii to live with my coach until I was old enough to live on my own. I didn't realize it then, but he only let me live with him so that he could have a say in my competition and sponsorship earnings. Even though I won a lot and should have had more than enough money to survive on by the time I was sixteen, with him being my legal guardian and signing all the contracts, he got control of my money. I eventually figured it out."

"What did you do?"

"I ran away and lived on my own for a while. I didn't really have a home, so I was couch-surfing for a while. But, after I won one competition, I suddenly had enough money to buy an apartment, and the rest is history."

I tilt his chin up to me and kiss him on the lips, letting him know how much I appreciate him sharing and how much I wish I could take away the pain from his childhood. Within seconds, the kiss turns to more. More kissing, more need, more passion. Asher's hand tangles in my hair, and mine goes under his shirt as Asher pushes me on my back. We make out on the old couch like two horny teenagers.

"Excuse me, Mrs., uh...um..."

We both freeze. We stop kissing. But our hands stay on each

other. Because it doesn't matter who is standing in the entryway. We need each other. We are desperate for each other. And, even though he is going to ruin our make-out session, we can at least still cling to each other for a few more seconds.

"You can still call me Ms. Hart," I say with my eyes closed as I press my forehead against Asher's for a little bit longer.

We each suck in a breath, and then I open my eyes back to reality as Asher does the same.

"I have to go," I whisper.

He nods. "I'll meet you back at your place."

I lean forward and kiss his lips one last time. Then, I get up to meet one of my employees who needs me at the door before returning to the hustle and bustle of the office.

"Ms. Hart, I need you to look over some plans, and then I need..." Kenny keeps telling me what he needs as he walks down the hallway, expecting me to follow him so that we can talk and get things accomplished at the same time.

I have to stop though for just a second and look back at Asher one last time before I enter the real world again.

He has a heart. Honestly, I wasn't sure he had one. But it makes my heart ache, just thinking about his.

I turn and hurry to catch up with Kenny. All the time, I'm thinking, *Asher has a heart. And it's a good heart that is capable of love. Who knew?*

16

SLOANE

MY WEEK IS ALMOST UP, and I can tell that Asher is getting restless at my place. He's accidentally broken a wine glass, a picture frame, and a glass figurine I had sitting on a shelf. It's not that he's clumsy; he's just not used to having so many nice things, and he didn't realize that one wrong movement could cause so much damage.

But Asher has done everything that he was supposed to do. He hasn't complained once about staying in my condo. And, anytime that he was close to complaining, he would just fuck me, and then he'd seemingly like my condo again.

He has spent most of the week at my office other than the few hours a day that he is surfing. He has taken I don't know how many of my kids out for surf lessons.

But he has also spent a lot of time talking with the kids. And, as much as I thought that I should be afraid of what he was telling the kids, I'm not afraid at all. I thought he would tell them that it was okay to drink, party, and do drugs. That it was okay to steal what you needed. But he didn't. He didn't exactly tell the kids that they needed to be models of perfection. He didn't sugarcoat and say that their life was going to be easy. He was completely honest and real with them. He's been doing a better job at connecting with them than many of our counselors have done. I would hire him full-time in a heartbeat if I thought he would say yes and if it wouldn't complicate things further.

Right now, it's a lazy Sunday afternoon. I'm working on my laptop, sitting on my comfortable couch, with my feet stretched out across his lap while he watches some baseball game on the TV. And all I can think about is how I can't imagine how we are going to spend our time at his place. I'm not even sure if his couch can support our weight for this long.

"Why are you staring at me like that?" Asher asks without taking his eyes off the television.

"How do you know I'm looking at you?"

"Because your typing on the computer stopped, and I assume it is because my body has distracted you. I need at least twenty minutes though before I can fuck you."

I laugh. "You're telling me that, if I stripped naked right now, you wouldn't fuck me?"

"Nope," he answers quickly.

"If I wore my black lace lingerie, you wouldn't fuck me?"

"Nope."

I frown. "If I rubbed oil all over my body?"

"Nope."

"If I brought in a model for a three-way?"

"Not even for a three-way. They are way overrated anyway."

I chuckle. "And when did you have a three-way?"

"A couple of years ago. After I won my first international competition. I won half a million in prize money alone. I had my choice of women after that."

I huff. "Why won't you fuck me? Why do you need twenty minutes at least?"

"Because this baseball game is tied, going into the bottom of the ninth, and I want to see who wins."

"I thought you didn't care about watching baseball."

He jumps up and starts yelling at the TV. "Homer! That's a homer. Go, go, go!"

I watch as the ball flies up and then lands in a guy's glove, inches from going over the fence.

"Shit," he says, slowly sitting back down, his eyes still on the TV.

"I thought you didn't care about watching baseball."

He shrugs. "Now, I do."

"And why is that?"

"Well, now that I have a nice TV to watch sports on every day, you've got me hooked to the thing. And there is a kid I'm helping tutor who is a Cubs fan, and I want them to win for once."

"You are tutoring a kid? I didn't know you were smart enough."

He tosses a pillow at me. I catch it with my hands.

"I'm not just a hot body—as much as that is all you use me for."

I roll my eyes. "Don't blame me for your newfound TV addiction."

"I'm definitely blaming you."

"Fine. Then, I'll blame you when I stink because I haven't showered in a week after moving into your place."

That gets his attention. He stares at me like I just spoke Chinese to him or something.

"You're still wanting to move into my place? I thought that was a joke when you said it."

I frown. "It wasn't a joke. I promised that, if you lived here for a week, then I would try out your place for a week without complaining about it. Then, we could make a decision together about where we lived for a while."

He raises an eyebrow. "You are always full of surprises."

He takes my feet back in his lap and begins slowly rubbing them. He might be waiting until the end of the game to fuck me, but I know that I'm at least still in the back of his mind.

He knows that rubbing my feet is one of my biggest turn-ons. I didn't realize it was until this week. I think he is the first guy to ever rub my feet. He did, and I've been putty in his hands ever since. So, I know this is his way of saying that the sex is coming the second the Cubs win or lose this game.

I pick my laptop back up and open it. I never imagined that Asher would be this nice to me. I never imagined that he would actually do anything to help my business. I never imagined I would ever want to do anything nice for him.

But here I am, sitting with my computer, frantically searching for the perfect gift to get him. Something to show him how much I appreciate him. Especially after I found out that his birthday is next week. I thought I would do something small. Take him to dinner or something. But, now, I'm buying him the most expensive gift I have ever bought anyone.

I look up at his grin as he watches the TV.

Damn it. I know this isn't going to end well. For either of us.

————

"What are you doing?" Asher asks.

I hold the tie out to him.

"I'm not wearing that," he says.

I laugh. "I didn't figure you would, and I don't want you to. Tonight is about celebrating you. Wear whatever you want."

"You're all dressed up though," he says.

I shake my head as I look down at my simple sundress. "I wouldn't call this dressed up."

"It's dressed up to me."

"I'm wearing a dress. That doesn't mean I'm dressed up."

"So, what is with the tie?" he asks.

I walk behind him and place the tie over his eyes. "I have a surprise that I don't want you to see until I'm ready."

I begin tying the tie behind his head, hoping it is enough so that he can't see.

"Do I want to know why you have a tie? It's not mine. Have you been cheating on me?"

I laugh. "Will you relax? You know I haven't been cheating on you. With the amount of sex we've been having lately, I don't think I would have time to cheat on you."

"True."

"I have a couple of outfits that look sexy with a tie. It's mine. It's pink. Not too many men wear bright pink ties."

I check to make sure that he can't see out of the tie by dancing around and acting goofy. When he doesn't respond to my craziness, I smile and grab his hand. "Follow me."

"I can't see. You could be leading me to my death, and I wouldn't know."

I grin. "I could. I guess you will just have to trust me."

I lead him out of my condo and start walking down the hallway to the elevators.

"You're lucky I like fucking you," he says as my older neighbors get off the elevator.

"Good afternoon, Mr. and Mrs. Shayfield," I say as we pass them and walk into the elevator.

"Stop talking dirty, and just do as you're told," I say.

Asher grins. "Fine. But it's my birthday. Aren't you supposed to be doing what I tell you to do? Not the other way around?"

"No. You're supposed to always do what I tell you. We are married, remember?" I joke with him.

He laughs. "Fine. I'll do whatever you want as long as I—"

I put my hand on his mouth, shutting him up, as the doors to the elevator open on the bottom floor. As much as I want to hear him say more dirty, filthy things to me, I want to still be able to live in my building without being completely embarrassed.

I grab his hand and quickly lead him through the lobby of the building and outside.

"Okay, now, I really think you are going to try and kill me. Or push me into the ocean, ruining my only pair of shorts that aren't swim trunks so that I will be forced to wear some suit or something that you have laid out for me upstairs."

I laugh and shake my head. "You are wrong on both accounts."

I keep leading him to my surprise.

"Then, what the hell are we doing?"

"Okay, stop."

He does, just inches from falling off the curb of the sidewalk.

I grimace, hoping he's not going to twist an ankle because of me. I grab his hips and force him to take a step backward.

"Are you ready for your surprise?" I ask excitedly.

He grins. "Ready as I'll ever be."

I pull on one end of the tie covering his head.

"Ow," he says when the tie jerks his head back instead of coming undone, like I expected it to.

I giggle. "Sorry. Here, let me—"

"No. You had your chance." He rips the tie off his eyes.

"Happy birthday!" I shout.

My eyes are glued to him as he looks at the brand-new truck I bought him for his birthday. It's exactly the same as his truck, just completely redone inside and out.

His eyes pop open as he looks at it.

"Well? What do you think?"

"You bought me a truck?" he asks hesitantly.

I laugh. "Yes. I bought you a truck for your birthday. I know you love that old thing that you are always driving around, but I know it's going to die soon. I thought you could use something new to drive that would also remind you of the old one you love so much. Just with a few new features."

"You bought me a truck," he repeats again.

I nod, and then my heart drops. "You don't like it, do you?"

"You bought me a truck."

I shake my head. "I can return it if you don't like it."

He turns to look at me. "You bought me a truck." A grin slowly curls up on his lips.

I bite my own lip, still not sure if he loves it or hates it. I don't know him well enough to know what this reaction means. It isn't how I expected him to react.

"You bought me a truck," he says, now fully grinning.

"If you say that one more time, I'm going to go insane. Yes, I bought you a truck. Do you like it or hate it?"

His arms go around me, and then he's twirling me around. I let out a little squeal, hoping to God this means he's happy with me whether he likes it or not.

"You bought me a freakin' truck! Of course I love it," he says.

He firmly kisses me and then carries me over to the passenger side. He throws the door open and lifts me up into the truck before running to the driver's side and climbing in.

"Holy cow! I thought you just bought me a new truck that was just like mine, but this thing..." He runs his hand over the dashboard that is full of buttons and lights. "This thing has everything."

I smile, but my heartbeat doesn't slow. It's beating on full blast, going about a million miles an hour, as I watch him try out every function of the truck.

"To be honest, I never wanted a new truck. And, when my truck died, I thought I would just buy another old used truck that would last a couple of years and then die. I beat my truck up enough with the sand and heat that I never thought I would want a nice truck."

Shit. He hates it. He thinks it's cool, but he will never use it.

"But, damn, was I wrong. This thing is awesome!"

I grin. "Really? Do you really like it? I can take it back."

He starts the truck and puts it in drive before pulling out onto the main street. I watch as he takes a deep breath of air when he puts down the sunroof to let in the cool ocean air.

"No way am I letting you take this thing back. This thing is awesome. I love it." He leans over and kisses me on the lips. "No one has ever gotten me anything this nice before. I don't care how much you spent on it. I don't care that we aren't really together. I'm not letting you take it back. You bought it and gave it to me. It's mine now."

When he looks at me, his eyes say that I'm his, too. Even though we both know that it isn't true. I'm not his. I can never be his.

"Take a left up here," I say.

"Why?"

I smile. "Because I have one more surprise for you."

He grins. "I like your surprises, Sloane. A lot."

"Good."

I like that, now that I bought him a truck, he will do whatever I want for the rest of the evening. He knows all I want is to do something nice for his birthday.

He parks the truck in the parking lot by the beach after I give him directions.

"You know I love the beach, Sloane, but I'm starving, and I spent most of the day here. So, it's not really a surprise to take me to the beach."

I shake my head. "You haven't seen the surprise yet. Come on."

I climb out of the truck and wait for him to savor the last few minutes of being inside the truck before climbing out. He finally does.

We automatically link our fingers together, and then I lead him down toward the beach.

When he sees it, he picks me up in his arms and starts kissing me. "Thank God you aren't taking me to a fancy restaurant for dinner."

I laugh. "I know you well enough to know that you don't like eating at fancy restaurants."

"I'm glad I stole you from Wes."

"You didn't steal me. I came willingly."

"Whatever you say, sweetheart. You're mine now. At least, you are tonight."

He finally places me down in one of the chairs and then takes a seat opposite me. The table is simple. It's a white table with white chairs. Nothing over the top. Nothing fancy. I knew he wouldn't want fancy although I did have the chef fix fancy food. I know he isn't opposed to fancy, good food.

The waiter brings over two beers, like I requested. "Would either of you like anything to drink other than beer?"

Asher grins. "Beer is perfect."

"I'll be right back with your first course," the waiter says before disappearing back up to his station several feet away.

Asher cocks his head to one side as he looks at me. "Why are you being so nice to me?"

"It's your birthday. It's, like, a law that you are nice to your husband on his birthday. You might even get lucky tonight," I say, winking.

He takes a sip of his beer. "I know that most wives are nice to their husbands on their birthdays. But we aren't really husband and wife. More like fake husband and wife. There is no requirement for fake husbands and wives to be nice. So, why are you?"

"Because I like you, and I want you to be happy. You are kind of growing on me, even if your heart is black."

He chuckles. "You're probably right about my heart, which is why you shouldn't get too close to me. I might just break it."

Too late, I think.

I suck in a breath. It can't be too late. I just have to remind myself how much of a monster he really is. Then, I won't care for him so much.

"Oysters, crab cakes, and calamari," the waiter says, placing a large plate of food in front of us.

We both stare at the appetizer plate. It looks delicious.

"I'll be back with more beers. Anything else you need?"

We both shake our heads.

The waiter leaves again, and we each dig into the food in front of us.

"This is amazing. Where did you order it from?"

I don't answer. I just keep digging into the food and eventually mumble something between bites, a bit ashamed that I ordered it from the nicest and most expensive place on the island. All week, I've been telling him this place has the best food on the island to try and get him to go with me after work one night. But he disagreed. He said anything that cost this much was full of crap and couldn't be the best food on the island. So, I don't want him to find out it's from this place until after dinner is over.

He grins. "It's from Azure, isn't it?"

My cheeks blush, and I nod as my mouth is still full of crab cake. I swallow slowly, waiting for him to argue with me about why I didn't pick a place that I already knew he loved for his birthday.

He takes another bite of calamari. "I hate losing. And I mean, *hate* losing. But I will concede. This is the best fucking food on the island." He takes another bite of oyster. "No, it's the best food I think I've ever had in the entire world."

I laugh. "I told you, you wouldn't win every time. Not when you're competing against me."

"I win when it's important to win."

His scoots his chair closer to me and then runs his hand up the center of my thigh. I tighten my legs to keep him from inching his hand up further.

"As much as I loved our first romp on the beach, I'm not sure I'm ready for another. Not when José is going to come back any second with more beer and food."

He chuckles and slowly removes his hand. "As much as I want you right now, this might be the first time that I'll be patient enough to finish a meal fully before I fuck you."

"You'll need your strength for sure for what I have planned for you tonight."

"It'd better be fucking. Followed by more fucking. Followed by a short nap and then fucking, fucking, fucking."

I run my tongue across my lip. "There will be no napping, and I think you are missing a fuck or two in there."

José brings us a cooler with beers so that we can grab our own whenever we want. He also brings us each a large steak and lobster even though we aren't even close to finishing our appetizer.

"Eat up. You'll definitely need your strength."

We both eat and chat about work or random thoughts we have. But we mainly just eat in silence as we watch the sun slowly start to set across the ocean while we celebrate Asher.

Somehow, we do manage to finish our plates. And then José brings the birthday cake out.

"I'm sorry. I tried to find out what your favorite dessert was, but I couldn't. So, I had them do a birthday cake at least, and you can order whatever you want for dessert. They have almost everything."

Asher blows out the candle. "I want the cake and you for dessert."

I grin and take my fork to dig into the cake when Asher smears a little of the frosting against my chest.

"We are not fucking on the beach again. I don't care if it is your birthday."

Asher glances up at his truck that is parked just up the beach. "I do know of a very nice place to fuck that is far too clean and could use a little dirtiness."

Asher and I exchange one look, and then we are both running up the beach to his new truck as fast as we can with Asher carrying the cake in his hands. My heart beats fast and not just because I'm running fast.

It does anytime there is a thought of having Asher. I've never needed sex as much as I do when I'm with Asher. I need it almost as much as I need food to eat and air to breathe. It doesn't even make sense to me why I need it with him so much. You would think, with how amazing he is at it, that I would need less to satisfy me, not more. But, every time we fuck, it feels like he hasn't touched me in weeks, months, years.

Asher beats me to the truck and already has the passenger door open for me when I get there. He lifts me up in the truck, so I'm sitting, facing him, and then his lips claim me. We kiss, and it makes me lose my breath. But I don't care. I would survive forever from his lips alone.

Asher slowly climbs up on the truck on top of me until I'm lying back on the front seat bench in his truck. He closes the door behind us, and then we are completely engulfed in our own world. People might be able to make out what we are doing or more likely guess, but they won't be able to really see what we are doing. The windows in this truck are tinted, and we are parked under a tree.

And, even if anyone could tell what we are doing, it doesn't matter. We don't care. We need each other too much to care.

I'm too entranced with his kiss to notice anything. But I feel it when the frosting covers my neck, followed by his tongue licking the sweet sugar off my body.

"I love this cake," he says as he spreads more of the frosting on my body. This time, it's over my breasts before his tongue slowly licks it off.

I moan every time he touches me with his tongue. I tangle my hand in his hair, keeping his tongue against my body. I can't really move. There isn't room in the truck. It's hot in here and getting hotter with every second that passes. I don't care about any of it. All I can focus on is Asher's tongue against my skin.

Asher's hand slides up under my dress and grasps my breast. I arch my back, needing him to touch me more.

"We will have to save this cake for later. I need you now," Asher says.

I feel his fingers run down my body and then slip into my panties. He pulls them down and rubs his thumb across my clit, making me wet in seconds. He slides a condom on before his cock replaces his fingers, and then he's inside me as my back arches, trying to push him in further and further, until he is fully filling me.

I bite my lip, and my toes curl as he thrusts inside me. Our lips touch, and our eyes stay locked as we fuck. I feel words on the tip of my tongue. Words that I never thought I would want to say to Asher. I force the words to stay down. I will not say them. I will not feel them.

I feel my orgasm take over, and it helps to keep down any words or feelings other than complete bliss. I come, and Asher comes as we are locked together.

Asher keeps looking at me after we both have come. His eyes look intense as he looks at me. He opens his mouth to speak but doesn't say anything either.

I hold my breath, waiting to see if he is going to say anything or not. I need him to say it and don't want him to say anything at the same time. Because, if he says anything, then everything will change.

A rattling at the door forces air into my lungs again. Asher pulls out of me and sits up while pulling his pants up. I jerk my dress down and look around for the cause of the noise. Most likely, I'm guessing that it is nothing more than a bird or something that hit his window.

But, by the look of terror on Asher's face, it's much more than just a bird. He stares out the passenger window. I sit up just as Asher rolls down his window.

"Hello, Officer," Asher says to the police officer standing outside the door.

I straighten up in my seat and try to remain calm, but I'm too afraid that the police officer just saw what we were doing and is about to arrest us for indecent exposure.

"Are you the owner of this vehicle?" the officer asks.

"Yes," Asher answers.

"Can I see your license and registration?"

Asher reaches into his pocket and pulls out his license.

"The registration is in the glove compartment," I say.

Asher slowly opens the glove compartment and pulls the papers out. He hands them all to the officer.

He quickly looks at the papers and then says to Asher, "Please step out of the car, sir."

Asher begins to step out of the car.

I stay frozen, not sure what I'm supposed to do.

"Asher Calder, you are under arrest," the officer says as he hand-cuffs him.

Shit.

I jump out of the truck, not thinking, and run over to them.

"What is he under arrest for?" I ask as I look Asher in his eyes, preparing myself to get arrested next.

"For stealing the truck," the officer says before walking Asher to the back of his cruiser and pushing him inside.

"What? The truck isn't stolen. I was the one who purchased it. It was a birthday gift. If you arrest anyone, it should be me! You have to let him go!"

I look at Asher sitting in the backseat of the cruiser, but he doesn't seem surprised at all to be arrested. In fact, he won't even look at me. He just looks straight ahead.

"Ma'am, I need you to step back," the officer says.

"You have it wrong. You shouldn't arrest him. I'll have him out tonight. You have to let him go."

The police officer shakes his head. "I can't do that. I have a warrant for his arrest. Do you have a way to get home, ma'am? Because I can't let you back inside the vehicle. It's now evidence."

"I'll get home just fine," I say, folding my arms across my chest in frustration.

This doesn't make sense at all. The truck isn't stolen. It must be a mistake or a mix-up.

The police officer climbs into the driver's seat just as two more police cars show up to take possession of the truck they think is stolen. I wrap my arms tighter across my chest, now feeling far too cold for the warm weather that is summer in Hawaii.

"I'm going to get you out tonight!" I shout as the car begins to slowly move away.

Asher looks at me for just a moment. His eyes don't tell me a damn thing. They seem completely empty. Cold. His whole body seems cold. He keeps eye contact with me a second longer, and then the car is too far away for me to see him.

I shiver, feeling completely cold and empty now that he is gone. I pull out my cell phone and arrange for a car to come pick me up. I will keep good on my promise and get everything straightened out tonight. It is all just a big misunderstanding. That's all this is. A misunderstanding.

But I can't shake the feeling that I should have said what I desperately tried to push down when I had the chance. Because, now that he's gone, even if just for a few hours, I regret not saying anything. I regret not telling him my true feelings. Because you never know when you are going to lose someone and never get the chance to say those words.

I shake my head. This isn't good-bye. And I can't say those words, no matter how much I need to.

17

SLOANE

I COULDN'T GET Asher out of jail the night he was arrested. I tried everything in my power, but they wouldn't release him. I had my attorney work on his case, and even he—someone I pay almost a million dollars in salary a year, working for days—couldn't get him out of jail. They claim they have evidence that the truck is the same truck that was reported stolen last week. That with Asher's prior history they won't release him.

It's been a week since his birthday. Since the night he was arrested.

I have spent the week staying at his place. Alone. I slept in his bed. I ate—no, mostly drank beer out of his fridge. I used his outdoor shower and toilet and actually started to enjoy it. I love every part of his shack. I love how simple he lives. And I love his place because it completely reminds me of him.

It took me a while to realize why the police weren't going to just let Asher go. Even if it was truly a mix-up. Even with proof that I was the one who bought the truck for him. That it wasn't stolen. His rap sheet is a million miles long. He has stolen countless cars, jewelry, money. Anything of value, and he stole it. He was in and out of jail most of his adolescence. He was once even charged with an armed robbery that would have put him away for twenty years. It was a miracle he wasn't already in jail.

Although maybe it would have been better if he were in jail. A lot less people would have been hurt if he were in jail this whole time.

I sit in my car outside the jail, waiting for Asher to come out, so I can take him home. It's a strange feeling. I know he didn't steal the truck, but he easily could have. It's been over a year since he was in jail for theft. But he could easily still be stealing and just not getting caught.

Or he could have changed.

I shake my head. He hasn't changed. He stole me. It's no different than stealing a car. Nothing's changed. He's a villain. A monster. I knew that. I just thought that maybe I could be the one to change him. That I could make him different. Better.

My fingers drum against the steering wheel as I wait. My heart beats fast, and my hands are sweaty. I'm nervous, waiting for Asher to come out. Because I'm afraid that one week has somehow changed everything. No, I know it has. I already think of him differently. Just knowing that he has gone to jail for such horrible things makes me feel differently. It reminds me of who he really is instead of the man who knows how to turn me on. How to fuck me and nothing more.

I see the door open and watch Asher walk out. He stops a second when he sees me, seemingly just as surprised to see me sitting in my car as I am at the sight of him. Because, looking at him now, I know that one week can completely change your whole world. One week can change everything.

Asher looks completely different than the man I knew who walked into the building. For one, the clothing he walked into the building with is gone. For some reason, he's wearing shorts and an old-looking sweatshirt that is far too big on him. He starts walking again, and the hood falls down. I gasp in complete shock. His long locks are gone, exchanged for a much shorter cut. His beard has grown out longer than it ever was before. And his eye looks bruised with a cut above it.

He's gone from a relaxed, beach-loving surfer to a hardened criminal overnight. I don't know what happened in there, but gone is the goofy, arrogant smile, and in its place is a menacing grimace. He looks even colder than when the police arrested him.

I'm not sure if he's going to walk to my car or not. He seems mad. I just don't know if he's mad at me, if he thinks I somehow set this all up, or if he is mad at the police and having to spend a week showering in front of other men and feeling afraid for his life at every second.

So, while he is walking down the sidewalk, I take the time to admire his body. I bite my lip as I take in his darker look. A look that I am just as desperate for as his surfer look.

He walks to my passenger door and opens it. He sits down without a word to me. We look at each other, just like we did when he fucked me in the truck, just like we did when he was in the back of the police cruiser. Both of us have so much to say, but neither of us is able to say anything.

I take a deep breath and say, "You hungry?"

He narrows his eyes and nods.

I smile weakly. "I know this great little place that does great American style food just up the road, or I can take you to get something else if you prefer."

He shrugs like he doesn't care.

I pull out of my parking spot and start driving toward the little diner in silence.

When we get to the diner, I stop and look at Asher. "This place makes great milkshakes. I figured we could both use one."

Asher chuckles. "A milkshake would actually be perfect."

I let out the breath I was holding since he stepped foot in my car. I smile. "Good."

We get out of the car, and our fingers brush against each other before Asher finally grabs hold of my hand and gives it a reassuring squeeze. I let out another deep exhale, but I still feel anxious.

We take a seat in one of the booths on the far side of the diner where no one else is sitting. We each order milkshakes and burgers.

"I'm sorry," we say at the same time.

"You have nothing to be sorry for," we say.

Asher relents and lets me speak.

"I'm sorry that you ended up in jail. I didn't realize the police would mistake the truck as a stolen one. I'm sorry your birthday sucked and that I couldn't get you out earlier."

Asher shakes his head. "I'm the one who should apologize. I should have told you the real reason I never have anything nice. Why I haven't replaced my old truck in years even though it's broken down. Why I live in a shack on the beach when I have millions sitting in the bank."

He takes a deep breath as he grimaces and then looks me in the eyes. "It's because I'm a thief. I used to steal cars; now, I steal women's hearts. But the police will always believe that anything nice I own is stolen. You need to know my whole story. It starts ten years ago..."

———

Ten Years Earlier—Asher

I'm not supposed to steal. I know that. I thought I had put the stealing all behind me.

But why is the temptation so great right now?

Maybe because I have had a shitty day. Although that doesn't make what I'm thinking about doing right. But I'm tempted all the same.

I've already done the hard part of sneaking into the garage without getting caught. I watched in my car as the family pulled out of their driveway. Gone for a weeklong vacation. It's not really a challenge. The family leaves the back door that leads into the garage unlocked so that the various people they've hired to take care of the pool and garden have access to their tools. And there isn't anything of value to steal in the garage anyway. They have a second garage for their fancy cars. But the garage is attached to the house.

I doubt they leave the door leading into the house open, but I try it anyway. It's locked, like I suspected. But I know where the spare key is. My friend, Sawyer, had to use the spare key to get into the house when he lost his while he was dog-sitting here last month.

I pull up the floor mat and find the key. I put the key in the door and turn it until it unlocks the door. I push the door open, holding my breath, hoping that they haven't installed an alarm system since I was here with Sawyer. No alarm sounds, so I make my way inside until I'm standing in the family's expansive living room that is two stories high. I can't help but look up at the huge ceiling and large windows that sit uncovered, revealing me to the outside world.

No one can see me, I have to remind myself.

It's dark outside, and I haven't turned any lights on. Man, I'm rusty at this.

I think about stealing one of their fancy cars. That is my favorite thing to steal. I love the thrill of driving out with a fast car that isn't mine. The only problem with stealing a car is getting rid of it before you get caught. I've done it several times in the past, but I've also gotten caught. And I don't plan on going back to jail anytime soon.

I find the stairs in the dark and begin creeping up them. I know enough from my past that, even if I think everyone has gone, it is better to be quiet. You never know if someone has decided to stay behind in the house even if you think they are all gone.

When I make it to the top of the stairs, I'm greeted by a small, fluffy dog that begins jumping at my feet. They left the dog, which means someone is going to be over at some point to let it out. It probably won't be till later since they just left, but to be sure, I have to move quickly.

I walk down the hallway until I find the master bedroom. The door is shut, and even though I'm confident that no one is behind it, I slowly and cautiously open the door.

The little dog decides to join me, still jumping at my feet whenever I walk. I hate dogs for this reason. They are horrible at protecting the home they are supposed to be guarding, no matter the size or breed. And they often just drive me nuts while I'm trying to do my job.

When I'm inside the bedroom, I quickly scan the room, trying to decide what to steal. I know the family is rich and most likely has a safe of some sort somewhere around here along with countless pieces of jewelry. I head toward the closet at the back of the room and find the safe. I'm tempted to break into the safe. The best items are in the safe. But the safe is the worst place to steal from. They know exactly what they have in the safe. The items they are less worried about, they keep in the bathroom or bedroom, and those are easier to steal without them noticing.

That's my target. Items that they won't even notice missing. So, as much as the safe calls my name, as much as I want to crack it because I can, I won't.

I turn my attention toward the bathroom and find the jewelry box sitting on top of the counter. I'm wearing gloves, so I don't have to worry about leaving my fingerprints behind. I open the box and slowly move the jewelry around, trying to find something valuable that doesn't look like it has been worn in a while. When I get to the back of the box, I find two necklaces in the same container.

I grin. This is exactly what I want. If I take one of the necklaces, it won't even look like anything is missing. I take the diamond necklace out and stare at it. It's not the most expensive thing in this house or even in the jewelry box. But the necklace is easily worth twenty thousand to thirty thousand dollars. It's enough to satisfy my urge to steal.

I place the necklace into my pocket. Then, I close the jewelry box and put everything back in its place. I start looking to see if there are other items in the bathroom or bedroom that are worth stealing when I hear the distant sound of sirens.

Shit. I glance around the room more thoroughly and see motion detectors in the corner of the room.

Shit. Shit. Shit. I must have triggered a silent alarm when I entered the house.

I start running down the stairs in the dark. The yipping dog is still jumping at my feet. I run fast enough that the dog can no longer keep up.

I make my way to the back door and open it. I move into the garage. The police sirens grow closer with every second that passes. I have to make a run for it. My car is parked a street back, so I begin running through the backyard to take the most direct route even though it's risky. The fence at the back is high and hard to climb, and any number of neighbors could see me and report me.

I run as fast as I can as I turn and look over my shoulder. I see the police cars arriving at the house. I dart behind a large tree as flashlights shine into the backyard. I take several deep breaths while I wait for my chance to jump the fence and disappear into the darkness.

If I admit it to myself, I love the excitement of the police being here. I love how my heart is racing. I love the thrill of getting caught. I just don't like actually getting caught.

The lights turn away from me and move toward the other half of the yard. I take one more deep breath before I run toward the fence that is ten feet or so in front of me. There is no turning back now. No place to hide. I have to make it over the fence that towers over me as quickly as possible before they decide to shine their flashlights back in my direction.

I reach the fence as beads of sweat pour off my neck. I run, jump, and grab hold of the large tree branch that is hanging over the fence from the neighbor's yard. I begin using my arms and legs to climb over the wooden fence.

I finally reach the top and throw my legs over before jumping down. I'm not safe just because I'm on the other side. In fact, I will never be safe again. I will always be on the run. Always on alert that I could be caught.

I begin running through the neighbor's yard. I trip and almost fall over a tree branch that I didn't see in the dark, but I keep running. I run until I reach the neighbor's gate. I carefully open it, hopeful that it doesn't squeak or make a sound, and then I make it through. I quickly shut it, and then I'm in the clear. It's a straight shot to my car.

I don't run now that I'm in clear view of the neighbors. Instead, I walk as calmly as I can toward my car. I quickly start it up and then drive at a normal speed, away from the area.

I stole again. I'm a thief. I don't even care about the money or things that I steal. I live for the rush I just experienced. I just don't know how to get this feeling without stealing. If I could find a way, I would never look back at this lifestyle again.

————

Five Years Earlier—Asher

My heart is racing. It always does on a night like this. The sun is just beginning to set. Before it rises again in the morning, I'm going to have a sweet-ass new car, and I'll be halfway to Mexico where I will sell it and then do it all over again.

I put my headphones on and then flip the hood of my sweatshirt up while I sit on the bench outside the dealership, waiting for the rest of the straggling employees to leave. The music is loud and steady. I try to use it to steady my heart, but I know that nothing is going to be able to do that. Not until I have the car in my possession, and I'm long gone.

So I sit and wait, hiding my face beneath the shadows of the hood. If employees drive by the bench, they will just think I'm waiting for the bus. They won't remember me. They never do. The few times I was caught were because I had been speeding after I stole the car or had friends who ratted me out. Neither is a mistake that I will repeat again.

I watch the last employee leave for the night, which leaves me exactly one hour until the janitor comes to clean. It's not quite dark, but it's dark enough to not draw too much attention to myself. I wait two more songs to ensure that no one is coming back because they forgot something inside, and then I get up, avoiding eye contact with the woman who just sat down on the bench next to me.

I walk slowly and carefully with my head down, making sure to avoid my face being caught on the security cameras that circle the outside of the dealership. I reach the door and then put on gloves before pulling out a lock pick. I enter the code I already gathered into the alarm system to prevent the alarm from going off and use the pick to unlock the door.

The door lock is loose and is easy to pick. It practically pops open on its own. I push the door, careful to keep my head down. Even though the alarm system is down, the cameras are still fully operational. So, I have to ensure that my head remains down to keep them from learning my identity. To stay out of jail.

I walk straight to the Lamborghini that is sitting in the middle of the showroom. The keys are, of course, not in it. I could spend minutes that I don't have searching for the keys, or I could hot-wire it. I go for option two.

I hot-wire the car, and then I get ready for the part that really gets my heart racing. The part that I live for. I stomp on the gas, going full speed ahead. I slam through the glass and drive as fast as I can away from the dealership.

I stole the car even though I don't need the money. Even though I don't need the car. Just because I want the freedom to feel how I do right now. I just want to live.

————

Present—Sloane

Asher finishes his story. "That's why I'm dressed the way I am. That's why I cut my hair off. I'm never going to be just a surfer. I'm always going to be part thief, no matter that I don't actually steal cars anymore. That is what the police think of me. I'm a thief.

"You knew that I was trying to steal you from Wes. But you don't treat me like I'm the monster that I am. You act like I'm just a normal person. You need to know that this is who I am. I'm a thief. This is me."

I nod, trying to take in what he said. "I know you are a thief. I've always known. Now, I just know how much of a thief you really are. But it doesn't matter. We aren't really married. Not in the way that counts. I've kept the story out of the news. I've just been telling everyone you were sick with the flu this week. No one knows where you really were."

He shakes his head. "You don't understand why it matters that you understand me. That you understand that I steal because I have to. I need that rush. I need that adrenaline boost that nothing else gives me. I need to feel alive. I need to fill a void that has never properly been filled. And stealing often does that for me."

He lifts my chin up to make sure I'm looking at him. "But I need you to know that I need you more." He hesitates a second and then says the thing that both of us have been avoiding for days, "I love you, Sloane."

18

SLOANE

"I LOVE YOU."

Three simple words with so much meaning.

He said them. I never expected that he was capable of love. That he would be able to love. But here he is, saying it, and I believe every word that fell from his lips. I know that he loves me. I've felt it for far too long now. We have both been avoiding it. But, now that it has been said, I wish he would take it back.

Every woman wishes for this moment when her boyfriend tells her that he loves her. I should be happy, over the moon, to realize that this arrangement has turned into something real. It has turned into something more than even I could have imagined.

But I'm not happy. I'm devastated. Because I now know what comes next, and I can't bear for it to happen.

"You don't have to say it back. In fact, I don't want you to say it until you feel it, too. I'll wait. I'm patient. I just want you to know that I want more. More than this arrangement that we originally set up. Because time in jail has taught me one very important thing. That I don't want to live without you. I know that I have to change. I have to be a better person, but being with you makes me that way. Being with you makes me want to believe that love can not only exist, but also last. I never thought that before."

I open my mouth to speak, but Asher continues, "When my father died, I was a mess. I hated that I loved him because the pain of losing him was too much to bear."

"How did he die?"

"He was shot."

"I'm so sorry," I say, wanting to know more because it's clear that he has more to say on the subject.

But he doesn't.

"I love you. Our pasts no longer matter. What matters is, if we have a real future together or not. What matters is, if you love me, too. Or if you could ever love me. If you could ever forgive me for what I've done."

I open my mouth to speak, but he beats me to it. "They are really taking forever with our milkshakes, huh? I should flag our waiter down and—"

"Will you shut up?" I say, laughing nervously.

Asher finally stops talking.

"I love you, Asher. I've felt it since the night of your birthday. I just pushed down the feeling because I thought we couldn't be together. We couldn't love each other. That wasn't the arrangement. The arrangement was to help each other. Nothing more. But I do love you."

Asher grins, and it is the brightest grin I've seen on him since I picked him up from jail.

"You love me?"

I smile because his grin is infectious. Even if I know that this is the start of our end, I still enjoy this moment with him. We love each other. No matter what happens after, this is a happy moment.

"I love you."

Asher reaches across the booth and kisses me on the lips.

"Here are your milkshakes and burgers."

"Can we get them to go?" we say at the same time.

We grin again.

"I'll be right back," the waiter says.

I dig out some cash and throw it on the table to cover our meals that aren't going to be eaten until later. We stand up and grab the to-go boxes, and then we practically run to my car. We jump in, and I step on the gas as soon as I can and peel out of the parking lot.

Tonight might be our last night together before everything changes, and I plan on making every minute count.

I speed back toward our home. I push that thought right out of my head. It's not our home. It's his home. It will never be ours.

Asher starts kissing my neck as I drive. With every kiss, I can feel it all over my body. Every nerve in my body is on fire, begging to be touched and kissed.

"You'd better stop that, or we aren't going to make it back to your place. And, last time we did it in a car, it didn't turn out so well in the end," I joke.

Asher stops kissing my neck for a second and has a solemn look on his face.

"I'm sorry. Too soon?"

He shakes his head and then kisses me again on the neck to show that it isn't too soon. "Why aren't we going back to your place?"

I swallow, trying to calm my breathing that is much too fast. "Because I fell in love with your place while you were gone."

A slow grin returns to his face as he sits back, staring at me. "You've been staying at my place while I was gone?"

I nod.

"I think I just fell even more in love with you, if that's possible."

I open my mouth to speak, but he kisses my neck again, and a moan comes out instead. All of my thoughts disappear. I try to focus on driving back to his place, but my attention is definitely on his soft lips that caress every inch of my neck.

I don't know how I make it back to his place, but somehow, I do. I jump out of the car, already knowing the perfect place that I want him to fuck me. I start running, and he chases me. He likes the thrill of the chase; I know that much.

And, now that he has me, now that he doesn't have to chase me anymore, will I be enough?

But I don't have to worry about that. Right now, I run until I find a secluded spot where the ocean tide is high.

Asher catches up to me and grabs me from behind, wrapping his arms around me. He kisses me again and again. He stops with his arms around me, and we look out at the sun over the ocean.

"Come inside. I want you in my bed."

I shake my head. "No. The beach is our place. I want you here."

He chuckles. "I'm not fucking you against the sand again."

"I'm not asking you to." I look down at the ocean in front of us.

I don't wait for him to give me all the reasons that the ocean is just as bad or worse of a place to fuck than the sand. I'm sure it is, but I've never fucked in the ocean before. And, even if it isn't perfect, it is what we both need.

Because, as much as he now looks like a thief, I need him to look like Asher again. The man I fell in love with, who has a heart. Who cares about other people, about me. Who loves me.

I grab his hand and lead him into the ocean until we are both waist-deep and covered with water.

"I need Asher tonight. The man I fell in love with, not the thief," I say.

"I can be whatever you want, Sloane. I wanted you to be mine, but instead, I'm yours."

I smile weakly and then stare at the sweatshirt that is covering his chest and body. Clothes that make him look so much like a thief instead of the man I fell in love with. I grab hold of the zipper and slowly lower it. His hard chest and abs come into view. I remove the sweatshirt and then hand it to Asher, who curiously looks at me.

"Throw it out into the ocean," I say.

He frowns. "You know this is littering."

I sigh. "Just do it. You need to let your past go."

He takes the sweatshirt and wads it up in a ball. Then, he throws it as hard as he can out into the ocean. We both stand for a moment, looking at it as it disappears beneath a wave.

When we look at each other, I jump into Asher's strong arms, and he carries me out further into the ocean. I grab on to his short hair that I know will eventually grow back into the long waves, and I wrap my legs around his waist. He rubs his hands up my thighs under the light sundress I'm wearing until he is grabbing my ass.

He kisses me, showing me how much he is mine. He pulls my lip into his mouth while I move my hand up and down his neck, grabbing hard, needing him desperately. He stops walking when we are both about chest-deep in the water.

He pulls our lips apart, just far enough that he can look me in the eye. I think he is going to say something serious about why he loves me or wants me.

"I don't have a condom," he says.

I laugh but realize that I don't have a condom either. I think he expects me to pull one out of my bra again or something.

"I don't have one either." I frown.

Asher takes a deep breath as we both realize that we are going to have to wait—at least until we can find one inside or go grab one at the store.

"I'm on the pill," I say out of nowhere. I don't know why I said it. Like the pill is magically going to fix our predicament.

"I'm clean. Although I don't expect you to trust me."

"I'm clean, too. And I do trust you."

We each take a deep breath in and out and then decide to trust each other even though I have no reason to trust him, and he doesn't know me well enough to trust me. Even though he thinks he does.

He thinks I'm perfect, incapable of doing anything wrong. He's wrong. I'm more than capable of ripping out his heart. But he trusts me. And, at least tonight, I don't plan on betraying that trust.

We kiss again, slower this time, as the waves crash around us. I reach for his pants, pushing them down so that I can feel his cock against my stomach. He lifts me up and gives me one last chance to back down before guiding me onto his cock.

I float in the water as Asher guides me up and down, our lips locked and my hands grasping on to his shoulders.

Maybe other people have had bad experiences of fucking in the water. But this is different than anything I've ever experienced. The ocean is the perfect place for us. We both understand it; we get it. The waves crash in, moving Asher in and out of me. I ride him over and over as the waves and Asher move me.

I feel freer than I have felt in a long time, fucking like this. But, when I look into Asher's eyes, I realize why this feels so much different than any other experience I have ever felt before. Because, this time, we aren't fucking.

"I love you," Asher whispers against my lips.

I can barely catch my breath, but somehow, I manage to say back to him, "I love you, too."

This time is different. It's making love, not fucking.

And, if I could take this moment with me forever, I would. Just live right here on the beach in Asher's arms and never return to the real world. The problem is, when the sun sets and this moment is gone, everything will be different. Because I know what I have to do next, and it's going to change everything.

19

ASHER

She said, "I love you."

That was music to my ears.

But I can't help but think, *What the fuck is wrong with me?*

I've thought it every day for the last week.

What the fuck is wrong with me?

I don't fall in love with women. I've seen the heartache that comes when that happens. Someone always gets hurt.

But, with Sloane, everything is different. I've fallen in love with her. I want her to be mine forever. I just have to make it official.

I know she loves me. Even before she said the words, I knew it was what she felt. But something has been holding her back. Something has been preventing her from moving forward. From actually letting herself be in love with me.

She let herself just be in the moment for one night. That one night when she said she loved me. But, the rest of the week, she has kept her distance. She's been busy at work. I don't know why though.

Is she upset she found out that I'm a thief, a criminal who has been in and out of jail too many times to count?

Is she upset that she fell in love with me?

Is she not convinced that I'm in love with her?

Does she think our lives are too different for us to be together?

Whatever the reason, I'm going to fix it tonight.

I haven't told her why I started stealing yet. She probably thinks I was just a crazy, wild child who liked hurting people. And, while that is part of the excitement for me, it's not the whole story. Not even close. I have to explain everything to her.

Sloane is working late again tonight, which gives me plenty of time to set everything up. I sling the bag filled with roses and flowers over my shoulder. I want tonight to be perfect for her. I'll start with decorating her bedroom. I figure we will stay at her place tonight since it's much nicer than mine. Tomorrow, I hope we can start searching for a new place together. Or maybe we will always split time between my place and hers.

I don't give a damn where we live. I just want her.

I have more decorations in the truck she bought me. I'm going to use them to decorate the beach later. I know it's cheesy to propose on the beach, but it's our place. Sloane won't care that it is cheesy. She will care that I put effort in. She will care that I love her. That's the only thing that is important.

But, still, I have no idea if she will say yes. I think most men who propose already know what the answer is going to be when they ask the question. They have already talked to their girlfriends about it. They might have even picked out a ring together, and then they go through the motions of proposing.

Sloane has no idea I'm about to propose. No man would propose so soon. But no man would have gotten himself in this predicament anyway. Fake married to a woman after he stole her from her fiancé, only to later fall in love with said woman. It's a crazy story that is only found in romance books but not in real life.

So, when I propose to Sloane, it has to be big. I'm going all out with decorations, music, champagne—the whole bit. I'm being the most romantic I can be.

But, first, I'm going to tell her everything. I don't want her to say yes without knowing fucking everything.

I walk over to the elevator where Archie, the elevator operator and security guard, greets me.

"Hello, Mr. Calder. How are you doing today? Here to see Ms. Hart?"

"I'm doing very well. I have a nice surprise tonight planned for Sloane. So, don't ruin it for me."

"I'm very happy to hear it. Ms. Hart has seemed very preoccupied and stressed lately. Hopefully, you'll be able to cheer her up."

I frown and nod as I step into the elevator. Even Archie has noticed that Sloane is unhappy. *Maybe I missed something else that has been going on. Maybe I should wait a little longer to propose.*

I feel the box that the ring is in burning a hole in my suit pocket. I can't wait to propose.

For one, as soon as Sloane sees me in this suit, she is going to know something is up. I'm wearing a suit, so she will know that I have changed. That I'm not just a thief or a surfer. I'm a man desperately in love with her, who will do anything for her. Including buying and wearing a useless suit.

The elevator doors open, and I step out and walk over to her door. I dig in my pocket and realize I forgot the keys to her place. I never lock my place, so I usually leave my keys in the truck. I know, if someone really wants to steal it, it won't matter if the keys are in it or not. I hate using my skills to break in her door today, but I'm not going all the way back to my place to get the keys to her place. I'm on a tight schedule because, at anytime, Sloane could call me and tell me that she's leaving work and ready to go out to dinner. That's all I've told her. That I'm taking her out for dinner. It is a Friday night after all.

I'll just pick her up and get her to change into a nice dress. I know her well enough to know that she has plenty of nice dresses hanging in her closet.

I pick the lock on the door and enter her condo. I take a deep breath as I always do when I enter her condo. It smells like clean linen. It's Sloane's smell. Clean and perfect, just like her.

I'm sure she has her faults, but these last few weeks, I haven't found any. She's perfect. Intelligent, sassy, caring, and beautiful. She's everything I never knew I wanted.

The linen scent that is Sloane is covering the condo. It smells stronger than usual, like she was recently here even though I know she's been in her office all day long. I could just stand here and smell her all day, but I have to work fast.

So, I start walking to her bedroom when I hear soft music playing. I shake my head. Her alarm clock plays music like that. She must have forgotten to turn it off when she left for work this morning. She stayed in bed while I got up to go surfing this morning, like usual.

I open the door and freeze.

I feel like I've just been stabbed in the heart.

Shot.

Broken.

And left for dead.

I can't move.

I can't breathe.

And I'm sure that my heart has stopped beating.

I close my eyes, hoping that this is a nightmare. That, at any second, I'm going to wake up and realize that what I'm seeing isn't really happening.

But, when I open my eyes, she's still there, lying naked, in her bed with another man.

It has to be a mistake.

She's perfect.

She loves me.

She would never hurt me like this.

Never.

I take a breath, finally able to breathe, when I realize that it is some sort of mistake. She has to have an explanation for what is happening.

"Sloane, what's going on?" I ask like I'm not witnessing what I am.

"I'm sorry," she says with tears in her eyes.

Two words.

"I'm sorry."

They tell me everything I need to know.

She cheated on me.

She broke my heart.

She made me believe in love and then destroyed me.

I'll never recover from this.

I know that.

I loved her more than I loved stealing.

I loved her more than I loved surfing.

I loved her more than I loved breathing.

But she didn't love me back.

Or, if she did, she was too scared to just be in love with me.

She had to ruin any chance that we had.

My initial gut reaction is to walk over and punch the naked man in the face. He deserves it.

But then, when women slept with me, I never thought I was the reason for them to have strayed. Well, at least, not the full reason.

People aren't supposed to get married. Everlasting love doesn't exist.

I knew that.

But I let myself fall in love with Sloane anyway.

I want to hate her. Yell at her. Do something to show her how angry I am with her.

But I'm not really angry. At least, not with her.

I'm angry with myself.

Love doesn't exist. And, when it does, it's selfish love that only lasts until that person falls in love again—with someone else.

So, as much as I want to yell at Sloane, ask her why, try to understand her, try to forgive her...

I can't do any of those things.

All I can do is turn around and walk back out the door, pretending like life didn't just fuck me over again. Like the only woman I've ever loved didn't just steal my heart and then destroy it.

20

ASHER

I HOLD out my shot glass. "Another."

Paige smiles sweetly. "I'll just leave the bottle here for you guys. Don't tell anyone."

Luca takes the bottle and pours me another one. "I hate to say this, but I told you so."

I glare at Luca as I lift the glass of tequila to my lips and pour the shot down my throat. I've lost track of how many shots I've done. I don't care anymore. I need something to numb the pain. And tequila is that something.

"Say it all you want. I need to hear it. I should have listened to you."

Luca laughs. "You shouldn't ever listen to me. You know that."

Luca looks down at the prenup contract. "You also shouldn't sign anything without talking to a lawyer first. You do understand that you are an idiot for signing this."

"I don't care."

"You are going to care when she takes everything you own. Your house, your money, your trucks—everything is now hers."

I shrug. "Let her have it. I don't want it."

Luca shakes his head. "You aren't sleeping on my couch when you have nowhere else to go."

"I'll make more money. I only get one heart, and it's gone now."

He shakes his head at me. "I don't know what you have turned into, but you are one giant mess, man. She's really fucked you up. You know that, right?"

I dump more of the tequila into the shot glass and take a drink. I don't care anymore. I have lost everything I cared about. All I want now is to spend the rest of my life here, at this bar, drinking. I no longer have a home. That's now hers. I no longer have either trucks. They are now hers. I can't go back to the beach, to the ocean. Everything I ever owned or loved is now hers.

———

"You need to leave this bar, man. It's been two weeks since the divorce was finalized. You weren't even married for real. You thought you were in love, but you can't fall in love with a chick that fast. You have to get over her. There are plenty of other fish in the sea, and if you got out of here and started training, you could actually earn some money and buy yourself another shack on the beach instead of sleeping outside a bar every night," Luca says.

I lay my head down on my folded arms on the table as I stare at the empty shot glass. After I puked about a week ago, Paige implemented a new rule where I can only have one shot every half hour. It doesn't matter though anyway. The pain is always here now. The alcohol is no longer strong enough to take the pain away.

Luca sighs. "Well, cheer up. I have great news for you."

My eyes dart up to him and then back to the glass in front of me. There is no way he has great news.

"I'm going to introduce you to my girlfriend. You can play your silly games on her. You can try to steal her and fuck her and do whatever you do to cheer yourself up."

"Get rid of your girlfriend yourself, Luca. I'm not going to do it for you."

Luca sighs again. "You really have to get over this girl. This isn't healthy. Have you even talked to her since she cheated on you?"

I shake my head.

"You need closure. Go talk to her. Yell at her. Whatever you need to do. Then, move on." Luca grabs my arm and lifts me out of my chair. "You are going to go talk to her. Now."

He walks me out of the building. "How much have you had to drink?" he asks.

"Not enough," I say.

Luca studies my eyes and then confirms that I haven't really been drinking. Not since Paige implemented her new rule. I've had maybe two drinks today since I also know, every other shot, she just fills with water, hoping I won't notice. I noticed though.

He reaches in his pocket and then flips me the keys to his car. "Go get closure. Get revenge. Get even. Apologize. Whatever you fucking need, go get it."

———

I started at her office, but she wasn't there. I talked to her receptionist, who said she hadn't been in, in weeks. Probably off fucking her new beau. I should warn him that she's going to do the same thing she did to me to him. Fuck him, make him fall in love, and then rip out his heart.

I thought I was a monster. But she's just as bad. No, she's worse. Because I tell people up front who I am. And, if they let me into their life, that is their problem. She pretends to be an angel for those less fortunate. She protects kids and gives them the help they need. But then she goes and hurts men without a second thought.

I tried her condo, but Archie wouldn't let me up to see her. He looked sad when he talked to me. I finally got him to tell me that she wasn't there, and her missing car from the parking lot confirmed it.

When I exited her building, I was swarmed with reporters. I ignored them all. I shouldn't have. I should have told them the real reason for our divorce. That she cheated. Not the crap that she has been feeding them about a whirlwind romance that ended because we were too different and we realized our love would never last. That we were just together to help each other through a difficult time. I should leak the prenup agreement that she had me sign that caused me to fucking lose everything. Then, we will see whose side the media is on.

I can't do that to her though, as much as I want revenge. I want her to feel exactly how I feel right now, but I can't. I just can't bring myself to do it. I can't bring myself to hurt her like that. Because, for reasons I will never understand, I still love her.

And, if she did one thing for me, she helped me realize that, even though I don't believe in lasting love, I shouldn't destroy it for those who do. Because, just maybe, if a couple has a fighting chance to last forever, then they actually will.

Even if they don't, I know I will never get the same thrill out of breaking a couple up again. Because every time I tried, I would be brought back to this feeling. This desperate, angry, sad feeling that I will never be able to escape from again because of her. But, for some stupid fucking reason, it makes me want to try again. Find some woman who can actually love me. That I could feel that way blows my mind the most.

I jump back in the car and start driving. First, I need closure. That is what Luca said. And, for once, I believe him. He's been in enough relationships to know that, that is what I need right now.

I don't know where else to look for her. I'm guessing that she's in that asshole's bed. But I have no idea where he lives, and that isn't the best place to get closure. All I would end up doing is getting in a fight that could land me back in jail.

So, I just drive. I guess I'll eventually go back to her place and see if she ever shows up. But, for now, I drive. I drive to our place on the beach and stop Luca's car. Maybe this is a way to get closure without actually having to speak to her. Maybe, if I tell the world how I'm feeling here, in our place, it will be enough that I can figure out how to move on.

I get out of the car, and a cold draft of wind blows, sending a shiver through my body. It doesn't really ever get cold here. Not enough to need anything but an occasional rain jacket. But that wind felt different. It felt cold, chilling.

I smile weakly. At least Hawaii still gets me. Still understands me and supports me. I just have to convince myself to get my ass back out into the ocean again.

I walk down the beach before I spot her blonde hair blowing in the wind. She has a light sweater wrapped around her shoulders as she sits on the beach, looking out at the storm that seems to be rolling in over the ocean.

I stop for a second. I could turn around, and she would never know that I was here.

Pussy, I think. *Just go talk to her. Get closure.*

I'll go pick up a six-pack of beer on my way back to Luca and drink the night away. But, first, I have to go talk to her.

I walk to where she is sitting and sit down next to her without a word. She doesn't glance over at me. She just tightens her grip on her sweater, and I know that she knows it is me sitting next to her.

I sit there, just staring out at the ocean with her, trying to figure out what I need from her. What I need to get over her. I don't have a clue. But the longer I sit next to her, the clearer what I need becomes.

I reach out and softly touch her chin to get her to look at me. She flinches at my touch.

I pull my hand back and wait for her to look at me. "Why?"

21

SLOANE

He asked, "Why?"

That's the first word I've heard him say since that night. That's all he gave me. One word.

No context about how he is feeling. Although I can tell, from the pain that is apparent on his face, the alcohol on his breath, and the brokenness of his body, I hurt him. More than I even thought I would.

I hurt Asher.

Ruined him.

Destroyed him.

And all he wants to know now is why.

I don't have to tell him. In fact, I thought I never would. But I think the story needs to be told. He needs to understand why. Then, maybe all can be forgiven. *Both* of us can be forgiven.

———

One Year Earlier

I hear the door to my condo slam as my roommate and best friend in the whole wide world walks in.

"Did you pick up groceries?" I ask from my spot on the couch. I don't know why I ask. I already know that she didn't pick up any groceries.

"Oh, Sloane, I just met the most amazing man!" Danielle says, flopping onto the couch.

I sit up, panicked now. "What do you mean, met? Like, as a friend? You're engaged, Danielle. You don't meet new men."

"Yeah, like a friend. Of course I didn't mean, like a boyfriend. I'm engaged to the most amazing man. But this guy, I could talk to him for hours. He just gets me. You know? I think he might be gay, or I would hook him up with you."

"I'm happily dating Wes," I say.

"No, you're boringly dating Wes. That guy is a complete bore. You need to find someone better. Hotter. This guy is hot. Did I tell you that?"

"No, but you shouldn't be determining how hot other guys are. You are engaged to Wade. Wade should be the hottest guy in your world."

Danielle rolls her eyes. "Of course Wade is the hottest guy in my world. But this guy, he's dreamy. But, like I said, I'm pretty sure he's gay."

"How sure?"

She shrugs and then skips off to her bedroom across from mine.

"Danielle, it's your turn to get groceries this week!" I shout from the couch.

But it's too late. Danielle already has her music turned way up, and I know she won't be coming back out for hours. I sigh and grab my keys to head to the grocery store. I really don't understand why I even bother with a roommate.

I open the door and smile. Sitting on our doorstep are three boxes filled with groceries.

I laugh. Danielle might never do things the same way as me or any other normal person would, but at least she gets things done.

———

I open the door to my condo and start walking toward my bathroom. I'm exhausted, and I need a hot shower to help me relax.

The hall bathroom door opens, and I step back as my mouth falls open.

A naked man steps out. Well, naked, except for the tiny towel wrapped around his waist. When he sees me staring, he rips the towel off and throws it over his shoulder as he walks past me and to Danielle's room. He gives me a little wink first and then disappears into her bedroom.

"Danielle!" I yell at the top of my lungs.

Danielle comes running out of her bedroom. "What's going on? I didn't leave the toaster on again, did I? I promise, I didn't mean to."

I sigh. Living with Danielle is like raising a little sister. "No, you didn't almost burn down our condo again. No, you did something far worse than that," I say, scowling at her.

"What?" she says, still not getting it.

"What is a half-naked man who isn't your fiancé doing in our condo?"

"Oh. That's Asher. He needed a place to shower after he was finished surfing. I let him come up here to use ours since we live so close to him."

"Asher, the gay guy?"

"Technically, he's not gay," Danielle says, not meeting my eyes.

"What do you mean, technically? He either is or isn't."

"That's not true. There are plenty of bi people in the world, you know."

I frown. "Is he one of those people?"

"No."

"Then, what is he doing in our condo?" I hiss.

"He's a friend."

"A friend you need to get rid of ASAP if you still want to get married next week."

She rolls her eyes. "I'm still getting married next week. He's just a good friend."

"Get rid of him."

Danielle huffs and then walks back into her room without saying another word to me. I doubt she talks to me for a few days. That's her usual way of dealing with a fight. She doesn't speak to me for days. She's still very much a child. But I'm not ready to be a mother yet. Well, not to any more kids than I already am a makeshift mother to.

———

I sit down on my couch with a bowl of popcorn and a glass of wine. I have a chick flick ready to go. I just got back from Danielle's rehearsal dinner, and I just want to sit here and relax before the chaos of tomorrow starts.

And I remind myself that it is okay that I'm not even close to getting married. Wes is nice, but he's not the kind of guy I want to marry. Even he knows that.

Danielle bursts through the door just as I'm about to press play on the video.

"What are you doing here? I thought you were staying in a suite at the hotel tonight."

"I was," she says through sobs.

I put the bowl of popcorn down as I look up at Danielle, who is soaking wet and sobbing.

"Sweetie, what is wrong?" I ask, getting up and running over to her. "Did Wade do something? Is there something wrong with the wedding? What's wrong?"

She shakes her head and walks over to the couch. I sit next to her, and she collapses into my lap. My arms automatically go around her.

"Whatever it is, I'm sure things will be better in the morning."

"No, they won't."

"Talk to me then. Tell me what is going on."

"I slept with him."

"Who?"

"Asher. And then he dumped me after."

"What do you mean? What about Wade?"

"I broke up with him before I slept with Asher. The wedding is off. There is no way he will take me back now."

My head is spinning, trying to understand what the hell just happened.

"I've ruined everything."

"Shh." I rub her back as she cries. "It's going to be okay. Everything is going to be okay. You still have me. You have your family, your job, your friends. We will figure this out. Together. And then everything will be better."

———

"Danielle, you have to get out of bed today. I want you to come to work with me today. I think seeing the kids will do you a lot of good."

"No. I'm staying in bed."

"Honey, it's been a month. I know it's hard, but you can't stay in this bed forever. You have to get out and join the real world again."

"No."

"I'll take you to your favorite restaurant for lunch, and then tonight, we can drink wine and watch movies all night long. That will be fun, right?" I say, trying to use bribes to get her out of bed.

"No."

I frown, and then I get desperate. I grab her ankles and start pulling her out of bed. She fights me the whole time, grabbing hold of her headboard to stay in bed.

"God, you're freakishly strong."

"I'm not going anywhere. I'm not up for seeing people who know what I did."

"No one at my work knows what happened. They don't know you or your story. And the kids sure as hell don't. Just come with me. I could use a friend today."

"What do you need a friend for? You have a perfect life that could never fuck you over. Your perfect job with your perfect boyfriend and your perfect body and perfect money."

"Wes and I split up."

She sits up just a little. "Good. That will just make room for a more perfect boyfriend to come in and replace him."

"Come on, Danielle. I could really use a friend today. I need you."

She throws the covers over her head. "You have plenty of friends. I can't help you."

———

Two months later, Danielle finally made an appearance. She got out of bed, got dressed, and walked right out of the condo without even saying a word to me.

I couldn't help but smile from seeing her out of bed.

And then, two days later, the same. And then the next day and the next until she was getting out of bed more days than she was staying in it.

I thought she was doing better. I thought she'd finally decided one day that the men in her life were no longer the most important things. I thought she was choosing living.

I didn't realize that she was still depressed. And that, when she started leaving, it was actually the most dangerous part of her healing.

"Hey, Danielle. I need to borrow that pink lace shirt that you said didn't fit you anymore!" I yell through her bedroom door.

She doesn't answer.

I knock. "Danielle?"

She doesn't answer.

I smile when I look down at my watch. I'm running a bit late today. Danielle must have gone into work early. She works at a marketing company.

I push the door open to just grab the shirt I need myself. We are always borrowing each other's clothes and never care when the other borrows something without asking first.

I scream when I see her and then immediately gather my composure to run over to her. A needle is sticking out of her arm as she lies in her bed.

"Danielle," I say, gently tapping her face.

She doesn't move, but I do see her chest rise and fall. She's still breathing—for now.

"Come on, Danielle! Wake up!"

She moans softly as I tap her face harder, but she doesn't wake up. I grab my phone and dial 911. I don't know what else to do. The operator gives me some instructions to try and wake her up. But, most importantly, I just need to make sure she is still breathing when the paramedics arrive.

I hold her head in my lap as I wait.

"I'm so sorry, Danielle. I'm so, so sorry." I pat her hair.

She looks so peaceful, lying in my arms like this, but I know she is anything but at peace.

"I'm so sorry I didn't realize what was going on. I should have known after this happened before. I'm an idiot. Just please don't die, and I'll be here for you. I'll make this better. I promise."

———

I place my hand on Danielle's tombstone and then fold my legs as I take a seat in front of it.

"I'm so sorry I couldn't keep my promise. I couldn't save you. I thought I could. I thought that, once you healed and went to rehab, they would be able to help you. They couldn't. I thought our friendship would be enough to save you. It wasn't."

I let the tears fall down my face.

"I thought that a lot of love could save you, but it couldn't."

I cry for a long time, just sitting there with her. I don't know if I will ever get over her death. It was so senseless. It was all because a stranger came into her life and played games with her heart. The coroner's report said that she died because of an overdose. That's not true. She died from a broken heart that was never able to heal.

"Sloane?" I hear Wes behind me.

I stand up and wipe my tears.

"I was in town and thought I would come see how you were doing. Not well, huh?"

I shake my head.

"I'm so sorry about your friend."

"Thank you."

"I wish there were something I could do to help you. I could go kick that guy's ass if you want."

I smile and then cock my head to the side, looking at Wes. "Maybe there is something you can do to help me."

"What do you mean?"

"You can propose."

He frowns. "I care about you, Sloane, and I would do anything for you, but I don't think you and I getting married is going to fix anything. You and I don't work as a couple."

I shake my head. "I mean, to help me get revenge. Propose. Pretend we are getting married. Let the asshole steal me from you. And then I'll rip out his heart, like he did to Danielle."

"But, to do that, he would have to want to steal you."

"He will. I know how his game works. I'll just dangle myself in front of him, and then he'll try to steal me."

"But won't you hurt your family when you don't marry me?"

I shake my head. "The only person that is left to hurt is my grand-mother. I'll tell her the truth."

He nods, still thinking. "This is a lot of work for something that might not work out the way you planned."

I nod. "I have to do it. For Danielle."

He nods, still thinking. "He has to fall in love with you to make this work."

"He will."

I look at Wes in the eyes, and I know he's still in love with me. Making men fall in love with me is never the problem. I always have the problem of falling in love with the man.

Wes nods, obviously agreeing that he will fall in love with me. "You can't fall in love with him."

I laugh. "I won't."

22

ASHER

"I KILLED HER," I say when Sloane finishes telling me her story.

Sloane nods solemnly.

"I knew I was a monster, but I never thought what I was doing was killing people."

I look at the tears that are now filling Sloane's eyes.

"I'm so sorry about Danielle. I never imagined that, that could happen. I'm so sorry she's gone. I'm so sorry that it was my fault. I'm so sorry I caused you so much pain."

"Sorry won't bring her back. That's the problem. I thought hurting you would make me feel better. Would get justice for what you did to Danielle. But nothing can change the only thing that would make any difference. Danielle is dead, and nothing will bring her back."

I feel my own tears welling in my eyes, looking at how much pain I've caused her. So much pain. And for what? So that I could play a game. So that I could have excitement in my life. It wasn't worth it.

"If I could take it all back, I would."

Sloane looks into my eyes, studying me for a moment. "I believe you would, but you can't. And, every time I look at you, all I feel is pain."

I swallow a lump in my throat. She doesn't have to say anything more. I can already tell she means it, even when I thought she was in love with me, all she felt was pain, hurt, and anger. None of it was real. That is what she is trying to say. I'm just not sure I believe her. She has to be one hell of an actress to have slept with me. To have gotten me to fall in love with her and not feel anything in return.

"I thought I came here for closure. So that I could move on with my life and no longer be in pain. So that I might have a real chance at falling in love again," I say.

She raises an eyebrow when I say *love*.

"But I realize now, that's not why I came here. I didn't come back here so that I could erase the pain you caused me. I came back because I love you, and I want to feel that pain every day.

"Now that I did something so unforgivable, I think it's only right that I live with that pain every day. And I want you to be that reminder whether you are mine or not. I have to try to repay my debt to Danielle, to you, to the world.

"So, even though I know there is no chance of you ever loving me, I will always love you. There won't be other women in my life, only you. There won't be any more stealing, only giving. I can't ask for forgiveness. All I can do is love you with all of my heart and deal with the consequences from what I caused."

Sloane hasn't taken a breath the entire time I've been talking. She just looks at me, frozen.

"Breathe," I say.

She does, and then I continue, "The first time I stole was after my father died. He'd died in an armed robbery. The thieves got a hundred dollars in cash. A hundred dollars in cash. That is what my father died for. Something so incredibly ridiculous. I couldn't make sense of it. The first time I stole, it was electric. I felt a rush like I'd never felt before. I realized that was why the thieves had stolen. Not because they wanted the money or reward at the end. It was the thrill of doing something you weren't supposed to do, something that you might get caught doing.

"I know you can't understand why I would steal when my father died that way. I guess it was my way of dealing and coping. I didn't ever carry a gun or any weapon when I robbed. I just wanted to feel alive again."

"You might not believe me, but I understand why. My grandfather died of smoking, which only made me smoke more. Cigars, anything I could get my hands on. It just helps you feel closer to that person in some way. I get it," she says.

I nod. "But, once I started, I was addicted. I couldn't stop. I ended up in jail countless times. And then, when I realized I had to stop, I couldn't.

"But then I accidentally stole a woman who was engaged. I got her to fall for me. I saw the pain I caused her and her fiancé. I became addicted to something new. I became addicted to stealing women. I thought it was better than breaking the law. I thought I was saving these women from what was eventually going to happen later. They were going to get married and then live miserable lives that would eventually lead to divorce. I didn't think love was real. And, if it was, I wanted them to prove it to me. Prove that love existed by staying away from me. By getting rid of me. None of them did though. Not one. They all gave in eventually."

"Danielle and Wade would have eventually divorced. And who's to say that she wouldn't have gone down the same path at that point? Not that it should make you feel any better," Sloane says.

"Don't worry. It doesn't. I'm done meddling in other people's lives. I did something so unforgivable that I will be spending the rest of my life trying to make things right."

"I did something unforgivable, too," Sloane says in a whisper.

Her words make my heart stop. I suck in a breath.

She cheated on me. She lied to me about loving me. She set me up to hurt me in the same way that I hurt Danielle. She might have had a good reason for doing so, but what she did is still unforgivable. I can never look at Sloane again without seeing his hands on her naked body. I can never hear her moan my name again without thinking about his name escaping her lips.

We each did something unforgivable.

I look at her eyes, and my heart stops again. "You loved me. That part wasn't a lie, was it?"

She doesn't answer right away. But she slowly shakes her head. "It wasn't a lie," she whispers.

My eyes widen. I have no reason to trust this woman. She has every reason to hurt me again and again and again. And I have every reason to not trust a damn word out of her mouth. But I trust her because, if there is one thing that I know to be true, it is that we loved each other.

"You still love me?" I whisper.

23

SLOANE

"Yes," I whisper back before biting my lip.

I hate myself for loving him. I shouldn't love him. He is the reason my friend is gone. Or, at least, a contributing factor. Although there are countless things I could blame for her death—Wade, drugs, Asher, Danielle, and myself—blaming anyone isn't going to bring her back.

What Danielle would have wanted, I hope, is for me to be happy. To keep living when she couldn't.

So, as crazy and stupid as it might be for me to love Asher, to trust that he has changed, I do. Because I love him.

"Can we try this again?" Asher asks, his little fingers brushing against mine in the sand.

I grin just a little. It's the first time I have in the weeks since I betrayed Asher. "Yes."

Our hands grasp each other's faces as we kiss. Our kisses are desperate, like we haven't seen each other in years, not weeks. Our tongues tangle together as well as our bodies in the sand.

As I kiss Asher, I realize how stupid I was for following through with my plan. I would have been walking down the same path that Danielle did instead of following my heart and finding happiness.

I feel the wind blow through us as we kiss. I shiver as it does. Asher wraps his arms around me tighter, kissing me, unable to stop.

The wind blows harder, and I get sand in my eye, causing me to stop kissing him for a second. When I get the sand out, he goes in for another kiss. I hold up my hand, stopping him. The look of pain on his face is so sad, it's almost cute.

"Are you having second thoughts?" he asks, his voice a little shaky.

I laugh because I love him so much that there is no way I could give him up, yet he still doubts how I feel. It's going to take him longer to heal than it will take me. But then I've had months to heal from his betrayal, and he's only had days to heal from mine.

"No. I just want to fuck you in a bed like normal people instead of here on the beach."

Asher laughs, and I immediately see his insecurity leave his face. He stands up and then motions for me to climb on his back. I do, and then he carries me while I kiss his neck on the way to his car.

———

We make it back to my condo building without completely stripping each other naked although it was hard to keep our hands off each other. At one point, I had to sit on my hands to keep Asher from crashing the car. He said he couldn't crash it. It wasn't even his car.

I'll have to ask him later where he has been sleeping since I took everything in the divorce. But I don't want to bring up negative things like that now. Right now, I want to remember one of the reasons that I fell in love so hard with Asher. Because of what he does to my body.

But we can't keep our hands off of each other any longer. Even though we still have to make it upstairs, into my condo, and then into bed.

Asher grabs my face and kisses me as soon as we are in the lobby. Sucking all of my breath away and making me wet with want and need for him.

"I can't wait to have you," I say between kisses.

"We need to move before they kick us out of the lobby," Asher says against my lips.

"Uh-huh," I say, tangling my hand in his hair that is starting to grow back out again.

Asher lifts me up, and I wrap my legs around his waist as he walks to the elevators.

"Miss Hart and Mr. Calder, it's so good to see you together again. I thought you might work it out," Archie says.

Asher sets me down while we wait for the elevator, but his hands stay on my waist as he kisses my cheek and neck, just giving my lips a break so that I can answer Archie.

"We are happy to be back together."

The elevator doors open, and Asher pushes me inside. "Thanks, Archie. We'll see you later."

The elevator doors close, and Asher pushes me against the wall as he kisses down my neck, then chest, and then stomach.

"Slow down, baby. We still have ten floors to climb."

Asher pumps his fist against the emergency button, and the elevator comes to a stop.

"What are you do—" I stop speaking or caring about what he is doing when he lifts my dress up and kisses my bare skin and then down the inside of my thigh.

"I know you want me to wait to fuck you until we get to your bed, but I can't wait to taste you. To make you mine again, especially after what he did to you."

I slip my panties down, and then he runs his tongue across my pussy.

"This is mine," he says against my skin.

I grab his hair as he licks over me, flicking his tongue across my clit, and then he slips a finger inside my pussy.

I bite my lip as he does it again and again, fucking me with his tongue, while I stand against the wall of the elevator. It's wrong and dirty and oh-so right.

He shows me exactly what he wants, what he needs, with his tongue. Me.

"I love this pussy," Asher says between licks. "Tell me you're mine. Tell me you want me. Tell me you need this," he says as he licks me faster.

I moan and feel myself getting close to exploding. I don't know how he expects me to say so much when he's doing what he is doing to me.

"Fuck, Asher," is all I can manage to get out.

I scream and come all over his face in the elevator that I'm sure Archie is frantically trying to fix.

Asher grins as he slowly stands up to see me breathing hard, my heart racing, and my cheeks flushed.

"I love you, Sloane."

"I love you, too. Although I think you need to do that at least a dozen more times before I start liking you again."

Asher laughs as he hits the button to start us moving again. He kisses me on the neck. "That can be arranged."

———

"See, I told you we would eventually make it to a bed," Asher says, holding me close, as I lie in my bed on his bare chest.

I grin. "All the other places are nice, but I still think I like the bed the best."

"Me, too. Although the ocean is a close second," he says, winking.

He runs his hand through my hair. "So, are you going to let me move in since you stole my house, my truck, and all my money?"

I wince. I was waiting for him to ask about it. "I kind of gave everything to the charity I run."

Asher laughs. "I knew you didn't like my shack."

I sit up and look at him. "I love your shack. It's the one thing I didn't sell or donate."

"I don't believe that you kept it."

"Of course I kept it. Besides, I don't think I would have been able to sell it. Nobody else would have wanted it, and if I had managed to sell it, I wouldn't have made money off of it anyway," I say.

Asher tickles me in retaliation. I giggle and squirm and swat at his hand to get him to stop.

When we both stop laughing, I say, "Can I move in with you though?"

Asher looks at me seriously. "You want to move into my place? You do know, I was telling the truth. That, that is my only place. You would have gotten any other place I had in the divorce if I'd had another place."

I nod. "I know. And maybe not right away. But, eventually, that is my hope. If you have taught me one thing, it is that I should live more simply. I live a life of giving back to others, yet I live in this place that has far too many things."

"I would love to have you share my shack with me as long as we bring this bed." Asher kisses me on the cheek. "This bed is far better than my bed."

I laugh. "We can bring the bed. When is your next competition?"

Asher frowns. "I have no idea. I haven't been training since you left me. Why?"

I grin and flip over, kissing his chest. "First, I want you to fuck me again and again in this bed."

Asher nods. "I'm listening."

"And then I want to talk about how you are going to work at my charity and continue surfing because you need to do both. You are great with the kids."

He kisses me on the cheek.

"And then we can talk about our future. When we are going to move in together, get married, have our own kids. Because, if there is one thing I know, it is that I love you, and I'm never hurting you again."

He kisses down to my breasts. "We can definitely talk about all of that. But I think we can wait to have the kids talk a little down the line." He takes my nipple in his mouth. "But I'm definitely up for practicing."

He grins.

"You did teach me the one thing you promised when you married me."

He thinks for a moment. "What was that again?"

"You taught me how to take risks. Because being with you is by far the riskiest thing I have ever done."

He grins. "Sometimes, taking the risk makes living worthwhile."

"And, sometimes, falling in love is all the adrenaline you need in your life."

He takes my nipple back in his mouth, ready for another round. One thought flashes through my head though, but I know I have only seconds left before the thought evaporates while Asher teases my body.

Should I tell him the truth?

No.

The truth isn't always needed to make a relationship work. Sometimes, a lie is needed to keep two people on even ground. Asher needs the lie to be true even if he suspects himself that it is false. He needs me to have done something unforgivable. Even though I didn't actually cheat on him with Chance, I did do something unforgivable. I lied.

I made Asher believe that I'd betrayed him. Cheated on him. I put images in his head that I know he will never be able to erase. But he needs to believe the lie. So, I will keep on lying about it. Just this once.

He stole to find love. I lied to keep it. But I have no doubts that our love will last because the one thing I don't have to worry about is that we will each do anything and everything to keep it.

EPILOGUE

ASHER

SIX MONTHS Later

I've been patient. Trying to give her a normal relationship. Trying not to rush us, like our relationship was rushed in the past, but it has been the hardest goddamn thing I have ever done. Waiting. I hate waiting.

But it has been six months since she said she was willing to give us a second chance. Five months since she moved into my shack. Four months since we thought she was pregnant. Three months since I won my latest competition and actually started earning money again. Two months since we sold her condo. And one month since we found out we are expecting twins. Twins.

She doesn't want me to propose or for us to get married until after the babies are born, but I am not going to let that happen. I want the world to know that she is mine. That these babies are mine before they are born.

If it were up to me, we would have been married months ago. But I know she wanted to do things right this time. I'm not waiting nine months though until the babies are born. I'm proposing tonight, and then whether she likes it or not, we are getting married within the next couple of months.

"You're wearing that to go to dinner?" I ask, looking at Sloane sitting on the couch, wearing shorts and a tank top with her bikini straps sticking out of the top of her tank.

"Yes. You were the one who taught me to always be ready to go into the ocean. I'm not going to swim in my sundress, like what happened last time."

I frown, but she doesn't look up from her magazine that she is flipping through. I don't know how I'm going to get her into a dress. I don't think the restaurant I'm taking her to would approve of shorts.

"But I love you in that pink dress you wear. You could wear your bikini under it, and that way, I could do dirty stuff to you while we are seated at the table."

Sloane sighs. "Fine, you win. I'll change." She gets up from the couch and walks over to the small closet she made in the corner. She pulls out the dress, starts to undress, and then puts it on.

"Thank you," I say, kissing her on the cheek.

Sloane picks up her magazine again.

"Look at these cribs. They are made for twins, but they're smaller. It would be perfect over in this corner," she says.

My eyes pop open. "We are not living here once the babies are born. We don't have enough space! They need their own rooms. Babies come with stuff. Lots and lots of stuff. We need to start looking for a new place. I would have said your condo would work, but of course, we sold that. But maybe this is the perfect opportunity. We could get a four- or five-bedroom house with a nice yard."

Sloane laughs. "Five bedrooms? We don't have any family that visits us. Why do we need five bedrooms?"

"When we have more kids."

She laughs again. "I think the two on the way are more than enough for now. And we don't need to move. We have plenty of space for them here."

I rub the back of my neck and take a deep breath. I will argue with her about getting a new place later. For now, I just want this night to go perfectly.

I glance at my watch. "You ready?"

She nods and smiles. I hold out my arm, and she takes it with a raised eyebrow, not used to me being so gentlemanly. She glances at my attire for the first time. I'm not wearing a suit. I figured that would be a little too obvious, but I am wearing khakis and a button-down shirt.

"You look nice," she says.

"And you look beautiful, as always." I chastely kiss her on the lips. I don't want us to get too carried away, like we have in the past, and not make it out of here.

I lead her out of the shack, and she stops in shock when she sees the limo I arranged for.

"Why are we going somewhere in a limo?"

I grin. "Because we have been dating for six months, and I want to celebrate without worrying about getting arrested for driving a nice car. Plus, we can do dirty things on the way back."

"Not on the way there?"

"No. I want to make sure my girls are well fed."

I lead her to the limo, and we climb in.

"What makes you think the twins are girls?" she asks.

"Because the universe knows better than to make another of anything remotely like me. If they are girls, then they will take after you, not me."

She laughs. "Well, I think, whatever they are, if they take a little after you, it won't be that bad."

I hold her hand as we drive to the restaurant I picked out. My hands are so sweaty though that I'm sure she has already figured out what is going on. I'm surprised she hasn't said anything about me not proposing tonight. So, at least, I'm happy with that.

We get to the restaurant, and I help Sloane out of the car. I hold her hand while we walk into the restaurant.

"Do you have a reservation, sir?"

"Yes, under Asher Calder."

"Just one moment, and I'll take you to your table."

"Hey, guys. What are you doing here?" Luca asks as he walks out of the bar area of the restaurant.

"Hey, Luca," Sloane says, giving him a hug. "Having dinner. Want to join us?"

I eye Luca, trying to let him know that he is not to have dinner with us.

"I'd love to. This place has great food. It's on me. I've heard that congratulations are in order," Luca says.

I grimace at Luca. He does not take a hint.

"You told him," Sloane says to me with a frown on her face, thinking that I told him about the twins.

I haven't.

"No. Luca likes to lie and joke a lot. Like I've told you before, you can never trust a word out of Luca's mouth."

Sloane ignores me though. "I can't believe you told him we are pregnant with twins."

"You're pregnant with twins! That's amazing! Good job, buddy," Luca says, slapping me on the back.

I glare at him, trying to make him stop, but there is no use.

"Wait...what were you congratulating us on if you didn't know about the twins?" Sloane asks.

"Your engagement, of course. All I've heard for the last month is, should he or shouldn't he use the same ring that he bought for you when he was going to propose last time? So, which did you go with?" Luca says.

Sloane turns to me. "Last time?"

I can see her wheels turning, and there is no use in making sure everything is proper and right. Not anymore.

I take Sloane's hand. I get down on one knee, and I pull the box out of my pocket.

"Sloane, I wanted tonight to go perfectly. I wanted to show you how much I love you with all the romance you deserve. But, as usual, that is not how things go with us. But I can't go one more day, minute, second without telling you that I love you more than anything. And I'm beyond excited to spend the rest of our lives together. Will you please, please marry me? I know I don't deserve it. But I promise to spend the rest of my life making it up to you."

She grins. "Yes."

I put the ring that I chose the first time on her finger and then stand up and kiss her, no longer caring if we have dinner or not. I can't contain my excitement.

"Good choice. I told you she would want the original ring that you were going to propose with until you found out that she was cheating on you," Luca says, staring down at the ring that is in the shape of a wave on her finger.

"Get out of here," I say to him between kisses.

"What? You don't want your best friend here to celebrate with you?" he asks.

"No, Luca," Sloane and I say at the same time.

"Fine, fine. I wouldn't want to hang out with thieves like you anyway," Luca says as he walks back to the bar.

I grin. "I wouldn't want to hang out with a liar like you either."

He smiles and waves. Then, he leaves Sloane and me to celebrate.

"So, what are you hungry for, future Mrs. Calder?"

"You. And, just so you know, I'm keeping my name."

I sigh. "As long as I get to call you my wife, I don't care." I stare at Sloane as she looks down at her ring and then back up at me. Her whole body is glowing with excitement. But even through the excitement I know that she is hiding something from me. And I know exactly what that secret is. I cornered Chance, the bastard lawyer that was in her bed. It was easy to persuade him to tell me the truth. I can seem pretty intimidating when I'm angry and threaten to cause him pain.

She never slept with him. She just paid him to pretend that they were cheating. And the look in her eyes now confirms his story.

I won't tell her that I know her secret. It's a lie I bet she plans on taking to her grave. It may not be as bad as ruining someone's life like I did, but it is still a lie. I stole her heart, she lied to claim mine. All that matters is that we love each other.

THE END

Keep reading for Heart of a Liar...

HEART OF A LIAR

BOOK TWO

He's a liar.
I know that. It's why I broke up with him almost two years ago.
But when he walked into my veterinarian clinic, my heart forgot all
about his lies. Instead, it ached for him. Begging my body to take him
back. Or at the very least fuck him.
It's been far too long since I've been fucked by a man that knows
exactly what I want in bed. And Luca knows how to make me come
alive in a way no other man can.
I need to stay away from him. But somehow one sexy grin and I'll do
anything he wants.

First, I'll fuck him.
Just one last time to get him out of my system.
And then, I'll kick him to the curb.
I just hope this time I can survive his lies. Should be easy since I don't
plan on keeping him around long enough to hear them. But what if
his lies are hiding a secret that I was never supposed to know?

1

IVY

"You're beautiful and sexy, and I can't wait to get you home so that I can do dirty, filthy things to you," Kirk says.

I choke on my wine as he speaks to me. I can barely breathe as I force the liquid down.

"You all right?" Kirk asks with a sexy grin on his face.

I nod and smile as my cheeks, I'm sure, blush the faintest shade of pink. It's not like he said anything that dirty, not really. I just wasn't expecting to hear anything of the sort from Kirk. He's been nothing but a gentleman to me since we went on our first date almost two months ago. I was expecting romance. I was expecting him to be subtler. I was expecting that tonight would be the night when we finally slept together. I just didn't expect this.

I take a deep breath and then take a bite of my lasagna in front of me. More to have something to occupy my mouth than because I'm actually still hungry.

"Ivy?" Kirk asks.

I look up from my food. "Huh?"

Kirk shakes his head and then takes my hand, stopping me from eating any more. "You didn't hear a word I said, did you?"

If my cheeks weren't red before, they are now. "I'm sorry. I'm just having trouble focusing, I guess."

"Too busy thinking about all the things we are going to be doing tonight?" Kirk asks, raising a hopeful eyebrow.

I grin. "Exactly."

Kirk rubs his thumb across my palm. I suck in a breath as I can feel the sensation all over my body.

Kirk is good with his hands. In the last two months, every time he has touched me, I have gotten similar feelings. The kind that makes me ache for him to touch me more. The kind that makes me want to see what dirty, filthy things he has up his sleeves. I have never been with a man who is this capable of turning me on by touching me in the most innocent of places.

Maybe it's because he is a doctor, and that makes him so good at understanding my body.

"Want to get out of here, or do you want dessert?" Kirk asks.

I bite my lip as he traces the lines in my palm. Again, this time, I feel it all the way to my toes. It's a hard decision because this restaurant has my favorite dessert ever—cannoli. But I also really want to see what his hands can do with my naked body.

It's been far too long since I've felt a man's hands on my body. Even longer since I've had sex. We should have done it weeks ago. It's not that I'm a prude. Our schedules are the main culprit. Most of our dates end early due to one or the other being called back to work.

But, if I'm being honest with myself, that isn't the only reason.

"Dessert to go?" I ask.

Kirk laughs. "Deal." He flags down the waitress to get my cannoli to go, pays the bill, and then he grabs hold of my hand as he leads me out of the restaurant and into his car.

Kirk grabs hold of my hand again when we get into his car, and he sweetly kisses it as he pulls out of the parking garage and starts heading toward his place.

I smile at his sweet kisses. *Maybe I was wrong. Maybe he is still a gentleman and going to be romantic. At least until he gets me back to his place.*

We drive for about five minutes when Kirk says, "Shit."

He lets go of my hand, and I look away to hide my disappointment. I didn't hear his cell phone ring, and it's not his day on call, so he can't be getting called back into work. So, whatever it is, it can't be that bad.

Can it?

"What?" I ask as I rest my hand, palm up, on the armrest, hoping that he will get the hint that I want him to hold my hand again.

He doesn't. Instead, he is staring down at the steering wheel, like he wants to rip it off.

"We don't have enough gas to make it home. We are going to have to stop for gas," he says, frowning.

I laugh. "I think we can make it five more minutes."

He glares at me. "I've waited two months. I don't want to wait five more minutes. I'm amazed that I haven't pulled over at the nearest hotel between here and my place and fucked you there." He runs his hand through his hair, not the least bit embarrassed by how badly he wants me.

I unbuckle my seat belt, and Kirk raises an eyebrow. Honestly, I'm surprising myself by being this bold. But I'm tired of being alone. Kirk is hot. He's good to me. He's a doctor. He's got his life together.

What more could I want in a man?

I can't fuck this up, like I do with every other relationship.

I scoot up in my seat and kiss Kirk on his smooth neck. He must have just shaved before our date.

"Pull over and get gas, and I'll make the drive back to your place fly by. You can drive while I do this, right?" I grab hold of his cock that is straining against his jeans.

He lets out a gasp. "You are a dirty girl."

I smirk. "You haven't seen dirty yet," I say. Then, I immediately regret it. *Why did I say that?* I'm the opposite of a dirty girl. Or at least, I'm not anymore. I'm completely out of practice. I don't know how to talk dirty anymore.

I shake it off. He won't care as long as he gets sex.

Kirk abruptly turns the car, and we fly into the gas station parking lot, coming to an even more abrupt stop. I grab hold of Kirk's arm to keep from flying into the dashboard.

Kirk grabs the nape of my neck and kisses me hard and fast. So fast that my eyes don't even have time to shut. I barely register the kiss, and then it's over.

"I'll be right back," he says.

He turns off the ignition and jumps out of the car to pump the gas. I can't take my eyes off of him as he does so. I expect that, as soon as he starts pumping gas, he'll be right back in the car to kiss me while we wait. Instead, he throws his hands up as I think I hear a curse escape his lips even though all the doors are closed. He points to a sign on the gas pump and then starts walking inside.

I squint to read the sign. It says the credit card reader is broken and to go inside to pay. I sigh. The world really isn't on our side today. But, unlike Kirk, I have a little more patience.

So what if we have to wait another five minutes? Either way, I'll still get to fuck him tonight.

I jump as a buzzing sounds in the cup holder next to me. I stare down and realize that Kirk left his phone in the car. I pick it up and stare at the caller ID. It's from the hospital. I frown. The world *really* isn't on our side.

I answer it in case it's an emergency that the hospital needs Kirk to come back into work for.

"Hello, Kirk?" the chipper voice on the other end of the line asks.

"No, this is Ivy. Kirk just ran inside to pay for gas. He'll be back in just a second, or I can pass along a message to him."

"Oh. I don't mean to bother him. I just had a break and thought I'd check in to see if we were still on for tomorrow night. Tell him to text me or leave a message here when he gets a chance."

"And who is calling?"

"Oh, sorry. Excuse my manners. This is Jodi."

I take a deep breath. I want to yell at her. I want to tell this woman that Kirk is mine and to back off. I want to ask a million questions about how long they have been seeing each other. *How serious are they? Does she know that he's dating another woman?*

I don't do any of those things though. Instead, I say, "I'll tell him." Then, I end the call.

I feel my heart racing in my chest.

He's seeing other people. And who knows how many? And he has the balls to complain about not having sex with me when he's been having sex with who knows how many other women.

I exhale deeply.

I can't be mad at him. We never said we were exclusive. We never said we couldn't date other people. I just thought it was implied. But I guess, in today's world, nothing is implied. People can date whomever they want.

I just haven't been dating other people. I've only been dating him. If I had known that this was what we were doing, I would have been dating other people as well.

I sigh.

Who am I kidding?

I wouldn't have dated other people. I'm barely able to manage dating Kirk as it is.

I see Kirk walking back to the car. I realize I'm still grasping the phone, and I put it back into the cup holder.

Why did I have to answer the phone? Why couldn't I have just let it go to voice mail? Then, I could have been blissfully ignorant to the fact that he's fucking other women.

Kirk walks closer to me as I try to regain my composure.

It doesn't matter that he is dating other people, I tell myself.

We aren't that serious yet anyway. After we fuck tonight and I show him the best time of his life, we can start talking about being exclusive.

I nod, reassuring myself. That's the plan. Pretend like the phone call didn't even happen. Maybe I'll mention it tomorrow, just to be nice. But, by then, he won't even be able to remember Jodi's name. I'll be the only thing on his mind.

He opens the door to the car, and before he can even sit down fully, I attack him with my lips. I kiss his neck. I kiss his lips. I kiss anything and everything that I can get my lips on. My hand caresses his cock that is growing hard beneath his pants.

I don't let him speak.

I don't let him breathe.

I just attack every part of his body, letting him know how much I want him.

"Ivy," he moans as I kiss his neck again.

I move back to his lips. I don't want him to be able to speak. I just want him thinking about me. I grab hold of his cock a little harder than I intended to, and Kirk lets out another moan.

He must like it rough. So, I continue massaging his cock as hard as my fingers and the denim will let me.

Kirk grabs hold of me and pushes me away.

I open my eyes, confused as to what's going on, and that's when I see the pained expression on his face.

"I like it rough, Ivy, but you are taking rough to a whole new level that I'm not ready for," Kirk says.

"Sorry," I mumble, trying to catch my breath from all the kissing I was doing.

"Don't stop. Just gentler."

I nod. I can do gentler. I start kissing his neck again, but I immediately feel the urge to be rough. It's been ages since I've been rough, so I'm not sure what has come over me. But I force myself to go slower, be gentle, as Kirk drives toward his home.

We finally reach Kirk's house. I stop kissing him long enough to see where he lives. It's a large home. Fit for a family of four, not a bachelor. I've never been to his home before. He said he lived in a house, but this is not what I was expecting. I know he has money. But this is ridiculous for just one person to live in. He doesn't even own any pets. He can't occupy more than a couple of rooms.

Unless he throws large parties here with naked women who he fucks in all the different rooms of his house. Maybe he has a different room for each woman he is dating, so he can keep us all straight.

Kirk grabs my neck to kiss me again before we go into his house, but as soon as his lips touch mine, my stomach feels sick. His touch that I welcomed and was dying to feel more of now makes me feel disgusted.

I don't want him to kiss me.

I don't want him to touch me.

I don't want anything to do with him.

I push him away. "I can't."

He cocks his head to one side, and his eyes narrow as he looks at me. "You can't?"

"I can't sleep with you."

He blinks several times and then rubs the back of his neck. "Okay. I guess we can keep moving slow. But can you tell me when you think you might be ready? Because we have been on almost a dozen dates. I'm not trying to pressure you, but I just thought we both wanted this."

I frown. I hate how nice he is being to me. But that is how men are. They are nice to me until they get what they want, and then they destroy me. At least, that has been my experience so far. They lie. They cheat. They hurt.

I should just swear them all off. Live alone with my houseful of pets for the rest of my life. Turn into the crazy cat lady. If the last few years have taught me anything, they have taught me that.

So, no matter how nice Kirk is to me right now, I'm not going to let it affect me.

"Jodi called while you were paying for gas," I say.

He frowns. "Okay. Thanks for the message. I'll call her back tomorrow." He narrows his eyes as he stares at me. That's all he says.

I shake my head. "I can't believe you. I know that we've never talked about us being exclusive, but I can't be with someone who dates other people. I can't handle it. I want the person I'm with to want only me."

I jump out of the car and start walking away from his house. I know I can't walk back to my house. It's more than a half-hour drive from here. Who knows how long of a walk it is from here? But I can't stay here.

So, I walk down the long, winding driveway. I'll worry about getting an Uber or something when I get away from the house. Right now, I want to get away from the pig that I thought was a gentleman. That I thought could be my boyfriend. Maybe even my husband.

"Ivy!" Kirk yells after me.

But it doesn't make me stop. I can't move that fast between the heels and the tight dress that I'm not used to wearing. I'm much more comfortable in scrubs and tennis shoes. I know he'll catch up to me soon if he wants to talk to me. But I'm through with him. My heart is already closed off. I don't give anyone a second chance. Not when I've been hurt like I have in the past. Once I'm through, I'm through.

Kirk can plead and ask for forgiveness all he wants. It won't work with me.

"Ivy," he says again, grabbing hold of my arm before I even make it all the way down his driveway.

I stop, but I don't look at him. I'm not sure I can look into his eyes again. I know he wasn't cheating, but that's what it feels like to me.

"What the hell just happened back there?" Kirk asks, his voice loud. He's not technically yelling, but it's clear he isn't happy.

I fold my arms across my chest and look at him. "You don't get to be mad at me. I'm the one mad at you."

He shakes his head from side to side. "What fucking reason can you give for being mad at me? I haven't done anything wrong."

Anger flares inside me. "You haven't done anything wrong! Are you fucking kidding me? Maybe not technically. You technically didn't cheat. I just thought I meant more to you. I thought you would want to be exclusive with me." I catch my breath. "You know what? Never mind. I don't want to talk about this anymore. I'm done. Have fun with Jodi tomorrow night."

I start walking down the driveway as I hear him say, "What are you talking about? You're crazy! I'm not dating anyone else. Jodi is one of my best friends. I'm not sleeping with her. I think of her as a sister." He pauses and then shouts, "I told you about Jodi on, like, our second or third date. That she was one of my closest friends."

I shake my head and shout over my shoulder, "I doubt that!"

Although I do faintly remember him mentioning Jodi to me once before.

No man can be just friends with a woman. It just doesn't happen. He has feelings for her, and I'm not going to stick around to see what those feelings are.

"Fine. Leave. I don't want to be with a woman who doesn't trust me anyway," he says.

Then, nothing.

I stop walking and freeze for a second, taking in a deep breath.

What is wrong with me? I shouldn't be this mad about his relationship with Jodi. I should trust him.

I just can't.

Men aren't to be trusted.

Still, I turn around because maybe Kirk is different.

Maybe I'll see the truth in his eyes. Maybe I'll see how much he truly cares about me.

When I turn around though, Kirk is gone. He didn't even bother to stick around long enough to fight for me.

I don't cry. I don't feel anything really. This is what I expected. For him to try to hurt me. I just can't be hurt anymore. I will do anything to protect myself. Because even nice men like Kirk will hurt me if I let them.

I won't go through that again.

I pull out my phone from my purse as I walk down the driveway and call for an Uber. I'm done with men. I'm happier when it's just me and my pets. I'm good at being alone. I don't need a man in my life. I just need to be happy.

———

I tie my curly black hair up into a high ponytail on my head. I can't believe I spent time fixing it or that I bothered to wear a dress and heels for Kirk. *Ridiculous.* I grab my white coat from the back of my chair in my office and put it on. I should change into some scrubs and tennis shoes before I try to work, but I might as well get some use out of the brand-new pair of heels and dress that I bought for tonight. Who knows when I will ever wear either of them again?

I walk out of my office at the same time that Skye walks out of one of the exam rooms with a Scottish terrier on a leash.

She frowns when she sees me. "What did you do? Did you break up with Kirk?" Skye asks.

"You know me too well."

"I would tell you to go home and pour yourself a big glass of wine and eat a pint of ice cream, but I know you wouldn't listen to me."

"I'd rather be here, working. Being useful."

She nods as the little black dog begins pulling roughly on the leash, getting bored with our conversation that it doesn't understand in the slightest and trying to pull as hard as it can to find something more interesting.

"Go on. I'll pick up the next patient," I say.

Skye looks at me with her sad eyes as she starts walking the dog back toward the kennels.

"Don't look at me like that. I'm fine. I'm just swearing off men for a while."

Skye nods and then disappears around the corner. I start walking toward the front desk to let Cynthia know that I can take the next patient. Although it's close to nine o'clock on a Friday night, and I don't expect many more patients the rest of the night. Except the occasional emergency that usually isn't even an emergency. Still, hopefully, I'll be able to see a patient or two to distract me tonight.

"Hey, Cynthia, are there any patients for me to see?" I ask as I open the door to our modest waiting room.

The clinic as a whole is small. We only have two vets on staff— Skye and me. We have the money and the patients to expand to a larger space, but we are happy here. Maybe, one day, we will move to a larger space, but for now, we will make do with what we have.

"What are you doing here, hon?" Cynthia asks.

I sigh. "I should ask you the same thing. Doesn't your shift end at seven?"

Cynthia smiles at me and tucks a strand of her blonde hair

behind her ear. "It ends when I get the work done. I had some paper-work to finish entering into the computer." She raises an eyebrow, waiting for me to answer her question.

"Kirk and I broke up."

Cynthia's smile immediately drops into a frown. "He wasn't good enough for you anyway, sweetie."

I walk over to pick up the chart that I see lying on the corner of her desk, indicating that we have a new patient to treat. "They never are."

"You should go home. Skye has everything covered here. I have a feeling it is going to be a slow night anyway."

I shake my head. "I can't do that. I need a distraction. And taking care of someone's sick pet is just what I need. You should go home though. That hubby of yours must be getting lonely."

Cynthia sighs as she shuts down the computer and then gets up. She walks over and gives me a tight hug. "You're going to be all right. You don't need a man in your life to be all right."

I nod. I don't say that I have already come to the same conclusion myself. But it is hard to accept her words when I know that Cynthia is secretly a romantic at heart.

"I put the next patient in exam room three."

"Emergency?" I ask.

Cynthia shakes her head. "No, not an emergency." She pauses a second as a smile creeps back on her face, but she doesn't say anything else.

"What's going on?" I ask.

"You'll see soon enough. Have a good night." Cynthia grabs her bag and then walks out the door to the parking lot.

She doesn't drive, but as soon as she walks out, her husband's SUV pulls up. He jumps out of the car and then runs over to her. He gives her a sweet hug and a kiss before opening the door for her. They both look so happy.

That's what I want. A man who will wait outside my office to pick me up, no matter how long. A man who greets me with a smile and hugs and kisses. A man who does simple, sweet things, like opening doors for me, no matter how old-fashioned that notion is.

I want an honest man who loves me. I'm just afraid Cynthia might have found the last man of that kind.

I glance down at the chart in my hand. I quickly flip it open as I walk toward exam room three. There is no name listed, which is pretty unusual. I keep reading further to see the breed is a German shepherd, and the age is approximately eight weeks. The dog is just in for a checkup and his puppy shots.

I shake my head. *What person schedules a new puppy exam for nine o'clock on a Friday night? The kind who doesn't have a life.*

I knock on the door to the exam room and then open it as I continue reading over the chart to see if there is any other information that I need to know before seeing the patient.

"Hi. I'm Dr. Ivy Lane. It says here, you are in for a new puppy exam?" I ask as I look up. My heart stops when I do. My hand is already extended to shake the owner's hand, as I always do, but I immediately pull it back. I'm not shaking his hand. I'm not going to do the exam. I don't want anything to do with this man.

Because standing in front of me is Luca. A man I never thought I would see again. And I wouldn't have if my eyes had traveled down far enough on the paperwork to see that he was the owner. I would have passed him right along to Skye.

I have so many questions for Luca.

What is he doing here?

How did he find me?

Why did he hurt me?

But my needing to know answers does nothing to make me want to stay in the same room with him for even a second longer. I don't say another word to him. I don't even look to see if he brought a dog in or if that dog needs my help. I turn and walk right back out the door.

I once thought I loved Luca, but then I realized you could never really love a liar.

2

LUCA

SHIT.

My plan backfired even faster than I'd thought it would. I'd thought she would at least stay and yell at me. Tell me how horrible of a person I was. How badly I'd hurt her. Maybe flash an engagement ring in my face if she were engaged or a picture of her new hot boyfriend. I'd thought she would at least take a look at the puppy lying on the floor, chewing on my shoelaces again.

Instead, she just left. Taking her gorgeous body and smart mouth with her.

I scoop up the puppy and then run out the door after her, trying to salvage what is left of my plan. I admit now that it wasn't a great plan. That, of course, she could run out and leave me all alone at any point. But, after seeing her again and feeling that ache return to my chest, I know I have to keep trying.

So, I run. Luckily, she doesn't move very fast in her heels, and there are only so many places to hide in the clinic.

I grab her arm. "Wait!"

Her head whips around until her eyes are glaring at me. She still hasn't looked at the bundle of fur in my arms.

"Why should I? You lied to me! You hurt me! You treated me like I was nothing. Like I was disposable. You're lucky I haven't called the police to have you arrested."

I can hear every bit of pain that I caused her dripping off of every word. I hate that she is in pain. I hate that I am at least partially to blame for the pain. But I'm not sorry about what happened between us. Apologizing for the past would just be another lie that we would have to overcome.

Ivy's nostrils flare, and her eyes shoot daggers as she stares at me. But then a soft black curl falls out of her ponytail, framing her face, and it's like a shield has been lowered between us. Her eyes don't seem as scary or angry with that curl gently hanging down in front of her face.

I hear a small whimper let out from the ball of fur that I have in my hands. She wiggles forcefully and then kicks me hard in the ribs. The puppy is doing everything it can to wiggle out of my arms. It firmly kicks me again in the ribs, and I can't hold on to the puppy anymore. Hopefully, puppies are like cats in that they can just land on their feet without injury. But I have no idea.

The puppy leaves my hands but doesn't fall to the ground. Instead, Ivy snatches the puppy out of the air, like she does this hundreds of times a day. I guess she does do this all day long. She easily holds the puppy and deals with the squirming like the professional that she is.

"How are you able to hold the puppy so easily without it kicking you in the ribs?" I ask, staring at her in amazement.

Ivy smiles at the puppy, who seems to have started to calm in her hands. She leans forward and lets the puppy kiss her on the cheek before she looks at me and glares again.

"Why did you get a puppy?" she asks, raising an eyebrow, challenging me to tell her the real reason I got a puppy.

There is no way I'm telling her the real reason—that I got a puppy, so I would have a reason to come see her.

"A friend of mine found her roaming his street. His girlfriend is allergic, and he couldn't keep it, so I did."

"It?" she says, her grimace deepening.

"Sorry. *Her*," I say, wishing I could take back my mistake. I'm not doing great at getting back on her good side. I'm not even doing enough to get her to tolerate me long enough to examine my puppy.

The puppy paws at her face again, and Ivy's grimace drops as the tiniest smile ever appears. Ivy's eyes dart back to me and then back to the puppy.

"Come on. Let's make sure you're in good health. You are going to need it if you are planning on living with your new daddy," she says, talking to the puppy, as she walks back to the exam room.

I follow behind Ivy with a large smile on my face. I just have to make it back into the exam room with them to know that she is going to give me a second chance. Maybe not a second chance at love, but a second chance to be in her life. I'll take it.

I almost expect her to kick the door closed to the exam room before I can even enter. When she doesn't and I'm safe in the room, I take a deep breath before shutting the door myself.

Ivy, on the other hand, isn't paying me any attention. She has the puppy on the exam table and is checking over her entire body. Completely ignoring me.

I sigh and rub the back of my neck, trying to figure out what I should do next. Yes, I have her in the same room as me, but it's not helpful if she won't even look at me.

I watch as she opens the puppy's mouth and listens to her heart as the puppy squirms on the table and tries to lick her. I take the moment to study Ivy while she is focused on the puppy, and I try to figure out my next move.

She's wearing a dress beneath her lab coat. A dress. I'm not even sure I ever saw her wear one in the year we were dating. Yet here she is, in a dress. The dress perfectly hugs her body, showing off how curvy her body is, even while the bulky lab coat tries to hide her body. I let my eyes drop down to her legs and then the heels I noticed earlier. Heels. She's in freakin' heels. Either she had a date that she thought was a lot more important than any date she'd ever gone on with me or something else important happened tonight.

I try to keep the jealousy at bay as I think about her with another man. I hate that thought. But I can't hate her for being with another man. We broke up about two years ago. I've been with other women since her.

But I haven't stopped thinking about her, no matter what woman I was with.

"So, how is my puppy doing?"

She lowers the stethoscope she was using to listen to the puppy's heart from her ears and leaves it hanging around her neck. She has a frown on her face, and I think it's because something is wrong with the puppy. I look down at the little squirt on the table. No way something could be wrong with something so adorable.

Could it?

"She's doing good. She seems healthy. I would guess she is around ten weeks old. Maybe a little older. She could use a good bath and a couple of good meals to fatten her up a little bit more. She's a little small for her age."

The lump in my throat eases. She's not worried about the puppy. She's just mad at me.

"If you leave her here with me, I'll make sure she gets fed and bathed. We will be able to put her up for adoption this week. She'll go fast. She's adorable."

I pick up the puppy from the table and hold her against my chest. "Why do you think I'd want to put her up for adoption?"

Ivy puts her hand on her hip and gives me a knowing look. "Because I know you. You don't like dogs. And I can get her adopted much faster now when she is still a puppy than six months from now when you realize that she is too much work and gets too big and you can't handle her."

"What makes you think I don't like dogs?" I ask.

"Because you told me that you liked them. And you lie. So, therefore, you don't like dogs."

I frown. I don't know how she came to the conclusion that I don't like dogs. I don't love them, but I don't hate them. I'm somewhere in the middle. More neutral. They are likable even if they are a lot of work.

"I like *this* dog."

She shakes her head. "What is the dog's name?" she asks.

I narrow my eyes at her. "I haven't decided yet. I've only had her for a day. I need more time to decide on such an important decision."

"Bullshit. The only reason you have a dog is so that you could bring her here and have an excuse to see me. You're not going to be able to take care of her when she's fully grown."

"That might be why I brought her to this specific clinic. Yes, I wanted to see you! But that's not why I have her. I have her because I like dogs!"

"And when the dog isn't trained and pees on your expensive rugs and rips up your couch and takes over your bed, how are you going to feel then?"

"First of all, I'm going to train the dog. And she wouldn't do that anyway," I say, nuzzling the puppy against my face. "Would you?" I ask the puppy, who licks my face. I turn my attention back to Ivy.

"And, second, she's a German shepherd. Those are like the easiest dogs on the planet to train. That's why they are used as police dogs. I'll have her trained to be the perfect dog in no time."

Ivy tries to stifle a laugh but then quickly gives up. "I'll make sure I have a bed for her in about six months. That's how long I give you until you realize just how wrong you are."

"Do you want to make any sort of bet on that?" I ask, hopeful.

She laughs. "No. I really hope I'm wrong. Because I don't want to see your lying ass again."

"That's too bad. Because I plan on seeing a lot of you. I plan on making you fall in love with me again. I plan on making you mine." Even if I have to adopt an animal a month to get her attention. I'm willing to do whatever it takes to get her back.

3

IVY

"I NEED TO GIVE HER, her shots, and then you can go," I say, turning toward the cabinet in the corner of the room that holds our basic medications and syringes.

"When do I need to bring her back in?" Luca asks.

I get the medication and syringes and then turn back to him. "Never. You should find a new vet. Or, at the very least, make sure to ask for Skye when you come back in a few months for more shots and to have her spayed."

I take the puppy back out of his hands, careful not to touch him as I do. I don't want the familiar feelings to return. I don't want my heart to start fluttering at his touch. Or my pulse to race because of his grin. Or my breath to catch because of his sexy deep voice. I'm not going to let any of those things affect me.

"Do I need to distract her while you do that?" he asks, looking at me with his deep blue eyes.

I forgot about his damn eyes. How they make me weak in the knees. How they make me say yes to anything he wants.

While Luca holds on to the puppy, I walk back to the cabinet and counter where there are a container of treats, and I pull a couple out. I walk back over and hand him the treats.

"You can feed her these while I give her the shots. But she won't feel a thing," I say as I get lost in his eyes that show genuine concern for the small puppy.

I shake it off. He lied to me before with his words. So, why not his body?

I give the puppy her shots while Luca feeds her the treats.

"See? Painless," I say when I'm finished.

I rub the adorable puppy's head. Maybe she will change him. Maybe she will make him learn to love someone else more than himself. I've seen it before. It can happen. I'm just not going to be around to see if it does or not. I don't plan on seeing him again after today, no matter what adorable creature he brings into my office to take care of.

Although I do wish I could see his reaction when he realizes the puppy isn't a German shepherd.

Luca picks the puppy back up and then places it on the ground to run around. It immediately begins chewing on his shoelaces, as most puppies do.

"Can I see you again?" he asks.

"No," I say immediately.

He sighs and takes a step forward instead of back. He was never any good at listening to the word *no*.

"Why not? We were good together."

"No."

"Not even as friends?"

"No."

He frowns. "Tell me what I did so wrong. The first date, I remember being pretty good, if you ask me. But maybe I was wrong to think that."

"Are you kidding me? You fucked up from day one. When the first lie left your mouth."

"Remind me."

"No. Why should I?"

"Maybe you'll be able to prevent me from hurting another woman like I hurt you."

Damn it. His eyes are going to make me say something stupid.

"Fine. What do you want to know?"

"Tell me what you remember from our first date. Tell me how I fucked it up."

I take a deep breath. I don't know why I'm doing this. But maybe, if I can go back to that time, if I can feel what I felt then, I can heal. Maybe I can figure out why I keep sabotaging myself.

———

Three Years Earlier: First Date

A volleyball comes flying toward my head. I put my arms up just in time to block it from crashing into me. Instead, it hits my arms and bounces off. I sit up from the towel that I was lying on, trying to get a tan on my only day off of work for the next three weeks. I can't even get a break when I'm lying on the beach, trying to relax.

"I'm sorry, miss," a man says as he runs toward me, most likely to retrieve the ball that is now lying next to me on the sand.

I pick up the ball and toss it to him. "It's fine. I should move farther down the beach."

The man stands over me, and I can't help but stare. My mouth falls open as I look at him. But at least my sunglasses are hiding my eyes that are currently devouring every ripple of muscle from his chest to his abs. I don't think I could have sculpted a man more perfect than the man standing in front of me. He must work out for a living. Or maybe he's a model or an actor. I am in California after all even if Hollywood is a bit away from San Diego.

"Or you could join us?" he asks.

"No. I'm not good at volleyball. I'll just move a bit farther down on the sand."

He removes his sunglasses, and his blue eyes seem to glow. To my surprise, they don't seem to be taking in my body. Instead, he is looking right into my eyes as best as he can with my sunglasses on.

"You sure?"

"Okay, I'll play. But don't say I didn't warn you about how horrible I am."

"We aren't really that competitive. Don't worry."

He extends his hand to me. I take it, and he pulls me into a standing position.

I pick up my towel and small bag of belongings to carry with me over to where everyone else is playing. My heart sinks when I look up and see everyone's eyes on me. *Not competitive, my ass.* They look like the most competitive group of people I have ever seen. Or maybe they are all models or something. They just look good, and they aren't that good at sports.

My heart starts beating again when I see the smiles on all the men's faces. God, they are hot. All the men are shirtless, just wearing their swim trunks, showing off their perfectly sculpted abs. My eyes quickly scan through all of them, but for some reason, no matter how hot the next guy is, I'm still partial to the one who invited me to play. He is standing to my left, his eyes still on me.

"Hey, Luca, is she playing or not?" one of the guys shouts.

Luca tosses him the volleyball. He looks to me and raises his eyebrows, asking if I'm going to back out or not.

I didn't realize that only guys were playing. I look over to the side where several women are tanning themselves as they watch the game. I'd much rather be over there, watching the show, than partici-pating in the game. But from the glares the women are giving me, I don't think they want me to join them. I think they'd prefer if I were anywhere but here.

I begin to tie my curly black hair up on top of my head. I grin when I see all the men's eyes staring at my breasts. I'm wearing a coral-colored bikini that makes my dark skin pop and that barely covers me. Not a bikini that is meant to play beach volleyball in. One wrong move, and I will be giving everyone a show. But I've never been shy about my body, so it doesn't matter to me.

"I'm in. Whose team am I on?" I say.

Luca smiles. "Mine. We are down six points."

"Well, I'm not going to be much help with making them up."

Luca leans close to my ear. "You're ho...beautiful. The guys on the other side will be plenty distracted by you. That is plenty of help."

I frown even though I'm not really upset that he's just using me as a decoy. It's mainly because he called me beautiful instead of hot even though I know that was the word on the tip of his tongue, and then he changed it at the last second.

"I'm more than just a beautiful woman, you know. I've just never played beach volleyball before."

"You'll do just fine. Trust me," Luca says, winking at me.

My heart flutters a little in my chest. I want this man, and he has barely said enough to even constitute a full conversation. I know nothing about him other than he is hot and enjoys playing beach volleyball. I never go for men just based on looks. I need to know a lot more about him first. I need to know if he is a doctor or a lawyer or a beach bum. I need to know if he likes animals or runs away at the responsibility. I need to know how he treats his mama. I need to know everything. But knowing nothing about him doesn't prevent me from dreaming of him in my bed.

"You ready?" Luca asks.

I must have been staring off into space.

"Yes, and it's Ivy."

Luca smiles. "Ivy," he says to himself, testing out how my name sounds when falling from his lips.

I could listen to him say my name all day.

But I don't have time for that because the volleyball is flying over to our side of the net faster than I thought a volleyball could move. One of Luca's friends digs the ball up, followed by another guy setting the ball up, and then Luca hits the ball down even faster than when it came over to our side. And, in the blink of a couple of seconds, the play is over.

Shit.

There is no way I can move fast enough to keep the ball in the air if it comes toward me.

"Next time, I'm setting the ball to you, Ivy," the guy who set the ball to Luca says.

I smile and swallow the lump in my throat. I don't argue and say he should just keep setting the ball to Luca. I don't want to look afraid. I want to impress Luca. And the only way to do that is to try. I doubt Luca expects me to look like a pro, but I don't want to be thought of as only a pretty girl who can't actually do anything. I can do plenty. If he only spent enough time to get to know me, he would know that I am plenty strong enough. That I can more than take care of myself.

I look over on the sidelines where the group of girls are still hollering, cheering Luca on even though he wasn't the only one on the team who did anything. He's got a girlfriend. I know it. One of those women is his girlfriend. I don't have a chance. I might as well save myself the embarrassment and just leave.

But the ball is being served over the net, and I don't have time to back out now. A second later, the ball is being hit back over to our side. Luca digs that ball up, and then his friend moves to set it toward me.

"You got it, Ivy," Luca says.

I got this, I think as I move toward where the ball is set close to the net.

I jump up, but I know I'm not getting up high enough to bring the ball down with the same strength that Luca did earlier, which is the only thing that will score us a point. So, instead of hitting, I barely push it over the net. Happy with myself that I was even able to make contact with the ball.

The ball trickles over and lands in the sand on their side.

I hear the guys on my side shouting in excitement.

Luca walks up to me and gives me a high five. "That was awesome."

I smile. "Thanks."

I like that he is giving me attention, but a high five just confirms that he has a girlfriend. There was no congratulatory hug. No accidental pat on the ass. Nothing.

We continue playing for a while. Me staying mostly out of the action until it is my turn to serve the ball.

"You can just serve the ball underhand. Like this," Luca says, holding the ball and motioning how I should hit it with my fist underhand. Then, he tosses me the ball.

He didn't even bother to use that moment as an excuse to put his hands on me.

Girlfriend, I remind myself.

"But that is not how any of you served," I say.

"It takes a lot of arm strength to get the ball over the net from there," Luca says.

I frown. He doesn't think I have enough arm strength. I'll admit that my arms look small, especially compared with theirs. But I have wrangled and lifted enough hundred-pound dogs and larger to know that I have plenty of arm strength.

So, I toss the ball into the air and hit it overhand, hoping it goes in the correct direction. It does. It floats over the net. It's nowhere near as fast as when they were hitting the ball over the net, but it still does the job. A few seconds later, it is flying back over the net, toward me. I try to dig the ball up. It hits my arms and then bounces off to the side.

I sigh and dust the sand off my body.

All the men are looking at me.

"What?" I ask, looking down at my bikini, assuming that it has moved around and my nipple is out or something. But I don't see anything out of place.

"You're incredible. Do you know that, Ivy?" Luca says.

I frown. "I just lost us a point. The ball just flew off my arms."

He shakes his head. "No. You just aced that serve. That was just them throwing the ball back over in frustration."

My frown lifts.

"This is match point. Just do the same thing again, and we'll win," Luca says, tossing me the ball.

I walk back behind the serving line, more determined than ever. I try not to think too much. I just do the same thing again. The ball flies over the net, but this time, the ball comes flying back over. One of the guys digs it up, and then Luca hits it over the net, not even waiting for someone to set it up for him. It hits the ground on the other side, and the guys on our side all start screaming and jumping up and down.

I start running over toward Luca, assuming everyone is going to go congratulate him for winning us the game, but instead, all the guys start running toward me. Before I have a chance to react, Luca runs under my legs and lifts me up and onto his shoulders. I grab hold of his thick blond hair.

All the guys start shouting my name as Luca parades me around on the sand. I can feel Luca starting to lose his balance, but there is nothing I can do to stop him. We both come crashing down. Somehow, I manage to fall on top of Luca more than on the sand. I can tell from his face that, when I land on him, it hurts, but he doesn't complain. We both breathe heavily as I lie on top of him on the sand. One of the guys extends his hand to me to help me up, and one of the other guys helps Luca up.

"You should come out and celebrate our win with us, Ivy. The losers always buy the winners drinks. I'm Troy by the way," Troy says.

I smile. "I really shouldn't. I need to get back and study."

"Study? Are you still in college, Ivy?" Troy asks.

I laugh. "No, I'm not. I'm studying for my board certification."

The guys all look at me, wide-eyed.

"I'm a veterinarian."

"Wow, that's impressive," Troy says.

"Thanks. I have the test coming up in a couple of weeks. Today is my only day off work this week, so I just wanted some time to relax on the beach. Thank you all for showing me a good time."

"Do you always have Thursdays off? Because we'd love to have you back to help us squash these guys again next week," Troy says.

"Thursdays are my day off."

"Good. Then, we'll see you here next week." Troy walks over and gives me a high five. "You're awesome."

I laugh. "Thanks."

I can come back next week. I smile, thinking about that. Even though I thought I wouldn't, I did really enjoy playing. I'd just moved here to take a job at a local clinic, and I don't have a lot of friends. It might be nice to come back here every Thursday and make some friends.

I start walking over to where my towel and things are, trying to decide if I want to go for a quick swim before I leave and go back to my normal life.

"You don't really have to go and study on your only night off, do you?" Luca asks.

I look up at him after I gather up my things. "I should. It's a hard test, and I don't have a lot of time to study because of work."

"Want to go for a swim with me first?" he asks.

"You don't want to go have a drink with your girlfriend and the guys?"

Luca laughs. "I don't have a girlfriend. Those girls are crazy. And I live with Troy and Shawn, so I see them plenty enough."

I grin. I can't help it even though I know it gives away how happy I am that he doesn't have a girlfriend.

"Come on," he says, running toward the ocean.

I run after him and jump into the ocean as the waves crash against us. Luca starts swimming out a little bit. He expertly moves fast in the water. Obviously, he's a good swimmer. I swim after him a little slower.

"If I didn't love animals so much, I would definitely spend all my time here, on the beach."

Luca smiles. "It's one of my favorite places; that's for sure."

"So, what do you do when you're not hanging out at the beach?" I ask.

"I'm a lawyer," he says.

He's lying to me. I just don't know it yet.

4

LUCA

"You lied to me. You were never a lawyer. We had barely known each other an hour, and you lied to me. You couldn't just tell me the truth. That you were unemployed and doing some surfing competitions to bring in some money. But, no, you had to lie."

I exhale deeply. "Is that all you remember about our first date?" I ask.

If that is all she remembers, I'm screwed. There is no coming back into her life if all she thinks I did was lie and lie and lie every time I was with her.

"What else is there to remember? I remember you lying to me. And then following it up with another lie and another lie and another. Why would I remember anything positive about that date?"

I frown. "Well, for one, the rest of that date was pretty great. Yes, I loved watching you be awesome at volleyball your first time. Yes, I loved watching you move in your bikini. But the rest of the date was what really made me fall in love with you."

Her face turns red, and her eyes are like fire. "You don't get to say that. You don't get to say that you fell in love with me. Even falling in love was a lie, remember?"

I don't respond. It's clear that, no matter what I say right now, she still isn't going to believe me. She thinks I hurt her on purpose. She thinks I lied to her on purpose. She thinks the only thing I want her to remember is how we swam in the ocean together. How our bodies occasionally brushed up against each other. She thinks I want her to remember how it felt to be sitting next to each other on the sand and how that first stolen kiss felt as the sun went down over the ocean before she stopped me from just having her there on the beach. She wasn't that type of girl, and I didn't want her to be. I wanted to take things slow with her. I wanted to fall in love with her and her with me.

I want her to remember all those things. But I want her to remember one other thing so much more. But she doesn't remember, and even if she did, I doubt it would change anything.

"What are you doing here, Luca? There isn't a beach here. There is nothing for you here in Albuquerque but a dry desert and disappointment."

I look into her eyes that are still filled with fire but also a tiny drop of fear. She used to be fearless. Not anymore. I caused her to be like this. I caused the pain and fear and all the rest of it.

"You already know the answer to that. I'm here for you."

"You should go," she says.

I nod and scoop the puppy up into my arms, trying to firmly hold it like she did as it squirms in my arms. I stare at her a second longer. This could be the last time I see her. She might never let me back into her clinic again. I don't know where she lives or where she hangs out, and I refuse to become a stalker. If she doesn't want me to find her again, then I won't. I knew it was bad enough, searching for her here. I know the only reason she is here is because of me. She left and went into hiding because of me. She thought I would never find her here or at least that I wouldn't want to come here because there wasn't a beach.

But she doesn't know me at all. The beach is the last thing I want.

"Good-bye, Ivy," I say. I don't know why I say it. I don't want this to be good-bye. But I don't know what else to say. And I guess, if I can give her closure so that she can move on and be happy, then that is what I need to do.

I walk out the door of the exam room and then out the door of the clinic. I walk across the pavement until I get to my Jeep that I bought just yesterday. I was living in Hawaii for the last two years and didn't bother moving anything other than one small suitcase here. I just sold it all and started over with all new things here. I need a fresh start, no matter what happens between Ivy and me.

I open the door to the Jeep and then place the puppy in the front seat next to me.

"Let's go home, pup," I say.

I climb in and roll the window down so that the puppy can stick her head out of it. She does for a second as I begin driving, but I think the wind is too much for her, so I roll the window back up.

"Ivy will come around. You already did a good job of helping me with that," I say to the puppy as I drive.

I pet her head. "She'll come around—if not to me, then to you. You're too adorable for her not to fall for you."

I take a sharp turn to head toward the apartment I am renting for the time being when I hear the puppy make a weird sound.

"You all right?" I ask the puppy like she is going to respond.

The smell confirms that she is not all right. I take a deep breath before I look over, trying to prepare myself for what I know I'm going to see. When I look over, I see a puddle of puke lying on the leather seat of my Jeep. I scoop the puppy up and put her on my lap to keep her from stepping in it.

"So, you get car sick, huh?" I shake my head. "I guess we are learning something about each other after all. No biggie. In the future, I will know that you get car sick, and I'll drive slower or bring a towel."

See? I can handle this puppy stuff, I think to myself. *Ivy is wrong. I'll have this puppy stuff figured out in no time.*

I stop the Jeep in front of my apartment and then contemplate what I should do next. Every second that passes, the puke is sinking further and further into the leather. But I don't have anything to clean it up with.

I look down at my shirt. It's either the shirt or the brand-new car. I take my shirt off and wipe up the puke. To my surprise, it comes up easily. Other than some Febreze and sanitizer, I don't think it will need much else.

I toss my shirt with the puke into a trash bin before carrying the puppy up into my apartment that is basically a bed, a couch, and a TV. I place the puppy on the ground.

"Go explore," I tell the puppy.

But she doesn't move. She just sits at my feet.

"Go on," I say, pushing on it to go run around and let me just be by myself for a second.

I automatically walk to the fridge before I remember that I haven't even had time to go grocery shopping yet. I don't have any beer to soothe my wounds right now. The puppy follows me as I walk from the kitchen to the living room. I take a seat on the couch and watch as the puppy tries to jump up onto the couch, but her little legs aren't quite long enough to propel her up onto the couch. So, I bend down and lift her up onto the couch next to me. She doesn't stay there long though. Instead, she climbs up onto my lap, and then she immediately lies down and closes her eyes.

"At least you like me, puppy," I say as I lift my legs up onto the couch so that I can take a nap as well. "I need to think of a name for you, puppy. If only Ivy could see you now, she would realize how much you do like me."

The puppy nestles into my stomach.

"Let me see. How about Molly?"

The puppy doesn't react. I shake my head. I'm talking to a dog. She doesn't care what she is called as long as I give her food and a bed to sleep in.

"Nah. How about Lucy?"

The puppy again doesn't react.

"No, I don't like it either." I pet her long fur, imagining her lying on me like this when she is about sixty pounds instead of the fifteen pounds she is now.

"You know, when you get older, you aren't going to be able to do this, right?"

She snores.

I laugh.

Being a dog parent is going to be easy, I think, *if she is this adorable all the time. I just need to come up with a name.*

"Bailey."

Nothing.

"Sadie."

Nothing.

"Sophie."

The puppy lifts her head and licks my face.

"You like that—Sophie?" I ask.

I swear, the puppy is smiling at me.

"Okay. Sophie, it is."

The puppy settles back on my stomach, and I close my eyes and allow myself to drift off to sleep.

I don't know how much later it is when I hear a high-pitched bark. I jump up from the couch, looking for Sophie. I find her peeing on the carpet in the living room a few feet from me.

I sigh as I go to the bathroom to see what I have to clean it up.

This might not be so easy after all.

5

IVY

I SLAM the door to my Jeep and then walk around to the back to gather my bags of things. I'm frustrated and angry, and I take it all out on the door as I slam it shut. I throw the back door open and sling bag after bag over my shoulder until all six bags are slung over my shoulder. I then slam the back door shut and start walking up the driveway to my house.

As I walk, at least half of the bags begin falling off my shoulders. I try to grab them to keep them from falling, but they don't stay up.

"Why the fuck do I have so many bags?" I curse loudly to myself, and then I look around at my neighbors' houses, afraid that they might have heard me even though I don't think it is possible.

I live in a very nice area. So nice that I doubt any of my neighbors have ever cursed in their lives. If they heard me, I'm sure I'd be kicked out of the neighborhood. But, thankfully, our houses are too far apart for them to have heard me. At least, I hope so.

Still, instead of yelling, I whisper the rest of the string of curse words that continue to fall from my lips as I try to carry the bags inside my house. I only make it halfway from my car to the front porch when I just can't take it anymore. I let the bags fall to the ground and just leave them there. There are a few medical supplies, a bag or two of my clothes that I have been meaning to bring home from the clinic and finally did, and a few bags with dog and cat toys for my pets. Nothing important in any of the bags. Nothing I need tonight.

And I no longer care what the neighbors think of me. Let them kick me out of the neighborhood. Honestly, now that Luca knows where I live, I'm not sure I want to live in Albuquerque anymore anyway.

I walk up to my door and put the key into the lock before I realize the door has been unlocked the entire time I was gone.

Shit.

"Please let all my pets still be inside," I plead before I push the door open.

I smile when I get attacked by my three dogs, happy to see me home and showing it by jumping on me, slobbering, barking, and wagging their tails. I have a pit bull mix, who is full of energy; a Great Dane, who is scared of everything; and a Chihuahua, who rules them all.

"Hey, guys. You have no idea how happy I am to see you."

I pet each of them and give them the attention they have been desperate for all evening. I don't leave them alone very often. I usually have a dog walker stop by, or I bring them into the clinic with me.

"You're all here. Now, how about your kitty friends?"

I start walking into the house with the group of dogs following me, and I call for the two cats. I spot one on top of my cabinets in the kitchen, and the other is under my bed. I take a deep breath when I find them. I won't be searching the neighborhood for any lost pets tonight.

"You guys hungry?" I ask to the dogs mainly.

My cats couldn't care less. They can find their own food via mice and so on if they really wanted to.

Zoey, my Great Dane, starts drooling immediately at the mention of food. Nala, my pit bull mix, starts turning circles. And Duke, my Chihuahua, starts jumping up and down.

I go over to the pantry that is filled mainly with dog and cat food and feed them. I then walk over to the counter in my kitchen where my fish tank sits and feed the fish. Then, I walk to one of the spare bedrooms where Jill, my turtle, lives.

"Hey, Jilly Bean, you hungry for dinner?" I gather her food to pour into her tank, and then I freeze. "Jill?"

She's not in her tank.

Shit.

I look all over the floor of the bedroom but don't see any sign of her anywhere. I walk back to the hallway where all the dogs are sitting, staring at me, and even the cats have come by to see what all the yelling is about.

"Who let the turtle out of her cage again?" I ask like they are going to answer me.

They all look back at me with guilty looks on their faces. I sigh. Even though I think animals can understand humans for the most part, they can't use words to talk back. So, asking them is really not that helpful. I spend a few minutes searching the house for the turtle but can't find her.

"Okay, Jill, come out when you're ready!" I shout like she is listening.

Unfortunately, this isn't the first time she has gone missing. She turned up about a week later last time.

Who knew a turtle would be the hardest animal to keep alive out of all the animals I have?

I walk to the kitchen and open the fridge. I have plenty of food, and most of it is even healthy. But I don't want any of that tonight. I open the freezer and pull out a pint of chocolate chip cookie dough ice cream, and then I pull a bottle of wine off my wine rack. I grab a glass and carry everything to my couch.

I pour a large glass of wine and then start eating the ice cream while my animals curl up in various places around me. Some are begging for ice cream while others know better and just lie down.

"Today has been a horrible day. I no longer have a boyfriend, and my ex-boyfriend, Luca—you remember him, Duke and Nala."

They perk up when I say their names.

"Luca came to the clinic today. I don't know why. I don't know what he thinks he will accomplish by coming back into my life. He lied to me. Not just once, but over and over and over again. Our whole relationship was one big lie."

Nala licks my hand.

"You're right. He was a nice guy to you. Even though he hates animals, he pretended like he didn't. I don't hate him. I just hate that he came back into my life and is trying to fuck everything up. I should just give up on men altogether. That's what I've decided. I'm happy without a man in my life."

Nala nudges my hand again.

"I know," I say, sadly looking down at her. "I know. It hurts. I still love him, but I can't be with him. He hurt me so much. After him, it took me over a year to even go out on a date with another man. It took me longer than that to trust another man."

Nala growls.

"Okay, you're right. I don't trust men. I might never again, and it's because of him. Maybe this is my push to learn to try to trust men again. I have to give it a chance. I have to learn to trust men again."

I pull out my phone, and I text Skye.

Me: I need you to find me a date.

Skye: When?

Me: As soon as possible.

Before I let Luca slip back into my life, I think.

Skye: One boyfriend coming right up. ;)

I smile. *Thank God for Skye. At least I can trust her.*

6

LUCA

I STEP into the hot shower as Sophie sits outside, pawing at the door, wanting to get in with me. She starts barking in her high-pitched bark that was once adorable. After a night of practically zero sleep because of that high-pitched barking and accidents in the house, I no longer find the bark adorable. I take a deep breath, trying my best not to take my frustration out on her.

Sophie decides that barking isn't getting her anywhere, so she lies down on the floor mat in front of the shower. I exhale deeply as I let the water run over my head. I can finally relax. I don't have to worry about her for at least a couple of minutes while I shower.

Instead, I can think about what has really been driving me crazy all night.

Ivy.

I came here because I want her, but now that I'm here, I have no idea how to win her back. How to tell her the truth or even if I should. Do I even deserve to have her in my life after how badly I treated her? If I loved her, should I bring her back into my life, knowing how much it could hurt her?

I don't have the answers.

I don't know if I will ever have the right answers.

249

I just have to make a decision.

But not right now. Now, I just want to think about Ivy.

My hand automatically goes to my cock, just thinking about her. I ache for her. And I can't believe that she didn't remember everything from our first date. At the very least, I can't believe she didn't remember what had happened after we swam in the ocean. How that first kiss had felt. It was the sweetest yet dirtiest kiss I'd ever had. One second, it was sweet. The next, we both knew it was going to lead to dirty things that we shouldn't feel after knowing each other for only a couple of hours.

And, as good as the first kiss was, the second was even better.

———————

Three Years Earlier: Second Date

I knock on the door of Ivy's apartment that she says she shares with her best friend, Skye.

The door flings open, and a woman is standing in the doorway. She doesn't look happy to see me. She has rainbow-colored hair and a pierced nose, and tattoos cover her arms. But none of that is what is shocking to me. What's shocking is that she is standing in the doorway in nothing but a bra and underwear. Her large boobs are spilling out of the bra, and, shit, the bra is see-through.

I keep my eyes focused on her face even though that is hard as well because her eyes are so focused on me. I'm afraid she is trying to break me with just her look.

"You must be Skye. I'm Luca. I'm here for Ivy."

Skye doesn't say anything. She just stares at me like she is waiting for me to hit on her.

I stand frozen in the doorway with a smile on my face. I don't know what else to do.

Suddenly, Skye's expression changes to something that resembles a smile but isn't actually a smile.

I cock my head to the side, and my eyes grow large as I wait for her to say something.

"I guess you pass. You can come in. I'll let Ivy know you are here," Skye says.

I follow Skye inside the small apartment. "Wait, that was a test?"

Skye shrugs. "Ivy has been hurt too many times. I don't want her getting hurt anymore."

I swallow down the lump in my throat. If I don't want to hurt Ivy, I should just turn around and walk out the door. Because, if my dating history tells me anything, it's that I hurt women. Over and over. Even when I'm trying to protect them, I hurt them.

But there is something about Ivy that I can't stop thinking about. I have to have her. I have to see. Because maybe she'll be the one I've been looking for.

"Are you going to put some clothes on now?" I can't help but ask Skye.

She laughs. "Why would I do that? I want to torture you as long as I can. You need to know that I will personally come after you if you hurt my friend."

I nod. "Understood."

"Good." She walks over to the hallway that I assume leads to their bedrooms. "Ivy! Get your ass out here!" she shouts down the hallway.

Ivy comes out, and my eyes grow wide at the sight of her. She's in blue jean shorts and a white lace bra that her dark nipples strain against. Other than her nipples being completely visible, she's not wearing anything different than she was the last time I saw her, but somehow, this seems more intimate than seeing her in a bathing suit. Her tightly curled hair is loose instead of up in a ponytail. She has spent time on her makeup. And she is wearing lingerie that I know is for me.

It's hard to tell if she blushes or not because of how dark her skin is, but I can tell from her eyes that she is both embarrassed and proud. Most likely embarrassed that she came out in this state of dress when she didn't realize I was here yet proud of her body that is getting more turned on, the longer we stare at each other.

"Is this another test?" I whisper to Skye, who is standing next to me.

She laughs. "Everything is a test. But I think, so far, you are passing with flying colors."

I grin as I continue to stare at Ivy. "If you don't go put a shirt on, I'm not going to be able to control myself."

Ivy bites her lip. "I'm not sure I want you to control yourself."

My eyes widen when she says that.

Is this the same woman from the beach? The same woman who only let me kiss her once and then pushed me away, wanting to take things slow?

Skye clears her throat. "I don't care if you guys go out to dinner or just stay in and fuck, but I don't want to hear you guys if you stay in. So, play your music loudly or go somewhere else."

Ivy and I both exhale at the same time.

"We'll leave," we say in unison.

Skye just shakes her head as she walks over to Ivy. She grabs Ivy's arm and then starts pulling her down the hallway toward her bedroom. I assume she's going to tell Ivy to finish getting dressed. I close my eyes when they both disappear around the corner and try to imagine anything other than Ivy.

I'm not going to fuck her tonight. She's too good of a girl to fuck, and I am not that kind of guy. Well, I'm not that kind of guy when I want to see the woman again after the first date. And I want to see Ivy again. No, I *need* to see her again and again and again.

Ivy is the woman I've been looking for. I know it. She's the one. And I'm not going to fuck it up by jumping her bones as soon as I get her alone. It's not going to happen.

I try to force my brain to think about food, about surfing, about the gross man I saw picking his nose in the car next to me on the way over here. Just when it starts working, I hear Skye clear her throat.

I look up, and Ivy is standing in a romper that barely covers her butt and reveals the top of her bra. My eyes pop open as I look at her. I had Ivy pegged all wrong. She isn't a sweet, innocent girl. She's a fierce firecracker, who is going to destroy me. I know it.

Not if I destroy her first, the voice in my head says.

Ivy devours me with her gorgeous dark brown eyes while I try to get my cock in check. But I know she can see how hard I am beneath my jeans when her eyes linger over it. I no longer care to take things slow. We are both willing to play with fire even though we know there is a good chance we will get burned.

I walk over and grab Ivy's hand as I rack my brain, trying to figure out where I can take her. I can't even remember what my original plan for our date was. I try to focus, but all I can focus on are Ivy's breasts bouncing as I pull her toward the door of her apartment. I force my eyes to focus on the door instead of Ivy.

Think, think, think.

I need to take her somewhere romantic. If we are going to fuck, at least I want it to be someplace nice, special.

A hotel maybe?

I try to think of the nicest hotel in the area, but my mind is blank.

Food.

I should get her some food first, and then we can fuck.

Romper. Heels. Dance.

I should take her dancing somewhere. I know that women who dress up like Ivy want to go out dancing.

But, again, my mind is drawing a blank.

Suddenly, we are at her apartment door. I open the door and step outside into the warm air as I pull Ivy with me. She shuts the door behind me.

Shit. I don't have long to decide what we are going to do.

I glance at Ivy again. I'm not going to be able to think of anything else ever again.

She smiles.

Damn it, I love her smile.

Love. That's not a word I think I have ever used.

But, God, do I love her smile.

She giggles when I look at her like I'm going to devour her at any second. And, now, I'm thinking about how much I love her laugh. Because, damn it, I think I love her laugh, too.

"What is going on in that head of yours?" she asks, cocking her head to the side as she looks at me like she loves my smile, too.

"I'm thinking about how much I love your smile and laugh."

Her smile gets bigger. "And?"

"And I have no idea where I was planning on taking you because all I want to do is taste that dirty mouth again. All I want is to fuck you."

I take a step closer to her. She doesn't back away. I grin and tuck a strand of loose hair behind her ear before I let the back of my hand trail down the side of her face. She closes her eyes, and her breathing gets slow and steady, like she is trying to feel every tingle in her body.

I lower my lips to hers before she opens her eyes. The kiss is supposed to be soft and gentle, just like how I touched her face. But I can't control my lips any more than I can control my thoughts or my cock. My lips crash against her soft lips that taste like strawberries from the lip gloss she is wearing. My hands grab her arms and push them high above her head, and my body pushes hard against hers, needing to feel every curve and every inch of her smooth skin against mine. I feel myself pushing her much too hard against the door of her apartment, but she doesn't seem to mind.

She opens her mouth, allowing my tongue inside. Soft, quiet moans purr from her throat as we kiss. Her arms and body don't fight me as I kiss her. Instead, they invite me in. Our bodies fit together as we kiss, and she moans louder when I push my cock into her stomach. It doesn't feel like the second time we have kissed, and the first time we had a serious make-out session. It feels like we have been doing this for years but with a fire that hasn't ever burned out.

Still, this isn't enough to satisfy either of us. But I can't think straight. I'm much too single-minded and focused.

First, I want her lip in my mouth. So, I bite her bottom lip and pull it into my mouth, sucking on it. Next, I want her neck. Boobs. Stomach. Pussy. I want to feel and taste it all.

"We," she says between kisses. "Should...ah, fuck," she says as I kiss her neck.

She pulls her arms out of my grasp above her head, and it's like that one kiss flipped a switch inside her. Before, she could think, and she could talk. But, now, the only thing she can do is moan and kiss and breathe.

Her hands go around my neck as she tries to pull me closer to her. I grab her bare legs and wrap them around my waist, like somehow having her fully in my arms is going to change something. But having her in my arms will make it so that I can carry her anywhere. She's mine while I have her in my arms.

And that is what I need right now. I need her to be mine. A feeling I never thought I would feel again.

Suddenly, the door opens, and I feel myself losing my balance. I barely have time to try to turn as we fall to the floor in the entryway to her apartment.

"You okay?" I ask Ivy.

I did my best not to fall on her, but I know that I did little.

"What are you two doing?" Skye asks.

I look over at Ivy, who is lying on the floor next to me with the largest grin on her face.

We both burst out laughing as Skye glares over us.

"When I told you that I didn't want to hear you, I meant it. I told you to leave, not barely make it out of our apartment and then make out so that I could see you."

I look at Ivy, not sure how to handle her friend.

"We'll go to my room," she says, looking at me with lust in her eyes.

I look up at Skye, like I have to ask her permission to take Ivy into her bedroom. To be honest, Skye scares the shit out of me.

Skye just looks at Ivy with a raised eyebrow and hands on her hips. "Really, Ivy?" asks Skye. "You're going to let this bum of a man do you without him even buying you dinner first?"

Ivy doesn't answer with words, but her eyes say it all. I stand up and help Ivy to her feet. And then I grab hold of each side of her face and kiss her again. My eyes close as I take in her lips. And kiss her again and again and again.

"Jesus. Fine, I'm out of here. I'll stay at my parents' house tonight if you need me, Ivy. But just realize that you owe me one after this."

I open my eyes just enough to see Ivy waving off her friend, but she doesn't open her eyes or stop kissing me.

As soon as the door slams, Ivy's lips pull away from mine, and I'm left wanting. Ivy grins again as she grabs hold of my hand and starts pulling me toward her bedroom.

"What?" she asks.

I shake my head. "Nothing. You are just nothing like what I expected."

"Is that a good thing or a bad thing?"

"Both."

As I walk toward her bedroom, Ivy leading the way, I can't take it anymore. I need my hands on her body. I need to have her now, not later. I scoop her up and carry her into the first room I see. I toss her onto the bed and then remove my shirt, watching her eyes grow heavy as they fall across my chest.

"Like what you see, baby?"

She rolls her eyes at me, but it doesn't stop her from looking. "I like you much better when you don't go for cheesy lines like that."

"I need you naked. Now."

Ivy bites her lip as she stares up at me. "Oh, yeah? And what if I obey you? What if I give in to your commands and do exactly what you want? Will you be out of my bed before I even wake in the morning? Will you lead me on for a few weeks to try to get all the sex you think you can get out of me? Will you call me up at random times, looking for a booty call but nothing else?"

My eyes darken as I stare at her, lying on the bed. I push my pants and underwear off and watch as her eyes grow even heavier. Her breathing is fast, her body flushed. I can tell from everything in her body that she likes what she sees, and she wants this.

So, despite her hesitation, despite her words saying that she's scared that this is just going to be a one-time thing, she is still willing to do it because this is what she wants. She wants me now, just like I want her now. We aren't waiting for anything.

I crawl up on top of her still-clothed body and sit just over her hips. My hands slide on either side of the fabric of her romper, and I pull hard. The fabric rips as easily as if it were a piece of paper. I wasn't expecting it to come apart so easily, just like I wasn't expecting her to want me so easily.

I lower my lips to the bare skin over her chest. I kiss gently, my lips barely brushing against her skin, as I hear and see her suck in a breath.

"I don't think I could ever give you up after this. I want this too much. I want to fuck you, and I want to love you. I want to take you to dinners so romantic that it's fit for a king yet fuck you in the dirty bathroom, like the dirty girl you really are but only show to me. I want everything, and you're not getting rid of me so easily."

She takes several deep breaths as she contemplates what I said. I know she thinks it's a line. Just something men say to get into her pants. I meant every word, but I know it will take more than words to prove that to her, especially after what I'm going to do to her later.

"What are you waiting for? Fuck me."

I grin. "Oh, I plan on it."

I slide the romper off her body, and then I reach back into the pocket of my pants and pull out a condom that I never thought I would use tonight. I stare at her body in her lace bra and underwear.

She leans forward and reaches her hand behind her back. "I seem to remember you saying that you wanted me naked." She undoes the hook on her bra and then pulls it off. She slips one leg and then the other out of her underwear and tosses them to the floor. She looks at me with a smirk on her face. My heart stops as I just look at her.

"Goddamn it."

She raises an eyebrow at me.

"I can't believe you're mine."

She looks at me, confused. "I'm not yours."

I look at her seriously. "You are tonight."

And then I flip her over hard, sucking the breath out of her. Because I know that I can't fuck her while looking her in the eyes. Not tonight. Tonight isn't about romance. Tonight isn't about love. Tonight is about the first time I get to claim her body before I claim her soul and hope that she survives it.

I slip the condom on and then grab her hips, loving how plump and curvy her ass is in my hands. I reach one hand up between her legs, ensuring that she is as wet as I think she is. When I get confirmation, I push my cock inside her.

She groans. Half-pain, half-pleasure. My head comes down, and I kiss her shoulder as I wait for a second to ensure the pain ends quickly.

"You're huge."

"You're tight," I moan happily against her neck.

I don't wait for her to catch her breath or to ease the pain for more than a second before I drive into her again. I grab hold of her hips and slam hard into her gorgeous ass as I thrust inside her.

"I need—"

"More," I finish for her.

Her head nods gently as she pants just a little. I give her more. I push in deeper, filling her completely, as her breathing speeds up.

"I need—"

I reach my hand, finding her clit between her folds and running my thumb across it.

"Yes...th-hat."

I feel her building and growing and tightening around me, and thank God, because I won't last either.

"I need—"

"Faster," I say as I move faster.

I don't know how I know her so well, but I do. I know her body. I know what she needs. I know everything, just like I know that I am desperate to have her forever.

"Come, baby," I whisper in her ear just as I feel her clench and unravel all over my cock.

Her orgasm pushes me into my own. And then we collapse on the bed, both breathing heavily.

She smiles as we lie face-to-face, our noses barely touching each other. She has the most beautiful grin on her face, like she knows something that she can't wait to tell me.

"What is it?" I ask.

She bites her lip, contemplating answering me, and then finally says, "This isn't my bedroom. It's Skye's."

———

Present

I come in the shower, just thinking about that night and how perfect it was. And then I went and fucked everything up. And then Skye, as I'd suspected, made my life a living hell after she discovered that I fucked Ivy in her bed. It's not as bad as whatever she's going to do to me now that I'm back in Ivy's life, no matter how short-lived it's going to be.

I turn off the water and grab the towel before stepping out of the shower when I hear a high-pitched squeal. I look down and see Sophie hobbling away from under my feet. Shit, I forgot she was down there.

I walk over to her, bend down, and scoop her up. "You okay, girl?"

She immediately begins licking my face. I smile and place her back on the ground before I start walking toward my closet to get some clothes to change into. As I do, I notice that Sophie, who is following me, has one of her feet raised.

I scoop her back up into my arms. "I guess it's another vet visit for you."

I'm just not sure if seeing Ivy again so soon is a good idea or not.

7

IVY

THIS CAN'T BE HAPPENING. That's all I can think when I get off the phone at the vet clinic. *This can't be happening. This can't be happening. This can't be happening. This can't be happening.*

I never thought, when I became a vet, something this crazy could happen to me. I thought being a vet was going to be all rainbows and happiness. Yes, I knew there would be the occasional death, the occasional sadness, but I knew how to handle that after my parents died when I was quite young. I had faced death time and time again. I wasn't worried about dealing with death or owners mourning their pets. I just never thought I would have to deal with this.

A tear rolls down my cheek as I realize my life could be changed forever. Skye puts her arm on my back, trying to reassure me, but there's nothing she can do to make this any better. Honestly, she's scared, more so than I am. Her life is just as much at risk. It doesn't matter how close Skye and I are to each other. There is nothing either of us can say to make it any better. The only difference between us is that I cry and show my emotions while Skye hides it, only showing a hint of fear in her eyes that only I can see.

Our intercom system buzzes. I click the button on the phone to answer the intercom, and Cynthia's voice comes on loud and clear into my office where Skye and I are gathered around my desk.

"I have a patient for you, Skye." "Okay. Give me five minutes. Who's the patient?" Skye says.

Cynthia's quiet for a minute, and then she says, "It's Luca. He says it's an emergency. Something about the puppy's leg."

Skye and I look at each other in frustration. Luca is the last guy that either one of us wants to deal with today.

I press the button for the intercom. "Are you sure he doesn't want to see me?" I ask.

Cynthia says, "No. He specifically asked for Skye. He was very persistent."

I sigh. "I'll deal with Luca. You shouldn't have to deal with him, Skye."

"No way in hell am I letting you deal with that asshole. Not today, not after everything we've been dealing with."

I shake my head as I get up from the desk. "I'm dealing with Luca. Let Cynthia know that I will be there in a minute."

I head to the restroom where I can quickly check my face and make sure that the tears are gone from my eyes. I don't want to let Luca know that I've been crying. My tears are quick to dry merely because I'm thinking about how angry I am with Luca for coming here again just one day after he was here previously. Just one day. He has some balls to come here, and I'm not dealing with his crap—not today, not ever again.

I don't care about how I look today. I'm wearing my scrubs that I usually wear and tennis shoes. I would actually prefer it if he were repulsed by me.

I shake my head. No, that's not what I want. I want him to find me so hot that he's desperate for me. I want him to hurt after what he did to me. I want him to see that I will never be *his* again. I want him to see me happy and in love with another man. I want anything but what my reality really is.

So, I spend a second pinching my cheeks and applying a little lip gloss—not for him, for *me*. I will not seem weak in front of him. I will not feel stupid or blind ever again.

And then I walk out of the restroom like a girl on a mission. As I walk, I realize I didn't even ask Cynthia which exam room she put him in. So, I have to poke my head inside two rooms filled with other patients. I apologize quickly each time before moving on to the next. I begin to expect another stranger when I open the door to another exam room and see him standing there, cuddling his puppy.

I don't expect what I see when I open the door. I was expecting to see Luca with a perfectly healthy dog, thinking he came in today just to torture me or to try to get Skye on his side. I wasn't expecting him to be scared and genuinely concerned about his dog. But that is what I see when I walk into the room. Luca is tightly holding the puppy against his chest. His eyes are focused on the dog, his body tense.

I shut the door and begin walking toward them. "How is she doing?" I ask.

Only then does Luca look up from his puppy and notice that I'm in the room.

"I'm not sure. I stepped on her foot on accident. She hasn't been walking on it since."

He doesn't ask me why I'm here instead of Skye. It's clear that part will come later. Right now, his only concern is the puppy's leg. Although I think he's probably overreacting, I'm happy to see him finally care about something other than himself.

"Here," I say, holding out my arms to take the puppy from him.

He hands the puppy over to me. She immediately starts licking my face and squirming in my arms.

I set her on the table and start doing a quick physical exam, checking that all her major organs are working correctly before focusing on her leg. As I examine her leg, I don't find anything that seems broken or suspicious.

"Her leg seems fine so far. I don't feel anything broken, but you never know with puppies. She most likely just sprained a muscle, or when you stepped on her foot, it was a little bit painful, so she's afraid to use it again." I pick her up and put her on the ground. "Call her to you, Luca."

Luca squats down. "Come here, Sophie," he says in a high-pitched voice, like most dog owners do. He also excitedly claps his hands together, trying to get the puppy to come to him.

The puppy almost immediately runs to him, and when she does, she walks just fine and without a limp.

I smile and go over to the computer where I start entering in everything I've found so far. "Looks like she's going to be just fine. She probably just twisted her leg a little bit. Puppies do that sometimes. But you did the right thing by bringing her in."

I glance up from the computer and see Luca playing with the puppy with a huge smile on his face. Gone is the expression of terror that was there just a moment ago when he thought he had broken his puppy.

I smile. I can't help it. I'm smiling more at the puppy than Luca.

"So, it seems I was wrong about one thing," I say.

Luca looks up at me. "I really did want to see Skye instead of you. I know it's too soon after you told me not to see you again. I was just concerned about the puppy."

I nod. "I realize that now. So, I guess I was wrong about two things. First, you didn't come here to see me. You came for the puppy. And, second, you actually do have feelings. You can actually care about something else even if it is only a puppy."

One corner of Luca's lips curls up ever so slightly. "I have feelings for a lot more than just Sophie, you know."

I roll my eyes. "I don't want to hear about who else you care about, just that you do have a heart. That was something I always suspected you didn't have."

"So, how much do I owe you for your reassurance that my puppy is okay?" Luca asks.

"Cynthia will be able to tell you that information when you get to the front."

My eyes flick back and forth between Luca and my computer. I find my eyes lingering more and more on Luca even though I shouldn't. I just need to get this finished, and then he can leave. Cynthia just needs to know how much to bill him. But I can't focus long enough to type out anything useful on the computer.

"You know what? Don't worry about it. This one is on me. I'm just happy you are taking better care of this puppy than I thought you would," I say, patting the puppy on the head. "I'll walk you out."

I walk past where Luca is staring at me, wide-eyed, and put my hand on the doorknob, just needing to get out of here as soon as possible. Luca's hand goes around mine, stopping me from being able to open the door.

"What are you doing?" he asks.

I don't look at him. Instead, I stare intently on the doorknob beneath both of our hands like it is the most interesting thing on the planet.

"I'm walking you out and covering your bill."

"You think I can't afford to pay for a vet bill?" he asks, his voice deep and angry.

My eyes dart to him. "I don't know if you can pay your vet bill or not. As far as I know, you are unemployed."

His face gets red. "I can pay the bill. It's not a problem. Just tell me how much I owe. I don't want you doing any favors for me because you think I can't pay."

"I don't have time to figure this out right now. I have other patients waiting. I'll mail you the bill," I say, happy that I came up with a solution so quickly.

I begin to turn the doorknob, but Luca tightens his grasp on my hand, preventing me from leaving.

"What. Is. Going. On?" Luca asks.

"Nothing. I'm just busy, and I need you to leave, so I can deal with the other patients," I say, my voice strong and steady.

He has no idea that I'm about to break on the inside. He has no idea how painful the last twenty-four hours have been since the last time I saw him. He has no idea that he is not the worst thing going on in my life. He has no fucking idea.

I glance down at my watch to show that I really am busy. Because

I am busy, just not with patients. I have a busy night planned of crying, feeling sorry for myself, and eating ice cream. Lots and lots of ice cream.

"I don't believe you," he says sternly.

"It doesn't matter if you believe me or not. I'm leaving. You're leaving. And, unless something else happens to Sophie, like eating something she isn't supposed to or you accidentally drop her on her head, I don't want to see you again until her next checkup."

"Puppies will really eat anything?"

I sigh. "Yes, they will eat anything. It doesn't have to be food, and it doesn't have to be small. I once had a dog come in after eating a whole couch."

He raises an eyebrow.

"So, closely watch her, and if you are going to be gone during the day, crate-train her."

He nods. "What is wrong, Ivy?" he asks with a voice so sweet that I think he actually cares for me.

But then again, I've fallen for that before. He's sweet until he's not. It's all just one big game to him.

"It's nothing," I whisper.

He trails a finger down my bare neck, like he always used to do. I get chills, just like I always used to do. I haven't had a man touch me like that since...well, since him. He always knew how to control my body and therefore me. He was the best at pretending to care. He was the best liar I had ever met.

Why couldn't he have taken that skill set and used it on something that would benefit the world? Become a police interrogator. A lawyer. A spy. A magician. Someone who needs to be good at lying and deceiving people. Instead, he used those skills on me.

"Tell me, and I'll leave you alone, Ivy."

"That's a lie," I say. It's not hard to guess when he is lying or telling the truth because he is *always* lying.

"Tell me, and I'll let you leave."

I suck in a breath because I'm not going to be able to hide my tears much longer, and I don't want him to think I'm crying because of him.

I exhale deeply. "I'm being sued for ten million dollars in a malpractice suit. They are claiming I killed their dog."

Luca's mouth drops, and his hand goes just slack enough that I can force the door open without him stopping me. I walk out into the waiting room and see Cynthia behind the desk.

Good ole Cynthia. She works far too hard to have to get fired because of my negligence.

"I'm leaving. Cancel the rest of my appointments, and let Skye handle emergencies," I tell Cynthia as I pass her desk.

She doesn't tell me that I still have six hours left on my shift and that I shouldn't cancel. I'm not too worried. Skye will want a distraction right now, and taking any emergencies that come in tonight will give her that. And, as for the patients with appointments being mad at me, let them be mad. Let them go find another clinic. They are going to have to find a new clinic soon enough. They can't hurt me anyway. I can't be more hurt than I already am.

I run out into the warm midday air that immediately causes me to sweat. It makes it hard to breathe because of how warm it is out here. But it doesn't stop the tears. The tears come full force. I squat down on the ground as the tears overwhelm me. I just want to go home. I want to snuggle with my dogs. I want ice cream. I just want to feel better.

But I didn't bring anything with me. I don't have my purse, my keys, nothing. When I finish crying, I'll have to go back inside to gather my things up before I leave.

"I think you are going to need this," Luca says.

I look to my left where he has squatted down next to me as he holds out my purse to me. Sophie is curled up around his other arm, half-asleep, just barely keeping her eyes open.

I take the purse. "Thanks."

I start digging through it, looking for Kleenex when he holds a tissue out to me. After staring at it for far too long, I take it from him. I wipe my eyes as the tears slowly stop. I don't know how he does it, but he always knows exactly what I want and even what I didn't think I needed myself. It always freaked me out when we were dating. It was like he had a sixth sense. Like he could literally read my mind and soul. Evidently being broken up and being apart for about two years hasn't changed anything.

"You didn't do anything wrong. You know that, right?" he says.

I look at him, and I want to slap him because it is the absolute worst thing he could have said in this moment. "Of course I did something wrong; otherwise, I wouldn't be getting sued. They would have had no case against me. I killed their precious puppy. It was my negligence."

He shakes his head. "You're wrong. I know you. You would never hurt another living creature. You don't even kill spiders in your house. You don't eat meat. I don't think you have ever killed another living thing. Ever. You didn't do this."

I exhale deeply, trying to find the words to explain this to him. "Yes. I. Did. I killed the puppy. The owners brought in a perfectly healthy six-month-old puppy. I thought I felt a lump and was concerned about cancer. The ultrasound and tests came back inconclusive. So, I wanted to do an exploratory surgery just to make sure. I did the surgery. But the lump wasn't cancer. It was a benign lump. He was perfectly fine. But he had a reaction to the general anesthesia. I couldn't wake him up. He died. I let him die. I killed him."

Luca places his fingers on the spot on my neck that always relaxes me and squeezes gently. *Damn it.* I feel immediately relaxed, immediately calm. I just wish those fingers weren't attached to this man. I wish they were attached to anyone else.

"You didn't kill him. He died. It was a freak thing that happens sometimes. If he hadn't died then, he would have died the first time they brought him in for any other surgery."

"Exactly. That could have been years from now. It's been eating at me since it happened two months ago. But, now that I know for sure that it was my fault, I can't handle it."

"It wasn't your fault. And, in the court of law, it definitely won't be your fault. There is no judge or jury in America that would find you guilty. You did everything you could to save that dog."

"How do you know that? How do you know that I didn't fuck it up? How do you know that I didn't kill that dog?"

"Because I know you. I've loved you. I've seen a side to you that no one else gets to see. I've seen you at your worst. And even your worst isn't capable of this. You are a perfectionist. You did everything right."

"Then, why do I feel so bad? Why does it hurt so much? Why am I being sued?"

"Because people are greedy. Because people need to blame others for unexplained deaths. This isn't your fault. You can't carry guilt around forever because of this."

I nod. I know he's right. I'm just not ready to hear any of this right now. "I should go."

"Do you have a lawyer?" he asks.

I sigh. "No, I don't. I guess I'll have to start looking. I never thought I would be in a position like this, but I guess every good thing in life has a downside." *Just like everyone who is bad has a good side*, I think to myself, looking at Luca.

"I can represent you," he says so quietly that I'm not sure I heard him correctly.

"You have a lawyer?" I ask although it doesn't really surprise me. I suspect he has gotten into plenty of trouble before that would have required a lawyer.

"No."

"No?"

"No, I am a lawyer."

I laugh. I can't help it. "You aren't a lawyer. And you realize this isn't something you can just lie about. When people actually need a lawyer, you can't just lie and fake it. You have to actually have a degree, a license to practice."

Luca sighs and reaches into his back pocket. He pulls out a card and hands it to me.

I skeptically look at the card. But it does have his name and a number, and it looks pretty official.

"It's fake. I know it is. It's a good fake, but it is still a fake."

Luca sighs. "It's not fake. I went back to law school after you and I broke up."

"What do you mean, back?"

"I had started going to law school before I met you. I hated it, so I dropped out. I was just a struggling surfer, barely making ends meet. I realized, after I met you, that I needed to get an actual degree. So, I went back and finished my last year. Now, I have my own practice."

My eyes are wide. I try to figure out what is the truth and what is a lie. My gut tells me that I can never trust him again. That every word is a lie. But I know that every single word can't be a lie. It's not possible.

"I don't believe you."

"I'm not asking you to. Yet. I'll prove it to you."

I frown. I'm pretty sure he could walk me into a law office that has his name on it where everyone called him by his name, and I wouldn't believe him. Hell, he could represent someone in court, a celebrity even, and I still wouldn't believe him. I don't think he can offer me any proof that would make me believe him.

"I'd like to see you try."

He smiles sadly. "I'll do my best. Can I take you home? I'm not sure you are in a good position to drive, and I want to make sure you get home okay. I can also leave you with some names and numbers of some really good lawyers if you don't want me to represent you." He touches me on the neck again.

"Yes," I say before I realize that he is using his touch to manipulate me into doing whatever he wants.

Luca stands up and then extends his hand to me. I take it.

"Does Skye need a ride home? Or do you need to be with her tonight?"

I laugh. "You are offering to take Skye home? I thought you were scared to death of her."

"I am. I just want you to be happy. Even if that means hanging out with Skye tonight instead of me."

"I love Skye, but she isn't great when it comes to emotional support. When it comes time to fight for the clinic, for me, she will be the best person to fight with. But she doesn't understand that some people just need to cry."

"Good. At least I don't have to worry about my balls getting kicked again tonight. Let's get you home."

I nod and lead Luca to my car. I toss him the keys to my car, and we both climb in. I tell him the directions while he puts the sleepy puppy into my lap. And then I close my eyes while I let Luca drive my car.

I'm trusting him to get me home. I'm trusting that he will drink with me tonight. Take care of me. I'm trusting that any lie he tells me tonight isn't going to destroy me.

8

LUCA

I PULL up in front of Ivy's large house and put her Jeep in park in the driveway. Her house is beautiful, and I have no doubt that she has at least a dozen animals housed inside. This right here is why I lied to her about being unemployed. She is the type of woman who expects the best and is able to get it for herself if her Prince Charming isn't able to. I don't want to be the kind of guy who offers nothing. I need to be useful. I need to provide for her. I need to be an equal with her.

I look over at Ivy, who is sound asleep in the seat next to me. Her head is resting against the window, and Sophie is curled up in her lap, snoring. I could look at them both like this forever. So calm and peaceful.

I know that today really hurt Ivy. She's been through a lot. I wish I could let her sleep like this until the pain was gone. Until the trial was over. Until she was proven innocent. Because I know in my heart that she is. And, soon, the world will know that for a fact. That Ivy Lane is nothing but perfect. She's an angel. She would never purposely hurt a puppy. There is no way.

But, as much as I want to let her sleep and forget about the pain, it's better if she deals with it now. And I don't want her to wake up with a crick in her neck from sleeping like that against the window. I'm done with causing her pain.

I get out of the car and walk over to her side. Well, at least I'm done causing her any more preventable pain. And this is definitely preventable.

But I will admit that a tiny part of me is happy with our current predicament. I'm happy that Ivy needs me tonight. I'm happy that I get to be here with her. I'm happy that I get to be the one who fixes things instead of fucking everything up in her life. I'm happy that I get a chance at telling her the truth that I tried to tell her almost two years ago.

I gently open the door on her side of the Jeep and ease her into my arms. She doesn't wake up as I lift her out of the Jeep, but Sophie, on the other hand, does. She jumps out of Ivy's arms and starts running down the driveway.

Shit.

"Sophie, come here!" I yell out to the puppy.

But she keeps running, her little legs carrying her much faster than I thought possible down the driveway.

So, I do the only thing left that I can think of. I start running down the driveway after her with Ivy bouncing in my arms.

"What—" she asks as she begins to stir in my arms. She flails for about a second when she realizes her body isn't on the ground and then grabs hold of my neck as she tries to keep herself from falling.

"Damn it, she's fast," I say to Ivy as I run down the driveway after Sophie, whose legs are carrying her tiny body faster than I thought possible.

Ivy laughs. "Put me down. You are never going to catch her this way."

I stop long enough to put Ivy down and then start running after Sophie again.

"Stop running," Ivy says, laughing at what I assume is how ridiculous I look while chasing after a tiny puppy.

I stop reluctantly. I don't know how stopping is going to enable me to catch Sophie.

"Sophie," Ivy calls out in a high-pitched voice.

Sophie stops running long enough to perk her ears up at the sound of her name.

"That's a good girl, Sophie," Ivy says, squatting down and holding her hand out. She makes clicking noises with her tongue and shakes something in her hand.

Sophie thinks for a second and then comes running toward Ivy. When she gets close to Ivy, she holds out her hand, and that's when I realize that she has a treat that she must have gotten from her pocket. She gently scoops up the puppy in her arms, and then she stands and looks at me.

I run over to where she is and take Sophie out of her arms, finally able to catch my breath, knowing that she isn't going to get run over by a car or something. Ivy cocks her head to one side as she looks at me with a strange look on her face. A look that I'm not used to seeing.

I pet Sophie on the head as I ask, "What is going on in that head of yours?"

The twinkle and light that was in her eyes just a second ago immediately vanishes. "You just surprise me; that's all."

"I know, I know. I shouldn't own a dog. I'm a terrible dog owner. I get it."

Ivy bites her lip, like she wants to say something but doesn't. "Come on. I need a drink."

"You still want me to come in and have a drink with you?" I ask, completely dumbfounded.

She stops walking to her front door and looks at me. "I need someone to pour me drinks until I'm so drunk that I can't move. Then, I need someone to carry me to bed and make sure I don't start drunk-dialing any of my exes. Can you be that guy who makes sure that all happens? Or do I need to call Skye?"

I laugh. "I can be that guy."

"Good. Now, come inside."

I follow Ivy up to her house. She opens the door and then is attacked by dogs, cats, and something that looks like a horse. Sophie immediately starts squirming in my arms and barking in her high-pitched voice, wanting to get down to join them all. I wait until I make sure the door is firmly shut, and then I let Sophie down. The dogs immediately turn their attention to the new puppy who has joined them.

"You remember all of them?" Ivy asks.

I nod. "Yes, that's Nala, the stinker who would come in between us anytime I got close to you. And Duke, the brave dog who would incessantly bark at me every morning, wanting me to take him out." I look around at the dog pack. "Where's Lucy?" I ask.

Lucy was always my favorite, Ivy's favorite as well. She was a sweetheart lab, and honestly, I think she was the only dog who liked me.

Ivy's eyes drop. "She passed away last year."

I feel the pain seep out of her body, surrounding us.

"I'm so sorry," are the only words I can say. I have nothing that will make the pain any easier for her.

"It's okay. She died peacefully in her sleep. She was a good dog. But it made more room for me to adopt Zoey here, who needed a good home," Ivy says, pointing to the animal who looks more like a horse than a dog.

I pet the dog on the head and then look up at Ivy as a tear falls down her cheek. It's strange, seeing her cry. I don't think she ever cried once in the year that we dated. Not once. But, since I've come here, she has cried twice. And I can't help but feel that I'm the reason the floodgate has opened.

"What do you want to drink?" I ask, trying to distract her from the pain.

I've also never seen Ivy drunk. And, if that is her goal, there are going to be a lot of firsts tonight.

"Moscow mule."

I chuckle. "Of course you want a complicated drink that I have no idea how to fix. Why couldn't you have asked for beer or wine or something?"

Ivy wipes the tear off her face. "I knew I should have called Skye to come over."

Ivy spends the next five minutes showing me exactly how to make a Moscow mule. She has to repeat herself a lot because I'm too distracted by being so close to her to actually pay attention to what she is saying. She's just wearing scrubs, but that doesn't stop me from imagining her breasts that are straining against the fabric. She smells like a mix of dogs, cats, and something sweet that is barely visible beneath the animal smells. But it's still there, and she smells just like I remember her smelling like.

"Luca!" Ivy snaps. "Seriously?"

"What?" I ask, not sure what she is referencing.

"You aren't paying attention to me at all, are you?"

I grin. "I'm paying attention to everything about you. Trust me."

She frowns. "Everything but my words."

"Yes. But your words aren't what matter. Your body is what matters."

She shakes her head as she carries her drink outside. The dogs immediately run outside, and I watch as Sophie enjoys herself in the pack.

"My words matter a heck of a lot. My brain matters. My thoughts matter."

I nod as I take a seat on the couch on her gorgeous patio that is big enough for twenty people. I glance out at the large field where the dogs are running around and then at the pool that has a fence surrounding it. I see now why she moved to Albuquerque. She has a lot more room for her money here than she did in San Diego.

"Of course your thoughts matter. That's not what I'm saying. I'm just saying that your body tells me a lot more of the truth than your words ever will. Even your thoughts, which I'm not privy to, lie to you."

She laughs. "The only person who lies to me is you. I don't lie to myself."

I raise an eyebrow. "Sure you do."

She shakes her head. "No, I don't."

We lock eyes, challenging each other without saying a word.

"You've never lied to yourself, like thinking a dress didn't make your butt look big even though you knew it did?"

"No."

"You've never lied to yourself when you told yourself that Skye was the right person to be your best friend?"

"No."

"You've never lied to yourself when you said you weren't going to get any more animals even though you knew you would?"

Ivy's eyes dart over to the group of dogs, and I know that she has gotten more cats since the last time I saw her.

"No."

"You've never lied to yourself when you told yourself that you didn't miss me when you did?"

She swallows hard, staring at me with anger in her eyes. "No," she snaps.

I grin and lean forward. "Liar. You've missed me. You've missed talking to someone normal who isn't Skye. You've missed my sexy grin. You've missed having a man who actually knows your body and how to handle you in bed. You've missed my cock between your legs. You might not miss the lies and pain. But you can't lie to me, Ivy. I can read you like an open book. You can't bluff. You can't lie. I know you, Ivy. I know that you've thought about me since we broke up."

"No."

"I can tell and not because of your words. Your words and your thoughts are saying no. That there is no way that you've ever thought about me. No way that you have missed me or thought of me in any way other than how cruel I was. Your words are lying to you and to me. Your body though is crystal clear about what you want. Your face is flushed. Your eyes are deep and heavy. Your throat is tight and dry. Your whole body is flushed and aching. Your words are trying to keep me at bay, but your body is inviting me in because, no matter how much you hate me, your body still wants me."

Ivy glares at me. "Fine. My body still wants you because, besides all your faults, you were decent in bed. But that is why I don't let my body make the decisions. My brain does, and my brain is telling me that fucking you tonight will do nothing but cause more pain tomorrow."

I grin. "You sure about that? Because I think even your brain is contemplating fucking me tonight. Weighing the pros and cons. Trying to decide if I am worth it or not. Just like deciding if, after drinking too much tonight, the hangover tomorrow is worth it or not."

"I'm not fucking you tonight. I'm getting drunk. That's the only mistake I'm making tonight."

I sit back and sip my Moscow mule. I've never had one before. It isn't bad. But, as I study Ivy, I know that, in about two-and-a-half drinks, she is going to be saying yes to a lot more than just alcohol. I just have to decide what body part of mine I'm going to be thinking with tonight. My brain or cock. I grin. I'm not sure if there is a difference.

"So, what would make you feel better right now?" I ask.

She needs something to distract her from the pain of thinking about being sued for killing a dog. That isn't why she is being sued. She's being sued because people are greedy.

"Watching you get run over by a car," she says with a straight face.

I laugh. "I have no doubt that is true. That that's what you want. But how about something that doesn't end with me in the hospital?"

She thinks for a minute while she drinks down most of her drink before jiggling it in front of me, indicating that she wants more. I take the glass and replace it with my own.

She frowns. "That's cheating. You are supposed to make me a new drink."

"Next time."

"You aren't going to drink with me?"

"I think someone needs to stay sober tonight to make sure we don't make a mistake."

"It doesn't matter if you stay sober or not. You don't make good decisions."

I nod. "You're right; I don't."

We stare at each other as she starts on her second drink.

"Why don't you yell at me for all the mistakes and lies I made? Would that make you happy—if you could tell me how horrible of a person I was?"

She thinks for a minute. "Maybe, but I try not to think about you when I can."

"Well, since I'm sitting here next to you, I think it would be hard for you not to think about me, don't you?"

She frowns and nods. "It was a mistake, having you drive me home, wasn't it?"

I nod. "Yes, but the game isn't to recount your mistakes. It is to recount mine."

"You'd better get a drink. We could be here all night."

I laugh. "It seems like you are stalling because you can't think of anything I did that hurt you."

She stares at me with intensity in her eyes. "You lied to me about your job, about graduating from college, about where you lived, about the fact that your parents had died when you were little, about liking dogs and cats even though you clearly didn't like animals, about not being able to surf even though you'd competed in endless competitions, about liking ice cream even though you were lactose intolerant. You lied to me about everything. Those were just the first things I could come up with without thinking too hard."

I nod. "I lied about all those things. But you are missing one pretty big one."

She sucks in a breath. "You lied about never hurting me. You lied when you said you loved me. You lied when you said you wanted to move in together and be together always."

I don't breathe when she says the things that were not lies. We both know that I loved her. We both know that I wanted to be with her forever. That I was willing to marry her. That I never wanted to hurt her, but it was a necessity. A necessity that she still doesn't understand because, when we broke up, I never got to finish telling her what I needed to.

"Tell me about our breakup."

"What? Why? You were there. You remember it as clearly as I do."

"It will make you feel better. I know you didn't tell Skye about our breakup—at least, not in great detail. I know that you are a private person, and none of your other friends really listen to you. So, tell me."

She shakes her head. "It's pointless. You were there. You know how it happened."

"I know I was there. But you need to vent about that night. You need to tell me how horrible it was for you. And I need to understand how much I hurt you."

Ivy stares at me for one second. Then, another. Then, another. One of the dogs barks, pulling her attention away from me for a second. When she turns back, she starts...

————

Two Years Earlier: Last Date
Ivy

"Tonight is the night, Skye," I say.

Skye rolls her eyes. "You don't think he is going to propose tonight, do you?"

"Yes. Of course he is. We've talked about it a lot. We love each other. We want to be together forever. We've been looking for places to buy together for weeks. Tonight is our one-year anniversary. He's a romantic. He's going to propose on some special night. He said he was going to take me to the beach tonight to play a game of sand volleyball."

"Then, why are you wearing a dress to play sand volleyball?" Skye asks, staring at my dress that hits me about mid thigh.

"Because he's not actually taking me to play sand volleyball. We don't play on Sunday nights. He's taking me back to the place where we first met, so he can propose."

"And what if you are wrong? What if he isn't going to propose?"

"He's proposing."

Skye rolls her eyes again. "I don't understand you two."

"That's just because you are a cynic and don't believe in marriage."

"Damn right I don't believe in that archaic tradition that makes women weak and submit to their husbands."

Now, I roll my eyes. "I'm not going to submit to my husband. That's not how our relationship works."

"You clearly don't know the history of marriage. Your father would pay a dowry for another man to take you away. You were property. You would be transferred from your father owning you to your husband owning you."

"Well, since I don't have a father, I don't have to worry about that. Seriously, Skye, can't you just be happy for me?"

Skye puts down the magazine that she has been staring intently at and walks over to me. She grabs hold of my shoulders and looks at me. "I'm only doing this because your parents are dead, and you don't have anyone to say these things to you."

I laugh. "Way to bring up that pain on one of the happiest days of my life."

Skye seriously looks at me. "I really do hope that today is one of your best days, followed by hundreds of best days. I really hope that for you. I want nothing but happiness for you. Whether Luca proposes tonight or not, you need to know that I love you. I always will."

I smile. "Thank you. I didn't know if you had it in you to be happy for another person who is getting married. I know you don't believe in marriage after all."

Skye sighs. "First of all, you are not getting married yet. You aren't even sure if you are getting engaged. Second of all, I can be happy for you if you are truly happy. It's just not what I want."

The doorbell to our apartment rings, and I light up. I raise my eyebrows at Skye, letting her know that this is it. This is the moment when everything changes.

I run to the door, unable to contain myself for a second longer. I throw the door open, watching it slam against the wall. I don't even wince like I usually do when Skye or Luca slams the door open. I don't care that the dent in the wall is getting bigger. I don't care at all. All I care about is getting to the person on the other side of the wall.

But, when I see Luca standing on the other side, my face drops. He's not wearing some nice outfit, like I was expecting. Instead, he's in his swim trunks, a tank top, and flip-flops. He doesn't even look like he's showered today.

His eyes travel up and down my body, taking in my dress, my curled hair, my overdone makeup. I look far too nice for just going to play sand volleyball.

He cocks his head to one side as he looks at me. "I did tell you that we were going to play sand volleyball, right?"

I nod. "Sorry. I just got home. I'll go change," I say, stuttering over my words.

I leave Luca standing in the doorway and run back into my bedroom to change. I don't look at Skye as I run past. I don't want to see an I-told-you-so look on her face.

I change quickly into a bikini and throw on a cover-up. I wipe as much makeup as I can off my face and then tie my hair up. Then, I run back to meet Luca, who is standing in the living room with his hands in his pockets, smiling at me as I enter.

"You ready now?" he asks with a knowing grin on his face.

He knows exactly what he is doing. He knows he is playing with my emotions. He knows that today is the one-year anniversary of when we first met. That I'm expecting something big.

And, if he proposes to me tonight when I look like shit and smell like ass, then...then...then...I'll still say yes because it's what I want. It would just be nice to have a nice picture of us. But I guess that doesn't really matter.

"Yep," I say, barely meeting his eyes as I walk out the door.

Luca follows me, and then he drives me to the beach in silence.

When we get to the beach, I see most of the guys from the volley-ball team already there. I frown. We really are just playing volleyball. Maybe, afterward, there will be something special.

But, after playing for more than forty-five minutes, I no longer believe that anything is going to happen afterward. Luca is acting exactly like he would on any other night, and it's the same with the guys. And I know at least two of the guys can't keep their mouths shut. Still, I haven't pressed them much, so there isn't much for them to keep their mouths shut about. Luca is on the opposite team as me tonight, so I have a good opportunity to question Troy, one of his friends and the guy most likely to spill the beans.

"So, Troy, is anything new going on with Luca that I don't know about?" I ask, trying to make it as obvious as possible that I know something is up and that he just needs to give it up.

Troy looks over at me, and I can immediately tell he knows something. His eyes are big, and he's sweating more than usual.

"No, I don't think so," he says as the ball flies over. But he misses it completely. Not something that Troy usually does.

"Really, Troy? Nothing going on?"

"Other than him getting into law school, I can't think of anything."

I freeze when he says that, and the ball comes flying over and hits the sand right at my feet.

"Oh, come on, baby! You can do better than that. You need to focus!" Luca shouts from across the net, teasing me.

I smile at him, trying not to let my fear and the fact that my world is crashing down on me noticeable.

"Oh, yeah, I already knew that. But Luca has still been acting weird. Do you know what it could be?" I ask, lying to Troy.

The ball comes over, and this time, I focus long enough to dig the ball up.

Troy thinks. "His ex-girlfriend has been driving him crazy. You know how she can get. Once he's rid of her, he'll be more relaxed. You know how he can get when she's around."

I nod like I know how he is with his ex-girlfriend, but in all honesty, I have no clue. I have no freaking clue how he acts when his ex-girlfriend is around because I have no idea who she is, and I had no idea that she was around.

"No, I don't think that's it. It's something else," I say, looking for more information out of Troy. Evidently, there is a lot of information that I don't have a clue about.

Troy sighs. "Fine. You can't tell him I said this, but Luca is planning a big surprise for you. We all know it's your one-year anniversary; that's why we are here. So, stop worrying. Let's play volleyball and beat these guys."

I nod.

We do beat them. We destroy them.

As it turned out, I'm actually pretty good at volleyball, and almost always, whatever team I'm on wins.

But all I could think about the whole time was that Luca had lied to me. About his job. About his ex-girlfriend. And who knows what else?

How can I say yes to marrying a man who has done that to me? How can I be happy tonight, celebrating one year together, when that year has been nothing but a lie, followed by another and another?

Luca runs over to me, giving me a high five and a kiss for a job well done. I try to smile. I try to pretend like nothing is bothering me. But he knows. He always knows how I'm feeling. What I need. I, on the other hand, know nothing about Luca. Nothing. He's smiling, but I don't know if that means he's happy and he loves me or he's happy that I haven't discovered the lies yet.

"I have something I need to ask you," he whispers into my ear before kissing my hair.

"I bet you do."

He frowns and pulls me aside. "What's wrong?"

"Nothing. Nothing is wrong whatsoever."

He studies me closer. "You're lying to me. What's wrong?"

I chuckle, but it's not happy. It's a chuckle full of sadness and regret. "You, of all people, can't be mad at me for lying."

He cocks his head to one side in confusion. "What are you talking about?"

"I'm talking about the fact that you have probably lied to me about everything!"

His eyes are wide, frozen. He's in shock. That much, I can tell. But it's also very obvious that he knows exactly what I'm talking about.

"Do you want to talk first, or do you want me to?" I ask, crossing my arms, like that is going to protect me.

He thinks for a second while I raise an eyebrow.

"Maybe you should tell me what you know?" he half-asks, half-says.

"Coward."

He sighs. "I don't know what you want from me. I don't know what lies you have been told."

"That's exactly the problem. What lies have you told me? What is the truth, and what is a lie?"

"The truth is, I love you. The truth is, I want you in my life forever. I want to marry you. I want to tell you the truth. I want you to know everything about me."

My heart melts the tiniest bit at his words because they are what I have been waiting for him to say every day since we first met. It's exactly what I wanted to hear today. He has a ring. He is going to propose. I was right.

"The lies are...everything else."

Now, it's my turn for my eyes to pop open. "What do you mean, everything else?"

He sucks in a deep breath. "Basically, everything else is a lie. I lied about my job. I lied about not dating anyone else while dating you. I lied about where I lived. I lied about simple things, too, like my favorite food and drinks."

I think my heart has stopped. "How could you have lied about everything? Why would you? I mean..." I can't form words. I can't process what he is saying. I can't comprehend how someone could do what he did. *How do you lie about fucking everything?*

Luca opens his mouth to answer, but I can't stay here and listen. I don't want the answers. I can't be with someone who has lied to me about freaking everything. I don't want a reason. I don't want to understand and feel sorry for him. I don't want to hear a sob story about abuse or how he wasn't loved as a child. There is no excuse for lying to me. There is no way I can ever trust him again. There is no way I can ever forgive him. No way to be with him.

"Just stop. I don't want to hear anything else. We're done."

I run away, completely broken by a complete stranger. I never thought a stranger would be able to do that to me. I never thought that someone I loved could be a stranger. But they both happened. I'm broken, and I don't think I'll ever be able to fix it.

———

Present

Luca

"That's how you remember it happening, huh?" I ask, studying her and waiting for the backlash that is sure to come.

Ivy frowns. "That is what happened."

"Minus one little important word that you got wrong."

She folds her arms across her chest, like she does when she is angry. "And what word would that be?"

"You said I had something that I needed to ask you."

She nods. "That is what you said."

"No, it wasn't. I wasn't going to propose that night, even as much as I wanted to. I hadn't bought a ring. It wouldn't have been fair to you if I had. There was too much you didn't know about."

"Obviously."

"I said, I needed to tell you something. That is the key difference."

"So, you are telling me that you were going to confess to me about everything that night? Was that what you were going to tell me? That you had been lying to me for our entire relationship?"

"No. That wasn't what I was going to say," I say, looking down at her glass that is empty again.

I don't think she is drunk. She's just had enough that what I'm about to say might be a little easier for her to take. Then again, she might slap me and say that I'm lying again. But she needs to know what I wanted to tell her that night. I need to tell her because it has been eating at me every day for the last two years. I thought it was better that she'd just left that night without me telling her. I thought that it was like the stars had aligned and prevented me from revealing one of my deepest, darkest secrets. I thought I had been saved. But, instead of being saved, I've been tortured with the fact that the one person I needed to tell this to didn't know the truth.

"Then, what? What could you have said that would have possibly made me think about you differently? What could you have possibly said that would have made me think twice? That would have gotten me to stay long enough for you to explain anything to me?"

I look into her dark brown eyes, considering what I might see in them after I tell her the truth. Happiness. Anger. Fear. Frustration. Sadness. Understanding. Pain.

I have no idea how she is going to react, and I think that is what I hate the most. I always know what is going on in her head. I always know exactly how she is going to feel when I do something. I knew that night that she expected me to propose, which is the exact reason that I never would have proposed that day.

I lied to her countless times. I told her countless stories. But the words that are about to leave my lips are the hardest words I've ever told her. Because how she reacts is going to decide everything.

"I'm a prince."

9

IVY

I FLUTTER my eyelashes quickly multiple times in a row, like that is going to change what Luca just said. I rub my ears, like it's going to erase the words I just heard him say. There is no way it is true. There is no way that anything he says is true.

So, why is my heart racing in my chest?

"You're a prince," I say slowly, repeating the words he said.

Maybe my mind has gone mad, and I just heard completely different words than what he said. Maybe it's a defense mechanism that I have developed to prevent me from hearing his bullshit. Maybe? Hopefully?

He nods slowly. "I'm a prince."

I rapidly blink again, looking at him. He doesn't look like a prince. He looks like the same beach bum I met three years ago. The only difference between then and now is his hair is a little shorter. Lines around his eyes are a little deeper, showing his age. But that's it.

"You're telling me you're a prince. Like the Prince of England? You know I'm not that gullible. You know that I know that the Prince of England is..." *Shit, I know the answer to this.*

"I'm not the Prince of England."

"Obviously. I knew you were lying."

"You know that more countries have princes than just England though, right?"

I nod. "But that is the only one that still does anything. I mean, even if you are telling me the truth. Even if you are a prince, it doesn't really matter. It's just a silly title that means you have people call you that. Like the same way with people who are knighted. You don't actually rule a country. If you did, you would be living in that country instead of lying to unsuspecting women like me."

"I'm a prince. Like a real prince who will someday rule a whole country. With responsibilities to a whole country of people."

I laugh. I can't help it. This is the most ridiculous thing I have ever heard. Sure, I've read books where the guy is secretly a prince. But this isn't a fairy tale. This is real life. This is my life. There is no way I dated a prince for a whole year and never figured it out. Someone, somewhere, would have noticed and told me. Tony would have told me if no one else did. Or has Luca lied to everyone in his life about who he is? I wouldn't put that past him.

Luca raises his eyebrows at me as I laugh.

"This is ridiculous. You know that, right?"

He nods. "It sounds ridiculous. I know that. But it's the truth."

I just shake my head, laughing. "There is not enough proof in the world to convince me that you are a prince."

Luca pulls out his phone. He types something in and then hands it to me. I stare at the screen and scroll quickly. There is article after article talking about him being the Prince of Monaco. About him attending balls. About him living in America to study law and meet a woman before he returns to the country to learn how to govern it.

"This is not possible," I whisper as I look at the phone and then back to Luca and then back to the phone.

It's almost like he is two completely different people. If I didn't know Luca well, I would swear that he is just a good body double. Just someone who looks similar to the prince but isn't actually him. But I know Luca well. And I know the guy in the pictures. I know the sexy grin, the lips that curl up just a tiny bit more on the right than the left, the tiny mole under his left eye, and the hair that, if you look closely, has just the faintest bit of gray coming through despite not being old enough to have gray hair.

It's Luca. Yes, he's a little more polished in the photos than he is in real life. Yes, in half of the pictures, he's dressed in formal clothing that is so different from anything I've ever seen him wear before. Yes, he has a woman in a nice ballgown next to him. But it's Luca. Charming, beautiful, lying Luca.

"Explain. Now," I say, needing answers even though I'm still not sure I believe him.

These could be fake. They could have been Photoshopped. I might never date or trust Luca again, but I have to have answers. I have to know why he hid this from me. I just need to know.

Luca takes his phone back and lays it on the end table next to him. He then sits for a second, and I watch his body exhale and then inhale and then exhale again. He's stalling.

"Luca, there is nothing you can say to me anymore that is going to shock me. Nothing that is going to make me hate you any more than I already do."

He looks up at me with puppy-dog eyes. "You hate me?"

I nod with a small smile. "I thought it was obvious."

He nods slowly as he leans back in his chair. "I guess it is obvious. I just hope so goddamn much that it isn't true. That you don't hate me."

"And why is that?" I ask, my heart racing in my chest.

He grins. "I thought it was obvious."

My heart races faster because it is, and as much as I hate Luca, my heart doesn't. My heart still aches for him. My heart still holds out hope that we can try again.

"Because I still love you, Ivy. I've never stopped loving you."

Luca leans forward, and I feel my body moving forward, leaning into him, needing to hear every word. Needing to see if his heartbeat is beating just as fast.

"I've tried to get over you, Ivy. Trust me, I have. I even proposed to someone else. I told her the truth. I tried to make her a princess because I knew she would be good at it. I knew it was exactly what she wanted. It's what my parents wanted. It's what the country wanted. But I just couldn't. I couldn't stop thinking about you."

I soak in his words. "You lied to me because you didn't think I would make a very good princess?"

He stops for a second and looks me straight in the eyes as I prepare for either another lie or a truth that will sting.

"There would be some issues with you being a princess," he says slowly, honestly.

"Like?"

He sighs and rubs his neck, avoiding eye contact with me for a minute. "Like the fact that you have this amazing job and career that you wouldn't be able to keep doing—at least, not long-term—once you became a princess." He pauses. "Like your past."

I nod, but it doesn't make any of the facts harder to hear. I already know the main reason that he would never want me as a princess, and it has nothing to do with the fact that I have my own career goals. My career is a challenge that we would have to overcome if I could even still work after the lawsuit, but it isn't a deal-breaker. The deal-breaker is that, if anyone digs far enough into my history, they will find out what I used to do to pay for vet school.

"You used to like the fact that I'd worked as a stripper," I say, smiling.

His eyes drop down my body, and I know he is undressing me with his eyes. I know he is imagining the many, many strip shows I used to give him. I know he is imagining how perfect our bodies fit together.

I hear the faintest of growls come from his throat.

"I love that fact. You would make my perfect princess. But you need to know why I lied."

He tucks a strand of hair behind my ear, and I lose it. I'm putty. I don't care about his lies. I don't care about the fact that we have absolutely no future together. I don't care about the pain that I will feel afterward. All I care about is one night.

"I lied to you to protect you. To keep you at bay because, no matter how great my life sounds, it's not. My life is horrible. I wouldn't wish my life on anyone. Especially not someone I love."

His answer is bullshit, and we both know it. But my body is too far gone to back out now. My mind has already made all the rationale I need. The decision has already been made.

I lean forward just an inch closer to Luca. Because, as much as I want this, I want *him* to make this mistake, not *me*. He says he still loves me. I'm not sure if that is true or not. But, if he does, I want him to feel just a tiny bit of what it feels like to be hurt by someone you love.

I lick my lips, and then I let my hand slowly trail down my body. I'm only wearing scrubs, so I know that I'm not in anything that is sexy enough to really get his attention, but I do know how to move my body. I do know how to look confidently at a man and tell him exactly what I want.

And the way that Luca is looking at me tells me how badly he wants me.

"Your move," I say, letting the words fall out of my mouth in a purr.

His eyes widen when he realizes what I'm saying. It's more to decide whatever we do next. Kiss. Strip. Fuck. It's all on him. This is not my mistake to make. This is his mistake because the one thing I've learned in the last three years since meeting Luca, is how to keep men at a distance. How to guard my heart. I know how to guard my heart, and I don't plan on letting Luca in.

I see the struggle in his eyes. I feel the tension in his body.

"No. Nothing is going to happen tonight. You're in pain, and when anything happens, I want it to be because you care about me and want to give us a chance again. Not because you just want to remember what it is like to fuck me."

"Fair enough. Just know that there is no way that is ever going to happen." I stand up and grab my empty glass. "Another?" I ask.

Luca shakes his head.

I smile as I walk to the door, making sure that my hips sway. He thinks he's won. He thinks he can control me, himself, and everything around us. Boy, is he wrong.

I grab the sliding door handle and begin to pull it open when I feel his rough hand on top of mine. It's hesitant but only for a second, and then his lips are on my neck, kissing up and down my skin, making me shiver every damn time his lips touch my skin.

I grin, and then my lips part when I feel him push up against me. I feel his cock already hard against my ass. I struggle to breathe—not from the pressure of him against me, but because I get to have him again. It's something I wanted, if I'm being completely honest with myself, for the last three years. Just one fuck. Just one night. Then, I can get over him. I will realize that it isn't as good as what I thought it was. I will realize that I was just making it better in my mind. That it isn't any better than with any other guy. Then, I will be able to move on.

I'm getting my chance.

Luca grabs my chin and turns my head so that he can kiss my lips. His mouth crashes with mine. His tongue tangles with mine. And I realize that I'm screwed. Because just this one kiss is better than anything I've experienced in the last two years.

It's just sex. Just because we are good at it doesn't mean anything. It just means that Luca has had too much practice. That's why he's so good. That's all this is. I'm not making a mistake.

Luca turns my whole body so that I'm facing him. He pushes my hands high over my head as his mouth claims mine. His body presses up against me, just like I remember.

I'm making a mistake.

"You sure you still want this, baby? I can stop at anytime. Can you?" he says, challenging me, letting me know that he is still in control.

But I'm done letting him have any control. I pull one hand free. I reach down and grab his hard cock a little too hard. "I'm just fine, baby."

"Where's your bed?" Luca growls.

I grab his cock harder as I grin. "You don't get to see my bedroom."

I push his head down until he is kneeling on the hard floor of my patio. His hands slide down the sides of my body as he moves down, and he slips his hand into the side of my scrub pants. He slips my pants and panties off in one motion. He looks at me one last time, giving me a chance to say no. His eyes show me how much he missed this.

When I push his head into my pussy, he obliges me. He attacks me with his lips, his tongue. I lose it. Fuck, he remembers exactly how I like it. And he does more with his tongue than I remember him being capable of doing. Or any other man being capable of doing.

"Fuck, Luca. Slow down, or I'm going to..."

I can't get any more words out because he is taking me there so fast. I'm going to come all over his face before I've even had a chance to enjoy him.

But then his tongue stops. His lips barely hover over my pussy.

"What? Don't stop. That's not what I meant," I groan.

He smiles against my pussy. "I'll kiss you again. In your bedroom."

God, I hate him. I absolutely hate him. How does he always find a way to take back the control?

"Fine," I growl, no longer caring if I have control right now.

I just want to come. I just want to forget about my shitty day and shitty ex-boyfriend. I just want to use him like he used me.

Who cares if he is in control of my body? I'm in control of his heart.

"Good girl," he says, lifting my body up because I can barely move after my almost orgasm.

He softly kisses my lips, like he knows that even a kiss is enough to send me over the edge and he isn't ready for that yet. He doesn't want me to come until he says I can come.

He glances back over his shoulder as we walk into my house. "Will the dogs be okay?"

I grin. "They will be fine. This is going to be quick anyway."

He frowns. "Quick first. And then long and slow. And then quick and then slow until I've had my fill. It's been too long. I need you in every way possible."

I shake my head. "I'm only promising one right now. Just one."

His frown deepens as he realizes what I'm saying.

"My bedroom is down the hallway, on the left."

He shuts the door behind him, but he doesn't start walking down the hallway. Instead, he walks into my kitchen and sets me on the counter.

"What are you doing? I said, my bedroom is down the hallway. Are you getting supplies for our one time?"

His eyes darken as he kneels down again and takes my pussy back in his mouth. I scream from his touch. I moan. I cry out. I lose my mind. And it is the last thing I remember before I pass out from the feeling.

10

LUCA

I DIDN'T FUCK IVY. I couldn't. I couldn't just have her once and then not have her again and again. But I realize now, as I lie in her bed and watch her sleep, just how much of a mistake that was. Anytime I turn down the woman I love is going to be a mistake. I should have her any chance I get.

I watch her sleep, wondering if she will let me have her when she wakes up. I gave her countless orgasms last night, just all with my tongue instead of my dick. I thought it was the right thing to do. I thought it would be easier than having her and not getting to have her again. But it just made it worse.

I thought it would give me the control back again. I thought that making her come would just make her want me more. Enough to give in to a whole night of sex instead of just one time. She didn't give in though. Instead, she passed out. I gave her the control—or so she thought. I gave her control for one night, but this is exactly why I never give her control. She makes bad decisions when she has the control. I know what she really wanted, and neither of us got it.

Ivy's alarm clock goes off, and she hits it automatically. She starts getting out of bed like I'm sure she does every morning. Ivy does everything with purpose. And, unlike most people, she actually loves her job and wants to get up early in the morning to go do it.

"Good morning," I say as I watch a naked Ivy walk toward her bathroom.

She jumps. "What the hell?" She grabs at her chest when she sees it's just me. "Jesus, Luca. You scared the crap out of me."

I grin. "Sorry."

She stares at me, not bothering to cover her naked body. I think she thinks she can use her body to control me. And she might be right. I've just had more practice at controlling others than she has. She's not good at it.

"What are you still doing here? And where did you put that puppy of yours? I'm sure she's destroyed half of my house by now," she says like she cares. She has this house because of her dogs, not because she loves nice things. She doesn't care if Sophie chewed anything up or not.

"I put her in the kennel I found in the spare bedroom."

She nods.

"And I wanted to make sure you were okay before I left."

She rolls her eyes. "You didn't give me that good of an orgasm, you know. I'm fine."

I lower the covers and watch as her eyes go straight to my naked cock that has been hard most of the night while I've thought about her. It was the hardest thing in the world, not to touch her. I walk over to her as she looks at me like she wants to devour me.

"That's not what I was talking about."

"Oh," is all she says, still staring at my dick.

"You could have had it last night if you had promised more than one time. You can still have it now," I say.

She quickly brings her eyes up and looks me in the eyes while crossing her arms across her chest. "What were you talking about?" she asks, ignoring what I said.

"I wanted to make sure that you were not still feeling like the world was going to end because you were being sued and that I was serious when I said that I would represent you if you wanted."

She shakes her head. "I'm fine. I've been through worse."

She means with me, I think.

"So, you will let me help you? You'll let me fix this?"

"This isn't something you can just fix. You have to actually be a lawyer. You have to know what you are doing. You have to be able to put your feelings aside and do what is right, not what is best for me."

"I'll always do what is best for you."

She looks at me with sad eyes. "No. You do what is best for you."

I sigh. "So, can I make you breakfast? Take you to work? Do anything for you today?"

"No. I'm not working today."

She starts walks into her bathroom, and I watch in disappointment as she puts on a robe before reemerging.

"Great. Then, we can hang out, and I can help you with your case."

She shakes her head. "I already have other plans."

"With Skye? You can tell her you're busy."

"No. Not with Skye."

"Then, with whom?" I ask.

She shrugs. "Some guy from Tinder."

"What?"

She smiles and shrugs again. "I have a date."

She starts walking out of the bedroom and is greeted by her dogs and cats licking her hands and wagging their tails—well, the dogs do anyway—all ready to be fed and let outside.

I'm stuck frozen, imagining her on a date with someone else. It's not fucking happening. She can't date someone else after I had my face buried in her pussy last night. She's not the type of girl that is okay with that. She is a one-man kind of girl.

I quickly move out of the fog and run after her. She is standing at the back patio door and opens it to let the dogs out. I notice that Sophie is in her arms. She pets her head one last time and is rewarded with a lick before she places the pup down to go run after the others. She leaves the door open and then walks over to the coffeemaker.

"You aren't serious, right? You're just mad at me and trying to get back at me."

"You want any coffee?" she asks, ignoring me.

I walk over to Ivy. I grab her shoulders and force her to stop moving around the kitchen. I need her to look at me. I need her to answer me.

"You aren't going out on a date tonight with a complete stranger. Right?"

She huffs, and then her big brown eyes look up at me with a tiny twinkle because she knows exactly what she is doing to me. "Yes, I think that is exactly what I'm doing."

My heart sinks. "You can't..."

She raises an eyebrow. "I can't? Are you serious right now? Who made you king over me?"

"Don't...please."

"It doesn't matter if I go on a date tonight or not. You and I are never going on a date. Last night..." She pauses and looks out at the dogs that are starting to run back inside. She walks over to where she keeps the dog food in the kitchen and begins to scoop some out into the bowls that line the wall of her dining room.

I slowly walk over and wait until she has finished scooping all the food into the bowls, and the dogs begin to eat the food.

I softly touch her arm. "Last night what?"

She takes a deep breath. "Last night was a mistake. For both of us. Let's just forget about it and move on with our lives. I'm tired of playing games with you. I think I finally got the closure I needed. That we both needed. I don't think you should represent me. I think we should just move on."

I narrow my eyes at her. "Can you really do that? Can you really just move on and forget last night even happened? Can you forget that I lied to you? Can you forget that I'm a prince?"

"Yes."

"Can you forget about our kisses?"

I lean down and softly, tenderly kiss her on the lips. And I know I'm stealing all the air from her body.

"Can you forget about how I touch you?"

I tuck a strand of her curly hair behind her ear.

"Can you forget about how I lick your pussy? Can you forget about how my dick feels inside you? Can you forget about how I love you?"

"Yes," she says in barely a whisper.

I nod. "If that's what you really want."

I walk over to Sophie, who has finished the bowl of food that Ivy laid down for her. I scoop up the puppy. "Have a good time on your date. I hope he's the one you've been looking for."

I look at Ivy one last time just in case this is the last time I ever see her, but I don't really believe that it could be the last time I ever see her. I can't believe that, not yet. I can't let her go this easily.

A plan starts forming in my head. She says she is tired of playing games, but that is exactly what we are doing. Playing games with each other for control until one of us breaks. She might have won this round, but the next round is mine.

11

IVY

I HAVEN'T BEEN able to think since Luca left this morning. All I've wanted to do all morning is pick up the phone and tell him to come back and fuck me. When I said I made a mistake last night, that mistake wasn't that I turned him down. The mistake was not saying that I would fuck him more than once so that he would fuck me. That was what I needed to get over. I needed to have that experience one last time, so I could remember how he was the same as every other man or could see that he was the best I'd ever have. But at least I would have known.

Sex isn't a reason to stay with someone. It isn't a reason to forgive someone. It's just sex.

And I want it desperately.

I've tried masturbating, but even a vibrator is not enough to rid my brain of Luca.

I've tried taking a long bath.

I've tried going for a run.

I've tried watching TV.

Nothing does anything to make me forget about Luca. But there is one last thing I haven't tried that could still give me hope to get over him. Tonight's date.

Skye found him for me on Tinder. I'm sure he would be up for a one-night stand. That's about all I can handle anyway. With everything going on in my life, I don't think I can handle balancing a guy and the lawsuit.

I do have to thank Luca for one thing. He's distracted me from the pain and fear. Instead, I'm just a horny mess.

I have an hour until my date is supposed to pick me, so I do the one thing I've been avoiding since Luca left. I run to my office and pull up Google. My fingers pause over the keys while I contemplate if I'm really going to do this or not.

After a few seconds, my fingers start typing *Luca Mores*. Dozens of articles pull up. I start with his Wikipedia page. He's a prince. It says it on the first line of the page.

Jesus, I think as I lean forward in the chair.

I want to read more, but my eyes can't get past that first line. Prince. It's such a crazy concept. But it will make a good story to tell the grandkids someday. That I once dated a prince. He was a lying, cheating scumbag. But he was still a prince.

I force my eyes to read past that line, and I scan until I find the next piece of information that I had been looking for. He graduated from Stanford with a law degree.

I sink back in my chair. He hasn't been lying to me this time. He's been telling me the truth. That means that he love—nope, I'm not going there.

I shake my head. This has to be some elaborate lie that I almost fell for. Again. He's not a prince. Just a liar.

I hear the dogs barking, playing down the hallway from my office, and I lean back further in my chair to see what they are doing. A second later, I feel the chair give out, and I'm falling to the floor.

"Shit," I curse as I hit the floor.

The dogs come running in and start licking my face.

I laugh. "Thank God for you guys."

But, when I look down at my shirt and pants that are now covered in dog slobber and hair, I remember the downside to having dogs. I sigh as I get up. I guess I'd better change before Van, my date, comes.

The doorbell rings, and I run to go open it with the dogs following closely behind me. I throw the door open, trying my best not to look frazzled, but I am.

My eyes widen when I see the man on the other side of the door.

"Hi, I'm Van," the man says, holding out a single rose to me while he leans against my doorframe.

"I'm Ivy," I say, slowing taking the flower from him before thinking I'm going to kill Skye later.

This man looks almost identical to Luca in every way.

"Do you want to come in for a drink first?"

I watch as Van looks down at my dogs in disgust. It's clear that he doesn't want to get dog hair on his designer jeans.

"Thanks, but I don't want us to miss our reservation."

I nod. "Let me just get my purse, and I'll be ready to go."

I don't bother calling the dogs away from Van as I walk back to my bedroom to get my purse. He might look like Luca—both have the too-long blond hair, fair skin, and blue eyes—but other than that, Van seems to be the opposite of Luca. Luca would have gladly come in for a drink even if that meant missing our reservation. He would have done anything I wanted. He just wanted to make me happy.

No, that's not true. He made me happy until he started lying his ass off, which was almost immediately.

I grab my purse. I'm going to give Van a chance. Although I don't know how I'm going to fuck him and not think of Luca.

"I'm ready," I say to Van, who is standing in my entryway, trying to keep my dogs from licking him to death.

"Good. Let's go." He immediately walks out my front door and toward his car without waiting for me.

I quickly lock up and then run out to where he is already climbing into his Porsche.

I sigh. Luca would have opened my door for me.

I walk over to the passenger side and climb in. Van starts pulling out of my driveway.

"So, where are we going for dinner?"

"I have reservations at Café DeLuce."

"Oh, wow. That's a nice restaurant. I should have worn something nicer."

Van glances down at me. "Do you have anything nicer? Never mind. Don't worry about it. We don't have time. They'll let us in. They always do."

I frown. I think I look fine. Better than fine. I'm in a dress and heels, for goodness' sake. I know I'm not wearing diamonds and a ballgown, but I still look nice. And I like this dress' hidden pockets for random things. Luca would have complimented me about how nice I looked and not given a fuck about a dress code at a restaurant.

I've got to stop thinking about Luca like this. It's not giving Van a fair chance.

I glance over at Van, trying to think of questions to ask him, when he reaches for the radio and cranks the music up. He puts the top down on his car.

I sigh. *So much for making conversation.*

We get to the restaurant, and the valet opens my door for me. I climb out and wait for Van to come over and at least walk next to me or hold my hand or place a hand on the small of my back. He does none of those things. Instead, he just walks straight into the restaurant. I can't walk as fast as him in my heels, so by the time I make it in, he is already arguing with the hostess about which table he wants.

I give the hostess an apologetic smile as she takes us to our table. But, if I had only known then what I know now, I would have left immediately.

He orders oysters even though I said I was allergic.

He orders a bottle of white wine even though I said I preferred red.

He sends our food back on three separate occasions, saying that our food wasn't cooked correctly.

He rambles on about his job. He's some kind of agent for actors or something. I don't really know because I wasn't listening.

Whenever I talk about my job, he just says that he doesn't like animals and doesn't understand how anyone else could.

His eyes stay on my breasts for at least three-quarters of our meal, and while I don't mind guys staring, it is a little much and creepy.

But none of this is the worst part of our meal. The worst part is that, the whole time, all I can do is compare him to Luca. How Luca would have ordered exactly what I wanted, even a cheeseburger from down the street. He wouldn't have care if I ordered red wine even though we were at a seafood restaurant and should order white with our meal. He would have stared at my breasts, but he would have made it known that it was because he found my body more beautiful than any other woman's in the restaurant, not because he was just a guy who liked boobs.

The waiter brings our check, and I'm thankful that our date has come to an end. I've definitely decided that I just want to take him somewhere and fuck him because there is no way in hell that I want to go on a second date with him. But he is good-looking, so it would be a shame not to fuck him. He's got to be good in bed. That's probably the only thing he has going for him.

But, when the waiter brings the check, he doesn't grab it. He just lets it sit there while he messes with something on his phone. Usually, I would wait a guy out who does this. I don't mind splitting a bill on a date, but I refuse to be the only one who pays, especially when I didn't pick the restaurant or have a good time. But I'm so desperate to get out of here that I pay for our meal.

"You ready to go?" he asks when I finish paying.

"Yes," I say sharply, not even sure if I'm going to be able to fake it long enough to have sex with this guy or not when he doesn't even thank me for paying for his meal.

I throw my napkin down and start walking out of the restaurant, not bothering to wait for Van. I walk outside and stand, waiting for the valet to get his car. I'm tempted to call an Uber to come pick me up, but at least his convertible is enjoyable to ride in, and I can decide on the way home if I want to fuck him or not.

I hear loud laughter coming from a couple walking down the

sidewalk. I turn in their direction and then freeze. Luca is walking with some blonde woman down the street. They are in casual clothes. Jeans and a nice shirt for him and a much-too-short sundress for her.

He stops when he sees me, like he wasn't expecting to see me here, but I know he has to be lying. He planned this. How? I don't know, but this has Luca's stench all over it.

"What are you doing here?" I growl at him.

He holds on to the woman's hand. "I'm on a date. This is Hannah. Hannah, this is Ivy. She's an ex. I am helping her with a lawsuit. She's the one I told you about, who is being sued," he says to Hannah.

I frown, my blood boiling. I don't like that he talked to Hannah about me. And especially not in such a negative light.

"Sorry to interrupt. You enjoy your date," I say, trying to keep what is left of my dignity intact.

They don't leave though.

"You should really go. My date was just getting the car, and then we are headed home to have some hot sex," I say. Then, my face turns bright red.

Why did I have to say the part about the sex?

Luca looks around me. "Isn't that your date leaving?"

I turn and look at where Luca is staring, and I start running after Van, who is driving away in his car. He either didn't notice that I wasn't in the car or he didn't care. Either way, he has left me stranded.

I stop running after him and just stand on the sidewalk in disbelief. This night can't get any worse than it already is.

"I can drive you home," Luca says.

I turn to look at him and notice that his date has disappeared in the three minutes that I spent running after Van. It takes me a second to realize what just happened, but when I do, I can't control my anger anymore.

I hit Luca on the arm over and over. "You lying bastard!"

"Whoa. What are you talking about?"

"Don't play dumb! I don't know how you did it, but you hired Van to treat me like that. You hired Hannah to make me jealous. You set this whole thing up. Van was texting you, telling you that we were just about to leave. That's why you were here when we came out. You're still playing games!"

Luca exhales. "All I did was pay Van, whom you were already going on a date with, to text me when you were leaving. That's it. Everything else he did, that was him. And, yes, Hannah is a friend whom I took out to dinner in exchange for making you jealous."

I shake my head, trying to keep the tears at bay. Because I want to hate him and love him at the same time. I hate that he is still playing games, but I love that he still wants me.

"I hate you," I say, telling him at least half of my feelings.

"I know."

"No." I cross my arms across my chest and turn away from Luca, not concerned. Not wanting to look at his smirk any longer.

He makes me so mad that I want to punch something.

No, him, I think.

I want to punch him. I hate him. I hate his games. But I know that he's never going to leave me alone. This is going to be a constant struggle between us until one of us finally wins at this game he's playing. I need to find a way to beat him at his own game. How? I have no idea. I have to find a way to make this stop.

I turn back to face Luca, who's still standing with a smug grin on his face. He thinks he's won. He thinks I've given up, and I'm going to let him drive me home. But the only way I'm going to figure out how to defeat him is by spending more time with him. Only then can I form a real plan, and if I have to spend time with him, there's only one way, but I'm going to find it enjoyable.

"That was fast. I thought it would take me following you, groveling at your feet, for blocks until I convinced you to let me take you home," Luca remarks.

I smile slowly and place my hands on my hips. "Oh, you're not taking me home."

"I'm not?"

"No. You're taking me to the nearest hotel that has at least three stars. And then you're going to fuck me until I forget all about the lies tonight. Until I forgive you."

"Forgiving me is going to take a long time, isn't it?" he asks, still grinning like an idiot.

I nod. "A very long time."

Luca pulls out his phone, I assume to search for a hotel. I stand and watch, crossing my arms, losing more and more patience every second.

"The offer expires in about ten seconds."

Luca looks up from his phone, still grinning. "I missed you, princess."

"Don't call me princess."

Luca tries to grab my hand as I start walking down the street, but I pull my hand free. This is not about romance. This is about sex.

"I've got a better idea."

"We are not fucking in a restroom again."

Luca rolls his eyes. "I thought my dirty princess liked that." He raises an eyebrow at me in challenge.

"I did enjoy that. But I prefer something with a slightly less chance of getting hepatitis afterward."

Luca laughs. "You and your outrageous demands."

We walk for a block and then another, and then Luca grabs hold of my hand, forcefully pulling me toward a building.

"Where are we going?"

Luca's eyes light up with excitement. "My office."

12

LUCA

I DON'T TURN back to look at Ivy as I pull her into the office building. Although I can imagine what she looks like. Eyes wide, brows raised, and her mouth slightly parted. I don't have time to look at her. I'm on a mission. A mission to have Ivy before she changes her mind. Because I know this is some sort of game with her. And I don't think that I can stop again. Last time was too hard. I'll die if I don't have her. Fuck her. Taste her. I'm desperate for her. And she knows that. I know that she is desperate for me, too. But I know that her self-control is stronger. She has more self-control than I do. She can still say no.

I'll die if I don't have her. I roughly hold on to her hand as I pull her further inside the building. I've only been inside a handful of times, so when I turn right down a hallway that leads me to a dead end, I curse and have to turn back to the lobby to read the signs to figure out which way I'm supposed to go to get to the elevators. I can hear Ivy behind me, laughing quietly to herself and at my inability to find my way around the building. She probably thinks it's just another lie I didn't think through before taking her here. But the truth is, Ivy makes me crazy. So crazy that I have no idea how to find my way around this building even though I've never gotten lost before.

I finally find the arrow that points us toward the elevators, and I drag Ivy down the hallway, pressing the button as soon as we get there. And then I stare up at the numbers above the elevator indicating what floor it is on.

Fourteen. Thirteen. Twelve. It stops at twelve for what seems like forever.

I can feel Ivy trying to break free of my grasp again, but I won't let her. My grasp is too firm for her to break free this time.

"I know you're lying. I know this isn't your office building. Let's just find the nearest restroom," Ivy says between heavy breaths.

I don't dare look at her. Because I know, if I do, I'll fuck her right here in this lobby. I won't wait. And she needs to see my office. She needs to see it to be a believer.

I crack my neck back and forth, trying to get rid of my angst, while we wait for the elevator to reach our floor. But it does nothing to release the energy that has built up inside me. Finally, the doors open, and I pull Ivy inside, practically ripping her arm off. I press the button for the eleventh floor and then the button for the doors to close.

"Can you hold the elevator for me?" a man's voice shouts.

I don't hold the elevator. The elevator starts creeping up, and I do everything I can to keep from looking at Ivy. I crack my neck, I tap my foot, and I stare at the numbers, reading what floor we are on, but I can feel myself losing control with each second that passes.

And then I feel Ivy's lips right next to my ear, her warm breath driving me mad. "I can't wait," she whispers in my ear.

I can't either. I grab her and push her up against the elevator wall as our lips collide, our bodies interlock, and our destinies change forever.

I kiss her over and over as my hands feel every inch of her body. My hand slips under her dress and grabbing her ass. I hear the ding of the elevator, and the doors prepare to open. I glance back but see we're only on the eighth floor. I move to pull away, knowing that someone else is about to step on the elevator, but Ivy bites my lip hard, keeping me in place.

My dirty princess, I think.

We both hear people step onto the elevator, but that doesn't stop us from making out in front of them. We hear the sighs. We hear the whispers from the guests in the elevator. But that doesn't stop us. Nothing can. Because we want each other too much to stop.

The elevator dings again. I glance up to see that we're on the eleventh floor. I grab Ivy's ass and lift her legs as she wraps them around my waist so that I can keep kissing her. I carry her off the elevator as Ivy's hands roughly hold on to my hair, our lips locked and eyes focused on each other. I turn right, at least remembering that my office is down the hallway. But I somehow manage to walk into every wall, door, and desk on my way to my office. People scatter as we walk by, looking at us with shocked looks on their faces. These are colleagues of mine—people I should be trying to impress, people I will have to work with—but I don't care. Right now, all I care about is Ivy.

We finally make it, and I push her back into the door, assuming the door is unlocked.

"Ow," Ivy says as I ram her back into the door.

I trying to push the door open, but it doesn't budge.

I gently set Ivy on the ground, and I turn the doorknob. But it still won't budge.

Ivy laughs. "Seriously, I think I saw a restroom at the other end of the hallway."

"No." I reach into my pocket and pull out my keys. I find the key that unlocks my office, and I push the key in until the door unlocks.

I look at Ivy, who has one eyebrow raised as she looks at the door that just popped open. I flick the lights on and watch with hungry eyes as Ivy walks cautiously into my office. I follow slowly behind her, waiting for her to tell me how much she doesn't believe me. I watch as her eyes scan the diplomas on the wall, showing I graduated from UCLA and Stanford. I watch as her eyes travel to my desk where there's a picture of me and my family dressed to go to a ball in full royal attire. She picks the picture up and stares at it for a minute before slowly returning the frame back to my desk. She looks over at the final picture on my desk and gasps. She picks it up, and her eyes fill with what I hope is love. Because sitting on my desk is a picture of me with her in my arms, sitting on the beach. We are both laughing and smiling and being our genuine selves. A moment that is pretty rare for me. A rare moment where I wasn't lying. I was just myself.

She narrows her eyes as she looks at me, studies me.

I shrug. "I told you I wasn't lying this time."

It takes her a second to decide what she's going to do next. But then she starts walking toward me, toward the door. And I don't know which one she's walking to.

Is she upset and going to leave? Or does she want me to fuck her in this office?

When her eyes meet mine, I know the answer. I push the door shut and turn the lock. And I meet her halfway, grabbing her ass as she grabs my neck, our lips locking again. We kiss and kiss, desperate for each other. Ivy's hands clutch my chest while mine grab her gorgeous ass. We're showing each other how desperate we are to have one moment where the lies or the truth don't matter. It's just about us connecting in a primal way that we both need, that we are desperate for.

"How does my dirty girl want to be fucked?" I kiss her neck while I wait for her response.

"I'm not so dirty anymore."

I bite her earlobe as she purrs.

"I think you're still plenty dirty enough."

In one swipe, I knock everything off my desk and onto the floor. Ivy gasps.

I laugh as I pick her up and set her on the desk. I spread her legs far apart and step in between them. I place my hand on her chin and pull her forward for one long kiss, trying to slow things down a little before we lose our minds. When I stop kissing her, I grab the hem of her dress and slowly lift it over her head as she grabs my shirt and does the same.

"Bra off," I command.

I watch as she slowly slinks out of her bra. I suck in a breath when

I notice something new and very dirty. Nipple piercings. She wasn't wearing them the night before.

I bend down and immediately take one of her nipples in my mouth, swirling around the piercing. "You're right; you're not such a dirty girl anymore."

She moans as I suck, and then she bites down hard on my shoulder as I take the other one in my mouth.

"I'm only dirty for you."

I grab and rip her underwear down her body, and my mouth drops to the floor.

"I've been very dirty," she says as her hands travel down between her legs, between her folds, to play with the piercing covering her clit. That she also wasn't wearing last night.

As much as I want her to keep playing with herself while I sit and watch, I can't let her continue. I grab her hand and take whatever fingers into my mouth, licking her sweet juices off of them. And then I lower my tongue to taste her.

"Fuck!" she screams much too loudly for someone in the building not to hear.

I stop when she screams and then bend down to grab the underwear that is lying on the floor. I shove it into her mouth to keep her quiet.

"If you scream, I can't keep doing this," I say.

My tongue flicks in between her full lips and over her clit. I can see in her eyes how good it feels and how desperate she is to scream again. I pull a condom out of my pocket and then push my pants and underwear down as I continue to lick her. I stroke myself once and then twice, but it's not necessary. I'm more than hard for her. I push the condom onto my dick and then grab her, pulling her off the desk. She whimpers just a little at the loss of my touch, but then I shove her hard against the window, face-first. Her eyes grow wide when she realizes that anybody can see her in the window, completely naked and exposed. But, when I start kissing her neck, she no longer cares. I push into her pussy from behind, and I watch as she bites down hard on the underwear in her mouth.

"You like that, my dirty princess?"

She moans her response.

I thrust over and over as I take turns grabbing each nipple and flicking its piercing. Her body was amazing before, but now, it's even more fun to play with. I love listening to the soft moans as I thrust inside her. I love feeling her body tighten and expand as I move inside her. I love as the look in her eyes grows heavier and heavier. I love knowing that she lets me have complete control, doing anything I want to her body, and that she only lets me. Have that control. Because, deep down, despite all my lies, I know that she trusts me enough to give me that control. She just won't ever admit it to herself.

"Come, princess." I see her getting close.

Her body trembles, and then she screams, "Fuck, prince!"

13

IVY

I CAN'T BELIEVE I just let Luca fuck me up against the window. I can't believe I just let him fuck me in a room with a building full of people. I still can't believe that he is a lawyer. And I definitely don't believe that he is a prince.

I don't look at Luca as I get dressed. I just quickly throw my clothes on and then try to determine how I'm gonna get out of this office with the least amount of embarrassment.

Luca comes over to softly kiss me. "I know you are ready to run, but I'm not ready to let you go."

"I'm not going anywhere. Not until I have some answers." I stare at the door.

"But I do need to use the restroom and get out of this office building as quickly as possible," I say. I blush.

"You're embarrassed because my colleagues heard you, aren't you?"

"No."

"Liar," Luca says.

"Fine. I'll own up to my lies, unlike some people. I don't want to see anyone after they heard me having sex with you."

"But I want to introduce you to everyone. Maybe then you'll believe that I'm a lawyer."

I walk over to the diplomas hanging on the wall to study them further. They look real. But then a piece of paper isn't that hard to fake.

"I'll believe you when you get the lawsuit against me dropped."

Luca smiles. "Done."

I wrap my arms across my chest, trying to comfort myself. I look over at Luca, who is looking at me with an expression I've never seen before. He opens his mouth, like he wants to say something but is holding back.

"What is it?" I ask.

Luca frowns and narrows his eyes. "I have so many things to tell you, so many things to explain, and I have no idea where to start."

I swallow down the lump in my throat. I don't want him to see how nervous I am. "Whatever it is, just tell me. It can't be any worse than all the lies you've already told me."

Luca walks closer until we are face-to-face. His hand gently caresses my neck, and his thumb strokes my cheek. His eyes search mine, trying to find the answers to questions that he hasn't even asked yet.

"I wish I had never lied to you."

I feel every single one of his words. I understand. I feel the sadness and pain he feels when he says those words. But it doesn't really lessen my pain.

"I wish your words could help me forgive you."

He closes his eyes, like my words sting. "I should have never come here. I should've let you be happy. Now, I've ruined everything."

I narrow my eyes, trying to understand. "But I wasn't happy."

In that moment, we don't think about the lies. We don't think about the fact that we don't have a future together. That there's no way to fix what's broken. We passionately kiss each other. We grab on to one another like this is the last time we will ever kiss, ever touch. And it could be.

As much as I love being in his arms, I can't keep doing this. I'll

318

always wonder if he is lying or telling the truth. I'll always wonder if he really loves me or is just playing games for some unknown purpose.

We slowly pull away. I blink back tears in my eyes. This feels like good-bye.

"I'm just going to go to the restroom, and then we can go." I don't wait for him to respond or to try to stop me.

Instead, I run out of the office and into the hallway, no longer caring if anyone sees me. I remember that I saw a restroom down the hallway on my left. I quickly walk there, trying to keep myself together for just a few more minutes until I make it to the restroom. But I don't make it that far. I take three steps and then crumple onto the floor, sobbing uncontrollably.

My life is such a mess. I'm in love with my ex-boyfriend, whom I can't trust. I'm being sued for everything I own. I'm about to lose everything, except for my pets. If Skye finds out that I slept with Luca, I don't know if I would even have her.

Someone walks by while I'm crying on the floor, but I don't care who it is or what they think of me. I cry a second longer, and then I grab on to the wall and stand up. Tears still stain my eyes as I walk, but I finally make it to the door.

I enter and am thankful that no one else is inside the small restroom. I walk over to the sink, and I stare at myself in the mirror. I grab tissue and begin trying to make myself look like I wasn't crying. I don't want Luca to know I was crying. If he knew that I was crying, he would probably use it to his advantage and do something nice for me that would make me fall even more in love with him.

I shake my head. *How can I be in love with such a lying bastard?* I should make an appointment with a psychologist because there has to be something wrong with me.

I splash water on my face, hoping that will help a little. I hear the door to the restroom open and close, but I don't bother looking up. I don't want to make eye contact with whoever just came in. I don't want to have that awkward conversation where someone asks me what's wrong when all they really care about is gossip. The woman enters one of the stalls, and I intend to be gone by the time she gets out. But she moves fast and flushes before I have a chance to leave. There's only one sink, so I know I need to let her use it.

"Sorry. Excuse me," I say as I dry my hands on a paper towel.

When I turn around and look at the person who just came out of the stall, I freeze. A man is standing in front of me. I look around, expecting to find a urinal, thinking that I went into the wrong restroom in all my haze of tears, but I don't see one.

"Excuse me," I say, trying to push past the man to exit the restroom.

But he doesn't move.

"Are you Ivy?" the man asks.

"Yes. And you are?" Maybe someone came to find me because this isn't really Luca's office. Maybe we're breaking and entering.

"Sorry, I can explain—"

The man doesn't let me explain. Instead, his fist starts flying toward my face.

14

LUCA

I RUN my hand through my hair.

I just had one of the best experiences and one of the worst experiences of my life at the same time. That was one of our best times having sex. But it also felt like good-bye. And I'm nowhere near ready to say good-bye to Ivy. I haven't had a chance to explain. She deserves the truth. Hopefully, she will give me a second chance. That's all I want.

But the way that Ivy just ran out of here, I know that I'm not going to get that second chance.

I bend down and start picking up the picture frames and papers from the floor. I slowly gather them up and then take my time as I put them back on my desk. I use it as a distraction really. A way to give Ivy more time to herself. Because I know that's what she wants right now. Time to think. And I want to give her a lot of time because it gives me time to think, too. I'm trying to figure out how I'm going to tell her the rest.

But, when I finish putting everything back together on my desk, I can't wait any longer. I walk out of my office and start making my way down to the restroom to wait for her. One of my colleagues, Bruno, stops me before I get to the restroom.

"Hey, bro. You're not supposed to be working tonight, are you?"

"No."

"Um, then why are you here?" Bruno asks, being nosy.

"Just showing my girlfriend my office."

Bruno's eyes widen, as he finally makes the connection. I'm sure he heard the sex noises earlier and is now realizing that it was me and Ivy.

"Sounded like you two were having a good time. Good thing the boss doesn't usually work on Friday nights; otherwise, you would've gotten a stern talking-to."

"Good thing then because I don't know if I can handle a stern talking-to," I say sarcastically.

"You definitely can't. The boss has a way of making you feel really horrible."

"I really should be going."

"Oh, yeah. I should be going, too. I should be working or something," Bruno says.

We go our separate ways.

I don't want to talk to anyone else in my office. I don't want to hear about meaningless things about our job. The people here think what we do is important. I'm sure it is to some people. But, to me, they are the little things.

I stare at the restroom door, waiting for her to open it, but after five minutes, it doesn't. I grow worried that Ivy is more upset than I thought. Or maybe she left and got a cab or something to take her home. Either way, I need to know now.

I push the door open as I say, "Ivy?"

I look around the corner at the sink, but no one is there.

"Ivy?" I shout again.

I bend down to see if I can find her in any of the stalls, but I don't see anyone. I push each door open, but no one is inside. She's not here.

Shit.

I run back out of the restroom and down the hall, toward the elevators. I see Marsha, our secretary, sitting behind her desk.

I stop abruptly. "Marsha, have you seen Ivy?"

She looks at me, confused.

"Have you seen the woman I came up here with? She's black. She has long, curly black hair. She's thin and beautiful. She was wearing a dress, and if you look closely, she is covered in dog hair."

"Oh. She just left."

"Shit." I run my hand through my hair as I start running down the hall after her.

"But you should know that she was with another man!" Marsha yells after me.

I freeze. Ivy wouldn't have been with another man. She's not that cruel or heartless to do something like that to me.

I backtrack to Marsha. "What kind of man? What did he look like?"

Marsha shrugs. "I don't know. Medium height, medium build. He was balding a little, and he looked upset about something. I wouldn't worry too much about it. Probably just a friend. There's nothing going on between them. You look about a million times better than he did."

This leads me to be even more confused. I pull out my cell phone and dial Ivy's number, begging her to pick up the phone. She doesn't.

I run to my car and drive as fast as I can toward her home.

I knock loudly on her door. No answer. I have to break the window to get inside her home, but I don't care. I'll fix it later. When I enter, I expect to find her angry and upset because I just broke the window. I expect to find her curled up on the couch with her dogs and cats. But I don't see any signs of her anywhere in the house.

I take the next hour to try to calm myself while I wait for her to come home with some other guy. She doesn't come home though. Another hour passes, and she still hasn't come home.

I try calling her again and again and again.

No answer.

I don't know why it takes me so long to realize I fucked up. It just hits me. And I know what happened.

I pick up my phone and dial Skye's number. "Skye, can you take care of my dog and Ivy's pets for me? Can you do that?"

"What the hell happened?"

"I fucked up."

15

IVY

I slowly open my eyes. Nothing feels right. My body is sore and stiff. When I move to look at where I am, my neck throbs. My hand moves automatically to grab my neck to keep it from aching. But, when I move my right hand, my left hand comes with it.

I see the rope tied loosely around my wrists. My heart races at the sight. My throat tightens up, making my breathing difficult. I use my arms to push myself into a seated position and try to figure out where I am. I look down at my feet that are also tied together with rope.

The room moves hard to the left, and I fall back on my side again, unable to keep myself upright due to the ropes.

I'm in a van, I realize immediately. *A dark, dirty van. Tied up in the backseat by myself.*

I've been kidnapped.

Kidnapped!

I feel the panic rising in my chest. I don't understand why I would be kidnapped.

Are they trying to get money from me? Are they going to rape me? This doesn't make sense.

I sit up again, and this time, I hold on to the handle on the door to keep myself upright. I try to remember what happened. I remember being with Luca. I remember having the best sex of my life and then nothing. I don't remember who kidnapped me or how I was kidnapped.

Maybe they drugged me.

My body hurts, but other than a slight pounding on one side of my head, I don't feel like I was seriously injured. I don't feel like any part of my body has been hurt. Still, not being injured doesn't do much to calm me.

I need a plan to get out of here. Now. Who knows where they are taking me or what they plan on doing to me once I get there? And I'm not going to stick around long enough to ask them what they plan on doing with me.

I start pulling on the ropes attached to my hands, trying to wiggle them free. It takes a minute and then another, but my hands finally wiggle free.

"Do you really think the royal family will pay big bucks to get her back?" a man's voice says from the front of the vehicle.

I freeze.

"Yes. We've been through this. They won't want another scandal. If she is the future princess, then they will want her back. They will want her back to keep her from talking at the very least."

Talking? Talking about what?

"I still think we should have kidnapped the prince. They would have paid more for him than the girl. We don't even know if they are serious about her being the future princess. What if she is just a fling? What if the prince doesn't really want to marry the girl?"

"They will still pay. Relax. We have photos of the two of them together. We will spread those pictures to the media. The royal family will have to admit that the two of them are dating. They will have to pay. They will have to do anything and everything to get her back."

"But I thought we wanted to get the royal family back? Make a big scandal?"

The other man who seems to be in charge says, "God, you're an idiot. We've been through this before. That is why, when we give the girl back, she'll have a bomb attached to her. We are going to blow them all up. That will make a big splash."

The other man laughs. "I can't wait."

I unfreeze. My hands start shaking. These guys are crazy. But they have convinced me of one thing. Luca is a prince. A fucking prince.

But I don't have time to worry about that. I have to get free. I have to warn him. Even if these two don't seem like the brightest guys on the planet. Even if they didn't even know how to tie my hands up tight enough so that I couldn't get out of the ropes. They might not have much experience with kidnapping, but I'm going to take them at their word and assume that, given the chance, they are going to kill me. And Luca, too.

My hands cling to the rope at my feet, desperate to get it off so that I can make a plan to get the heck out of here. The rope is tied in a bizarre knot, and my fingers are still shaking and sweaty. I struggle to get the rope untied. With each second that passes, I feel my time is running out.

My mind drifts to Luca. He was telling me the truth. For once in his goddamn life, he was telling me the truth. I want to tell him that I know he was telling the truth. I would give anything to be in his arms again. I would give anything to kiss him one last time. I would give anything to tell him how I really feel even though I shouldn't. That I love him more than anything even though he hurt me. I need to tell him that I love him. Even if I don't know what that love means.

The van turns hard to the right, and I tumble over to the floor again. I hit my head as I fall. The pounding in my head returns and forces me to focus on the task at hand. I have to get free. I can't think about Luca.

I work furiously, trying to get the ropes off my feet as fast as possible. Each second that passes causes my heart to speed up to a dangerous level. My hands are shaking so badly that I'm afraid I'm never going to be able to control them again.

I pull hard on one of the ropes, and my eyes widen as I watch the rope start to unravel. I pull harder and harder, forcing the rope to slither off my ankles. I pull so hard that it is burning my legs as it rubs against my ankles. But, within seconds, my legs are free of the rope.

I'm free, I think.

But that's not quite true. I'm free of the rope, but I'm still stuck in this smelly, disgusting van with two lunatics who want to kill me and the entire royal family.

I pull myself up into a standing position as quietly as I can, trying my best not to alert the guys in the front of the van that I'm free.

I walk over to the side of the van that has a sliding door on it. I unlock the door and then hold on to the handle, waiting for the two guys in front to slow down to give me a chance to jump out. But seconds pass and then minutes, and the van never slows down. The driver speeds around corners, never really stopping. The windows in the back are blacked out, so I have no idea where I am. I have no idea if I'm in a busy city or out in the middle of nowhere.

I feel my time running out, so I take a chance. I throw the door open. I see concrete whizzing by my feet, but I don't take a second to think about how badly it's going to hurt. I just jump.

I don't land on my feet. Instead, my body collapses on the hard concrete. But I don't wait to see if I broke any bones or if I bruised any part of me. Instead, I push myself up and start running. I don't look back to see if they're following me. I just run until I find a small store and duck inside.

I breathe heavily as I enter what I realize is a small coffee shop. I walk to the back and take a seat in a corner table, trying not to draw any attention to myself. The waiter brings me a menu, and it's immediately clear that I'm not in the US anymore. The menu is in a language I don't recognize, and as I glance around the coffee shop, I realize the building is quite old, possibly built hundreds of years ago.

I take a second to think about what I should do next. I need to get ahold of Luca. I feel in the pockets of my dress, trying to figure out if I have any cash on me or anything to give the waiter in exchange for using a phone. My heart suddenly stops when I feel the cold metal of my phone.

Those idiots, I think.

I pull the phone out and dial Luca's number. It rings once and then twice.

"Ivy?" Luca asks into the line.

"Yes." I exhale, finally able to breathe again, just from hearing his voice.

"Oh, thank God! Where are you?"

"I am...not sure. I don't think I'm still in the US but I'm not sure."

"We've been tracking you for a while and I'm triangulating where you are right now. I'll be there in about five minutes."

I smile and sink back into my chair. Luca is on his way. I'm saved. This nightmare is over.

"Hurry," is all I say.

"I will, love," Luca says before ending the call.

I look around, trying to find the restroom to clean myself up before Luca gets here. I find the one small restroom in the back and go inside. I look at myself in the mirror. I have a bad gash on the hairline of my head. My face is pretty bruised up, but I don't think it'll even need medical attention. I splash some water on the cut to get rid of the blood and then run my hand through my hair, trying to make it look more normal so that I don't shock Luca too much when he sees me. I look down at my wrist that is a little red but not really noticeable. The rest of my body seems perfectly fine.

I try to collect myself and get rid of the anxiety still pulsing through my veins. That was by far the craziest, scariest thing I'd ever been through. And, hopefully, it will be the scariest thing I will ever go through. It all happened so fast, and I was only conscious, thankfully, for a very small part of it. But it's still crazy to think that this is what my life might be like if I dated Luca, a prince.

Will my life be filled with running from crazy lunatics who want to kill me? Will my life be lived in fear? Or is this a one-time fluke that will never happen again?

I take a couple of deep breaths. I don't even know why I'm worrying about it.

I don't want to be with Luca, I remind myself.

Who am I kidding?

After almost dying, I don't care that he lied to me. I just want to be with somebody I love and who loves me back. Despite all the lies.

I walk back out of the restroom to go look for Luca, who's hopefully going to be here any second now. As soon as I step out, I feel a man's hand grab hold of my arm. I freeze because I know it's not Luca's hand. I slowly look up to see a large man dressed in a suit, holding on to my arm. I don't think it's either of the two guys who kidnapped me earlier. But it is also definitely not Luca.

"Come with me."

"No," I whisper.

"You don't have a choice," he says as he starts walking me forward.

He's right; I don't have a choice. He has more strength in his hand than I do in my entire body. I don't know what's going on with the royal family. *Why are people so desperate to kidnap me?* But it looks like my luck has run out. I'm going to be kidnapped twice in a twenty-four-hour period. And, unlike my last captors, this man seems much smarter and stronger.

I walk as slowly as I can, hoping that Luca will come before I'm shoved back inside of another van. But we make it all the way out of the small coffee shop, and he hasn't come.

I see a large blacked-out SUV sitting in front of me, only about five feet from the entrance of the coffee shop. The man holding my arm picks up speed when we are outside. Like he thinks I'm going to make a run for it or something. I'm not. His grip is still as strong as it was before. There is no getting out of this. This time could be the end. My only hope is that maybe they don't want to kill me. That these guys actually want a ransom.

He walks me to the door, opens it, and shoves me inside.

This is the end. I'm never going to see Luca again. I'm never going to be able to tell him that I love him despite everything. That I would give up my entire life for him. Marry him tomorrow and always live with the fear. Because I love him.

16

LUCA

I fucked up.

I've done some horrible things. I lied. Cheated. Stole. Done anything and everything to hide my one secret. The one secret that no one could ever find out. I'm not even sure that I can tell Ivy my secret. But getting Ivy involved in my life might have been the worst mistake I've ever made.

I can't lose her. I won't lose her. But, now that she's so entwined in my life, I don't know how to protect her. I have no idea how to keep her safe. I don't even know if it's possible to keep her safe. But I have to try. I have to find a way. She's too important to me.

I've been a nervous wreck for the last twenty or so hours since she went missing.

Even though I knew that our country had the best military, detectives, people looking for her, searching for her, it still wasn't enough to reassure me. Even though I knew that they would find her. I believed they were the best, and they knew what they were doing.

I wasn't sure, when we found her, if she would still be alive or dead. That was the one thing my security team reassured me. They kept telling me that, most likely, she had been kidnapped because the kidnappers wanted a ransom. If the prince had finally found his princess, they thought that I would pay anything to get her back.

Who knew that she would be able to rescue herself? Who knew that I wouldn't have to do a damn thing to save her?

It just makes me love her more. Want her more. It makes it even harder for me because the only way I will truly be able to keep her safe is to say good-bye. To stop loving her. Because my life is anything but safe.

So, when Andy jumps out of the SUV to go into the small coffee shop where Ivy is, I can barely breathe. I know they won't let me out of this car, not until they find the men responsible for Ivy's kidnapping. Not until they know that it is safe for me. But it takes everything inside me to stay put, and the only reason I really do is because I know that they will do everything to keep me inside, including tasering me to keep me safe.

He disappears inside, and it seems like hours are passing even though I know it hasn't been more than a couple of seconds. But each second that passes, my breath gets shorter, my heart beats faster. With every second, my body turns cold, as I imagine a life without her, which would simply be no life at all.

Then, suddenly, the door to the coffee shop is thrust open, and Ivy is being pushed through as Andy tightly holds on to her arm. But, still, I can't breathe. Because, as she walks to the SUV, she looks terrified. I can still see the feistiness behind her eyes, the defiance at trying her best not to follow his orders. But she doesn't feel safe. It's a feeling I wish I could take away from her, but I can't. She'll never be safe again, and it's all my fault.

Andy opens the door and shoves her inside, and I want nothing more than to throw my arms around her to protect her and love her and never, ever let her go again. But it's clear, as she's being shoved into the car, that she doesn't know I'm here. I'm afraid that, if I grab hold of her without her recognizing that it's me, it's going to scare her even more. I'm also slightly scared that, when she does recognize me, she is still going to hate me. For bringing her into this mess.

But I can't hold my arms back when I see that she's been hurt. Her head has been sliced open, her face is bruised, and her wrists are red, most likely from rope.

"Ivy!" I throw my arms around her, needing to feel she's actually here.

I feel her take a deep breath when she instantly knows that I'm here. That it's me.

I feel the tears rolling down her cheeks before I see or hear them.

"Shh...it's okay, baby. I got you. I'm not going to let anything happen to you ever again," I say, telling her a promise that I can't guarantee or keep. "I'm so sorry, baby. I'm so sorry," I say, rocking her back and forth in my arms in the backseat of the SUV.

"I thought I was never going to see you again," she whispers through the tears, like it's difficult for her to even speak right now.

"Oh, baby, I would never let that happen. You're my whole world. I wouldn't be able to survive without you."

"Don't ever let me go again," she says.

I exhale deeply. "I won't. I'll never let you go again," I say, relieved that she wants to be near me even though I hate that this is what it took for her to want to be around me. I didn't want her to fall in love with me this way. So, I won't let her tell me that she loves me today. I want her to love me on her own terms.

I see Andy eyeing me in the rearview mirror, and I already know what he's asking without saying. *Am I taking you to the hospital or the palace?*

We've known each other too long to not be able to read each other at a moment's notice.

"Are you hurt anywhere else? I can see the cut on your head, the bruises on your face, the redness on your wrists, but it would really be best if we took you to the palace first and had a doctor meet us there rather than going to the hospital. Or do you need medical attention first?" I ask.

Ivy rests her head on my chest while I stroke her hair. "I'm not hurt. You can take me to the palace," she says.

When she says *palace* without hesitation, it's clear now that she believes me. That she believes that I'm a prince.

"Palace," I say, looking at Andy in the rearview mirror.

He nods and mumbles something into his headset, letting the other bodyguards know where we are headed, so they can follow suit as he begins driving in that direction.

"What happened, Ivy? Tell me everything."

I feel Ivy swallow hard as she wipes the tears that have slowly stopped flowing down her face. "I'm not sure entirely. I remember being in the restroom at your office in Albuquerque, and then the next thing I know, I woke up in the back of a van with my arms and legs tied together."

I try to keep my body calm and just continue to stroke her hair. The last thing she needs is for me to get anxious or angry. She needs someone calm who can keep her calm and reassure her that everything's going to be okay from here on out. But that's the last thing I want to do. I want to find these guys, punch them, and kill them. No, killing them wouldn't even be enough. I want to make them feel like they've lost everything because that's how I felt when I realized she was gone.

"How did you escape?" I ask. I'm in shock that she is lying here, in my arms, and not trapped in an abandoned building somewhere, most likely with a bullet between her eyes.

"I don't think the men who kidnapped me had much experience or had done this many times before. My arms and legs were tied together, yes, but the ropes were loose. I was easily able to get my arms and legs untied by myself."

I nod as I listen to her every word, imagining her being in that position, scared to death.

"I knew I had to untie myself and get out as fast as I could because they were talking about strapping a bomb to me and using it to kill you," she says, lifting her head and looking at me square in the eyes. "And I couldn't be the reason you died. I couldn't let them kill you. It was the only thing that kept me going."

I can't breathe. She loves me. If I didn't know before, I know it for sure now. She wasn't worried about herself. She was worried about me.

Andy swerves the car over to the side of the road, coming to an abrupt stop. He jumps out of the SUV while he mumbles something into his headset, and all the other bodyguards stop around us, forming a protective shield.

Andy runs around to Ivy's door and throws it open. He grabs her and throws her outside. I glare at Andy as I jump out of the car after her.

"What the hell are you doing?" I scream at Andy while his hands travel all over Ivy's body. I run to where he has thrown her against the wall of a building, her legs spread and her arms up. But I don't make it far, only a couple of steps, before several of the bodyguards grab me and force me back to the SUV.

"Let me go. Now!"

"I can't do that, sir. I have to keep you safe," one of the bodyguards I don't recognize says.

"I'm the prince. Let me go. Now," I say.

"I can't do that, sir. My orders come from the queen. I must do everything to keep you safe for her and the country."

"Ivy's not going to hurt me. Now, let me go."

I watch in horror as Andy requires Ivy to take off her shirt in the middle of the sidewalk while a dozen other bodyguards stand, surrounding her, some with guns drawn. Others are looking away, keeping a small crowd that has formed, while others seemingly search for another threat on the street.

Andy skims something long and black over her bra while I search for Ivy's eyes. She can't see me though, as the guards have shut me back inside the SUV, and the windows are tinted dark black. But I can see her beautiful brown eyes. She doesn't look scared. In fact, she looks incredibly calm and still. She is not focused on what Andy is doing. Instead, she is looking straight at me even though she can't see me. With just the expression on her face, she's trying to reassure me that this is okay even though I have no idea how it could be.

I glance back to see what Andy is doing, and that's when he reaches his hand inside her bra. I about lose it. I throw myself at the bodyguard who is babysitting me in the car. He wasn't expecting me to attack him, which gives me just enough time to unlock the door and shove him out. I jump out after him, ready to pummel Andy to the ground even though he is twice my size.

I start running toward her when Ivy says, "Stop."

I stop even though I think she's wrong.

A second later, Andy pulls a small device from her bra and hands it over to one of the other bodyguards. The bodyguard begins running away from us. Andy then looks at me and nods. I run the rest of the way toward Ivy, finally understanding what's been happening.

We throw our arms around each other. We each let out a long exhale. We kiss again and again and again. I don't care that Ivy's standing in the middle of the street, half-naked. I don't care who is watching. We just need each other more than anything else. We slowly pull away, both breathing fast and heavy.

"I didn't save myself. I almost killed you. I almost killed us both. They didn't let me go. They let me escape on purpose so that I would bring the bomb to you. Andy saved us."

I shake my head. "You saved us both when you told us the story. And don't ever think otherwise."

I begin to hear and see the flashes of light that I'm sure have been going off every second since I stepped out of the SUV. Paparazzi are here, taking pictures of us, invading our privacy, letting the whole world know that Ivy is mine. If I thought it was too late to protect her before, it's for sure too late now. She'll never be able to walk the streets of Europe again without being noticed, and it won't be long before the US realizes who she is and who I am, too.

"Come on," I say, throwing my arm around her.

I lead her back to the SUV with Andy walking in front of us, trying his best to protect us from the invading lights and cameras. I help her into the car and then climb in afterward. Andy starts driving again, slowly this time, trying to get around the people who are swarming our cars.

In all the commotion, I realize that we forgot her shirt. It is still lying on the sidewalk on the street behind us. I take off my shirt and hand it to her. She puts it on but not before eyeing my body up and down, eating me up with her eyes. I'm desperate for the feeling of our bodies being so connected together.

"I'm sorry," I say.

She cocks her head to the side with a small smile on her lips as she adjusts her shirt. "What do you have to be sorry for? It's not your fault that some crazy people decided to kidnap me and then tried to kill us both."

I see the feistiness in her eyes, and her bright smile has returned. It seems that she thinks she's truly safe now. She doesn't realize that this is going to just keep happening over and over and over again.

"I'm sorry that, by the time we get back to the palace, your half-naked body with me pressed up against you, kissing you, is going to be all over the news, all over social media, all over everything here," I say, looking at her with remorse, trying my best to show her how sorry I am that her first experience with the media is going to be this.

She laughs, and I raise my eyebrows at her.

"Good thing I'm not ashamed of my body then."

I laugh. "I don't know what I did to deserve you."

And I don't know what I'm going to have to do to keep her. But I'll do anything. Including lie to her.

17

IVY

I DON'T KNOW why I feel so calm, but I do. Maybe surviving a near-death experience twice now in twenty-four hours makes you appreciate every moment even more. Maybe that is why I feel calm right now. Maybe it has something to do with the adrenaline that has been pumping through my body. Maybe that's what science would say, but I don't think it's the truth. I think the reason I feel so calm right now is that my head is currently resting on Luca's chest. I think it's the fact that I get to hear Luca's heart beating again. That I know that he is still alive and that the threat has now lessened. That is what is keeping me calm.

It's because I love him. I just haven't had a chance to tell him yet. I'm not gonna wait for the perfect moment, like I initially thought I was going to do when I finally saw it was him in the back of the SUV. I can't wait. I have to tell him because every second that passes is precious. Who knows how many more seconds either one of us will have?

I try to sit up, but Luca tries to keep me from moving by holding me tightly in his arms.

I chuckle. "I'm just sitting up, so I can look at you. I'm not going anywhere."

He firmly kisses me on the lips, like he has for about the thousandth time since I got back into the SUV after Andy found a bomb attached to my bra. They really were experienced kidnappers. They just made me believe that they weren't, and I fed right into their plan. It's something that I don't think I'll ever get over. I'll never forgive myself for having someone use me to try to hurt Luca.

He stops kissing me and lets me sit up. But his hand still firmly holds on to mine. I glance to Andy, who is sitting in the front seat, seemingly preoccupied with driving us to the palace and keeping us safe. And, honestly, after he saved both of our lives, I don't care if he hears what I'm about to say to Luca.

I take a deep breath and then say, "Luca, I have something I need to tell you. Something that I discovered about myself while all of this was happening."

Luca looks at me with concern. His eyes narrow at me as he tries to figure out what I'm about to say. But I know he has no way of guessing. He thinks I still hate him for lying. He thinks there is still no way that we could ever be together again. But he is beyond wrong.

"Luca, I lo—"

"Look, the palace," Luca says, pointing out the window.

I lose my focus and look up to see a mighty castle growing larger over the long drive in front of us. It's the largest, most beautiful building I've ever seen. It's straight from a fairy tale with the way it seems to rise up into the clouds, overlooking the beautiful lush green forest below it. He's really a prince, and this is really his castle. His mother's really the queen, and his father's really the king. Fairy tales really do exist.

The castle itself takes my breath away. I can't imagine growing up here. I knew that places like this existed, that people grew up being real kings and queens, but I never realized how close to the fairy tale they really were. It's something I've always wanted—the fairy tale with Prince Charming and everything. It's not that I wanted to be rescued, just that I wanted to be loved and looked at the way that Prince Charming did with Cinderella. But, when I imagined the fairy tale, I never imagined this.

I look back at Luca. "It's beautiful. You grew up here?"

He stares out the window at the castle that he calls home. "I spent quite a bit of time here and then spent quite a bit of time in the US with my grandparents as well. They gave up the throne to my parents, and my parents wanted me to have some semblance of a normal life. But this was always home, I guess."

"Well, you have quite a beautiful home. I can't wait to see the inside."

Luca doesn't say anything after I speak, and after I get another few seconds to take in the castle, I look over at him.

"What's wrong?" I ask.

Luca shakes his head. "It's nothing. I'm just sorry that I have to introduce you to my life this way. The media is not going to be nice to you. And my parents..."

My eyes widen as I realize what he is saying. I'm going to meet the King and Queen of Monaco today. I'm going to meet his parents today, and I don't even know what we are. Friends? Lovers? Boyfriend and girlfriend? Or something more?

I know nothing about them. Not even what their names are.

"Are you sure you want me to meet the king and queen today? Surely, we should wait until we've had a chance to talk and figure out what we are," I say.

Luca tucks a strand of loose hair behind my ear. His eyes sweetly study me. "They are just my parents if it makes you feel any better. They are going to love you, no matter what we are, because I love you. We don't need to figure things out right away. I just want to show you my world and make sure you're safe. After that, you can decide to go or stay."

I feel the car slowing as we inch closer to the entrance of the palace. I'm running out of time before I'm sure I'll be whizzed into a different world. A world where he won't know if I love him simply because he is a prince or because I actually love him.

"Luca, I need to finish what I was about to say earlier. I—"

Luca kisses me hard on the lips, forcing me to stop mid sentence again. He slowly pulls away when he thinks the thought has been wiped from my brain. The SUV stops, and Andy gets out, leaving us alone in the backseat.

"We'll talk later," Luca says.

"But—"

"Later."

Our doors are thrust open, and hands are extended in to help us out before I can protest any further.

"Welcome to Monaco's castle, Miss Lane," the gentleman says, holding out his hand. He pulls me out of the back of the SUV.

I look at the middle-aged man who is dressed nicely in something resembling a suit. He has a large smile on his face, and it's clear he was expecting us even though I have no idea who he is.

"Thank you, Mr...."

"Thomas, the butler. If you have any questions at all about your stay, I'm the guy to find."

I smile. "Thank you."

I glance up and see more than a dozen staff members standing around me, all with large smiles on their faces.

Holy crap, I think.

My mouth drops open as I stare at all of them. I assumed a large staff would run a castle. I just didn't realize they'd all be standing outside when I arrived. It's a bit overwhelming. Luca runs over to my side as he pulls on a shirt that one of the staff handed to him. He takes my hand from Thomas's, linking our fingers together.

He leans down so that only I can hear and says in my ear, "You're going to be fine. I'm going to do my best to ease you into this. Just introduce you to everyone for a little bit and then give you some time alone in your room."

"My room?"

He nods and smiles.

I frown. I don't like that I won't be sharing a room with him. But I guess I shouldn't expect that the Prince of Monaco would want me in his bed every night with his parents sleeping next door.

"Let me introduce you to some of the staff," Luca says as he guides me forward on the driveway outside of the castle. "This is Sarah, and this is Jamie; both are housekeepers. That's Jonathan, Jordan, and James; they are some of our groundskeepers. That is Catherine, Kate, and Stephanie—some of the chefs and cooks."

Luca continues to rattle off names, and each person steps forward, smiling, curtsying, and bowing in front of Luca as he introduces them. I stare, wide-eyed, knowing that I won't be able to remember everyone's names. The longer he rambles, the more confused I become.

"And this, everyone, is Ivy Lane. She's a veterinarian, currently residing in Albuquerque, New Mexico. She has traveled a long way to be here today, and she's very special to me, so take good care of her when I'm not around. And, if I hear so much as a whisper of gossip about her, anyone accused will be fired on the spot. Understood?"

The staff nods.

Thomas says, "Completely understood. We will treat her as one of the family while she's here."

"Good. Now, where are Margaret and Murray?"

"Murray just finished with a meeting and is in his sitting room. Margaret isn't going to be home for another hour," Thomas answers.

"When Margaret gets here, hold her off for as long as you can. Let her know we'll see her around three." Luca squeezes my hand tighter and says, "You ready?"

I nod even though I feel anything but ready.

He grins. "Come on. Haven't you always wondered what a castle looks like?"

His grin is infectious. I find myself smiling just as big, despite how anxious I really am. Luca leads me around to the front entrance where we parked.

"Who are Margaret and Murray?" I ask.

"Oh, sorry. Those are my parents."

I squint my eyes, a bit confused as to why he calls them Margaret and Murray, but I let the thought go as he grabs hold of the big oak front door that is surrounded by stone and pushes it open.

"Holy shit." I step inside the large entryway as my mouth falls open.

I don't even know how to describe it. It's so beautiful and large and magnificent. There isn't just one chandelier hanging over the entryway. There are at least five that I can see hanging at least five stories up. A large spiral staircase sits before me with a large balcony leading to who knows how many rooms up above. The stone that surrounds me on all sides is gorgeous and detailed and nothing like I've ever seen back in the States.

I look at Luca, who is studying me with a large grin on his face.

"It's beautiful, isn't it?"

"It's better than beautiful. It's one of the most exquisite things I've ever seen."

"Well, I'm not going to let you enjoy it for long."

"Why?" I frown.

"Because there about one hundred fifty more rooms to check out, if my memory serves me right."

My mouth drops open again. "One hundred fifty! That's crazy. Who sleeps in all those rooms?"

Luca shrugs. "Well, my parents, me sometimes, some of the staff. And a lot of people stay when we have parties and banquets and things. We also have a lot of offices and rooms for other royal leaders and presidents to stay and meet with my parents and me when I come home. Plus, at least half of the rooms are designated for my future children."

I shake my head. "Well, you'd better get to having kids then."

Luca pulls hard on my hand, pulling me toward his body, before his hand slides over my ass, and he pulls me in for a passionate kiss. "And, if I'm lucky, maybe you'll give me some of those babies."

I swat Luca on the arm. "Don't count on it," I tease.

"Come on, let me at least show you a couple of the other rooms before I have to take you to meet my father."

"Don't you want me to change or look a little more presentable before I meet your father?"

Luca looks me up and down. I'm still wearing my dress but now it's dirty with a small tear at the hem. I'm sure I smell, as I haven't showered in over twenty-four hours, and my hair is a mess from the blood and scrape on my head.

"No. Murray will barely notice that you're a woman. He's not all there, and even when he was, he didn't truly care about anything really. I'd rather introduce you and get that over with quickly. Then, I'll show you the room and allow you to clean up before my mother sees you. She is the one you've got to look out for."

I sigh. "Take me to your father."

18

LUCA

Ivy's nervous. I can feel it exuding off of every inch of her body and out through her fingertips as I hold her hand and walk her through the castle. I wasn't expecting her to be nervous. I was expecting her to be skeptical. I was expecting to have to woo her with all the amazing things that come with living in a castle. But I wasn't expecting her to be nervous about meeting my family. She doesn't have anything to prove to me. I already know that she's amazing, strong, and talented.

I, on the other hand, have everything to prove. She's never known me as anything other than a bum and a liar. But, for some reason, unlike her, I'm no longer nervous. My anxiety disappeared the second I had her back in my arms and when I realized that she would get to live, not die because of me and my selfishness. I don't care if she likes my family or impresses them. All I care about is that she is still breathing and that I get to be a part of her life for one more day.

I pause outside of Murray's sitting room and grab hold of both of Ivy's hands, doing my best to give her a reassuring smile to calm her nerves before she meets my father.

"You have nothing to be worried about. You don't need to worry about impressing Murray or anyone else. You're already better than anyone else."

Ivy bites her bottom lip as she looks up at me with big brown eyes. "But what if I want to impress him? What then?"

I shake my head. "Then, you will."

She nods and fakes a small smile.

I keep holding on to one of her hands as I lead her into the sitting room. She stops about two feet in, and we separate for just a second. I look back, confused as to why she stopped, and then I see the look of amazement on her face. I glance up at the expansive ceiling that is at least three stories tall. One wall is covered in books, and another has massive artwork done by one famous painter or another. The other two are floor-to-ceiling windows that look out over the hillside and forest that stands for miles. It is a sight to see if you've never seen it before. I take a second to appreciate it like she does. It's amazing how she makes me look at things differently, like I haven't really seen it in years.

A snoring sound quickly brings me back to reality. I look over at the armchair where I already know I'll find Murray in. I nod my head at Ivy, pointing to Murray sleeping in the chair.

She stifles a giggle when she sees him with his head back in the armchair, a tiny bit of drool dripping off his lip, while a newspaper is spread out over his large belly. I walk over to the old man, who is sound asleep, and slap him hard once on the shoulder.

"I can see you're hard at work, as usual," I say loudly to ensure that he wakes up and hears me.

Murray startles awake, grumbling to himself, and then he sees me. He smiles—or at least, he opens his mouth and shows his teeth in what I know is a normal smile for Murray.

"Good to see you, boy. It's been a while. And, of course, I'm hard at work." He begins folding up the newspaper and sets it on the table next to him before he gets up and gives me a rough hug, as usual.

"I have somebody I'd like you to meet, Murray," I say, running back over to grab Ivy's hand. I pull her forward. "This is Ivy Lane. She's—"

"She's beautiful and talented and smart. I can already see it, just from looking at her. I think you have a good one here, Luca." Murray holds out his hand to Ivy. "I'm Murray Mores. It's a pleasure to meet you, Ivy."

Ivy surprises me by hugging Murray, just like I did earlier.

Murray chuckles. "You've definitely got a keeper. But I'm sure you've already gone and messed it up, like usual, Luca," Murray says, his eyes going back and forth between Ivy and me.

Of course he already knows that I screwed it up. He can read me that well.

"He hasn't done anything that is unforgivable. And he's done quite a bit in these last twenty-four hours to show me that he might be worth forgiving anyway," Ivy says, looking over at me with a gleam in her eye.

I smile back, but honestly, I would hate it if she forgave me right now. Not until she knows everything. Not until she understands what's at stake. Then, she can decide.

"Well, you just come and talk to me if he mistreats you in any way. I'll give him a stern talking-to again, like when he was a boy," Murray says.

Ivy laughs. "Will do, sir."

"Please call me Murray. And definitely don't start calling me all that King and Your Highness nonsense that the staff will try to convince you to say."

"Thank you, Murray. I have enjoyed the tour of your home. It's quite spectacular," Ivy says.

"Has Luca shown you the secret castle ruins yet?" Murray asks.

Ivy's eyes brighten as she looks up at me. "No. He seems to have missed that stop on the tour."

"Well, he definitely has to do that. My favorite place on all the grounds. You'll love it, Ivy."

"We should make it our next stop," Ivy says.

I shake my head. "I'm going to show you your room first and give you time to freshen up before Margaret gets back," I say.

Ivy frowns.

"Oh, yes. My dear wife will definitely have a comment if you meet her in a dress that has a spot of dirt on it, even if you do look beautiful. And I'm sure you want to rest. I've heard about your adventures today," Murray says.

"Adventures?" Ivy asks, a little annoyed that he called her kidnapping an adventure.

Murray sighs as he walks over to the small TV in the corner of the room and flicks it on. Immediately, her face appears on the screen. The image is most likely from her driver's license, and it appears next to footage of her shirtless, making out with me on the street. There is no mention of her kidnapping, just that the prince has returned and found himself a rather promiscuous princess prospect.

I run my hand through my hair and then rub my neck hard. I knew this was bound to happen. I was just hoping I could get Ivy settled before she saw this.

"Why are they not mentioning my kidnapping?" Ivy asks as she walks closer and closer to the TV.

Murray and I exchange glances.

"Because we didn't—" I start to say.

"Because the media are shitheads that only care about selling magazines and newspapers and will paint you in whatever light they feel. Don't worry; Margaret will have you in a pretty ballgown by the end of the day, and they won't have any choice but to see you as a beautiful, intelligent woman who made one past mistake," Murray says.

"But I didn't make a mistake. It's not like I just went on the street and took my shirt off to make out with Luca."

Murray sighs. "Honey, don't worry about it. This family has seen worse scandals than this. This is nothing. They already think Luca is rather promiscuous anyway, and once they really get to know you, they'll realize that they don't have a story—at least, not the one that they think they do. Don't worry about it. The country will love you if you choose to let it."

My eyes go from Murray to Ivy, trying to see if she buys it, if she understands, or if I'll have to explain more of why we aren't doing anything to clear her name and explain the reason she was half-naked on our streets.

Ivy looks from Murray to me. She looks deep into my eyes, trying to decide if we're telling the truth or not. I put my hands in my pockets, trying my best not to encourage her one way or the other. All I've ever done is lie to her, and I don't really want to have to do more of that now if I don't have to. I'd rather let Murray fib a little bit along with the truth other than flat-out lie to her myself. She takes a second longer and then seems to accept Murray's words.

"I guess I'd better get used to it if I'm going to be hanging around this one," she says.

"No. You don't need to get used to it. In fact, if you're smart, you will stay far away from us all. But, if you do end up as part of this family, know that you won't have to face it alone. You can ignore all the horrible stuff that is said about you anyway," Murray says.

"Thank you," Ivy says.

I take Ivy's hand back in mine. "Let's get you to your room, so you have time to change before you have to face the last obstacle of today —Margaret."

Ivy nods. "It was nice meeting you, Murray. I'm looking forward to talking with you more tonight," Ivy says.

Murray chuckles. "Good luck with that. Margaret rather likes to hog conversations, but I'm sure we will be spending more time together in the future."

Ivy raises an eyebrow at me in fear.

I just shrug. I can do my best to protect her, but I can only do so much to protect her against Margaret.

I lead Ivy out of Murray's sitting room and head toward her bedroom.

"Wait," she says.

I stop and look at her. She has a sexy grin on her face.

"What's going on in that head of yours?" I ask with a grin because her grin is infectious.

"Show me the ruins." Her grin brightens even more.

I laugh and shake my head. I look down at my watch to see the time. "We have forty-five minutes, tops, before Margaret gets here."

Ivy places her hands around my neck and then closes her eyes as she leans up and kisses me on the lips, slipping her tongue into my mouth, enticing me to give in to what she wants along with my own desires. She pulls away but not before she sucks on my lip just a second longer. When I open my eyes, I can see from the look on her face that she knows she's won. That I've given in and that I will do whatever she wants.

"I'll show you the ruins, but we have to be quick."

Her face lights up, and she starts skipping as I lead her down the long corridor and outside to the warm fresh air where the sun beats down on top of us.

"You know, you can't always use that to get your way," I say as she skips in front of me even though she has no idea where she's going.

She starts skipping backward so that she can face me. She looks so beautiful when she's this happy. I wish I could make her this happy every day, but I'm thankful that she was so quick to get her spark back after what had happened to her only hours before.

"I'm guessing it'll work at least ninety to ninety-five percent of the time. I'll play my odds," she says with a wink.

I sigh and shake my head. "You're probably right. It's just because I find you so irresistible."

She smiles. "I know," she says before biting her finger. Then, she slowly runs her finger down her body before slipping her hand beneath her dress and underwear, touching herself. Turning herself on.

I stop walking, frozen, just looking at her touch herself in the backyard, but there's at least two dozen staff within eyesight of us at the moment. I don't tell her that because I don't want to embarrass her, and more importantly, I don't want her to stop.

"You're a dirty girl, you know that?"

"I'm your dirty girl," she says, removing her fingers from her panties. She sticks one finger in my mouth, followed by the next one and then the next, until I have tasted all her juices off each finger.

"Your Highness, is that you? I need—" Thomas's voice rings out over the gardens.

"Run!" I shout to Ivy as I give her a mischievous look with my eyes.

We both take off running down the hill that leads to the initial gardens, then past another large field filled with fountains between two large pools on either side.

We keep running even though I know Thomas can no longer hear, see, or find me to ask me some silly question like, *What should be on the menu for dinner tonight?* I honestly couldn't care less.

But we keep running anyway because I don't want any other staff members to stop us and because it's fun. Ivy starts running toward a clearing on the right, assuming that's where we're going. I run harder to catch up with her and then scoop her up and throw her over my shoulder. I start running in the other direction where there is no trail.

She squeals, "What are you doing? I can run, you know. Just tell me where we're going."

I smack her ass. "But this is way more fun."

We both laugh again as I run through the woods, ducking left and right to avoid tree branches that have fallen and bushes that are overgrown. I go on a very small trail that is only visible to those who know it's here. Mainly, me and Murray. But, unlike Murray, who hasn't been back here in years, I come back every summer. It's my favorite place on earth, and I would live here if I could. I don't get lost along the old almost half-mile trail that leads down to the abandoned ruins of the castle that is now part castle, part garden, and part forest. When I get close, I stop and put Ivy down so that she can get the full image as the castle comes into view.

I look at her breathing heavily as she stares at my favorite place on earth. She starts walking closer but very slowly, like she doesn't want to disturb anything around her. I follow right next to her so that I can see her face and the castle ruins at the same time. She stops, and her face is as beautiful as the place. All I can think about is how much I want her right now. How beautiful she is when she's like this. Her lips are lush and red, her hair relaxed and natural, her body so focused on something. The rest of the world no longer matters. I want her to look at me the same way that she looks at these ruins.

"What do you think?" I ask.

She doesn't say anything. She just takes another couple of steps forward.

I ask again, "What do you think?"

But she again takes a few steps forward, like she doesn't hear me. We continue this pattern over and over until we are both standing inside the ruins in the center of the large room that used to be a ballroom with only three of the four walls remaining. The ceiling is gone, and roses and all sorts of flowers crawl up the walls and take over the floor, making it the perfect hideout.

"What do you think?" I ask again. Even though I already know what she thinks, I need to hear it. I need her to love this place as much as I love her.

She still doesn't answer. Instead, she lies down on her back, looking up at the sky and everything around her. I lie down next to her, feeling the thorns of the roses and the sticks that cover and layer the ground stick into my back. But the pain is soon forgotten because of the beauty that surrounds us.

"I know that this is a little overwhelming for you, Ivy. But I need to know what you think. I'm desperate to hear that you love this place as much as I love you." I hesitantly look over at Ivy, hoping she'll finally give me an answer.

Ivy turns over, so we are looking at each other. Nose-to-nose. Body-to-body. Our lips just barely touching, just enough to call it a kiss.

Then, Ivy says, "I love it as much as I love you."

19

IVY

I SAID IT. I finally said it. *I love you.*

He now knows that my feelings have changed, but I don't know where we'll go from here. Right now, honestly, I don't care.

He doesn't say anything back, but hearing him say I love you again is not what I need right now, and he knows it. Instead, he wraps his arms around me, looks deep into my eyes, and then kisses me while rolling me on top of his body. His kisses are primal, showing me just how hungry and desperate he is for me. He holds nothing back as he kisses me over and over. Not letting me go, even when I try to provide him some relief from the thorns that I know are sticking into his back. He doesn't let me take the pain away. He takes it all himself. I know he is trying to protect me from the thorns, but it also feels like he's trying to protect me from something else. I just don't know what.

I sit up, straddling him, trying to provide him a little relief under the guise of taking my dress off, followed by my bra. We stare at each other, both breathing hard and fast, each of our hearts barely controllable in our chests.

"You don't have to protect me all the time, you know. I can take care of myself," I say.

I roll onto my back until the thorns jab into my skin. I'm sure I'm causing scars that I might never get rid of. Luca studies me to see exactly where the pain is and how badly it hurt me. He then removes his own shirt when he realizes that the pain is bearable.

"I know you can take care of yourself. You can handle the pain and face any obstacle in front of you. But you shouldn't have to because of me. You shouldn't have to when I can protect you." He roughly grabs hold of me again and rolls us back over so that he's taking all the thorns and pain himself. His hands touch the back of my skin as he kisses my shoulders where I can see little drops of blood trickling down.

"I promise you, you will never have to feel pain like this again."

He kisses my shoulder again, making what little pain is there instantly disappear, as his hands travel over my body until he finds a small thorn still trapped in the skin of my back. He sits up with me sitting on his lap. He gently pulls it out while kissing my neck, so I don't even feel him removing it.

"And any pain that you have to deal with, I promise, I'll take it away as soon as I know you're in pain."

I firmly kiss him on the lips, hating that he feels like he has to protect me. Hating that he feels responsible for my well-being. That, in some way, he is responsible for protecting me. I know his promises are sincere, but there's no way for him to keep them. He can provide more bodyguards, more security, to prevent some crazy person from kidnapping me, raping me, or killing me, but he can't guarantee it. Honestly, I'm not sure I want him to because a life like that would surely be filled with many given-up opportunities, all a mistake to keep me safe. And I know that's not what either one of us wants.

He stands up with my legs wrapped around his waist. He undoes his jeans, and I push them and his underwear down. I kiss him hard over and over, my hands tangling in his hair, his hand running all over my body while the other holds me up. He slowly eases us back down to the ground, but I know it's difficult for him to keep his balance because we can't keep our hands off of each other. We can't stop kissing. We can't stop being connected as one in any way that we possibly can. Somehow, he manages to get us back on the ground without letting one single thorn grace my skin.

His hand slips into my underwear while my hands travel over his hard pecs and abs and then to his back. I'm trying to hold him up to protect him, but I can't. He won't let me. Every time I try, his back goes more firmly against the thorns, causing him even more pain. I know he feels it even though he tries not to show it to me. He moans when I kiss him, but I can still detect a hint of pain, not pleasure.

He tugs at my panties, trying to get them off, but he can't get them fully off in the position we're sitting in. There are only two choices. Stand up to remove them, which would cause the least physical pain but would mean separating our lips and our bodies for a couple of seconds. Right now, I just can't handle that. Or roll me back over onto my back so that he can remove my pants for me.

I open my eyes and see Luca staring back at me, already coming to the same conclusion.

"No. No more," he says before going back to kissing me again.

I don't have to say anything now. I just look at him, and he knows what I want, what I need. He rolls me over as gently as possible, basically still holding me up with his arms behind my back. I lower my panties, all while he holds me up, keeping me from the pain. When my pants are pulled below my knees, he flips back over, and I come down on his thick, hard cock. He growls in obvious pain and pleasure. I just can't tell which one is stronger. When I start thrusting up and down over his hard body and I can see the pain gone from his eyes, I know which is stronger. I know that I want to be careful, but I can't, not with him. I thrust over and over, and his body meets each of my thrusts.

We kiss in unison, tangling our hands in each other's hair. It doesn't take us long to grow so close to bursting after the emotions of the last couple of days. We both just keep moving faster together while our eyes lock, our mouths claim each other, and our bodies become one. We fuck, sure, but more importantly, we make love.

"Fuck, baby," Luca says I move faster.

I need him to come, need him to feel the ultimate pleasure.

"Are you close, baby? Because, God, I need you to be close."

"Yes!" I scream.

"Come, princess," Luca growls as he thrusts harder and harder, his hard body hitting me, rubbing against my clit.

His cock pushes deep inside me to a place I never knew he could hit. My heart.

I scream as I come, and Luca does the same. I try to collapse back on the ground, but he doesn't let me. Instead, his arms wrap tightly around me as we both breathe heavily on each other's chests.

"So, that's what it feels like to make love." Luca sighs, still breathing heavily.

"I guess it is."

"It's still not too late," he says.

I lift my head to look at him. "What do you mean?"

"I mean, you can still take back your *I love you*. You still don't know everything about me. I still have too many truths left to tell. And, as much as I love hearing those words fall from your lips, I can't really believe them, not until you know all of me."

"It doesn't matter what else you have to say. I know the lies. I know that, when you lie to me, you're just trying to protect me. So, whatever you say to me now, it doesn't matter. I'll still love you. I don't need to take my *I love you* back. Ever."

"I hope that's the case. But, to protect my own heart, I can't believe you just yet."

I frown as I study Luca's eyes, going back and forth between them, trying to understand what could be so bad. I don't know what more he could say. What lie he could tell me that would hurt me. I know that the only lie he could say that would hurt me is saying *I love you* and not really meaning it.

"I really think you could've found a better use for your time, like figuring out how to fix this family scandal, than by fucking my son in a garden where anyone could see you," a woman says from behind me.

I jump at the startle of someone being here when I wasn't expecting anyone. And then realize I'm completely naked. I grab my clothes lying next to me, and I do my best to cover my naked butt and back while staying pressed to Luca's naked body. I look at Luca, who looks like he's about ready to kill someone. He doesn't seem to be bothered at all by the fact that his mother just found us having sex.

"What are you doing here, Margaret?" Luca growls, his voice dark and heavy, filled with an anger I'm not sure I have ever seen before.

I take a chance and glance back at the woman that I now realize is his mother. She's standing just barely at the entrance with her arms folded across her chest and a scowl only a mother could give on her face.

"The question is not, what am I doing here? The question is, what are you doing here with her?" she says.

Luca shakes his head. "What the hell do you think we are doing here, Mom? We're fucking."

I wince just a little.

"Oh, so it's *Mom* now. You haven't called me that since you were twelve."

"Well, it shows you just how angry I really am."

"Get dressed and meet me at the back patio in ten minutes, preferably with clothes on. I need to talk to Ivy alone. And, Luca, you need a haircut before tonight's ball."

Luca doesn't protest or say anything to his mother. He just lies, frozen.

Eventually, I know she has left because the coldness I felt upon her immediate arrival is gone, and the warm sun begins to shine back down on us.

"We need to get dressed and go," Luca says as he helps me into a standing position.

He hands me the rest of my clothes, and I start getting dressed. Both of us are careful not to step on any of the sharp thorns.

"Your mother's pretty scary. You weren't lying when you said your mother was going to be an obstacle."

"No, I wasn't," Luca says with a coldness that I didn't expect after we just made love so passionately a moment before.

It's clear that moment is long gone.

I try not to be anxious about having to speak with his mother alone, but I am. She clearly didn't get the greatest first impression of me. And it's clear he has his own issues with his mother that he needs to deal with. She can't be that bad. Maybe a little protective of her son.

I finish dressing first and watch Luca put on his jeans before he turns and bends down to pick up his shirt still lying on the floor.

I gasp when I see it. His back is covered in thorns, deep scratches, and blood. But I don't know what to say to take that pain away. He turns around as he slips his shirt back on and walks over to me. His eyes look at me for the first time since his mother came in.

He softly kisses me on the forehead and then says, "Don't worry, princess; the scars are worth it. Because, every time I look at them or feel them, I'll remember how I felt in this moment, how happy and loved I was, if only for a short time. Because it won't be long now until you hate me; I'm sure of that."

"And what will I be left with?"

"Your heart."

20

LUCA

I SEE Margaret scowling at us as we get closer. Her arms are crossed, and her high-heeled foot taps loudly over and over again against the pavement. It takes everything in my body not to run over and strangle her after I finally realized what she did. I knew it the second that she came and found us in the ruins. I knew that was all a test. And I'm sick of it. I'm sick of her games, especially when someone's life is at stake.

I lean over to Ivy, who's standing next to me, probably scared to death by the woman standing in front of us. But there's nothing that I can say to ease those fears.

"Ivy, go wait inside for me a minute. I need to speak with Margaret alone."

Ivy's grip on my hand tightens, telling me that she doesn't want to leave me all alone with Margaret. I turn and look at her. I nod, letting her know that I really need her to do as she's told.

Ivy softly kisses me on the cheek. "I'll be right inside if you need me."

I keep my eyes on Ivy as she walks back inside the castle. But all I can think is, *What have I brought her into? What danger?*

I feel my heart breaking, trying to figure out what my next move is. *Do I follow through with the plan to try to make her mine and a princess for our country? Or do I do what's best for her and set her free again? This time, forever.*

I turn my attention to Margaret, who doesn't seem surprised at all that I want to have a one-on-one conversation with her.

"What did you do?" I ask through clenched teeth, trying with everything inside me to remain civil and not cause a fight.

Because, as much as Margaret can be the biggest pain in my ass, I also know that she is one of only a handful of people who genuinely care about me and know all my secrets.

"You already know what I did. I tested her strength and ability to be in this family. If you are going to insist on bringing a complete stranger in, then I'm going to insist on doing whatever test I deem necessary to protect this family, this country."

"You should've at least told me. I was scared to death that she had really been kidnapped."

"She was really kidnapped," Margaret says with an even face, like she is reporting the weather to me.

I step closer, feeling my anger overtake any feelings of love I have for this woman.

"What do you mean, she was kidnapped? I know you hired them."

"You're right; I did hire them. They just didn't know that I was the one who'd they hired them. They thought I was a terrorist, just like all the rest of them, who would pay them well when they kidnapped and used the girl to try to kill us all. How else do you think anyone would have known that you two were dating?"

My heart breaks at how ruthless Margaret can be. How willing she is to do anything to protect her family and her country. I understand because I've made plenty of sacrifices myself, all in the name of protecting this country that I love so much.

"You took it too far. She could have died. We could've all died. What then?"

"Then, we would've all died. But it was a sacrifice I was willing to make to ensure that our country was safe and didn't fall into bad hands."

"But I'm not willing to take that risk. I'm not willing to risk her life."

Margaret steps forward, looking me straight in the eyes. "If she is going to be a princess, you'd better be willing to risk her life for this country. If not, let her go now, and stop wasting everybody's time."

I glare at Margaret, our faces inches apart, neither one of us backing down. My breathing is fast, my heart is racing, and my fists are clenched, trying to hold in the anger and fear that I feel.

"You have to decide, son. Do you love her? Do you love her so much that you're willing to let her go to save her life? Or are you going to be selfish and destroy her? The decision is yours."

Margaret backs away, giving me my space while I deal with the facts that I know are true. It's one of the reasons I let Ivy go so easily last time. Because I know deep in my heart that setting her free is the right thing to do. But I also know that I'm far too selfish now for that to happen. My heart isn't willing to let her go.

"In the meantime, while you decide what your decision is going to be, I'm going to continue to test her and you every time I can. Because, if she's going to be in this life, she needs to be prepared for everything that comes with it. Our life isn't easy. Loving you will never be easy. And she deserves to know that before she commits herself to this life."

"I'm telling her tonight. I'm telling her the whole truth. She needs to know that, too. You don't have to worry about her hiding our secret. Unlike the rest of them, she will."

She turns back, pausing just at the door to look at me. "You're right; I don't think she will reveal our secret. But just realize what you are doing because, after the truth has been said, you can't take it back. After she has agreed to be part of this life, death is the only way out."

21

IVY

I SEE Margaret throw open the door to enter the castle, and my heart stops. I spent the last twenty minutes trying to eavesdrop on their conversation, but unfortunately, the walls of the castle are far too thick for me to have heard anything.

Margaret stares at me with a blank expression on her face. I have no idea what she's thinking or what's going on in that head of hers.

"Follow me," Margaret says.

I glance back over at Luca, who is still standing outside, pacing, making no move to come inside. So, I follow Margaret. She walks with purpose as she strides through the castle. I follow her close behind. She doesn't say anything as she walks, and I try to keep my mouth shut despite all the questions running through my head. I try to focus on the beauty of the castle and the new rooms we pass as we head upstairs. But I've never been one to just blindly follow orders.

"Why does Luca call you Margaret?" I wince when the words leave my mouth. Of all the questions to ask this woman—like where we are going or telling her how beautiful her home is—that's what I said.

Margaret stops and turns to look at me. She cocks her head to one side as her eyes pierce through to my soul. "He used to call me Mother." She sighs, letting in the tiniest human moment. But then, when she looks back up at me a second later, her face is hard and cold again, just like I figure her heart is. "But something changed over the years. As he grew older, taking on more responsibilities as a prince, and as I molded him into the man he is today, he no longer thought of me as a mother. He now thinks of me as his queen. I didn't like him calling me Your Highness all the time, so now, he calls me Margaret and his father Murray."

My mouth drops open a little bit as I realize the toll that being the prince has taken on Luca. He no longer even calls his mother, Mother.

"Now, if you don't have any more nosy questions for me, then I'll show you to your room and help you prepare for tonight."

I smile. "I have a lot of questions. But I'll let you finish showing me to my room and doing the things you need me to do before I ask them."

"Good."

Margaret continues up the long staircase, and I follow behind her, taking in the details that seem to be so ingrained in every aspect of the castle. It takes us almost five minutes of walking down long corridors and up more stairs until Margaret stops at a door.

"This will be your room while you're with us. I think you'll find it has more than enough things to fit all your needs. And it might keep you and my son apart long enough to do something other than fuck."

I about choke as I swallow at her bluntness.

"I'm sorry you had to see that. Our goal was never to upset you, which is why we went off to the most secluded place we could find before we fucked, as you said. But do know that it was more than just fucking. I love your son very much. I wouldn't be here if I didn't."

"I have no doubt that is true. I know you love my son, but it takes more than love to do this job, and that's what I'm here to show you— what your real life would be like if you moved in here, not the fairy tale that my son has tried to make you think it would be."

She opens the door and steps inside. I follow behind her. My mouth drops open, something that I've grown used to since I've been inside the castle. The one bedroom alone is almost the same size as the whole first floor of my house. A bed sits on one side that is large, much larger than a normal king-size. It has beautiful canopies hanging down all around it. There is a large fireplace with at least three or four chairs and two large sofas sitting around it. There are large, expansive windows that look out over a small stream outside my window. There's so much more to take in inside the large room. I could spend all day staring at all the intricate details. But I know that Margaret isn't going to let me spend all day relaxing and enjoying the room, like I would imagine in a fairy tale.

I give Margaret my full attention.

"Good. Now that you have seen your room, we have a lot to get done before tonight. We have to get you fitted for a dress, cleaned and washed up, do something with your hair so that it's presentable, and educated for tonight."

"Educated?"

Margaret ignores my question and snaps her fingers as a couple of staff members appear seemingly from nowhere. They run over to me with tape measures in their hands and start measuring all parts of my body while I awkwardly stand, letting them do it. I look over at Margaret, who is standing and studying me, while the staff measures me.

"You have a beautiful home here."

Margaret's scowl deepens. "It's not my home. It belongs to the kingdom, not to me."

"Oh, um...well, it's beautiful anyway."

I wait for her to thank me, but she doesn't. I expect she never says, *Thank you.*

"Who usually stays in this room?" I ask, generally wondering what other guests have stayed in this magnificent room before.

But it seems I said something wrong again because Margaret frowns.

"No one in all my time here at the castle. This room has always been set aside for the future princess. It's the best single room in the castle, and we always figured whoever married Luca would be a spoiled rotten princess who would want the most expansive room with the best view."

I frown. "But I'm not—"

"We are finished with the measurements, Your Highness," says one of the staff who just had her hands all over me, measuring me, invading my privacy and my personal space.

"Then, hurry along and tweak the dress that we picked out," Margaret says.

The staff scurries off but not before curtsying before Margaret.

"I really don't need the nicest room in the castle. And I'm also more than fine with Luca and I sharing a room if we were to ever get married," I say, not really believing that this is the most beautiful room in the castle. Not because it's not beautiful; it is. In fact, I don't think I can imagine a more beautiful room. But it's because I think those rooms are reserved for the king and queen.

"If you marry my son, this will be your room. He will have his own. And, although I'm sure he will be spending many nights here, in your bed, there are going to be more than enough times when you come back and need your own space, away from him. Trust me, this job is more taxing than your vet job."

I open my mouth to argue but then shut it. I'm getting nowhere with this woman, and if I want her to like me, I need to keep my mouth shut at least part of the time.

"Now, get in the shower and quickly wash off the dirt and filth. We are already a half hour behind schedule."

I glance around the room and see at least four different doors that lead off of it. I have no idea which one is the bathroom, which one is the closet, or where the other two doors lead to.

"Um...which way to the bathroom?"

Margaret rolls her eyes and then points to my right. I run into the bathroom, thankful to have a few minutes away from Margaret and to myself. If this is what my life would be like if I married Luca, I can see why my life would be taxing. She is the reason.

I don't take the time to admire the double sinks or the marble floor or the chandeliers hanging over my head. Instead, I head straight to the large shower that could fit at least half a dozen people inside of it. I turn on the main showerhead, not bothering to figure out how to turn on the other four showerheads. That will have to wait until another time when I have the time to truly relax and enjoy my shower. For now, I just need to hurry so that I can get back out to Margaret to make her happy. That's what I do. I hop in and out of the shower in less than two minutes while still trying to ensure that I'm squeaky clean. When I step out, I put the robe on and then come back out, only to find my room empty.

"Margaret?"

Instead of Margaret, three staff members scurry to my sides, telling me that they're here to do my hair and makeup. So, I sit for the next two hours, getting every inch of me pampered and taken care of. My hair and makeup are done to perfection even though the hair-stylist had to try a couple of different updos until she figured out how to deal with the texture of my hair, as it's so different from what she's used to here. But it's the most beautiful thing I've ever seen done with my hair, also hooked up with curls hanging down.

Just as they finish, Margaret comes back into the room, holding a couple of boxes. She nods at the staff, and they all scurry out of the room as she sets the boxes down on the dressing table in front of me.

"What's your full name, Ivy?" Margaret asks.

I flutter my eyelashes, surprised that she doesn't already know my full name since she seems to know so much else about me.

"Ivy Catherine Lane."

"No."

I scrunch my eyes, completely confused as to why she said that.

"Your name used to be Ivy Catherine Lane. But, if you want any chance, any possibility, of being anonymous when you go back to the US, then your name tonight cannot be Ivy Catherine Lane. Your name is Ivy Burke."

"But what if I stay?"

"Then, your name will still forever be Ivy Burke until you marry my son; in which case, it will be Ivy Mores. Ivy Lane will never exist here. Your past will never exist here."

"What do you mean?"

"Your past no longer exists here," she says more slowly. "Your name is Ivy Burke. You grew up mainly in the US. You had grandparents who lived here, which is why you know the country well. You've visited often. You met my son, Luca, three years ago in law school. You've been dating for that entire time. You both realized that you wanted to be serious about your relationship and take things to the next level. You were not kidnapped yesterday. Your life has never been in danger. That is what you are going to tell the press and everyone else. Those are the lies you will tell tonight."

I raise my eyebrows and take a deep breath as I try to understand what she said. Why she wants me to lie about everything.

But I'm too shocked to ask any questions or say anything.

"I need you to understand this, Ivy. If you want to live in our world, you have to play by our rules. And, if you fuck up, you're gone. We can't afford to give second chances. You tell the lies that we tell you to, or you are gone."

"But Luca——"

Margaret roughly grabs my chin, forcing me to look at her close in the eyes. "You must understand this, my dear, as it's the most important rule. You must do exactly as I say if you want to be with Luca. Exactly as I say. You can ask Luca yourself when we are through here. He'll tell you exactly the same thing. There's too much that you still don't know about yet. Too much that you don't understand. He will let you go just as fast as I will. You have to be willing to lie, or this all ends. Do you understand?"

"I understand," I say slowly.

Margaret lets go of my chin and slowly backs away.

I said so, but I don't really understand it.

Margaret goes back to the boxes and begins opening them until she finds what she is looking for. She pulls out a box and turns to me. That's when I see the beautiful tiara she's holding in her hands.

"You'll wear this tonight, so you'll be reminded all night of what you're giving up if you decide to leave here."

I swallow hard. She walks behind me and places the tiara on top of my head. It's gorgeous, and it's crazy that I'm wearing it. It instantly makes me feel like a princess even though I really have no idea what is required to in fact be a princess.

What would my duties be? What would my real life be like? Would I really never be able to treat animals again?

I look at myself in the mirror though, and I see a princess. But Margaret is wrong if she thinks that, by putting the tiara on my head, I would understand what I could be giving up. Because I couldn't care less about being a princess. I care a lot more about being Luca's wife.

"Why?"

Margaret sighs and sits down on the chair next to me. "Why what?"

"Why do I have to lie? Why can't I just be myself?"

"You'll understand much more as time goes on. You'll understand all the intricate details about what this role means, but the gist is, you are not what the country wants. The country wants a princess of their own making. Not a promiscuous stripper who is being sued and who is about to lose her license."

I swallow down my pride a little bit. I must learn to not ask questions that I don't want to hear honest answers to. For as much as the family lies, they sure do know how to tell the truth in such a way that rips you right to your soul.

"And what do I say about the pictures of Luca and me kissing on the street while I was half naked?"

Margaret stands up and walks over to the door. Staff members enter, carrying a large cream-colored ballgown. It has the most beautiful lace corset I've ever seen. It's more beautiful than what I would even imagine my wedding gown to look like. But I have a feeling that, if I was to marry Luca, my wedding dress would be at least twice as nice as this dress.

"Make them forget, which they are likely to do if you can carry off this dress," Margaret says.

22

LUCA

I PACE back and forth outside of Ivy's bedroom, waiting for her to finish getting ready and come out. I've spent the last three hours apart from her, and it's been killing me. I know that it is necessary. Margaret wouldn't have had it any other way. But, still, I hate being apart from Ivy. These last few minutes, waiting for her to finish getting ready and come out so that we can be introduced as a couple at the ball, have been the absolute worst.

I shouldn't complain. The last three hours for me really haven't been that bad. I got a haircut, so I look more like a prince and less like a beach bum or lawyer from the US. I showered and got dressed in a new tux. And I spent most of the time with Murray, discussing how things have been going since I left. Discussing what my life is going to be like in the coming months as I start taking over a lot of Murray's responsibilities, which he is no longer physically capable of doing because of his health. I had a rather relaxing afternoon. Whereas Ivy has been thrown into a world she never thought actually existed with Margaret scolding her, I'm sure, the whole time.

I can't wait any longer, but I know Margaret will kill me if I see Ivy before she's completely ready and before Margaret is through with setting up whatever test she has for her now. It doesn't matter what her test is. Whatever it is, I'm not leaving Ivy's side again tonight. And, by the end of the night, Ivy will know everything. If she's smart, she'll make the decision to go back home and forget that any of us ever existed.

I knock on the door, growing impatient. "Almost ready?" I ask.

"Patience is a virtue, my son," I hear Margaret's voice ring out.

I frown and walk away from the door, clenching my fists and then unclenching them over and over, and then my heart stops when I hear the door opening.

"Don't turn around just yet," Margaret says.

I hear her walking toward me. I look at her, a bit confused. She gets to the staircase, and then she quietly nods to me. She makes her way downstairs to go change into her own ballgown before dinner and the ball tonight.

It's moments like these when I love Margaret. She might be the strictest mother on the planet, but she also knows well enough when to leave us alone and let us have our own moment.

I take one more breath before I slowly turn around and see Ivy standing in the doorway with a large smile on her face. I pause for a second, not doing anything, as I look at her and take in all of her beauty. For a woman who is used to wearing scrubs every day, she sure knows how to wear a ballgown. The light color of the dress complements her dark skin well, and the gown pushes her breasts up, making me want to devour them. Her hair is done up with curls framing her face, and she's wearing a tiara, like the princess that she is.

I suck in a breath, suddenly realizing that I haven't breathed since I saw her. "You look beautiful, but then you always do."

"You look handsome as well. You really clean up well." Her eyes soak up every inch of my body.

I walk toward her and hold out my arms, which she takes. Then, I start guiding her down the stairs, trying my best to remember to breathe. But all I can think about is that this is the dress she's going to be wearing when both of our lives change forever. I just don't know if it'll be for better or for worse.

"I'm a bit nervous. Margaret explained a lot of things to me, but she didn't explain what's expected of me at the ball. Am I expected to dance? Because you know I'm horrible at that," she says.

I laugh. "Of course you're expected to dance. But you'll be dancing primarily with me, and it's pretty simple. You'll catch on easily."

"Do people think you and I are going to get married, and that's why I'm attending the ball now instead of at some point in the last three years?" she asks.

I stop. "Margaret told you about what we have to pretend tonight then?"

"You mean, the lies."

I nod. "Yes, the lies. Just do this for me, and I promise, when tonight is over, I'll explain everything."

She takes a deep breath. "Let's get this over with then," she says.

I smile and then firmly kiss her on the lips. "You know, most women would be excited about attending a ball, being the princess, having all the attention on them."

"Yeah, but I'm not just like any other woman."

"That, you aren't." *You're my woman*, I want to say.

I guide her to the back entrance of the ballroom where we will be introduced in just a minute.

"They're going to introduce us to the world. And then there will be some dancing and some eating and then more dancing. But, unfortunately, there won't be enough eating. But don't worry; I'll have the cook make us a burger or something later after everyone has gone home. And, to answer your earlier question, yes, everyone thinks I'm introducing you because we are about to get engaged."

"Oh. So, no pressure, right?" she says with a worried smile.

I kiss her again. "No pressure. Remember, these people have already seen you shirtless. Tonight's going to be easy compared to that."

"Thanks for reminding me," she says sarcastically.

Thomas comes to the door and asks, "Ready, Your Highness?"

"Yes." I nod.

He speaks into his headset, and then the double doors are opened as we are announced as a couple to the world.

We walk into the room, both with fake smiles plastered on our faces. I guide her out to the center of the dance floor as music starts up. I take her hand and look her in the eyes, and then right on cue, I move. She moves, too, but it's more of a stumble than a glide.

I try to hold back a laugh. "You've got this. Just dance with me like it's just the two of us."

She starts moving with me and quickly catches on to the simple rhythm.

"Why didn't you tell me we would be the only two people dancing and that everyone's eyes would be on me?" she hisses through clenched teeth.

I laugh. "Because it wouldn't have helped anything. There wasn't enough time to teach you how to dance, and we would've still had to do it anyway. It would have just made you more nervous at the beginning," I say. "Don't worry; my parents are going to be introduced. Then, the party will really start."

Just as I finish speaking, my parents are introduced. They don't dance, but everyone else finally joins us on the dance floor.

Several more songs pass with us dancing the whole time. Ivy slowly gains more and more confidence with every song that passes.

"How much longer do we have to dance? My feet are killing me in these heels."

I laugh. "We can stop anytime. But, when we do, that's when the questions will start."

She plasters a fake terrified expression on her face that just makes me laugh more.

"God, I hope you say yes," I say.

She pauses at my words. "What? Are you going to propose tonight?" Ivy asks.

"No. That would be too much of a perfect fairy tale. No, I have a far more important question to ask you."

"What could be a more important question than asking me to marry you?"

"I guess you'll have to wait and see," I say with a grin that I know she wants to smack off my face for torturing her with that info.

I slow our movements until we are barely dancing, seeing someone approaching us.

"Hello, Luca. It's been a long time since you've been to one of these balls," Jennifer, my ex, says from behind me.

I wrap my arm around Ivy's waist and then turn to face Jennifer. "Hi, Jennifer. I'd like to introduce you to my girlfriend, Ivy. Ivy, this is Jennifer. We used to date in high school," I say, introducing them, being as honest as I can to try to make Ivy comfortable.

Ivy holds her hand out to Jennifer. "It's nice to meet a friend of Luca's," Ivy says.

Jennifer shakes Ivy's hand, sizing her up and down, looking at how much she doesn't fit into our world. I know her dark skin is different, that she is an American. She didn't grow up here; she's never even been here before, making her look like an outsider. When I compare Ivy to Jennifer, Ivy looks like a total outcast while Jennifer could easily hold her own as my wife.

"Do you mind if I have the next dance?" Jennifer asks, pushing her luck too far.

"Ivy and I were about to go get some food actually."

I lean over and firmly kiss Ivy on the lips. I can feel Ivy's hesitation as I kiss her while Jennifer's and everyone else's eyes are on us, but I couldn't care less. I need everyone to know without a shadow of a doubt that I'm with Ivy, not anyone else.

"And I'll actually be dancing all my dances with Ivy for the rest of the night and my life, if I get to be so lucky."

23

IVY

I AM amazed by the way Luca handled his ex. He treated me like I was the only woman in his world while still telling me the truth about who Jennifer was. To be honest, I think the Luca here is far more of a gentleman than the man back in the States. It's something I'm not quite used to, coming from him. But he's been that way the entire night so far. Only having eyes for me. Only dancing with me. Waiting on me hand and foot, making sure that I'm completely comfortable, basically treating me like a princess.

And, boy, have I felt like a princess tonight. Everyone's eyes have been on me the entire night. My glass of champagne has never been empty; a staff member comes to fill it up every few minutes. Everyone curtsies and smiles before coming to talk to us.

It's a strange feeling being pampered. Something that I might have a hard time getting used to.

Could I get used to it for Luca?

Could I give up my entire world to live in his and be waited on hand and foot?

It doesn't take me long to answer the question. I would do almost anything for this man. Because I've fallen much harder than I thought I would ever fall for a man.

"I've got to get off my feet. They're killing me. I don't know how your mother or any of the other women here are doing it."

Luca laughs. "None of them have any feeling left in their feet after doing this for years."

"That must be the case," I say, laughing, too.

"You can have a seat at our table over here. I need to go speak with Thomas. He's been eyeing me all night, trying to get me to come talk with him."

I nod. "You can do that as long as you sneak off to the bathroom or coat closet with me when you get back."

Luca kisses me hard on the lips, slipping his tongue into my mouth, making me want him even more. I've wanted him since the second I saw him in his tux-like outfit.

"Deal," he says before walking away.

I sink back into my chair, lifting my feet on the chair across from me, not caring if it's not ladylike and that Margaret will probably scold me later. I just need a few minutes with my feet up while Luca's gone, and then I need a few minutes with my feet up in the air while I'm lying flat on my back as he fucks me, so I can get through the rest of this night.

Of course, as soon as I sit down, I see Jennifer and a couple of other girls walking toward me. I try to smile as the girls all sit down at my table without asking me for permission first, something I know they would never do if Luca were sitting here, based on my experience so far by how everyone treats him.

"I wanted to introduce you to a few more of Luca's friends," Jennifer says.

"That's nice of you, but I'm sure Luca would've gotten around to it if he had wanted me to meet you all," I say a bit snarky.

I know girls like this. They play games. They throw shade and start fights without actually throwing any real punches. That's how they attack and hurt and get what they want, and I'm not going to let them do it to me.

"Well, since I'm Luca's closest friend, I know him better than most. I know he would like me to introduce you to his other friends here. You need to get to know them all if you have a chance at making this work," Jennifer says.

I slowly stand so that I'm higher than all the women now sitting at my table.

"I know Luca better than all of you, and I know that he'd rather introduce me to all of you himself, if at all, so I ask that you show some respect and wait to introduce yourself until Luca returns."

Jennifer rolls her eyes. "This is Samantha and Catherine. Ladies, this is Luca's new bitch for the moment. What was your name again? I can't quite remember," Jennifer says, smiling.

"You know damn well what my name is. It's Ivy Lane. You'd better get used to it because I'm not going anywhere. I would recommend staying far, far away from me for the rest of the night if you know what's good for you and if you want to remain in Luca's life."

I storm off from the table. I'd hoped that Luca had dated better women, but I guess not.

I search the room, looking for Luca, when I see Margaret eyeing me from two tables over. *Shit.* She's probably upset with me because I spoke so poorly to those women. She will probably scold me later. I don't care. They deserved it, and it was worth whatever scolding's coming my way later.

I see Luca on the outskirts of the ballroom. He smiles when we lock eyes and then nods, signaling that he is ducking out the door and that I should follow him. I walk quickly across the floor and run over to where he stood before slipping out the door. When I'm out in the hallway, I don't see him anywhere.

I start walking forward as I whisper, "Luca?"

I walk a few feet further before Luca pops out of a door and pulls me inside. It's pitch-black in here.

"Where are we?" I ask.

"A coat closet," Luca answers as he backs me up against the wall before his lips claim mine.

"I think I made a mistake," I say between kisses.

"Not possible."

"No, really—"

Luca kisses me again, and I forget what I wanted to tell him. All I think about is his lips on mine and the liquid that is drenching my panties.

"I don't know how I'm going to fuck you in this dress," Luca says suddenly.

And then we both laugh.

I stare down at the fabric covering my body and say, "I don't think it's possible without removing it."

"If I remove it, we're never gonna be able to get it back on," Luca growls.

"I really hate balls," I say.

"Well, we can't have that."

Before I know what's happening, my arms are thrust over my head, and something soft, like silk, is being tied around them. I gently pull on them. I can't move them off the rod in the closet above my head.

"What are you doing?"

"Making you like balls more."

And then I feel him under my dress, his lips and breath over my panties.

"You have to be quiet, princess, or I'll stop. Do you understand me?"

"Yes," I whisper, showing him that I can be quiet.

His fingers plunge inside me as his tongue goes over the piercing on my clit. His fingers taunt me while his tongue builds me, but it's not enough. It's not what I want. And he knows it. Within seconds, his touch disappears. I take several deep breaths while trying to be patient to see if he's going to come up with any solution. I feel my dress being lifted but nothing else. He doesn't touch me, and I begin to lose faith that he ever will until long after the ball is over.

"Luca, I need you," I let out in a whimper. His cock slides inside me as I say the last word. I try to scream out, but his hand covers my mouth, as he anticipated that I would scream.

His cock thrusts easily in and out, turning me on more and more. All my senses are heightened. My hands are tied up, and my sight is gone. My inability to make a sound makes it so that all I can do is feel him. I feel his cock, feel his touch, feel him fucking me. I moan into his hand seconds later as he makes me calm, and I feel him calm inside me.

"I love you, princess," he whispers into my ear.

"I love you, too."

Luca slowly removes the tie around my wrist, and I immediately collapse to the floor.

"Sex with you is exhausting," I say.

"We'll just have to build up your stamina then, so I can fuck you more."

I bite my lip at the thought of that. At the thought of more. At the thought of being able to do this anytime of any day.

"I'll step outside first, and then you can follow a few seconds later in case anyone sees us. They won't know if it's a coat closet or a bathroom."

I nod. His lips land back on mine one last time, and then he's gone. And I don't ever want to leave this coat closet again. I just want to stay here where I can think of how perfect and simple our life could be if he weren't a prince.

24

LUCA

I step back into the ballroom, trying my best to pretend like nothing just happened. It's going to be impossible to hide how good I feel right now. Everyone's eyes are on me, as usual. But, this time, I feel like they can peer into my soul. Like they know exactly what dirty, filthy things Ivy and I were just doing in a coat closet.

Several people pass me, intently staring at me, and I nod and smile at them, but I get a strange feeling about it all. I see Thomas running over to me with a worried expression on his face. And that combined with all the awkward stares I've been getting makes me worried that something happened when I was gone.

"What happened?" I ask Thomas when he gets close.

Thomas tries to catch his breath. "I..." He sucks in a breath. "Don't know how..." He takes another breath. "But they found out Ivy's real last name."

"Shit," I curse. I must say it far too loudly because a couple of the women standing nearest glance up at me with a disgusted look, like I shouldn't use such a disgusting word.

"What have they found out?" I ask.

Thomas nervously looks at me. And then he pulls out a phone

and hands it to me. I type in her name to see what all the news outlets are saying about her.

"Shit. They've found out everything."

Thomas nods.

"Does Margaret know?" I ask.

Thomas doesn't have to say a word. I already know from the expression on his face that she does know.

"Shit." I run my hand through my hair, trying to think about what we should do. How we will salvage this. How to keep Ivy in my life but also as protected as she can be. But my mind is racing so fast that it's hard to come up with anything.

I turn to Thomas. "I'm going to go talk to Margaret. You handle getting Ivy somewhere where she's safe and protected. Understood?"

"I'll make sure she's escorted back up to her room, Your Highness."

"We don't have time for all that Your Highness. Don't let her back into the ballroom. I don't want her to deal with this right now. Tell her nothing, just that I will be up soon and she's not to worry."

I start running across the ballroom in search of Margaret. She's seated at her table with her usual scowl on her face. But, this time, she looks even angrier than before. I hear the commotion behind me, and I freeze. I'm standing in the middle of the ballroom when I slowly turn around to see that Ivy has entered. She gets swarmed immediately by press and others asking her questions, trying to figure out why she lied about who she really is. And what a stripper is doing here. Because, of course, that's the only thing the press report on. Her past as a stripper. Not the fact that she saves animals every single day.

I lock eyes with her over the crowd, doing my best to reassure her that I'll be there in just a second. But I feel someone's hands on me, holding me back before I have a chance to take a step toward her.

"We need to get you somewhere safe before all hell breaks out," Andy says.

"We have to get Ivy first."

"We have a team going in for her. It's best that she go out the other way instead of through the crowd. I'll have her brought around to you."

I don't move. I'm too worried about Ivy. She is clearly in shock. I wasn't expecting the chaos that has now broken out around her. But I spy several of the other bodyguards moving toward her, only seconds away. So, I let Andy start pulling me away even though it kills me that I can't see her for even a second.

I promised I would protect her. But it's clear in just the twenty-four hours she's been here that I can't. I can't protect her from anything. I should've never brought her here.

Andy pulls me into a small room that he secured. I see that Murray and Margaret are seated on two of the couches in the small sitting room that hardly ever gets used. It's just the closest room to the ballroom where Andy thinks he can keep us safe.

I walk over to Margaret. "So, what's the plan? How do we resolve this?"

She looks at me with pain in her eyes. "We don't."

"What do you mean? There has to be some sort of plan. This isn't Ivy's fault. And this isn't even the worst scandal that we've been through. It'll all blow over. We just need to do some damage control about her past. And, if she chooses not to stay here, I just need to find a new woman fast to spark the public's interest."

Margaret runs her hand through her hair with a worried expression on her face that I haven't seen in a long time. I sink down onto the couch next to her, so they can look at me.

"What is it?" I ask even though I'm afraid to.

"She's not the one, Luca. I desperately wanted her to be, for your sake. I thought she was strong enough. I thought she was intelligent enough. And maybe she has those things."

"What are you talking about?"

"She didn't keep the secret. She didn't keep the lie. She told Jennifer her real name. She is the reason that the press now knows her entire past. And, if she can't keep a secret that simple, how can she keep any of ours?"

My mouth drops with all the air sucked out of my lungs. I can't marry Ivy. I can't even ask her. It doesn't matter that it was an honest mistake. If she slipped up with any of our lies, everything that we've built the last twenty years will come crashing down. This country will be in turmoil. Everything will be destroyed.

I have to stop loving her. Period. Because she can't be the princess.

25

IVY

I STEP BACK inside the ballroom, and everything is chaos. Everyone is staring at me. As I take a step forward, everyone starts running toward me, all asking questions, saying my real name, revealing a past that I never thought would come back to haunt me. Cameras are thrust into my face as more and more questions are asked.

I eventually stop listening, trying my best to tune them out, while I search for the only thing that does matter in my life—Luca. I spot him in the center of the ballroom and make eye contact for just a second, long enough for him to reassure me that he is on this and is going to figure it out. That he's going to protect me, like he always does.

I take a deep breath and try to calm my beating heart and my heavy breathing as I watch Andy approach Luca and start leading him out of the room. As much as I wish that Luca were standing right beside me, I'm actually happy that Andy has him. He'll keep him safe, and I'm sure that I'll be reunited with him soon enough.

I feel a hand on my arm, and I try to pull it away, but the grip is far too strong—something that I have gotten far to used to since coming here. I look up to see whose hand is holding on to me.

A bodyguard, I realize. *Thank God.*

I think he says something to me, but the crowd is much too loud for me to hear, so instead, I just let him guide me with his hands out of the ballroom and away from the crowd.

"What is going on?" I ask the bodyguard.

He continues to hold on to me as he focuses on getting me somewhere safer than this hallway. I glance around and notice at least three more members of the security team surrounding us.

"There's time for explanations later. Right now, I need to get you to safety."

We move forcefully and quickly down the hallway and toward a door at the other end. A few people have started emerging from the ballroom, but the security team doesn't give me enough time to worry about them as we move quickly past them. Still, I can't help but notice the closer that we get to the other end of the hallway, the more people come spilling out of the ballroom, trying to get to us.

So that they can ask more invading questions to sell newspapers, I think.

The door opens at the end of the hallway, preparing to let us in when we get there, and I can see Luca. But before we can get there, the crowd breaks loose and shots ring out. I stare at Luca in the room and see his eyes, the fear in them for just a second before the door is slammed shut in our faces, and then I'm being pulled away to a nearer room.

I have no idea what just happened or when I'll see Luca again. I don't think any shots were fired into the room for the split second that the door to Luca was open, but I can't be sure as more shots ring out around us. The security team surrounds me and carries me off, not giving me time to think. They don't stop until I'm outside, shoved into a car, and driven far away from here. Far away from Luca. Giving me no idea if Luca is safe or already gone.

————

It's been two days. Two freaking days, and they haven't told me anything. I've been locked in a hotel room—albeit a nice hotel room, but with no access to the outside world. They didn't even give me access to a TV, so I don't even know what happened that night.

I haven't heard from Luca in all that time either. Not one single word.

It makes me automatically fear that the worst has happened. *Were more shots fired? Was Luca killed?* I never even heard if they caught the guys who had kidnapped me. *Did they come back that night? Were they the ones behind the shooting?*

I'm about to lose my mind, being alone in the hotel room with no answers, when I hear the hotel room door open again. The security team usually comes in and checks on me a couple of times a day to provide food and any other basic necessities I need, but they never answer any of my questions, which is the only thing I really need.

I run to the door, expecting Drew, the security guard that has been protecting me, or one of the other guys whose names I've learned, planning on doing everything I can to get some answers.

It's not any of them though. It's Luca.

I run to him and tightly wrap my arms around him. He does the same, hugging me back, tightly holding me like he's never, ever going to let me go again.

"Oh, thank God that you're alive," I sob into his neck. "I thought that something had happened to you. I thought that you had been killed."

Luca slowly lets go of me, taking a step backward. "Something did happen, Ivy."

I wipe my eyes and step closer to him, but he retreats quickly backward, like he can't stand to hold me or touch me anymore.

"What happened?" I ask.

"Let's go sit down," Luca says, walking toward the chairs in my living room.

He takes his seat, and I take a seat in the closest chair to him.

"What happened?" I ask again.

"There was another attack. A different group this time, but they tried to kill us."

"Oh my God. Was anyone hurt?"

"A bullet grazed my arm, but it was nothing serious."

My eyes immediately go to his left bicep where I notice a small bandage for the first time.

"My father's dead," he says next.

My heart sinks. "Luca, I'm so sorry. I know how much you loved your father."

I touch my hand to his, trying to provide him with some comfort, but he pulls his hand away.

"It wasn't a bullet that got him. It was a heart attack. Something that could have happened at any time, under any level of stress."

"I'm so sorry," I say, not knowing what else to say.

We both sit in silence for a long time—Luca thinking about his father and me frustrated that he won't let me comfort him.

"Why do people keep trying to kill you and your family?" I finally ask.

"Because they want power. And they wouldn't have to go too far down the succession line to get the power they want. All they need now is my mother and me gone. I don't have an heir. I don't have anyone else to pass the crown on to if I were killed."

"I'm so sorry, Luca. I wish I could've been there for you when that happened."

"I'm glad you weren't."

"What do you mean?"

"Because, as horrible as losing my father was, something else happened that night that devastated me even more."

"What could be worse than losing your father?" I ask, not believing that anything worse could have happened.

"Losing you."

"What do you mean? You still have me. I'll marry you tomorrow if it could be arranged that quickly. If this last week has taught me anything, it has taught me that life is far too short to let little things get in the way."

"You see, that's just it. I'm running out of time. And you couldn't keep the lie. Not one single lie."

I suck in a breath, realizing why he is upset. "I didn't do it on purpose. It was just a slip of the tongue. I was going to tell you, but then we got distracted, and everything else happened. I didn't mean to tell Jennifer who I really am. What my real name is. I didn't mean for all my past history and scandal to become yours, too." I pause. "I'm sure we can do some damage control. We can fix it. Especially with everyone mourning your father's death."

"It's not about that, Ivy. It was all one big test to ensure that you were the right fit for me. Because I don't get to choose a woman based on whom I love. I have to choose a woman based on what's best for this country. And what's best for this country is my family staying in power, and that means keeping secrets. Secrets that we can no longer trust with you because you failed the test."

I sink back into my chair. "It's my fault you got shot. It's my fault your father is dead, isn't it?" I ask. I already know the answer that he's going to give will be a lie.

"No," he says.

But I know he's lying. I know that it's all connected. That if my scandal hadn't caused chaos that night, giving the shooter the perfect opportunity to take a shot at Luca, then his father might still be alive.

It's then when I realize that, even if Luca wanted me right now, I wouldn't take him back. He is right; I'm not what's best for him or this country. I put him in danger, and I don't want to do that.

I have to let him go even though it is going to be the hardest thing I've ever done. I have to make him realize that, that is what I really want. Because I know him. He broke up with me before because he knew in his heart that we weren't a good fit for his life. But then he came back. I have to make sure that he doesn't come back this time. He needs to marry someone like Jennifer, someone who understands this world far better than I ever will. Someone who will keep him safe and protect the power that they need to hold on to, for the sake of the country.

"Well, I guess there's no point in hiding anymore," I say slowly, carefully choosing my words.

Luca leans forward in his chair.

"I told Jennifer on purpose. I never forgave you for all the lying and pain you caused me. I thought the scandal would destroy you. I thought it would hurt you to be dating a woman with such a scandalous past. I just didn't realize how full of scandal your family really was."

I stand up, intent on going to the bedroom and getting out of here as quickly as I can so that Luca doesn't see me cry.

Luca grabs my arm, stopping me from ducking into the bedroom where I plan on crying my eyes out. "That's a lie."

I slowly turn to look at him because he needs to see that I'm brave enough to look him in the eyes when I say it. He needs to never question that what I'm about to say is anything but the truth. I need to break his heart to protect him.

"I never loved you. I just said it so that I could make you hurt like you made me hurt."

"That's a lie?" Luca asks.

I smirk. "I guess you'll never know."

Luca drops my arm as he gives in to the lie, just like I did with all of his before. He starts walking to the door, completely done with me. He pauses for just a second. "I'll have the security team pack you up and get you on the next flight home. Don't worry about your safety. You will have a small security team follow you around until it's determined that you're safe again." He pauses a second longer. "Good-bye, Ivy."

And then he's gone. He walks out my door and out of my life forever.

My heart breaks into a thousand tiny pieces, and I know there's no hope of ever getting over him again.

26

LUCA

LOSING MY FATHER WAS HARD. Losing Ivy was worse.

I replay our last exchange over and over again in my head. I still don't know if she was telling the truth or not. She felt so sincere when she said it. But I thought I knew her. I thought I loved her. And I thought she loved me back.

But I guess lying to her and hurting her before did too much damage to her for her to ever forgive me. She wanted to hurt me back. And she got her wish.

But it's probably for the best. Because, that way, I didn't hurt her again. She had already guarded her heart, which made it easier for her to leave.

While I'm stuck here. Margaret will have a new princess for me to marry within the week. I'll be married, and then shortly after that, I'll become the king. This is what my whole life has been building toward. This is what all the sacrifices I've made were for. For this moment right now.

But, instead of being ready for the moment, I'm in incredible pain. There's a hole left in my heart that will never be filled again.

I shake my head. It kills me that Ivy will never know the truth.

She will never understand that all the lies were not really lies at all. And, worst of all, she'll never know I was willing to give all of this up for her.

27

IVY

Three Months Later

My life has gone pretty much back to normal in the months since I left Luca. I've buried myself in work, trying my best not to think about him. But, unfortunately, since he visited the clinic, everything there reminds me of him. Just like everything at home does.

But, somehow, I've managed to get back into a routine again. Wake up extra early to go to work. Stay late. Come home to my dogs and cats. Drink or cry until I fall asleep, and then get up the next day to do it all over again. That's my life now. Staying as busy as I can so that I don't have any time to think. And that's how my life is gonna remain forever if I have the choice.

Skye has been the one who surprised me the most. I thought that she would be happy that Luca and I broke up. I thought that she would be throwing guy after guy at me, trying to get me to move past him and on to someone bigger and better. But she hasn't. Instead, she's encouraged me to do the opposite. She wants me to call Luca.

Every damn day that I go into the office and see her, that's what she tells me to do. To call Luca.

I finally snapped at her the other day. I yelled and screamed and told her to stop meddling in my life. We haven't talked since. It is really a shame because I have a court hearing today for the lawsuit that was filed against me, and I could really use a friend.

I walk into my closet and put on the jacket that matches the skirt and heels I bought to wear to court. That's what my lawyer suggested —that I wear something pretty and feminine yet businesslike. So, that's what I'm wearing.

My lawyer is confident he can win my case, and he should be for the amount of money that I'm paying him. He is one of the best lawyers in the country. He just wasn't good enough to get the case dropped before having to go to court.

I feel something cold and wet lick my hand. I look down to see Sophie licking my hand. I sigh as I bend down and pet her, knowing that the dog hair is going to go all over my skirt and jacket. But maybe that's a good thing. Maybe it'll make it seem like I actually give a shit about the animals that I treat. Instead of the coldhearted, businesslike woman that my attorney wants me to look like.

"It's going to be okay, Sophie. I'm going to find you a good home. I just don't think I can keep you here. I can't have one more daily reminder of Luca."

Sophie licks my face and looks at me with her sad puppy-dog eyes.

"Don't look at me that way. He hurt both of us. Abandon us both. We deserve better." I stand up and pet Sophie one more time. "Good girl."

I walk through my house, gathering my purse and keys before I leave, trying not to think about the fact that, when I return, my life could be vastly different. I might no longer be able to afford this house. I might no longer be able to practice veterinarian medicine. I might have lost everything that I had left. But, somehow, that thought doesn't scare me. At least, not like it used to. Because I know I'm capable of starting over and doing something amazing with my life. If I lose everything, I'll just start something better. Something stronger that no one will be able to break down. I have to.

I jump in my car and turn on the radio to distract myself as I drive to the courthouse. I turn it to a rap station and listen to my favorite

Eminem song as I drive. Mainly because I just want to listen to music that doesn't always have a happy ending.

The music fades and the DJ's voice comes on the radio. I hear the words that I've been dreading every day since I left Luca. "Luca Mores is engaged to Sarah Thompson. They say they'll get married later this year in an intimate wedding just for family and friends. Luca was recently linked to his longtime US love, Ivy Lane. A woman who went from rags to riches, but it wasn't enough to steal the young prince's heart. Ultimately, a scandal ripped the two apart. This must be devastating news for the young American. But we must say that we're all excited to see what another beautiful royal wedding could be like with a prince as hot as him."

I turn the radio off, not able to listen to another word. I knew that he would get engaged fast and marry even faster. I know that's what he thinks he needs for his country. But it breaks my heart that he can move on so fast. I know that he loves me. And I know that he doesn't love her, not yet anyway. But it still hurts.

So, I have no idea how to handle the news. Cry. Yell and scream. Or be at peace with his decision. None of the choices seems like the right one.

And it also means that I'm running out of time to decide if I want to share my own secrets with him. Because I know that, once he marries Sarah, I will keep quiet forever, burying my secrets deep down in my heart and never letting him know the truth. I just have to decide what I'm going to do.

But I'm just as clueless as I was the day I left. I have no answer as to what's the right thing to do. But I do know that, if I saw him again, I would have a hard time continuing to lie to him.

Nothing. I will do nothing.

We both made our decisions. To protect each other, we can no longer be in each other's lives. So, that's what I'm going to do. Live my life and let him live his. I will try my best to find some purpose and happiness without the only man I have ever loved.

I park outside of the courthouse, take a minute to gather myself, and then walk inside to find my lawyer. The second I walk inside the courthouse, it makes me feel like a criminal. I walk through the metal detectors and then toward courtroom number two where I sit down on the bench outside, waiting for my turn.

Twenty minutes later, I glance down at my watch, realizing that my attorney is late. *Shit.* I don't know if that's a good sign or bad. Maybe he has worked out a last-minute deal that he's settling before he comes to meet me. Or maybe he's decided to drop my case because he knows he can't win.

I dig out my phone from my purse and dial his number, but I get his voice mail. I look at the clock. Less than five minutes before I'm due in court.

What if he doesn't show? Does that mean I'll just have to represent myself? Will they appoint me a lawyer at the last minute? Or will they postpone this hearing?

I watch as the seconds and minutes tick by, growing more anxious by the second. So anxious that I even consider calling Luca, like he would be able to give me some sort of advice on what to do next. But I don't call Luca.

"Ivy!" I hear my lawyer's voice ring out in the hallway.

I stand up and look at him. "Where have you been, Brett?"

He runs toward me, very out of breath. "I'm so sorry. But I got you a last-second deal."

My eyes widen. "What do you mean?"

"Well, I shouldn't say *I* did. Your previous lawyer spoke with the couple this morning. They dropped the lawsuit."

"What? What do you mean, they dropped the lawsuit? How much money do I owe them?"

"Nothing," my lawyer says, smiling. "You owe them nothing. They said they realized that the only reason they were doing this was for the money. They thought you had done an excellent job, and your previous lawyer was able to convince them to drop it, saying how badly it would hurt you if they won the money. It would make you stop being a vet, and that wasn't fair to you. Apparently, they agreed."

I sink back down onto the bench.

Luca. Luca did this. He saved me from the lawsuit, just like he'd promised.

He still loves me. He'll still do anything to protect me.

And I know what I have to do. I have to go talk to him. I have to tell him my secret. I have to let him know that I love him, too. And then we can make an honest decision about both of our futures.

———

I booked the first fight I could to Monaco. I ran home, packed a bag, convinced Skye to take care of my animals, and then headed to the airport. And, now, I'm sitting, waiting impatiently for my flight to board. I haven't texted Luca or called him to let him know that I'm coming. I don't even know if they'll let me in when I just show up at the castle. But I have to try.

I take the phone out of my purse and contemplate my next move. *Should I send him a text, letting him know that I'm coming? No.* He'll just tell me not to come. I need to get to Monaco first, and then I'll try to figure out how to get him to see me.

I hear them announce that they are boarding my flight. I jump up and get in line. I wait anxiously as the line slowly moves forward. When I get to the front, I hold out my boarding pass, waiting for them to scan it so that I can board the plane and be one step closer to Luca. I watch as the gate attendant scans my boarding pass and then frowns.

"I need you to step aside for just a moment," the gate attendant says to me.

"Why? What's wrong?" "Your passport has been flagged for further screening. An agent will be here any second to help you."

I sigh and step aside, hating that they won't just let me immediately on the plane. But I know that being on the plane isn't going to make the plane move any faster. So, it doesn't matter if I wait here or in a seat on the plane. I'll get to Luca equally as fast either way.

"Miss Lane, come with me, please," I hear a man's deep voice say.

I turn and look at a man in a dark suit, clearly not a uniformed officer.

"And you are?"

"Airport security." The man nods at the gate agent, and I know I have no choice but to follow him.

I follow the man, not having a clue as to what's happening, but I'm ready to fight if I have to. I'll do anything to get to Luca.

The security officer opens the door and waits for me to go inside. I hesitantly look at him, trying to decide how much of a threat he really is, and then I step inside.

"Luca," I breathe, not understanding what he's doing here.

Luca is standing in a small room by himself. His hands are in the pockets of his jeans, and he's wearing a button-down shirt with the sleeves rolled up. His hair has grown a bit longer again and is no longer styled perfectly. He slowly walks toward me while keeping his hands in his pockets.

"Is there a reason you were going to Monaco, or was it just to see me?"

"I was going to see you."

He nods with a confused expression on his face. "Why?"

"Because I have some secrets that I need to tell you the truth about." I pause. "Why are you here? Do you have some business in the US, or are you here to see me?"

Luca slowly looks up at me. "Everything I do is because of you."

I take a deep breath in and out, not prepared to be facing him quite yet. But here he is, and I know I'm only going to get one chance at us.

"Luca, I—"

"Stop. I need to talk first," Luca says.

Luca glances over at the small couch in the room. I nod, and we go take a seat on the couch, facing each other.

Luca takes a deep breath in and out. He opens his mouth and then closes it several times, like he's about to say something but doesn't quite know how to start.

He finally begins, "Ivy, letting you go the first time was hard. It stayed with me for the three years after. It killed me. It consumed me until I had no choice. Until I had to come and make you mine again. Losing you the second time was tragic. Worse than that. I haven't been able to sleep. I haven't been able to eat. I haven't been able to deal with any of my duties because all I can think about is you. Last time, it took me three years to come to this realization. This time, less than three months.

"I've tried doing what I'm supposed to. I've tried going through the motions, finding a new woman to marry and make the princess. And, if after everything is said and done here and you still don't want me, then I'll do what I'm supposed to. I'll marry another woman and never come back for you again.

"But I need you to know the complete, honest truth, and then you can decide if you still hate me. Because I need to do everything I can to fight for you. I'll regret it for the rest of my life if I don't."

I open my mouth, but Luca shakes his head, not letting me answer. I sigh, trying to be patient even though I feel the exact same way about him. I need to listen to whatever he has to say. Because his words might make all the difference.

"I want to tell you the truth about everything. Because I trust you and love you, and I know that you will never reveal the truth to anyone."

I nod.

Luca reaches into his back pocket and pulls out a picture. He hands it to me. I slowly take it from him and look at the picture of two young boys, maybe ten. One, I immediately recognize as Luca. The other though, I can't place, but he has an uncanny resemblance to Luca. They look like brothers. Twins even.

I look up at Luca. "I don't understand."

"That's a picture of me and my cousin, Luke, the Prince of Monaco."

I blink rapidly, not understanding the words that are coming out of Luca's mouth.

"I'm not the prince. He is." He pauses and takes a deep breath. "Well, was. My cousin was the prince. He was born a prince.

"I was just born into a middle-class family. My parents died when I was quite young. I went from foster home to foster home. I didn't even know that I had a cousin who was a prince until I was about ten years old.

"Margaret and Murray decided that Luke needed some family his age to hang out with, so I spent an entire summer with them, hanging out with the only family that I had left. Luke and I became the best of friends that summer. We did everything together, shared everything in common. We became like brothers.

"So close in fact that Margaret and Murray decided that they wanted me as their second son. They let me live at the castle, but the summer before they were going to announce their plans to the country, before they were going to introduce me as their new son, Luke was kidnapped and killed."

I feel the tears streaming down my face as I feel his pain at losing the person he felt was like a brother.

"Margaret knew she couldn't have any more kids, and even if she adopted me, I wouldn't be heir to the throne. Murray's uncle and his son would be next in line. So, Margaret made a decision to keep the crown out of the hands of those she felt would bring devastation to the country. She turned me into her son. I went along with the plan because it meant leaving my life, hopping around from foster home to foster home, to living permanently in the castle. It was all just one big game to me, pretending to be Luke.

"Margaret taught me everything I needed to know to become her son. Slowly, the name Luke turned to Luca, which made it easier for me to respond to when called. I was mostly out of the public eye until my late teens through early twenties, enough to quiet any questions about the changing prince's appearance. But then again, I looked so much like Luke that only those closest to the family would have even noticed a difference.

"Then, in my early twenties, I started to rebel and get in trouble. I was having a hard time with accepting that I had given my life away to become a prince. I wound up getting caught for speeding or getting caught in various women's beds. So, Margaret and Murray let me go

404

for a while to the US to get away from it all to try to find myself and make sure that this was the life I really wanted. All the while saying that I had joined the military and was gaining some discipline. During that time, I graduated college and got a law degree.

"I was on my way back to being a prince and accepting my role when I met you. I was always supposed to marry another when I returned. Someone that Margaret had picked out in order to keep her secret. She would do everything in her power to keep me safe. Because I had truly become a son to her, and she couldn't bear the thought of losing me after everything she sacrificed the last twenty years.

"But, when I met you, that was all I could think about—you and me. I even considered giving up the throne to be with you. I tried to stall by reapplying for law school again—this time, under a different name. To give me more time with you. To give me time to convince Margaret that you could lie and keep our secrets. That a foreigner would be willing to give her life up to protect our country—knowing that, at any moment, she could be kidnapped or killed, especially if she ever carried an heir. Because the people who kidnapped and killed Luke have never been found.

"But then you thought I was lying. I realized that I would be making a huge mistake if I gave it all up or couldn't convince Margaret you were the one. So, I let you go. I went back to law school for the second time and then prepared to marry someone else. Just like I'm doing now. Except I can't marry someone else, not while you're still breathing.

"I know that I said we could never be together because I didn't trust you with our lives or to pretend like I'm a prince even though I'm not. But that's not true. I trust you with my life, and even Margaret has come around to agree with me. I tried to break up with you to keep you safe. Because I know that, once you carry an heir, your life is going to be in even more danger. These people will stop at nothing to try to regain their power for my great-uncle and who they feel is the rightful heir to the throne. I thought I was protecting you by giving you up, but I need you to know the truth. The only real thing I've ever lied to you about is being a prince even though I'm not. Everything else I ever told you was the truth.

"I love you, and I know how much you would have to sacrifice to be with me. And I know that you probably hate me and want to see me miserable, but I couldn't live with myself if you didn't know the truth."

After he finishes speaking, I sit for a long time, trying to understand everything.

He's not a liar.

He's not a prince.

Yet he is a prince.

His life is in danger every second of every day.

And mine would be, too, if I chose to marry him.

"You might have never lied to me. But I lied to you."

Luca leans forward, trying to understand what I'm saying. "It doesn't matter what you lied about. I just want us to be together."

"See, that's the thing. Last time we were together, I lied to protect you. Because I thought that I was the reason they shot at you. I thought I was the one causing so much turmoil in your country. So, I lied and told you that I didn't love you, but I do."

A slow smile creeps up on Luca's face. He crashes on top of me, grabbing my face, while our lips kiss, desperate for each other. When we kiss, I know it won't take much for our clothes to be gone and for us to be naked and making love on this couch. But there's more to be said before we do.

"Ask me the question you were going to ask me that night," I say.

Luca grins and reaches into his back pocket, pulling out a rose full of thorns and handing it to me. I take it from him.

"You've seen the highs and lows of what it's like to rule Monaco. You've seen the good and the bad, just like this rose is beautiful yet has thorns. I know the sacrifices you are going to have to make to do the job, but I know that you're more than capable of doing the perfect job. Ivy Lane, will you be Monaco's princess?"

I look up from the rose, slightly disappointed that there's not a ring attached to it. But I know it's a good first step and that he wouldn't be asking me to be a princess if he wasn't also willing to marry me.

"Yes."

"Oh, yeah. I should probably ask you one more question, too."

He softly kisses me on the lips and then says, "Open."

I look up at him like he's crazy. "Open the rose?" I ask.

He laughs. "Yes."

I begin digging into the center of the rose, and I realize now that it isn't completely real. When I get to the center, I find a latch and open it. Inside is a large diamond ring.

I look up at Luca.

"Marry me?"

I laugh. "Yes!"

Luca slips the ring onto my finger and then starts kissing me again, ripping the clothes off my body as he does.

"Let's practice making some babies now," Luca says, kissing me.

I laugh. "I have one more secret to tell first."

Luca kisses my neck. "Whatever it is, it will have to wait. I need to fuck my dirty princess and fiancée first."

I laugh again. "I was just going to say, there's no need to practice making babies. We've already succeeded."

Luca stops kissing me with his eyes wide open, and he stares from my eyes to my stomach. "You're pregnant?"

Tears start rolling gently down my cheeks as I see them falling down his.

"I'm pregnant."

EPILOGUE

LUCA

"Skye should be here any minute with a surprise for you," Ivy says with a mischievous grin on her face.

She goes back to combing her hair in the mirror while I stand up from the couch and walk over to her, putting my arms around her large belly as I kiss her on the cheek.

"You know, I think I've really had enough surprises for a lifetime. Just tell me."

"No. I want to see the expression on your face when you see the surprise. It's a good surprise anyway."

I sigh, knowing that there is no way that Ivy is going to tell me the surprise. I sink back into the couch while Ivy continues to get ready.

"You know, we have staff that we specifically hired to do your hair and makeup, right?"

Ivy smiles as she looks at me in the mirror. "I know, but tonight is just going to be close family, and I don't mind doing it myself."

"But you shouldn't have to lift a finger, not in your state."

She rolls her eyes. "I'm pregnant, not sick. I can do plenty of things myself."

I glance at my watch that tells me that Skye should be here any second. "I can't wait to see Sophie and the other dogs. I bet Sophie has gotten so big by now," I say.

"I bet she has," Ivy says with a large grin on her face.

We hear a knock on the door, followed by Thomas saying, "Skye has arrived."

But, before I can get up to go to the door, the door bursts open as Skye and all the dogs and cats come tumbling in. She even brought Ivy's turtle. The dogs and cats all run over to attack Ivy, but I don't see Sophie in the bunch.

I turn to Skye. "Where's Sophie?"

Skye's eyes go from me to the largest dog in the group.

"Oh my God," I say when I see her.

At the sound of my voice, Sophie comes running over, tackling me to the ground. "You've gotten huge, buddy," I say as she licks my face while I wrestle on the floor with her. "I didn't think German shepherds were supposed to get this big."

Skye laughs. "You thought she was a German shepherd this whole time? Oh, you're evil, Ivy," Skye says.

Ivy laughs. "She is a Great Dane and St. Bernard mix. That's why she's so big."

I look at Sophie. "Well, it's a good thing the castle is so big then."

Ivy's eyes light up. "Does that mean we can get more animals?"

"Why not?" I say, giving in.

"Who knew that I could save my animals by being a princess?" Ivy says.

I laugh as I walk over and give her a kiss. I hear another knock on the door, and then Margaret comes in.

Margaret glances around the room and looks over at Ivy. "Can I have a few moments alone with you, Ivy?"

I raise my eyebrows, surprised that she asked permission from Ivy instead of commanding it.

"Of course," Ivy says seriously.

I look back and forth between the two women. "What's going on?" I ask.

Margaret looks at me. "Can't a future mother-in-law talk with her future daughter-in-law about plans for the nursery without getting questioned?"

"No, you can't."

Margaret rolls her eyes and walks over to kiss me on the cheek. "You worry too much. I just want some alone time tonight with Ivy to talk with her before you two get married. Just mother-to-daughter type stuff since Ivy doesn't have a mother."

My eyes dart between all three women who are clearly hiding something from me. And it doesn't feel like they're hiding something good. Unfortunately, I trust all three of these women with everything that I have. So, if they say they need time alone, then I'll give it to them.

———

Ivy

I'm anxious as I sit next to Luca at what is basically a rehearsal dinner tonight. Margaret and I have a plan to fix things that have long needed fixing. But I know Luca is going to hate the plan. And he'll kill us both for doing it if the plan goes south. But we don't have a lot of choices left. If I want to keep my family together, this is our best shot at doing so.

"What did you and Margaret talk about?" Skye asks, who is sitting on my left. She ended up taking the dogs outside after Luca left so that Margaret and I could talk in private.

She's also clueless to the plan because she would also kill me if she knew. Margaret and I are the only ones who are willing to make significant sacrifices to protect our family.

"She just commented on the fact that she wanted your hair to be normal-colored and for your piercings to be gone tomorrow for the wedding."

Skye frowns. "Why? I thought it was going to be a small, private wedding."

"It is. But the pictures are still going to be all over everything. So, she'd rather you looked like a normal human being."

Skye rolls her eyes. "Who wants normal? And it's not like you don't have piercings as well."

"Yeah, but mine aren't visible in pictures, you rebel."

Dessert is served, and I know that's my cue to enact the plan.

I lean over toward Luca's chair. "I have to go pee. I'll be right back," I say as nonchalantly as I can before kissing him on the cheek.

Luca suspiciously looks at me the same way he's been looking at me all night. He knows that something is up. But he nods, and I get up from the table, my pregnant belly very obvious to our small table and the guests who are just close family and friends.

I walk to the restroom and then wait. I've set the trap now. I just have to wait to see if he'll take the bait.

I go into one of the stalls because I actually do have to pee, and when I come back out, I take my time with washing my hands. But no one has come for me. I'm beginning to think the plan won't work when I walk back out of the restroom.

I take my time and walk the long way back to the dining room when I feel a hand go around my mouth and another wrap around my waist, pulling me hard, backward. I try to scream, but I can't. His hand is placed firmly over my nose and mouth. I realize quickly when I cough that he's using a cloth to cover my nose and mouth, and it has some scent on it that is making me feel more and more light-headed by the second.

Shit.

We didn't think this through well enough. If whatever drug is on here does anything to the baby, I'll never forgive myself. That is, if I even have long enough for that to happen.

I try to remember what the plan was. We had a safety net. A way to call for security when they tried to kidnap and kill me. *But what was it?* I can't remember. All I can feel is the pain and burning in my throat and nose as he continues to drag me backward, away from the roomful of people.

I claw at his hands, trying to get them away from my mouth, but he pushes my hands away. I feel the bracelet slide up and down on my arm, and that's when I remember. I grab for my bracelet, pushing the button that signals to the security team that I need help. But I'm afraid it's too late because I feel myself drifting off into a deep sleep.

––––––––

Luca

Ivy's eyes open, and I can breathe again. I throw my arms around her while I kiss every inch of her face and body that's visible beneath the sheets wrapped around her.

"You scared me to death," I say.

Ivy blinks, clearly confused. "What happened? All I remember is being at dinner."

I shake my head. "You did what you always do, Ivy. Saved us."

Her eyes widen, but I still think she doesn't remember.

"I can tell you this much. I'm never leaving you and Margaret alone in a room together again. All you do is come up with horrible plans to get you both killed."

She stares at me with a blank expression on her face. I lean down and softly kiss her on the lips.

"You set a trap to get my great-uncle to try to kidnap you and kill you so that he could be caught red-handed and thrown in jail for the rest of his life."

"Oh my God. I remember now. He drugged me with something. The baby!"

"Shh..." I say. I stroke her face, trying to get her to calm down and lie back in bed. "The baby's fine. The doctor said that not enough of the drug got into your system. And that you were most likely dehydrated to begin with, which is why you passed out."

"Thank God."

"Yes, thank God that you're both safe because I don't know what I would have done without either of you. And, just so you know, I'm not leaving your side for a second ever again, and neither is Andy," I say, glancing over my shoulder.

"Nope, I'm your permanent shadow from now on, so you'd better get used to me. I'm not to leave you alone ever, not even to go to the bathroom."

Ivy laughs. "Fair enough."

"But we don't have to worry about my great-uncle. Not anymore. You've saved us all from a lifetime of fear and danger. You've saved me and our child, Ivy. I don't know what I'm going to do with you." In front of Andy, I'm not able to say that she also finally got Luke's killer. But, when I look into her eyes, I know that she understands what I'm thankful for.

"Well, you can marry me tomorrow," she says with a laugh.

"That, I'll do."

I lean down and firmly kiss her on the lips, thinking about the beautiful wedding that I have planned for tomorrow. She thinks it's going to be in a small chapel down the street with all our friends and family. She doesn't know that I turned the castle ruins into a wedding venue.

"You know, you aren't the only one with surprises up their sleeves," I say.

Ivy's eyes brighten. "I love any surprises from you, my prince."

"And I look forward to a lifetime of surprises with you, my dirty princess."

THE END

Keep reading for Heart of a Prick...

HEART OF A PRICK

BOOK THREE

I need a man.
I've got this relaxing thing on the beach down. The bartender is wrapped around my finger, bringing me drinks the second mine is remotely empty. Now I just need a man in my bed for the week, and I'll be all set.
Not just any man will do though.
I want wild animal sex.
The kind that involve tying each other up and spanking and all things kinky. The kind that no guy back home would dare to do.

Really I need a distraction. Someone to make me forget about all my troubles waiting for me when I get back home. Trouble that I have no idea how to get out of. I'm not even sure how to stay alive.
There are plenty of hot men at this resort just waiting to serve as a perfect distraction. **But how do I find a guy who will give in to all my darkest desires?**

1

SKYE

Him, him, definitely him, not him, so hot, gross, him, him.

My mind scans all the men within eyesight as I lie on my chaise lounger by the pool at my all-inclusive resort in the Bahamas. I'm here for exactly seven days, and I plan on making the most of it. That means men. Lots and lots of men. Lots of sex. And zero thoughts about my real life, which has taken a turn for the worse recently. This week is all about relaxing and having a good time while I do it.

I take a sip of my piña colada. I've got the relaxing thing down. I have my chaise lounger, I have a bartender wrapped around my finger, bringing me drinks as soon as my glass is empty, and I'm surrounded by some of the most beautiful scenery in the world. I just need to find a man for the week, and then I'll be all set.

The problem is finding one that will fit my needs for this week. I want *wild animal* sex. The kind that involves tying each other up and spanking and all things kinky. The kind that no guy back home would dare to do.

I just don't know how to find that guy. There are plenty of hot men at this resort. And plenty that seem single. But how do I find a guy who will give in to all my darkest desires?

"Another, Miss Skye?" my favorite bartender asks as he holds out another piña colada to me.

I grin behind my sunglasses and large hat. "Thank you, Bayron." I take the drink from him.

"You look like you're thinking hard. You shouldn't be thinking so hard. You're in paradise! You should just relax and let what happens, happen."

I nod. "Maybe. But what if I have specific needs for this trip? Needs that I'm not sure how to go about getting."

"You mean, a man?"

I nod, grinning.

He chuckles. "I don't think a woman as smart and beautiful as you should have much trouble finding a nice man."

I smirk. "But what if I don't want a nice man? What if I want a bad boy? A very, very bad boy."

He glances around at the choices currently surrounding the pool. "I don't think you should have much difficulty with that either." He winks at me.

I laugh. "You're right. But how do I choose? What if I have too many options?"

He thinks for a moment and then glances over at the small stage set up near the pool where they often have a band play music or occasionally entertain with competitions and poolside games.

"How about a competition? Winner wins a date with you."

I bite my lip as I stare at another man strutting by with muscles that contract with each step, begging to be put to use in bed with a woman like me. It could take me all week to find a man who is good in bed. But, if I can put them through a series of tests to figure out which one has the qualities I'm looking for, then I can find the guy in half the time and get on to the good stuff.

I take my hat off and push my sunglasses up on my head as I sit up on my lounger. "Let's do it!"

Bayron smiles and holds out his hand to me. I take it and let my long, dark hair with blue highlights flow down my back, matching the dark blue bikini I'm wearing. Between my hair, tattoos, and piercings in my nose, eyebrow, and ears, any man should know that I'm not looking for a good man.

Bayron leads me around the pool over to the small stage where he takes the microphone and turns it on.

"You sure about his?" he asks, whispering to me.

"Yes." I've never been so sure about needing anything. I'm desperate to find a man who can help me forget.

"Hey, Royal Bahamas Resort! Are you guys having a good time?" Bayron says.

The crowd around the pool shouts back, "Yes!"

"Awesome! I have a special treat for you today. This lovely lady here is looking for a date, and we are going to help her get one."

The crowd cheers again as I scan the pool, trying to determine which guy I want the most.

"This is Miss Skye. She's from New Mexico. She's smart and beautiful, and she's looking for a bad boy to keep her company this week. If you think you fit that bill, I want you to run onto this stage in the next ten seconds. And then the real competition will begin."

I bite my lip as the anxiety and anticipation build.

"Go! One...two...three..." Bayron starts counting, and men start running up onstage.

Some very, very good-looking men join us onstage. Men with muscles, men with beards, men with dreamy eyes, and men with tattoos. Almost all the men running up onstage look like men I'd love to take back to my room and have a test run with. But I need to choose just one. Or at least one for now.

"And time!" Bayron shouts.

He starts walking up and down the stage area, counting how many men have decided to enter. "It looks like we have fifteen men who would like to compete for a date! That's far too many." Bayron walks back to me and whispers in my ear, "What would you like them to do first?"

"Strength. I want a strong man. So, knock out the weaklings."

He nods and holds the microphone back to his lips. "Skye wants a man who's strong. So, for this competition, we are going to do as many push-ups as you can in sixty seconds. I'm going to need a little help with this one."

Bayron waves over to more of his staff to come join him. The staff line up around the men, helping them spread out around the pool area and stage.

"Everyone ready? The top ten will move on to the next round."

The men and staff nod.

"Go!" Bayron says, staring at his watch.

I watch, drooling as the men start doing push-ups as fast as they can. I can already tell by watching them which ones are truly in shape and which men aren't. And which men are too drunk to even attempt a push-up.

Two men, in particular, grab my attention. A blond man with arms for days. And a black man who is killing everyone. Both of them have excellent bodies. Either one could handle my body with ease.

"Time!" Bayron yells.

He walks down, asking the judges how many the men got.

"Okay, if you did less than a hundred, you're out!"

Five men slump back to the pool or loungers after having their egos crushed.

I look at the contestants that are left. All look fit. All look gorgeous. All look like men I'd gladly share a bed with.

Bayron again asks me what I want them to compete on next.

"I need a fast man," I answer.

He raises an eyebrow. "Skye wants a guy who is fast. I'm guessing she's still trying to weed out the in-shape guys from the ones who aren't—and she doesn't mean fast in bed. So, for our speed test, we are going to divide you into two swimming races. The fastest three in each race will move on."

I watch as the first group jumps into the water. One of the men glances over at me with hungry eyes, and my heart about stops. That's what I want. A man who desires me. I want a man who will fight and compete for me.

Bayron starts the first race, and I find myself cheering for the man who looked at me with hungry eyes. He wins easily.

The second round starts, but I find myself still entranced with the man who won the first race. I'm not even paying attention to the second race.

The winners are decided, and again, I watch as the losers sulk off, disappointed.

"What do you want me to test next, sweetheart?" Bayron asks.

"Pain."

He nods, thinking for a second. "Next, we are going to test to see who can handle pain the longest. We are going to pass out two weights to each of you, and you will hold them out to your sides, arms extended. The last six men still holding on to their weights will continue."

The weights are distributed to the six remaining men, which consists of Hungry Eyes from the swimming round, both of the men I noticed from the strength round, and three other men I haven't paid much attention to yet.

"Go!" Bayron shouts.

I watch in pain, hoping that my favorites survive to make it to the next round.

All are doing well and holding their own, but I see the blond starting to falter. He won't hold out much longer. After a few more seconds, his arms fall. Either the push-ups from earlier wore him out or he couldn't handle the pain. Either way, he's not my bad boy. Too bad.

Other men start falling, leaving me with four men. The winner of the swimming round. The winner of the strength. A new winner from the pain round. And then another man who hasn't won any but hasn't lost either.

"What's up next?" Bayron asks, jogging next to me.

"Two rounds left. The first round is dirty. Who can tell me the dirtiest, filthiest thing?"

Bayron nods. "You heard her. Prepare your best lines. We want you to get dirty. Tell her the filthiest thing you can think of."

The first man walks forward. The winner of the strength round. I want to eat up his juicy, dark muscles.

He leans down and whispers in my ear, "I want to kiss you. Claim you. Make you mine."

I smile at him as he takes a step back. It was good but not really that dirty.

Next up is the man who won the last round. He's taller than the rest, and he has deep, dark eyes. He leans down and whispers, "I want to spank your gorgeous ass while I fuck you into ecstasy."

I grin. Better.

I bite my lip while I wait for the next guy. The winner of the swimming round and my favorite so far.

He tucks a strand of my hair behind my ear, giving me goosebumps, as he says, "I want to tie you up to your bed, so you can't move. Then, I want to lick honey off your bare skin before I spank your ass until it's bright red. I won't stop until you are screaming my name, begging me to stop because you can't come anymore."

Damn. He's the clear winner so far.

Last up is a man I've barely noticed before. He says something into my ear, but I'm still so lost in the last guy's words that I don't even hear him.

"So, who is the loser?" Bayron asks.

I take a deep breath, not liking having to choose a loser.

"Number one," I say.

"Sorry, number one. You're out. We have one final round, which is..."

"Best kisser, of course," I say with a large grin as I stare at the final three men that I get to kiss.

Any one of them could be amazing in bed and give me exactly what I'm looking for this week. It all comes down to who can make my toes curl the most. And I think the man who said the dirtiest line is most likely going to be the winner.

The first man steps forward, forcefully grabs my head with both hands, and presses his lips to mine. He's aggressive. I like that. But he's so aggressive that his lips miss my mouth initially. He quickly corrects himself, pushing his tongue into my mouth like he's trying to suffocate me.

My eyes stay wide as he kisses me. I'm in shock as to what exactly he's trying to do to me. I try to grab on to him to keep from falling backward, but when he releases me, I stumble backward, unable to keep my balance.

Bayron shoots me a look, asking if I'm okay.

I nod and bite my lip to keep from giving away how horrible that kiss was, so I don't completely embarrass the poor man in front of everyone.

"All right, number two, give her your best kiss," Bayron says.

I take a deep breath to prepare myself for his kiss. I know it can't be any worse than the first. I know his kiss is going to be the best. He's won everything else. He's the one. I know it.

He walks toward me and takes me into his arms. He dips me backward as his tongue moistens his lips before he places a flawless kiss on my lips with just the tiniest hint of tongue. It is perfect. The right amount of moisture. The right amount of force. The right amount of control.

It's a pleasant kiss that warms my insides.

He brings me back up as he ends the kiss to hoots and hollers from the crowd, obviously liking the performance he put on. I liked it, too. But something was missing. Maybe it was the fact that we were in front of a large crowd. Maybe it's that I don't even know his real name, and it's keeping me from feeling more. But whatever it is, I intend on finding the missing piece to that kiss once I declare him as the winner.

I smile at him, giving him a wink, as he steps back in line with the other men.

"Woo, that was one hot kiss. I'm not sure if contestant number three can beat that, but give it your best shot," Bayron says.

I still have my eyes glued to contestant number two when contestant number three approaches.

One of his hands goes around my waist, and the other tangles in my hair as he pulls my body tightly to his, forcing me to stop looking at any other man other than him. I get one glimpse of his dark eyes before he kisses me. And then my eyes are forced closed, his body commanding that I give everything to him in the kiss. He takes his time, not rushing it, as he expertly slips his tongue into my mouth. His hand glides down from my waist to my ass as his hard cock pushes into my stomach, making it clear how badly he wants me. I feel a shock wave shoot throughout my body as he deepens the kiss, pushing me to my limit.

He stops the kiss, but I can't open my eyes yet. I'm panting heavily as he holds me in his arms. I feel his hand stroke my cheek, tucking a strand of hair behind my ear. Being so gentle after being so rough.

I open my eyes and stare into his, not sure what the hell just happened other than something amazing. It wasn't perfect. It was rough, primal, a panty-melting kind of kiss. The kind that only a bad boy with years of experience in getting dirty with plenty of women can give.

He slowly lets me go and takes his place back in line with the other men. I know that Bayron is going to ask me who the winner is. I thought it was going to be number two in a landslide. But number three just made things way more complicated. And, now, I'm not sure who I'm going to choose.

2

BRODY

I STEP BACK INTO LINE, knowing that she is going to choose the guy to my left. Number two. She's had eyes only for him since the competition started. But, damn, that kiss was hot.

I've kissed strangers before but never like that. When I kissed her, she submitted to me. She wanted me to take control. Was begging for it. And I was more than happy to take it. That's what my whole life is. Taking charge and loving it.

I stare at her, commanding her to pick me with my eyes. I don't think it will work, but it's worth a shot. She's the opposite of the type of woman that I would usually go for. She's a troublemaker; it's clear from this little game that she convinced the staff to play along with. I'm into corporate women who always dress classy with clean, sharp looks. But this woman doesn't care that she breaks all the norms when it comes to her looks. She has blue streaks in her dark hair, piercings and tattoos cover her body, and the way her body moves is like nothing I've ever seen before. She's confident and independent, but she seems tired of always being so in control of herself when it's clear from her appearance that she would rather be free, going whichever way the wind pushes her. Something is stopping her. But maybe this is her way of trying to break free of whatever is holding her back.

Behind me, I hear Noah, Harry, and Levi cheering for her to pick me. They were the ones who pushed me into this ridiculous competition in the first place. I'm here to get a break from the chaos, and I brought a few members of my team along with me. I thought they had earned a much-needed break from our daily grind at the office. They jumped at the chance to push their boss into a pissing contest over a complete stranger. I regretted bringing them the second they pushed my ass onto the stage.

Now, I'm thankful. That kiss brought me back to life again. It reminded me what taking a chance with a woman feels like and how good it feels to have a woman's lips on mine. I've taken a break from extracurricular activities, like fucking a woman, for far too long. That ends tonight. I want it to be with this woman in front of me, but if she doesn't want me, there are plenty of hot women here that I can have. I'm here for seven nights. Seven women in seven nights sounds like an excellent plan.

"Can I get a drum roll, please?" Bayron says to the crowd.

Everyone begins banging on things and shouting loudly for who they want to win.

She bites her lip—a habit of hers when she doesn't know what she wants I've noticed, or at least guess since she's done exactly that half a dozen times since the competition started. Or she does, but she is not ready to say it yet.

Her eyes are bright and wild as she looks from the first man to the second and then finally to me. I smirk at her. She won't pick me, but I want my face burned into her memory, so when she is fucking him later, my face will pop into her mind, making her second-guess her choice. I want her to regret not choosing me every day.

"And the moment of truth! Will it be contestant number one?" Bayron says as the first guy's friends cheer him on. "Contestant number two?"

The crowd cheers loudly for contestant number two.

"Or contestant number three?"

Again, the crowd cheers loudly at the same level they did for the guy in front of me.

"And the winner is..." Bayron holds the microphone to her luscious lips, which she is still biting into.

I should have bitten her lip when I had the chance just to see what all the fuss was about.

"Number three."

The crowd cheers while I try to keep my bewilderment at winning off my face. No one needs to know that I'm not a cocky ass who thought I had this in the bag from the beginning.

The other men sulk off, disappointed that they lost. I stride forward to claim my prize and bite the lip that I've been thinking about for the last few minutes.

But Bayron stops me in my tracks before I can even get close to her.

"You hurt her, I'll kill you. And I know where you sleep at night. Understand?"

I nod, not understanding why the staff would care so much about one of its guests.

Bayron escorts me over the few feet to her.

"Skye, this is Brody. Brody, this is Skye."

"Brody?" she asks, raising an eyebrow at my name.

"Yes. You have a problem with my name?"

She laughs. "No, it sounds like a name for an arrogant man who knows how to treat a woman in bed. Just my type."

My eyes dart over her body again, taking in her breathing that has sped up as her chest rises and falls beneath the bikini top that barely covers her body. Her eyes dilate as she looks me over as well, and from how she moistens her lips, she is more than happy with what she sees me. She might have struggled with her decision between me and the other guy, but tonight, I'll make sure she forgets that any other man exists.

She licks her lips again, and I know she is preparing for another life-altering kiss. Her whole body is on alert, waiting for me to make my move now that she has chosen me. I don't know anything other than her name, but I already know from her expression that she is ready for me to sweep her off her feet and go fuck her in the nearest bedroom. I'll happily answer her wishes.

I take a step forward. I grab her and pull her close to me again. I love how her heartbeat picks up while her breathing all but stops when I simply hold her in my arms. I can't imagine what her body will do when I actually take her back to my room and strip her naked.

"Excuse me," Bayron says, pushing between us, cockblocking me.

I glare at him like I've never glared at a man before. I won. She chose me. I played all of his stupid games. Now, let me have her.

The only thing keeping me from punching him right now is that, if I do, I know I'll get thrown out of the resort, and I won't ever be able to have her.

"The resort would like to give you both a gift," Bayron says.

"That's really not necessary, Bayron. I appreciate you playing along with my stupid game," Skye says, not looking at Bayron. She's looking at me like she's about to devour me.

My cocks twitches at that thought.

"Oh, but it is. You are one of our favorite guests, Miss Skye, and we want to make sure you are thoroughly taken care of while you are here. And that means giving you a special gift to celebrate your new relationship."

Don't kill him. Don't kill him, I repeat in my head. *I can't have the girl if I kill him.*

"And what gift is that?" Skye asks, her throat dry and raspy as she speaks.

"We want to make sure your first date is spectacular. So, we will go all out tonight to throw you the best first date possible. It will be the most romantic moment of your life."

"This isn't about romance," Skye says.

Bayron grabs her arm and turns her from me, whispering loud enough that I can still hear him. "A little romance never hurt anyone. I have a full day planned with a spa trip to prepare you for your date tonight." He turns his head back to me. "The date starts promptly at seven. I'll have someone send more information to your room shortly, Mr. Brody."

And then he takes Skye and walks her away from me. I don't get my kiss. I barely even got to put my hands on her. I want to run after her and kidnap her out of his pushy hands.

Skye glances back at me one last time before Bayron leads her around the building and out of view. The look she gives me is one that asks me to save her. I want to. But I know that the asshole who has a grip on her arm won't let me.

Tonight. I'll have to find a way to put an end to the romance and get to the fun part. It's clear that Skye is on the same page with me on that one.

I walk back to where the guys are still sitting.

"You won. But why do you look like you do when we are in a meeting and you hate everything that we have presented to you?" Noah asks.

"Because I'm in a foul mood."

"Where's your woman?" Harry asks, laughing.

"Bayron took her for a day of pampering before our date tonight."

"Ooh, date. I can't imagine you dating," Harry teases.

"That's because I don't date. I never have. And I don't plan on going on one tonight."

"Then, what are you going to do?"

"I'm going to kidnap the girl that I won from the bastard who thinks he's in charge of her well-being, taking back control into my own hands."

———

The seven hours until our "date" creep by slowly. The guys thought I should spend it getting drunk, which would have been the more fun way to spend the day. But I hardly ever get drunk. I don't like losing control. And, tonight, in order to get Skye away from Bayron and his staff, I need to be clearheaded.

So, instead, I spent it working out, working on my computer, and trying to get Skye out of my damn head. I've never had a woman take over my head before. Work always keeps me plenty busy enough to push away any flickers of thoughts about boobs or ass. But even work wasn't enough to keep the sway of her hips as she walked away from me out of my mind.

I hear a knock on the door to my suite. I growl, not wanting to see whoever is on the other side of that damn door unless it's Skye. The last time I answered the door, a nicely dressed man delivered my outfit for tonight. Like I was incapable of picking out my own clothes for a date.

I walk over to the door and throw it open. "What?"

Bayron frowns. "You're not wearing what was delivered to you."

I glance down at my khaki shorts and a dark V-neck T-shirt. "I'm sure I'm dressed well enough for whatever it is you are having us do."

He ignores me and pushes into my room. He walks over to the floor of my bed where I tossed the bag that was delivered to my room an hour ago. He picks it up and pulls out a light-blue button-down shirt, khaki pants, dress shoes, and a tie.

"Get dressed," he says, walking back to the door.

"And if I don't?"

"Then, I guess I'll have to find Matt, the runner-up, to take your place on the date with Skye tonight. And shave, too."

He slams the door. I rip the shirt off my body and throw it at the door, hoping it will help me not kill him. I still want to, but I try to be a good boy. I shave. I get dressed in the clothes that were delivered to me. I'll play along until I have my chance to steal Skye away to do something with a lot less romance.

I open the door when I'm dressed. Bayron scans me up and down and must approve because he waves me to follow him. I follow him out of my suite and down the hallway to the elevator.

We step on.

"So, what is this grand date you have planned for us tonight?"

"You'll find out."

"So, why are you doing this again? Trying to make tonight so perfect for us?"

The doors open to the ground floor, and we both step out.

"Because Skye is a very important guest to us."

"You mean that she is related to the owner."

He shakes his head. "No, she's just special."

"You have a thing for her or something?"

"No, Mr. Brody, I just care about her. You can ask Miss Skye why if you want more details," he says, ending the conversation.

I put my hands in my pockets as I follow him out toward the beach, waiting for a clue as to what we are doing. I find none. We stop suddenly in the sand.

"Wait here," he says.

I sigh but do what I was told.

I watch Bayron jog back up toward the resort and then disappear. I glance around me, waiting for someone to jump out and mug me if Bayron has his way. Just when I'm about done with this waiting crap, I see her.

She walks down the beach toward me without Bayron in sight—thank god. She's wearing a light-gray dress that is cut low in the front and then hugs tightly to her body before flowing around her legs. It shimmers a little toward the bottom as she walks, as if each step she takes makes the sand beneath her feet sparkle. The wind blows and tousles her hair over her head while the dress blows at her feet.

He told me to wait. Like a dog. I'm not waiting anymore.

I jog toward her far too fast for someone who is going on a date with a woman he doesn't even know. But I don't care what she thinks of me right now. Today has been hell, waiting after our kiss this morning.

She starts running toward me as well until we crash into each other, our lips locking together immediately before anyone has a chance to tell us otherwise. Our hands grab on to each other, holding us together instead of exploring each other's bodies like I really want to be doing.

Her tongue darts into my mouth, begging me to take the kiss further and making it known just how badly she has wanted to kiss me all day. It makes me hungrier. I need her now.

431

I deepen the kiss, pushing her lips apart wider as my tongue pushes inside her, massaging her tongue. I hear the purr in her throat in response. She loves it when I kiss her. It's what caused me to win. One kiss changed it all.

We hear a throat clearing, and she reluctantly starts to pull away, but I won't let her. Not until I've had one last taste.

I pull her bottom lip into my mouth and gently bite down. I feel her body tighten in my arms as she tries to keep the intense feelings of desire at bay.

I let her go then. Satisfied with finally getting to taste her lip.

"Right this way," Bayron says as he starts walking us down the beach.

I wrestle with myself between grabbing Skye and taking off now or waiting until later. I decide on later. I'm sure he just has a dinner or something set up. We can eat quickly and then get out of here.

Our hands interlink as we follow Bayron down the beach, still not saying a word to each other, but not needing to. We know that we want each other. In a bed. Right now.

We round the edge of the property and see a large yacht sitting at the end of the pier.

"Your date awaits," Bayron says, pointing toward the boat.

My mouth drops open. I know how much a yacht like that costs. There is no way that this is our gift from the resort. Even if we only go out for an hour, it would cost them more than both of our rooms for the entire week, combined.

"You're kidding, right?" I ask.

Bayron smiles. "Only the best for Miss Skye."

He starts walking down the long wooden peer. The yacht gets larger and larger with each step we take.

"He's joking, right? If this is really our gift, you know they are going to expect us to pay them back somehow," I lean over and say to Skye.

She shrugs. "Let's just get the romance over with, so we can move on to the fun part." She winks.

I squeeze her hand tighter. "Done."

We keep walking toward the yacht, and the boy part of me that still gets excited about shiny things with fast motors and expensive boats gets me far too giddy as we stop in front of it. I've never been on a yacht before, and all I want to do is go explore every inch of it. Talk to the captain about how it works, how expensive it is, and how fast it can go.

But then I look over at Skye, and I forget about the damn yacht. We could be riding a bus for all I care as long as I get to hold her again. Kiss her. Fuck her. Nothing else matters. Not even figuring out the crazy reason we are getting to ride in this yacht instead of just getting a romantic dinner on the beach, like every other couple who stays at this resort.

Bayron holds his hand out to Skye. She lets go of my hand and takes his as he helps her into the yacht.

I grind my teeth to keep from chewing Bayron out for taking Skye from me for a single second. I really need to get my anger in check. Bayron is just doing his job. He's not hitting on Skye. And it's clear Skye is only interested in me. But I can't. I've never felt such claim over a woman before, especially one that I've only ever kissed.

I climb up onto the yacht behind Skye.

"Have a good date. If you need anything, just ask one of the wait staff on board or the captain."

I turn back to look at Bayron. "How long are we going to be on the yacht?" I'm starting to think that he's going to trap me on this boat so that I can't escape and am forced to be romantic with Skye.

He smiles. "Are you well taken care of, Miss Skye?"

She gives me a sideways glance with a sparkle in her eyes before she takes my hand again. "I think I'm in very good hands."

"How long?" I ask again, not about to be trapped on this yacht for my entire vacation.

"Don't worry, Mr. Brody; there are beds on the yacht," he says with a wink.

The yacht starts moving gently away from the pier. I could jump back onto the pier. But I don't think I could get Skye to come with me. I hate not having control. I hate not knowing where we are going or when we are coming back. But, until this yacht turns around, I'm going to have to find a way to let all of that go.

"Come on," Skye says, pulling me toward the front of the yacht as we head out into the ocean, toward the sun that is just beginning to set.

We stop at the railing at the front of the boat, still gripping on to each other's hands while resting them on the railing. We stand in silence just staring at the ocean.

"I'm sorry," Skye says as she looks out at the ocean.

"Why are you sorry?"

"For Bayron. He means well, but sometimes, he takes things too far. You never agreed to being kidnapped on a boat with me."

My eyes widen a little at just how on the nose she is about my feelings. But, as soon as she says it out loud, I realize how absolutely ridiculous my feelings are.

I stroke her cheek. "Don't be sorry. For any of it. There are worse ways I could be spending my time than trapped on a boat with a beautiful woman like you."

She blushes a little. "Let's try to survive for a couple of hours, and then we can have them turn it around."

I arch an eyebrow. "You can have them turn the yacht around at any time, and they'll listen to you?"

Skye turns toward me with an amused smile. "You really thought they were kidnapping us and holding us hostage until we had the romantic date that they wanted, didn't you?"

I shrug. "Bayron came to my room, forced me to wear this outfit, and then escorted me down to the beach where he told me to stay. Then, he forced me onto a boat, and I have no idea how long I will be on it. Seems like kidnapping to me."

She places her hand on my chest, running it over the smooth fabric, feeling the muscles that ripple beneath her hand. "You're right. This shirt is horrible." She winks at me. "And I'll let you repay the favor by kidnapping me anytime." Her hand dances across my chest as she looks to her right. "It looks like dinner is ready." She sighs.

I look to my left and see three waiters with a fancy table with a white tablecloth and red roses everywhere. This is going to be the most romantic date of my life in the most romantic of places. This is meant to be the start of an epic love story. It's just not the love story that either of us wants.

I walk over to the table and pull out the chair like the gentleman that I am for Skye to sit.

She shakes her head and walks over to the other chair. She pulls it out herself and takes a seat.

I rub the back of my neck, completely bewildered by this woman.

"This isn't a date. Take a seat, Romeo," she says, pointing at the chair that I just pulled out for her.

I take a seat. "I thought that was exactly what this was. A date."

"What do you want to drink?" she asks me.

"Wine."

"No, not wine. What else do you want?"

"Bourbon."

She looks at the waiters. "Bring us a bottle of bourbon and tequila and two glasses. Then, leave us alone until we call for you."

The waiters nod and then leave to I assume follow her instructions.

"Why can't we have wine?" I ask.

"Because wine is for people on a date."

"And we aren't on a date?" I ask, still not understanding what we are doing then.

"Exactly. We aren't on a date." She reaches into the middle of the table, grabbing the red roses sitting on the table. "Get the petals," she commands.

I quickly sweep the flower petals into my hand, not sure what we are doing with them. Two waiters return with the bottles and glasses.

"Set them on the table in the center," Skye commands.

They do without hesitation or blink of the eye.

"Now, take these, and leave us alone. We will come inside to grab food later." Skye holds out the flowers, and I do the same. The waiters take the flowers and petals and leave us alone.

Skye grabs the tequila bottle and glass and pours herself a glass almost completely full with way more tequila than what she should be drinking. She takes a swig as she leans back in the chair until the front legs are off the ground. "Better. Now, it's not a date."

I nod as I look around at the yacht. She might have taken away the flowers and the wine, but we are still on a boat with gold-colored edging and dark wood floors, which costs more than quadruple the price of most people's houses. We are still alone on a yacht in the middle of the ocean with the sun setting before us. Getting rid of a few flowers doesn't get rid of the fact that this is definitely a date.

"Now, you just need to get rid of the sunset and start burping or something so that I stop thinking of you as this beautiful woman I want to fuck."

She burps.

I laugh.

"I can't do anything about the sunset. And I want you to want to fuck me, just not date me."

I grab the bottle of bourbon and pour myself a reasonable glass.

"So, what are we doing if we aren't on a date?"

"We are negotiating."

I take a drink of my bourbon. "And what are we negotiating?"

"What I want from you."

She takes another drink of her tequila, emptying almost half of the glass, before she leans forward, the front legs of her chair touching back down on the ground. She harshly places the glass back on the table, and she folds her arms in front of her.

"Here are my terms. I want one week of filthy, dirty, *tie me up*, *spank me till I come*, dangerous sex. I want the kind of sex that makes me forget about everything. I want the kind that makes me feel alive again. The kind you only read about in naughty romance books or when watching porn. That's what I want. Can you give me that, Brody?"

Her eyes are dark and serious when she talks. Her voice is stern and unwavering. Something happened to her to make her need this or at least think that this is what she wants. And I don't care to know what it is. I don't want to get involved in her clearly messy life.

I lean forward on the table so that I'm eye-to-eye with her. "I can make your darkest fantasies come true."

She grins. "Good. I chose my man well then."

I nod.

"Now, the terms. You are mine for the week. You don't get to go around, fucking other women and then fuck me. I'll have sex with you as much as you want this week, but I'm not willing to share."

I smirk. "I don't share either."

"Good. I also don't do attachment. We aren't dating. We aren't a couple. This goes nowhere after this week."

"I don't date, so it won't be a problem—as long as you can keep your emotions out of this." I eye her with suspicion.

She growls. "Just because I'm a woman doesn't mean I have emotions that need more controlling than you do. When I look at you, I feel nothing but the need to rip your clothes off."

I narrow my eyes, searching hers for a bit of untruth. I find none.

"Satisfied?" she asks.

"Yes."

"Lastly, we don't discuss anything personal. We don't talk about what our jobs are or where we live. We don't do last names. You don't introduce me to your friends. I don't hear about your past girlfriends, and you don't ask about my past lovers. We learn nothing about each other, except how you like to fuck me and what each other sounds like when we come. That's it."

"I couldn't agree more."

"Do you have any terms or requests?"

"Just one. That you remember the word *red*. It's your safe word when you can't handle the pain or the sex anymore, and you are going to need to use it."

Her eyes deepen, and her lips curl up just a little at that thought.

"I don't think there is anything you can do to make me use that word. But I'll remember."

My eyes scan hers. She's been hurt. Really, really hurt. She wants me to take away her pain with more pain and sex. She's right that it will help her for the week. I'm just glad I won't be there when she goes back to her normal life and has to deal with whatever crap she is hiding from me.

"Food or sex first?" she asks.

I smirk. "I forgot one final rule. You want BDSM, right? You want me to tie you up, spank you, whip you—the whole package, right?"

She nods, her mouth open and panting.

"Then, you have to give up control. You do exactly what I say, when I say it. You don't get to say no to anything. You just do without thinking. If it's too much, you tell me *red* to stop. Otherwise, you don't think for the rest of the week."

"Exactly."

My inner demon comes out the second she says that. She just gave me complete control over her body. And I plan on taking advantage of having that control.

"Excuse me," one of the waiters says.

I exhale deeply. I'm pretty sure steam blows out of my ears from my pent-up anger with Bayron, but it is now getting directed at this new man who I won't let cockblock me. Not now that I finally get her with no strings attached.

Skye gives the man an equally perturbed look. "What?" she snaps.

"I'm very sorry to interrupt you, but the captain's cat we think is having a seizure or something. We can either turn back or you can—"

Skye sighs, getting up from the table, looking me dead in the eye. Then, she breaks her own rule, telling me something about herself. "I'll take a look at the cat."

3

SKYE

Damn it!

All I wanted to do was have some filthy, dirty, mind-blowing sex with a hot stranger who wants the same thing that I do. How hard is that to get? Between Bayron forcing me into this date and now the captain's cat, I'm not sure if I will ever get what I want.

I quickly follow the waiter back to the captain's quarters where they have the cat lying on a bed. I try not to think about how many rules I'm breaking by showing Brody that I'm a vet. I just want to take care of the cat and then get back to the part where Brody fucks me. The cat is probably fine anyway.

But, when I put my hands on the cat, I know that the cat isn't fine. He needs help. *Immediately.*

"Get me the first aid kit. Now," I say calmly, looking at the waiter.

"Is he going to be okay?" the captain asks.

"I need you to get me towels, his food, and favorite toys. Understand?"

He nods.

"Go," I say sternly, just trying to get him out of the room, so I can do what I need to do. I don't need any of the things I just asked him to get.

The waiter returns with the first aid kit and puts it on the bed. The cat isn't breathing. I quickly look in his mouth to see if anything is obstructing his airflow. I can't see anything, but most likely, there is something, and I just can't see it. If he was having a seizure before, he might have thrown something up that is now lodged in his throat.

I start performing CPR, but air isn't getting into his lungs like I expected.

"Are you squeamish?" I ask the waiter as I throw open the first aid kit, hoping it has everything I need.

"Yes."

"Then, get out."

It has a scalpel and gauze. "I need a straw," I say, glancing around the room.

"Here," Brody says, handing me a straw as he kneels down next to me on the bed.

I give him a wide-eyed stare. I don't have time to ask how or where he found it.

"I'm not squeamish," he says.

I nod, not having time to deal with if he is or isn't. I have a cat to save.

"Start opening those gauze packets."

He does while I grab the scalpel. I don't have time to shave the cat like I'd like or give the cat anything for pain. Instead, I palpate and then make a quick and exact cut into the cat's lungs.

I grab the straw and carefully place it into the opening. I grab the gauze from Brody to stop the bleeding.

"Come on," I say, waiting for oxygen to get into the cat's lungs.

His lungs slowly start filling and then emptying with air, and I let out a deep breath.

"Hold him still," I tell Brody.

His hands hold the cat that will start feeling more alive now that he is getting oxygen.

"Do you have your phone on you?"

Brody pulls out his phone and hands it to me. I turn the flashlight on and open the cat's mouth to get a better look while I take the tweezers. It takes me several minutes to find the obstruction, but I finally find the piece of plastic that is lodged in his throat. I pull it out, and then slowly, the cat starts breathing on his own.

"Good kitty," I say, petting his head. I wait a few more minutes to make sure he is breathing well on his own before I take the straw out and cover the small wound with gauze and wrap.

The captain runs back into the room. "I couldn't find his favorite toys."

I smile. "It's okay. Your cat is doing much better now. You should have your vet take a look at him tomorrow to make sure he's still doing okay, but he's in the clear."

I can see the relief all over the man's face. It's one of the best parts of the job—watching owners realize that their beloved pet is going to be all right.

He runs over to the cat and wraps his arms around him while I take a step back.

I don't dare glance over at Brody. I don't want to know what he's thinking. We were supposed to remain a mystery to each other. That was how we would be able to remain unattached. But, in a matter of seconds, I destroyed all of that.

I walk out of the room, knowing that Brody is following. I walk back to the front of the boat as the first part of darkness starts covering the sky. I walk back to the railing to look out as the stars begin to take over the sky.

Brody slowly walks over next to me. He doesn't touch me. He just leans on the railing and looks out at the ocean and sky with me.

"I wish I could pretend like I didn't just see that, but I'm not a very good actor."

I sigh. "It's okay. It was stupid to think that we could spend a week together and not learn some basic facts about each other." I turn toward Brody. "I'm a veterinarian, if you didn't figure that out already. I like animals more than I like people. And, if you think what I did back there was impressive, don't. I don't want you thinking I'm this amazing human being you should date after this. I'm not that good of a person. If that had been a human back there, I would have let them die. This changes nothing."

He smirks.

"What's so amusing?"

"You are the strangest human being I've ever met."

My lips slowly curl up. "You think I'm strange. Good."

I walk back to the table, pour us each another drink, and then walk back to the railing, handing Brody his drink.

"So, tell me something about yourself since you now know too much about me."

Brody takes a slow sip of his drink as he stares deeply into my eyes. "You don't want me to tell you anything about myself."

"Yes, I do."

"No, you don't."

"Yes, it's only fair."

He grabs my hand and roughly pulls me to him. He's done that a couple of times now. And, every single time, it shocks and excites me. My body comes alive with a fire that I don't know how to extinguish and don't really want to get rid of. I want more and more of his body. I want to feel and see every glorious inch of his hardness that he teases me with but hasn't shown me enough of yet.

He looks at me like he wants to devour me.

My body screams back, *Yes, yes, yes. Kiss me. Devour me. Do whatever dirty things you think of in your mind but haven't dared to do yet. I need it. I want it. I can't live without it.*

"My favorite movie is *The Lord of the Rings*."

My head snaps back as I look at him incredulously. I was expecting a kiss; instead, I got a lousy fact about him.

"If you are going to share something about yourself, you could at least share something interesting. Your favorite movie doesn't count."

"I just told you one of the most important things about myself."

"No, you told me a random trivia fact. What your favorite movie is tells me nothing about you."

He pulls me tighter, and I try to keep my body from getting too excited because, apparently, we are going to argue about what makes a trivia fact worth caring about. And, after we are done with that, I'm sure we will be interrupted again by the staff to handle another crisis, and we will never actually have sex. But my body doesn't care about any of that. My body thinks that, anytime our bodies are within three feet of each other, we are about to have sex.

"Actually, it tells you everything."

"How?" I ask, breathing heavily.

"Well, if I had said my favorite movie was *Die Hard* or *The Godfather*, what would you have thought?"

"That you are like every other hot-blooded male on this planet, who can't think for themselves."

He nods. "Exactly."

His hand tangles in my hair, and I can't think anymore about anything other than his hand.

"So, what does me liking *The Lord of the Rings* tell you about me?"

"Um..." I can't think. *Why can't he tell that, when he touches me, I can't think at all?*

He smirks, and his damn dimples catch my attention now as my mouth goes dry. I glance up at his eyes that are laughing at my predicament. He knows. He knows exactly what he is doing to me. He's teasing me while trying to have a stupid conversation. But I don't want to be teased. I want to be fucked.

I can play this game.

I take a drink of my tequila as I take a step back. I toss my hair over my head, forcing him to let go of my hair as I expose my bare neck to him. His eyes deepen, and he clears his throat as he stares at me.

"It tells me that you are a nerd who likes watching people fight over a ring."

He frowns and takes a step toward me. "No, it tells you that I'm an intelligent man who has a dark imagination and isn't afraid to go after what he wants."

It's my turn to swallow hard. I watch him watch my throat as he thinks about what dirty thing he is going to do to me.

"Fuck me before some other crazy thing happens that stops us," I say.

Before he can respond, a loud popping sound makes us both jump. We turn out toward the ocean where the sound is coming from.

Fireworks.

He arches an eyebrow at me.

"Yes, Bayron planned the fireworks for us," I say, groaning.

It's beautiful and romantic, and it would be perfect if I were actually on a date with a man I thought was capable of dating when I got home. But that's not what this is.

I don't want to watch the fireworks. But the resort spent far too much money on them for us not to watch. So, I lean over the railing, hoping that the show ends soon.

Brody walks behind me, wrapping his arms around me as his body presses against my back.

"We should watch, but it doesn't mean that you need to make this any more romantic than it already is," I hiss.

His mouth moves to my ear. "Don't react; the staff is watching."

"What?" And then his hand slips into the front of my dress, grabbing my breast.

I gasp.

"Don't react," he commands with a growl to his voice.

I suck in a breath as I feel an ice cube dance over my nipple. His mouth lightly kisses my exposed neck, and the combination sends chills shooting through my body.

"You've wanted me to kiss your neck all night."

"Yes," I whisper.

"I've wanted to do this all night." He hikes my dress up, and his hand slips into my panties.

I groan as his fingers slip inside my drenched pussy.

"Not. A. Sound," he says.

I bite my lip to keep from screaming. I don't know why it matters if I moan a little. The fireworks would more than cover up any sound I made.

His fingers slide in and out of me, and my hips start buckling as he moves.

"Don't move, sweetheart, or I'll stop." His voice is serious and threatening.

I don't know how not to move. I don't know how not to make a sound. But I'm so desperate to get fucked by him that I'll do anything I can to give in to his demands. I grab the railing hard, forcing myself to remain still, as I continue to bite my lip.

His fingers slip back out of me, and for a second, all I feel is his heavy breathing on my neck. He kicks my legs apart a little more, and then his cock enters me without warning.

I bite my lip hard, causing it to bleed to keep from screaming.

"Good girl," he whispers into my ear when I do everything I can to follow his command.

I don't know if he has a condom on or not. I don't know if the entire staff can see us right now or not. But neither matters. My body is his. He can do whatever he wants to it. I instantly trust him. And the way he controls my body shows me just how correct I was in giving him that power.

"Aw, baby, I can already feel your pussy starting to tighten around my cock."

I pant, unable to bite down on my lip any longer.

"You want to come so badly."

"Yes."

"But you don't get to come. Not yet. You're not ready."

I swallow, trying to push down my orgasm that I'm on the edge of having.

"I can't."

"Don't come, Skye," he commands as he fucks me, making it almost impossible for me not to.

I try to hold on to his words. I try to do exactly what he says when every part of my body is begging me to do the opposite. I need to come. My body won't let me hold back much longer.

He grabs on to my hips as he pushes his thick, long cock into me harder, driving me so close to the edge that I'm not sure there is anything that can keep me from coming.

"No, Skye," he warns.

I stop. I don't know how his words are able to control me despite his body pushing me to do the opposite. But my body listens. At least, one more time.

"You want to come, Skye?"

"Yes."

"You think you've earned it?"

"Yes."

He snickers. "You think this was hard, but you don't know how bad I can be."

I suck in a breath, trying desperately to hold on as he continues to thrust harder, making the task impossible.

"Come."

One tiny word, and my body responds. My pussy tightens around his cock as my body explodes more fiercely than the fireworks still shooting off in front of us. I don't know if I'm still supposed to be quiet or not, but I can't be quiet. I open my mouth to moan, and his mouth captures mine. I moan into his mouth instead of screaming into the night.

I don't know if he comes. I don't notice the fireworks. I don't notice if anyone is watching us. All I can do is come over and over until my body finally stills.

I'm a strong woman. I work out daily. But I have no strength left. I collapse into his arms, unable to even stand.

He grins like the asshole he is.

"I think I chose correctly," I say, trying to catch my breath and strength.

He tucks his cock back into his pants before he scoops me up into his arms. "I didn't do my job very well if you are still thinking about other men."

My head rests against his hard chest. I want him to get naked in one of the bedrooms. I want to do that again and again, but I can barely move.

"I'm not thinking of them."

He smirks. "I know."

He carries me inside and down a hallway, stopping outside a door that has our names written on it in hearts.

"What did Bayron think? That he would put our name on a couple of hearts, and by the end of the date, I would be proposing to you?" he asks as he pushes the door open.

We both stare at the bed that is covered in rose petals and has two swan towels kissing. There is a bottle of champagne chilling with chocolate-covered strawberries sitting on the table next to the bed.

I sigh. "I think that is exactly what Bayron was thinking."

"I don't want to put you on the bed."

"Why? You think I'll catch romantic fever if you let me near some rose petals?"

"No, I think we are both going to fall asleep before I get to fuck you again."

He looks down at me, and I see the lust that I feel reflecting in his eyes.

"But, if I put you down anywhere else, I'm afraid you will collapse from exhaustion."

I laugh. "Whose fault is that?"

"Fine. I'll let you sleep well tonight, but you'd better get plenty of rest because, tomorrow, I plan on making up for lost time."

I bite my lip, liking that thought. "Deal."

He tosses me onto the bed and climbs into bed next to me.

"You're not going to undress?" I ask, disappointed.

"If I undress either of us, I'm going to fuck you again. And, since you trusted me with your body, I know I need to pace ourselves so that I can have a full day with you tomorrow."

I sigh. "Fine."

His arms wrap around me, and I snuggle against his body. I'm not sure if snuggling breaks the rules of getting too close or doing anything other than sex, but right now, I'm too tired to think about it.

"Why did you pick me instead of the dickhead?" he asks.

My eyes open, and I turn. "Why does it matter?"

447

"Because I'm a man, and I need to know that I blew away my competition."

I laugh. "Sorry, the competition was close. I chose you because you kissed better."

"Not because of the naughty things I said?"

I blush. I don't want to tell him that I was so caught up with the other guy that I didn't even hear what he said.

He shakes his head. "That's what I thought. You didn't even hear what I said, did you?"

I blush a deeper shade of red. "No."

He growls, "Well then, you missed out."

"What did you say?"

"I guess you'll have to find out tomorrow."

I sigh. "Tell me."

"I'll show you later. Now, sleep, and if you dream about dickface or even think about him again, I'll punish you."

He pulls me close against his body, and I close my eyes. He thinks I thought of another guy for even a second after he fucked me. That's his goal—to eliminate any thoughts of any other man from my brain. He just doesn't realize that he's already done it.

He's fucked me once, and my body already belongs to him. I can't remember any other man ever fucking me. And, as much as I want to sleep, all I can think about is forcing my brain to try to remember what dirty, filthy thing he said to me so that I can figure out what naughty thing he has planned for me tomorrow.

4

BRODY

WHY THE FUCK did I bring up dickface?

Because I'm a jealous asshole who can't tolerate her thinking about any man other than me. I needed to hear her say that she was mine. Because I'm a controlling fucker who wants complete control over her body.

I'm already close to controlling her body. Her body followed almost every command. I could have made her come anytime after my cock entered her pussy. She would have done anything I wanted. But she still tried to scream. That was the only command she couldn't completely follow.

One fuck, and I already own her body. But my dark heart wants to control more than just her body. I want to control everything about her. Her every movement. Her every breath. Who she talks to. What she does. What she thinks.

I've gotten one tiny taste of what controlling her would be like, and now, my thoughts have turned into an asshole. Only a giant prick would want this much control over another person.

I thought I came here to get away from the control that I was used to at home. But, instead, I came here and got more control over another person than I'd ever thought they would give me. I got a taste of what I'd always wanted but never thought I could have. And, now, I want more.

She stirs in my arms. She's been out since about five minutes after her head hit the pillow. Yesterday was exhausting for her. But today is going to be much worse. I have too many dirty thoughts playing in my head that I need to experience with her. We only have a week together. And I plan on making the most of it by playing out every dark fantasy that either of us has ever had.

She grins when she sees me.

"Sleep well?" I ask, already knowing the answer.

She stretches her arms over her head. "Yes."

"Good. Now, get off my arm. You've been lying on it all night."

She rolls off my arm with a giggle. "You're not serious, right? I haven't actually been lying on your arm all night."

I rub my arm, trying to get the feeling back into it. "I'm dead serious."

"You could have just moved me."

"But then you might have woken up."

She narrows her eyes as she tucks her hair behind her ear. "We should probably get going. I want to get out of this dress, and the staff would probably like time to clean before their next excursion."

She walks out of the bedroom without giving me a chance to respond. I follow her, hating that she is making a decision without me. I wanted her one more time on the yacht first, but by the time I chase after her, she is already thanking the crew and exiting the boat.

I run after her. "What are you doing?"

She turns and looks at me, still staring at me with her big eyes. "Exactly what I said. Getting off the boat and going back to my room to shower and get ready for the day."

I frown. "I'm the one in control this week. You do what I say. You don't get to make decisions anymore."

Her eyes brighten in amusement. "No, you get control over my body when we are having sex. We aren't fucking right now, so that means I have control over my own decisions. Understand? If not, I'll find a new man."

I take a step toward her and tower over her. "You wouldn't find a new man. You want my cock, not anyone else's. And, as far as our agreement, fine. I control your body when we are fucking, nothing more."

"Thank you. Now, I'm going to go up to my room to shower and put my swimsuit on. Meet me in my room in twenty."

I nod and watch her walk off to go change. I agree because it's what I want. I want her in her swimsuit. I want to fuck her again, but just because I want to fuck her doesn't mean we have to stay in the bedroom.

———

The door to her suite opens, and my jaw drops for more than one reason. The swimsuit that she is wearing is racy as hell. It's white and simple, but that is where the innocence of it ends. The front barely covers her breasts, and her nipples push hard against the fabric into peaks that I'm desperate to suck.

"Come in," she says, turning, and that's when I get the view of her ass in a thong bikini.

Goddamn, her body is amazing. It's clear that she works out regularly, and whatever she is doing, it's working. Really, really working. The muscles in her legs and ass draw me in and make me think of a few too many crazy positions to try. I know last night took a lot out of her, but it wasn't because her body couldn't handle it. It was more like her mind wasn't prepared for it. It makes my naughty plans for today that much more exciting.

And then I get a view of her suite, and my jaw drops again. She either is the highest-priced veterinarian in the country to be able to afford a suite like this or she has other money. The suite is three times the size of mine. I thought mine was outrageous and one of the best suites, but clearly, I was wrong. She has her own private pool in her room along with two hot tubs, an amazing view of the ocean, a living room, a dining room, and it looks like at least two or three bedrooms that jet off from the main room.

"What do you think of my swimsuit?" Skye asks, flaunting her body in front of me as she puts sunglasses on her head.

I growl.

She laughs. "That was the answer I was hoping for."

I bite my lip to keep from asking my questions about how she makes this kind of money. We promised we wouldn't share anything personal about each other, but now that I've seen her room, I have a better understanding of why we got the yacht yesterday. The resort didn't pay for it. She did. Either through her payments on this room or separately, it doesn't matter. She paid for it.

"Want to go to the beach or stay here and do something naughty?" she asks as she bends over, flashing me a view of her plump, tight ass.

I want her. But I can't have her here. Not right now. My ego can't handle it. Not until I figure out how she has this much money. I need to know if she earned it or if she has a rich daddy or something that is paying for all of this.

"Both."

Her eyes light up.

I walk over to the bag she has been packing for the beach and pick it up, throwing it over my shoulder before I take her hand.

She gives me a disappointed look. But I don't let it stop me. I lead her out until I find a private spot on the beach with two lounge chairs and an umbrella. I dig her towel out of the bag and put it on one of the chairs.

"I'll go get you a drink. What do you want?"

She frowns. "You don't need to get me a drink. A bartender will be around in a few minutes."

"No need to wait. I'll get you something now. Do you just want whatever the drink of the day is or a piña colada or what?"

"Drink of the day is fine," she says.

I expect her to smile or give me some indication that she is happy that I'm doing something nice for her. Instead, I get a blank expression. I walk away up the beach and toward the bar that sits on the edge of the property.

I pull out my phone as I walk and type in everything that I know about her, which isn't much. Her first name and that she's a veterinarian. And then I hope that something comes up.

I take a seat on one of the small circular barstools attached to the bar.

"Can I get two drinks of the day?" I ask while I wait for my Wi-Fi connection to kick in and pull up the results.

The bartender nods and begins making our drinks.

Slowly, the search results start coming up. I click on the first article and watch as her big eyes and sly lips come up on the screen. The only difference between her now and in this picture is that her hair was red then and, now, it's blue. I didn't expect to find out much about her so quickly without even a last name to go off of. I glance to the two other people in the image next to her and read the caption. But I guess, when you are friends with a princess and prince, Google assumes you are searching for that famous Skye and not someone else.

I continue reading through the article but don't find out much more about her. I search through other articles, but all I can find out about Skye is her connection to her princess best friend. I don't find anything about a rich father or that she sold a company that made her millions. She has a rich friend. That must be why she is treated like royalty when she comes here even though she isn't a princess herself; she knows a princess.

I close my phone as the bartender hands me our drinks.

"Thanks," I say, taking the drinks and walking back to Skye.

My ego feels less crushed, knowing that she doesn't make outrageous amounts of money; she just has a rich friend who takes care of her.

"Here you go," I say, holding her drink out to her.

"Thanks," she says, forcing a fake smile onto her lips.

She sits on her lounge chair, half in and half out of the sun.

"Do you want me to move the umbrella, so you are out of the sun? Or do you want to work on your tan?" I ask.

"I'm fine as is."

I take a seat in the lounge chair next to her, and we both stare out at the ocean while drinking our drinks. I'll give her a few minutes just to enjoy the beach before I make my move. It's a quarter till eleven. I'll start my plan on the hour. It will make it easier for me to execute.

She eyes me out of the corner of her eye as she drinks, but she doesn't say anything. She just drinks, like I'm not even here, obviously lost in thought.

I take her hand and gently kiss it.

"What are you doing?" she asks, her voice exploding with her anger toward me, which she has obviously been hiding all morning.

"Kissing your hand," I say, confused as to why she is so upset.

She pulls her hand away and sits up, straddling the lounge chair. "No, what are you doing, being so nice to me? The opening doors for me and carrying my bag and fetching me drinks and, now, kissing my hand. It has to stop!"

I wrinkle my forehead because I think she has absolutely lost it. "I can't do nice things for you? Why?"

"Because that's not what we are. We aren't boyfriend and girlfriend. We aren't dating. We aren't doing anything with emotions. We are just fucking. The rougher, the better. So, stop being so nice to me."

I laugh. I can't help it. "I can't be nice to you? Seriously? I get that you want the bad boy in the bedroom, but what I've done so far isn't even that nice. I got you a drink and carried your bag. So what? Next time we need a drink, you can go get it if it will make you feel better."

"It will."

"Fine." I slurp down the rest of my drink. "Then, get me a refill."

She smirks and storms off toward the bar to get us new drinks while I try to figure out what the hell just happened. She's an independent firecracker. I know that. I just didn't realize that doing anything for her would turn into such a fight. There is something I'm missing. I know that. I just don't know what it is or if it matters.

I have six days left with her. I just have to let more of my asshole nature out so that she doesn't feel like I want something after the six days are up. I don't. And not trying is easy. I'll just pretend like she doesn't exist, except when I want sex from her.

"Here," she says, roughly handing me my drink.

I take the drink from her without saying thank you, without a grin, without anything.

She carefully watches me as she takes a seat next to me. "You're not living up to your end of the deal."

I exhale deeply, closing my eyes and leaning back. "How am I not living up to the deal?"

"You're supposed to be giving me hot, *I can't move for a week* sex. Not lying around, giving me compliments, and getting me drinks."

I don't open my eyes. "Seven minutes."

"What?"

"I'm giving you *I can't move for a week* sex starting in seven minutes."

"Why seven minutes?"

"If you had listened to me instead of your favorite to win yesterday, then maybe you would know the answer to that."

She sighs while I grin on the inside. She's flustered and confused. She says that she wants me to be in control, to be an ass, but when I do it for even a second, she hates it.

I hear her shift in her seat, not able to get comfortable while she waits for what's going to happen in seven minutes. I listen to her breathing get faster and faster. She sighs every few seconds, annoyed that she gave up control to me and this is how I use it. To torture her. She slurps from her drink, trying to calm her mind. But it won't work either. She wants me too badly.

I, on the other hand, have never been more relaxed.

"It's been seven minutes," she says, her face right over mine as she waits for me to open my eyes.

"Six minutes. It's been six minutes."

"How do you know that? Your eyes have been closed the entire time."

"I know because you are far too restless to wait the entire seven minutes, so that means that only six minutes must have passed."

I open my eyes, and she bites her lip as trying to keep it from curling up in a smile.

"What happened to you giving me complete control?"

She narrows her eyes as she tucks her hair behind her ear while she still hovers over me. "I've realized that I'm not very good at it."

"No, you're not. But you're going to be."

I tackle her back onto her lounge chair, and she gasps. I pin her body beneath me. With my eyes, I make my intentions clear of exactly what I want to do with her.

"No, we can't," she says, looking around at the other people on the beach.

"We are."

"Brody, we can't—"

My mouth presses down on her soft lips, which are trembling as she has thoughts of getting caught having sex on the beach. She thinks she has a choice, but she doesn't. If she wants me to continue to fuck her for the rest of the week, then she has to do exactly what I say.

"Fuck me right here. Anyone could see us. We could get kicked off the resort for this. Arrested even. But none of that matters because you can't help but fuck me," I say into her lips as I continue kissing her.

She writhes beneath me, trying to fight between what she wants and what she feels is right.

My hand slips down between her legs, beneath her bikini bottoms. I rub over her clit and then into her pussy. She wants me. Now. She can't hide what her body is telling me.

"Decide, Skye. Fuck me here, or don't fuck me ever again."

Her eyes search mine. "You couldn't stop fucking me if I didn't fuck you here."

I smirk. "There are plenty of other women I could fuck. You said you wanted a bad boy, a man to take charge and play out your wildest fantasies. So, either let me have the control or find someone else."

"Fuck me," she says without hesitation. Whatever doubts she had before are gone. She wants me, and that's all that matters to her now.

"Good girl," I say, settling between her legs as I bite her bottom lip hard for hesitating in the first place.

She whimpers at the sting of the pain, but it does want I intended it to do. It makes me the sole focus of her attention. She's forgotten that we are on a beach chair, only feet from the nearest couple.

I move my kisses down her neck, and my fingers trace circles between her folds. Her breathing is slow and heavy, but I know it's soon going to turn fast and desperate.

"Grab my cock," I say into her ear.

Her hand finds the waistband of my swim trunks, and she slips her hand inside, finding my hard cock, stroking it over and over.

"That's my girl," I say, loving how she strokes my cock with just the right amount of pressure.

I pull a condom out of my pocket and place it in her other hand.

"Put it on," I command.

Her eyes grow heavy as she rips the condom wrapper open with her teeth.

"Don't move," I say as a couple walks by us, hand in hand.

I can feel her heart racing in her chest. She holds her breath, not moving an inch. And I'm afraid she's going to back out and not let me fuck her.

The couple passes, and I look her in the eye again, trying to get her focus back on me. "Put the condom on."

She takes a deep breath with a sexy grin. "Don't worry, hand-some." She leans forward, firmly kissing me as her tongue darts into my mouth. "I don't think I could ever stop fucking you."

I growl and shove her hand holding the condom toward my cock, needing the damn condom on now before I fuck her whether it's on or not.

She gets the hint and places the condom on. I shove her bikini bottoms down and pull my cock out, not caring who is looking as I slide it into her slit. Her hands tangle in my hair, pulling me closer to her, and I push harder inside her.

I know I need to make this fast, but I could stay buried deep inside her forever if she let me. And I have a feeling, from the look of ecstasy on her face, that she would.

But I can hear people coming. I know that our risky moment can only be that—just a moment. That, if I want to fuck her properly, I'm going to need to find a place more private than the beach. Because, if we get caught, I'll lose her trust and ability to take control of her body. And I won't give that up.

So, I fuck her hard. Fast. Thrusting quickly without giving her a second to breathe.

"Come, Skye," I command as I come deep inside her, not waiting for her.

She comes as she buries her face into my shoulder to keep from crying out.

"Hey, guys! Look, I found the two lovebirds," Noah says.

I quickly slip out of Skye as my face turns redder—not because of embarrassment, but because my douche-bag friends were the ones who caused me to end that romp much sooner than I wanted to.

"I'm not talking to you until we are back home and in the office and I don't have a choice but to talk to you. Until then, leave me alone," I say as I turn my attention back to Skye, who is still pinned beneath me.

I know I wanted to fuck her every hour on the hour, but I'm not sure I can wait a whole hour to have her again. She's far too addictive for me to wait.

Noah laughs. The other two look at us with an amused grin on their faces, arms folded across their chests.

"You know they have bedrooms in this place for you to fuck in," Noah says with a wink.

I glare at him. I'm going to fire him when we get back home.

Skye laughs and pushes me off of her. I sit on the edge of the lounger while she turns and hangs her legs off, facing the men who are still standing, looking at us like they just found gold. But, if they think they are going to hang this over my head for the rest of eternity when we get back, they are wrong. They forget I'm their controlling boss who will fire them all if it comes to it.

"Actually, you were just who I was looking for," Skye says.

My glare turns from them to her. "What are you talking about?"

I know that Skye wants some kinky sex to make her forget about whatever she came here to forget, but if she's going to suggest a three-some with any one of these guys, I'm going to throw her over my shoulder and trap her in my room for the rest of the week. I won't share her. Not even with my best friends.

She ignores me, looking at them.

Noah sits down on the other lounger, curiously looking at her. "How can I be of help?"

"Well, this was supposed to be a *no-strings attached, hot romance* kind of thing for one week. But, unfortunately, a cat needed some rescuing the other day. The cat is fine now, but I had to show off some of my fabulous veterinarian skills, revealing far more about myself to Mr. Romantic here than I wanted. Now, he won't share anything with me to even the score. Care to share and get me caught up on him?"

"Noah is not saying anything," I say, looking at him dead in the eye, threatening more than his job if he says anything to her.

He smirks. "What do you want to know?" he asks, leaning closer to Skye.

"Something juicy. Because Mr. Romantic over here is acting far too perfect, and I know he has a darker side that he isn't showing me yet."

He glances at me while I continue to frown.

"He's being too romantic, huh?"

She nods.

"Hmm, that's shocking. I didn't think he had a romantic drop in his body."

"What do you mean?"

"I mean, he's a ruthless, controlling boss to us. A man who doesn't date. He doesn't do romance. All he cares about is money and pussy. Back home, he has a woman for every day of the week. So, whatever romantic he's pretending to be here, he's the exact opposite. It's a lie. He's nothing but a prick who will rip your heart out if you let him get too close."

I'm going to kill him. Here. Now. I won't even let him go back home. He's dead to me.

Skye smiles, placing her hand on his folded hands. "Thank you. That's just what I needed to hear."

I look at Skye like I'm looking at her for the first time. I thought she just wanted me to act cold toward her to help her keep from getting attached to me. That way, she couldn't have feelings toward me, and we could easily go our separate ways after this week. But I'm beginning to think it's more than that. She doesn't just want me to act distant toward her; she wants me to be cruel toward her. I'm missing something. A piece of her puzzle that I may never understand.

5

SKYE

HE'S A BAD BOY, just like I wanted him to be. Every drop of romance he's given me has all been an act, most likely because he thought that was what he needed to do to get me into his bed. But, hopefully, now, he understands it's the exact opposite of what I want. I don't want a man who does anything more than kinky sex.

But still, from the look on Brody's face, he isn't too happy with his friends for revealing his true self to me. He doesn't realize that it's a blessing, not a curse, to know the truth. But he will.

"Skye, go to your room. I'll meet you there in five minutes," Brody commands.

I feel the familiar knots form deep in my belly at the thought of what he wants to do with me in my bedroom. We just had sex, but I'm nowhere near satiated, and it seems he isn't either.

I glance at his friends, silently wishing them luck, before I give in to Brody's command and head to my suite. I have a feeling that he's about to chew his friends out the second I leave, but I don't care as long as he keeps his promise and is knocking on my door within five minutes. If he doesn't keep his promise, I might have to punish him for not keeping his word.

I wait in my room for what seems like far longer than five minutes before I finally hear the rattle of his fist on the door. It's not a patient knock. Instead, it's an *if you don't open the door in three seconds, I'm going to knock the door down* kind of knock. So, as much as I want to swing the door open and jump into his waiting arms, I also want to make him even more pissed off than I'm sure he already is. The angrier he is, the better the sex is going to be. And I want the true bad boy he's been hiding from me to come out and play.

I make my feet drag on the tiled floor as I walk to the door in nothing but my bikini. I get to the wooden door separating us and take a deep breath as I hear him pound his fist on the door again. He's pissed. It's exuding off his body through the door to me. I bite my bottom lip as my lips curl up into a smile. I flip my wavy blue hair out of my face, and then I open the door with an amused smirk on my face as I look at Brody standing there with both hands grasping the doorframe. His face is dark, his nostrils are flared, and his eyes are full of rage. He looks like he doesn't know whether he's going to rip the door off the frame or punish me for taking so long to open the door. But I already know the answer. He's going to punish me. Hard. And I can't wait.

"Would you like to come in?" I ask smugly.

He drops his hands and walks into my suite, looking around at it like he wants to destroy every sparkling glass, every bottle of wine, every fancy lamp, and every piece of furniture in the room.

"Something wrong with my room?" I ask as I follow him into the bar area, which is large enough to function as a kitchen despite not having an actual stove or oven because there is no way anyone would actually cook on a vacation here.

He takes out a bottle of tequila and pours himself a drink before he turns and glares at me as he rests his back against the counter.

"Nothing's wrong with your room. I have to remember that you didn't pay for it."

"Excuse me? I didn't pay for it?"

He gulps down the entire glass of tequila. Then, he grabs the bottle and pours some more into the glass. "Nope, you didn't. Your rich friend did."

I asked for a bad boy. I asked him to show me no emotions. I just didn't expect he'd turn into such an ass in a matter of seconds.

"First, I did pay for this suite. So, if your ego can't handle dating a woman who can afford a much nicer suite than you, you can leave."

I've never been so angry with a man in my life. He doesn't get to be pissed at me for having money that I earned.

"My ego can handle you making more money than me. I just don't believe that you do."

I frown. Hating him. That's all it took—one comment to make me go from begging for his body every second of every day to hating him.

"Second, you weren't supposed to Google me. We weren't supposed to know anything about each other."

He snorts. "Yeah, just like you weren't supposed to ask my friends anything about me."

"I asked one question about you because you already found out a fact about me. I was just returning the favor, but now that I know you were Googling me behind my back, I should have asked a lot more questions. Like why you are such a complete dick."

His lip twitches at that comment before he drinks down the rest of the tequila.

"Get out!" I say, not able to stand another second of his arrogant, chauvinistic ass.

"No." He pours himself another drink.

"You don't get to tell me no. I said, get the fuck out!"

He walks over to where I'm standing in the center of the kitchen, shaking from my anger. He holds the glass out to me, but I knock it onto the floor. The glass shatters as it hits the tiled floor. I don't care about the glass though. I care about getting this prick out of my life.

"I'll leave—after you admit what you really want, sweetheart."

He takes a step closer, and I take a step back until my back hits the counter behind me. He grins like the bastard he is as he traps me with his arms on either side of me, his body pushing up against me.

"I want you to leave," I say slowly, trying to squash the sparks flying around my body and lighting it up with a fire that only he has been able to start, and I have no idea how to put out the flames. I just want him gone. Then, I can get myself off in my Jacuzzi.

"No. What do you want? You said you wanted a bad boy. You wanted a man who didn't care about you. A man who takes what he wants from you with no regard for your feelings. You said you wanted a man to make you feel alive again and to make you forget about whatever you came here to forget. But, now that I am that man, you want me to leave. What. Do. You. Want?"

I can't breathe. I can't fucking breathe. His eyes are bearing down on me along with his entire body. Trapping me and consuming me. My body has never wanted him more than I do right now, and I hate myself for what I'm going to say next.

"You're right."

He cocks his head to one side with an amused expression on his face.

"What did you just say?" he asks even though he heard me clearly the first time.

"You. Are. Right. I wanted a bad boy, a man who didn't take care of me. A man who would play out all of my naughty fantasies in bed. Nothing more."

He nods. "And what do you want now?"

My eyes travel down his body. Over his hard chest and rippling abs that I want to trace my tongue over until I've felt every hard ridge. Down to his swim trunks that barely contain his erection as it pushes in my bare stomach. I want his body. I want his indifference to me. I want him to treat me like shit, so when we go our separate ways, I will feel nothing toward him, except hatred and a longing to find another man who can fuck me like he did.

He can treat me like an ass, and I'll do the same right back. That's the only way this will work.

"I want you. I want you to fuck me. I want you to be your true self. An asshole. A prick. A man I will never think of again after this week, except for how his cock felt when he fucked me."

"Done, baby," he says as his lips claim mine.

The kiss is aggressive, carnal, full of threats about what he's going to do with my body. It's exactly what I want even if it feels a bit dangerous at the same time.

I kiss back, throwing everything I can into the kiss. My tongue pushes into his mouth, dancing with his, letting him know that I might want him to take control, but I won't give up that control easily. I nip at his lip, nibbling hard.

He growls and grabs my face, forcing me to stop.

"I don't know what happened to you to make you hate men so much, but you're about to hate and love me so much that whatever happened in your past is nothing more than a blip on your radar."

I suck in a breath at his admission. He can Google me all he wants, but he'll never learn enough about my past to really know me. He can guess all he wants about what man broke my heart in the past and how, but he'll never know the truth.

He smirks. "You want dirty?" he whispers into my ear.

"Yes," I exhale as he kisses my ear.

"You want to be tied up and in pain?"

"Yes."

"You want me to tell you what I whispered in your ear during the competition?"

"Yes."

He turns his head and glances at the clock that says two minutes till one o'clock. He turns back around with a sly grin on his face.

"I said that I was going to tie you up and fuck you every hour on the hour for twenty-four hours straight. That you wouldn't be able to sleep or eat or sit straight because all you could think about while the minutes passed between fuckings was my cock. How desperate you were for it. How you ached between your legs for me to fuck you. How your lips begged to be wrapped around my long, thick length. How your body trembled, waiting for me."

My mouth drops as I think about it. I've never fucked a man more than twice in a day. I can't imagine twenty-four times. I don't think he can do it. That's impossible. But I watch the clock as the seconds tick by behind him, inching closer to the next hour. We started at noon. That leaves twenty-three more times. That's far too many and somehow also not enough. I'm not sure if a week is long enough to get Brody out of my system. But I need to try.

I watch as the clock changes to one o'clock, and Brody's face comes alive with a darkness I haven't seen from him before.

He spins me around before I realize what's happening. My arms are forced together behind my back, and then I feel something slick going around my wrists as he forcefully ties them together.

"A tie?" I ask, confused about where he got it.

"Yes. I grabbed the damn thing from my room before I came here. It's the one that Bayron pressured me into wearing last night. I've finally found a way to put it to good use."

He tightens it, roughly tying it around my wrists, so tightly that there is no way I will ever be able to break free. He grabs my arm and leads me out toward the balcony that overlooks my private pool. He pushes me down until I'm kneeling in front of him before he pulls out his thick, erect cock.

"Suck," he commands.

I want to, but I don't want to at the same time. I want to feel his cock filling my mouth. I want to suck the pleasure out of him, but I don't want to give him any pleasure at the same time because he's a dick.

"Suck," he says again as he pushes his cock at my lips.

My eyes light up in defiance, as I open my mouth to let his cock in, but I don't plan on letting him get the pleasure that he is seeking. I barely let my lips cover his tip as I suck him, licking the pre-cum off that has settled over the tip.

He grabs my hair in his fist, and I know he is going to force my head further over his cock but not until I rake my teeth over his length hard enough that I know it isn't entirely pleasant.

"Cunt," he curses with a wicked grin on his face.

He likes it when I defy him. He wants me to. Just like I want him to punish me for defying him.

And then he pushes his dick so far into my throat that I can't help but gag.

"Breathe, gorgeous," he says before he pulls his cock back out of my mouth before slowly pushing it back in again.

This time, I'm prepared. I breathe calmly as the tears stain down my face from the pain, but the look on his face makes it all worth it. The groans leaving his throat make me want to suck him in deeper. And the pain pushes all of my real pain away, just like I thought it would. I want more and more and more of this. More pain.

He sees it in my eyes when I surrender to the pain, and instead of fighting it, I crave more. His lip twitches, and his eyes come alive when he realizes that this is actually what I want. That I'm not going to say *red* when he pushes his cock down my throat, I'm not going to say it when he hits me too hard on the ass, I'm not going to say it when his cock is thrusting too hard inside. Instead, I'm going to beg for more.

He grabs my arm, forcing me back onto my feet. He kisses me, tasting himself on my lips. My body aches for him every time he kisses me. My pussy aches for him, desperate to have the same cock that was filling me earlier inside me.

"Trust me, Skye," he commands. It should be a question, but it isn't. I realize nothing with him will ever be a question again.

He grabs my thighs and lifts me up, spreading my legs open as he sits me on the railing. I squeal as he does it. Both from the sudden movement and from being thrust up onto a railing where I could fall over the edge and die.

I glance over my shoulder. We aren't that high up, not even a full story. I might not die if I fell, but I would definitely break something. The problem is, my hands are still tied behind my back. I can't hold on to anything. I'm entirely under his control. My life is literally in his hands.

"Brody, no—"

But then his tongue is licking my pussy as his hands spread me wider, and I forget that I could die. At least I'd die happy. He licks me, taking in every drop of liquid that pours out of my body. His tongue dances over my clit as I make sounds that I didn't even know my throat could make. I went from incredible pain to incredible pleasure in a second. From fear to ecstasy. And I know that, in a second, he could flip a switch and bring me right back to the pain.

"God, don't ever stop," I groan so loudly that I'm sure all the rooms next to us can hear me.

"God, huh? Why does he get the credit for all my hard work?"

He flicks his tongue over my clit again.

"Brody," I cry out.

"That's better," he moans against my clit, causing me to shake from the electricity that he just shot through my body.

I feel my body falling backward. I tense my abs, holding myself up, an almost impossible task, even for someone as in shape as I am, while he's doing what he's doing to my body with his tongue.

"Brody, help," I cry.

He stops for a second. "You'd better hold yourself up because I'm a little busy here," he says with a wink.

"I hate you," I cry as he tortures me again with his tongue.

"I know, but you don't know what hate is yet."

I try to focus on keeping my balance instead of what he's doing to my body, which is almost impossible because he's far too good at what he's doing. I'm about to come, and I'm not sure how I can keep my balance and come at the same time.

He won't let you fall, the voice in my head reminds me. *He's just teasing you.*

I hope.

So, instead of focusing on staying upright, I focus on his tongue lapping over my clit. I focus on that feeling deep in my gut that keeps getting stronger.

"I'm going to..."

The second I start to come, he stops, and I come on nothing. His fingers disappear from my pussy, his tongue stops licking my clit, and my orgasm is far less exceptional than I expected. Because he fucking stopped.

His hands let go of me, and he licks my juices off of his fingers, one by one. I stare intently at him, not believing what he just did, as I forget that I'm the only one now holding me up onto the balcony.

I start falling. I try to engage my abs and my legs to keep myself from falling, but I'm not sure if I'm strong enough to hold myself up. Not anymore.

My body slips off backward, and I know my last chance is if I can hook my leg under the railing to keep me from falling to the ground below me. My leg catches at the same time that Brody's hands grab on to my waist.

Together, we pull me back up.

"You almost let me die!" I pant and scream.

He puts his fingers over my lips, shushing me. "No, I pushed you to your limit to teach you how to live."

I breathe hard and fast, wanting to yell at him more, but he's right. Deep down, I loved that. I loved the thrill that anything could happen. The only part I didn't love was not getting to experience my full orgasm because of him.

"What's wrong, princess?" he asks with a smirk.

"You didn't let me come."

"I know. But you will now."

He grabs me, shoving me face-first toward the railing with my ass in the air. His hands grab my hips, and I feel his cock pushing at my ass. He's going to fuck me in the ass. I know it. I bite my lip to keep from begging him not to. I've never been fucked in the ass before, and as scary as it sounds, I want to feel it. I want to know how dirty and painful sex can be. I want to feel all of it. It's the only way I can move on with my life.

His cock pushes at my ass as it taunts me but doesn't actually enter me.

"You want me to fuck your ass, don't you, Skye?" he asks, his voice sultry and full of promises that I'm not sure I'm ready for.

"Yes," I groan, keeping my eyes closed rather than looking down at how far I could have fallen.

"Oh, I will but not yet. You aren't ready. Your pussy, on the other hand"—his fingers dip inside me, two, three, four, stretching me wider than I've ever been stretched—"is very ready." He pulls his fingers back out and immediately replaces them with his cock

469

pushing hard into me.

"Jesus," I growl as I'm pushed hard into the railing as he fucks me from behind, sliding in and out of me like he's been fucking me his whole life and knows exactly what my body craves.

He thrusts, and I know that, after not coming hard enough earlier, it won't take me long to come. And I plan on coming hard on his cock. I won't let him take my pleasure from me again.

"You almost there?" he asks, not needing to ask the question because he already knows the answer.

I pant hard because I can't form any words or process what he's saying. I can't concentrate on anything but the wave consuming me. An explosion of feelings as my orgasm starts deep in my belly and then takes over every fiber in my body.

I feel his palm on my ass as he hits me hard at the peak of my orgasm. I've never experienced pain like that during sex. I thought it was meant as a punishment, but when his palm touches my body, I finally understand what the pain is really meant to bring. A pleasure I've never felt before and a connection to the man who gives me that feeling. I let a man tie me up, hold my life in his hands, and slap my ass hard. It's not something I would trust every man with. But, after this, I would trust Brody with any part of my body. I trust him with bringing me the best sex I've ever felt or ever thought I could feel.

He pulls out of me, and I feel my body falling to the floor in complete exhaustion. I love running and working out. But I have nothing left in me. I've never felt so exhausted after sex.

I feel his arms scooping me up and lifting me off the ground. My head falls against his chest as I close my eyes. I could easily sleep in his arms just like this if he held me. He carries me back inside and gently lays me on the bed. I wait for him to go around to my arms to untie me and then climb into bed with me. I'm sure he is just as exhausted as I am.

He leans down, and I feel his lips against my ear. "Sleep tight, baby. You have thirty-five minutes until you'll be coming with my cock deep inside your gorgeous pussy." He nips at my ear and then stands back up.

I glance at the clock. Thirty-five minutes. It's not nearly enough time to rest if every time is going to be like that. But, somehow, my pussy is already aching for another fuck with him. I've turned into a greedy monster that can't get enough of his body.

I watch him walk away from the slits that my eyes have become. I can't even bring myself to open them all the way.

"Where are you going?" I whisper. Even my voice is not working properly.

He smirks as he stops, standing naked at the foot of the bed, before he grabs his trunks and pulls them back on.

"To get some new toys to torture you with to play with in thirty-three minutes," he says, somehow always knowing exactly how much time remains without ever looking at the clock.

I swallow hard, thinking about what he could be bringing back. A whip, crop, rope, butt plug, what? I doubt that he thought to bring all those things with him when he didn't know that he was going to find a woman who craved those things, but maybe he did. Or maybe he's going to find a creative solution to finding new toys to play with. Whatever he does, I don't care. I want him. The toys are just a bonus.

He's the most exciting thing I've ever felt. I've never been so consumed with the need for sex, but now, I don't know how I've lived without sex that takes over everything.

He starts walking toward the door.

"Are you going to untie me?"

He stops and turns his head to look at me, deadpan. "No."

And then he turns and walks out the door, leaving my arms tied behind my back, as I lie in the bed, naked except for my own cum still dripping down between my legs. Damn this man. Even when he's gone, he makes sure that all I can do is think about him. I close my eyes while I try to decide if choosing Brody over all the other men was the best or worst thing I've ever done in my life. It's too soon to decide. But I do know one thing. Brody has just ruined sex for me with all other men.

6

BRODY

This woman.

I can't get her out of my head. She owns me. My thoughts. My body. My cock. Everything. It's hers.

I've only known her a week, but in that week, I've fucked her in almost every way my dirty brain can come up with. I've tied her up in ways I thought no woman could actually bend. I've pushed her limits, fucking her in public places, over balconies, in restaurants. I've made her bleed, caused bruises, and heard her cry out from the pain of my hand or a whip on her ass or thigh. None of it was enough.

It wasn't enough for me.

And it sure wasn't enough for her.

I know everything there is to know about her body. I know the whimpers she makes when she is begging me for more. I know just how far her body can last before she's lost to her orgasm. I know exactly what buttons to push on her body to make her come seconds after our first kiss. I know how hard to hit her ass to make her cheeks just the right shade of pink.

I know all of that, yet the only personal thing I know about her is that she's a veterinarian who has a rich friend, who's a princess, and that she came here to forget something. I know that I'm the first man she's been with who she's had dark, dangerous sex with and that, most likely, after today, when she goes back home, she'll go back to her normal ways. She will date normal men who take her on normal dates and have normal sex.

She won't beg them to tie her up. She won't ache for them to control her body with whips and chains. She'll pretend she is a nice, sweet girl that wants a nice, caring man. She'll search for a man to marry, to raise kids with. She'll forget about her dark urges and me.

I'm not sure if I can handle that. I won't let her forget about me. I need one more fuck that will make it impossible for her to forget me. Something that will push her limits further than I've ever pushed her. Which is going to be hard since I fucked her on the hour for twenty-four hours straight and then at least three times a day the rest of the week. Each time I fucked her, I tried to come up with something that would make her use her safe word to make me stop.

She never did. Not even close.

Skye rolls over in bed with a grin on her face. Even though her eyes are still closed, she knows that I'm in bed with her. It's a strange feeling at first—to wake up in a bed with a woman, but how quickly that faded after the first night we spent together. Now, I can't imagine not waking up to her sweet face and getting a good fuck in before we even leave the bed.

"What are you thinking?" she asks, able to read my body and mind without even opening her eyes.

It's freaky how well we know each other's bodies.

"About how I want to fuck you on our last day together."

Her eyes flicker open as she licks her bottom lip. "What do you have in mind?"

I can't help but smile at her reaction. I've never been with a woman who wanted sex as much as I do, but Skye is definitely that woman. She's never satiated. I think I could spend every second of every day trying to make that happen, and it never would.

I stroke her face, trying to memorize every feature of her face to take with me.

"What is something you've always wanted to do on vacation?" I ask.

"You," she says, giggling a little.

I shake my head. "Other than sex, my dirty girl. What's something you've always wanted to do but never did? Or have you done it all? The snorkeling, the swimming with dolphins, the zip-lining."

She thinks for a second.

"You've done all of that, haven't you?" I ask.

She winces. "Yeah, as much as I've probably convinced you that all I do on vacations is fuck complete strangers for a week, it's not true. I usually spend my time going on adventures. It beats just sitting on the beach and drinking alone every day."

I frown. I can't imagine her ever being lonely, but it seems that, for at least part of her life, she has been.

I tuck her hair behind her ear as I gently and lazily kiss her on the lips, not wanting it to go any further than a kiss right now but needing to taste her to make her not feel alone at least for a second.

She smiles sweetly when I stop kissing her.

"Why do you want to know?"

I shrug. "Just trying to think of a way to spice up our last few fucks together."

She laughs. "I don't think that's possible, not after last night."

My eyes glaze over as I think about last night. I fucked her in the ass while she was tied up to one of the curtains backstage at one of the performances that the resort puts on. All the time, any of the performers had to do in order to see her was glance to their left, and they would have seen us fucking. Only one ever did at the very end, but I don't think she got a good look at what was happening.

"You're probably right. That was a great night. Almost as good as the fifth time I fucked you."

I watch her eyes glaze over with thoughts of that night. It doesn't take her long to get the fire in her eyes as she finally remembers that time. It was the first time I used a whip on her. I can still remember the excitement and shock that covered her face when I first touched the cold whip to her bare skin.

A rattling sound on the door tears us both from our reliving our highlights of the week.

"Room service?" I ask, raising an eyebrow as I climb out of bed.

Her eyes follow me, lingering over my dick as I pull my boxers on.

"Maybe," she finally says, thinking.

I shrug and walk to the door. I never order room service unless I plan on eating the food off her body. In fact, I haven't done a nice thing for her all week unless you count giving her too many orgasms. The only reason I'm even opening the door to her suite for her is to keep her in the bed, naked, as long as I can.

I open the door, expecting breakfast and instead find Bayron.

I frown and stand firmly in the doorway. I would slam the door in his face without saying a word, but I'm guessing he's here to tell Skye when people will arrive to pack her things and about her leaving instructions. I only allow him a moment to tell me that's what he's here for because ensuring that other people are taking care of her packing means I get more time with her today.

"I need to speak with Miss Skye," he says, ignoring me.

I fold my arms across my chest, standing more firmly in the doorway. "You can tell me, and I'll make sure she gets the message."

He shakes his head like he expected me to say that and it's ridiculous. "Fine. Tell Miss Skye I have a message from Gabe. I'll be waiting here for her to tell me what she wants me to do about it."

I roll my eyes as I slam the door in his face and walk back to Skye. I don't know who Gabe is, but whoever he is, I'm sure that she won't give a fuck what he has to say, not when she has me to keep her fully occupied the rest of the day. Gabe can wait until tonight when she's back in the real world.

"Was that Bayron?" Skye asks, amused. She knows how I feel about Bayron.

"Yes," I say, falling back onto the bed next to her. I was going to wait to fuck her until I came up with some crazy way to fuck her. While parasailing or something, but my dick needs her pussy now. I don't even feel like tying her up or spanking her. I just need a good, fast, hard fuck.

I grab her and pull her on top of my body until she is straddling me, my dick growing hard underneath her pussy that will quickly drench me as her hips thrust over me. I grab her hair that is tangled from sleep and pull her face to mine so that I can kiss her luscious lips. She easily gives in, always prepared for sex because she wants it as badly as I do.

She moans into my lips as I push my tongue hard into her mouth, dancing with her tongue as I press our bodies tighter together. I watch her eyes roll back in her head as my cock pushes against her tight cunt.

"What do you want, baby?" I ask. I never ask what she wants. There's no need. I know. Her body gives me more than enough clues of what she wants.

"I want—"

Rattling on the door stops Skye in her tracks as she looks at me again, amused at what Bayron could have possibly said to me that would make me come back and fuck her to distract her and me.

"What did Bayron want?" she asks.

I shake my head. "Nothing. Here's your last chance to get anything you want from me. You want it slow and easy. You want to take control. You want to tie me up. I'll do anything you want. A one-time chance. What do you want?"

Her grin widens as she leans down and kisses me hard and firm on the lips but doesn't push her tongue into my mouth like I want her to.

"You're being bad, trying to distract me, because you don't want me to do whatever nonsense Bayron wants me to do, but if I miss my flight because of you, you're going to be in big trouble, mister. So, tell me what Bayron wanted, and then you can get back to fucking me however you want."

I glare at her, trying to convince her with my eyes that she doesn't want to know what Bayron said, but it only makes her more adorable. She won't give in to my glares or charm.

I sigh. "Something about you having a phone call from someone. It was nothing. He said he'd wait out in the hallway for a few minutes until you decided what you wanted to do about it. I wouldn't worry about it. You're going to be home in twelve hours, and you can call them back then."

She nods and leans down, her lips hovering over mine to kiss me again when she stops.

"Who?" she asks suddenly.

I shrug. "Gabe."

"Oh," she says, her body freezing as her eyes grow wide.

I raise an eyebrow at her reaction, but I don't ask the obvious question. *Who is Gabe?* I want to know. *Is he her brother? Father? Child? Her dog? Best friend? Or Lover?*

I'd be fine with most of those answers. I don't care if she has a kid. But I don't want to know about a current or ex-lover. She's still mine for the next eight hours until she has to leave for the airport.

She rolls off me and onto her back before she bounces off the edge of the bed and begins putting her clothes back on.

"What are you doing?"

She ignores me and continues to put clothes on.

I jump out of the bed, still only wearing my boxers and now a hard-on that won't go away anytime soon.

"Skye?" I ask, standing in front of her, not letting her go talk to Bayron until she talks to me first.

She shakes her head, snapping out of whatever spell she has been under the last few seconds that made her forget that I was even here.

"Sorry. I should go speak to Bayron. Just give me five minutes, and then we can get back to what we do best," she says, smiling. She quickly kisses me on the lips and then slips under my arm and out to the door.

I don't know what just happened, but I don't have a good feeling about it. She smiled at me, but it wasn't genuine. She kissed me, but she kissed me like she was kissing a brother. With nothing behind it.

I consider chasing after her and dragging her back inside to demand she tell me what the hell is going on, but I don't. That's not what we are. We are fuck buddies. I don't get to ask about her life, and she doesn't get to ask about my life.

I consider jacking off while I wait. It will give me something to keep me distracted, but I'd rather jack off in her. So, I wait. I walk to the kitchenette and pull out leftovers from our meal last night. I start eating them to stop my mind from thinking too hard. I quickly eat the fried chicken, annoyed that she isn't back. I start pacing, walking all the way to the front door to try to listen to her conversation with Bayron before I walk back to the bedroom. Whatever she is talking to Bayron about, she isn't angry or upset or frustrated. She seems calm, happy even. That only makes my own frustration grow.

Finally, the door swings open, and a bouncing Skye walks back into the bedroom, but her grin quickly disappears the second she sees me frowning at her.

"Did your conversation go well?" I ask.

"Yes," she says, swallowing hard.

"And?" I ask, waiting for her to elaborate.

She bites her lip, and I know whatever it is, it's very bad for me. She only ever bites her lip when she's nervous or she wants to be fucked. And, right now, I think it's a little of both.

"I have to leave...now."

My mouth drops open at that. Of all the things I imagined her saying when she returned, that wasn't one of them.

"Why?"

"Does it matter?"

I narrow my eyes, walking toward her. "Yes, it fucking matters when it takes away time I was supposed to have with you."

Her eyes look away from me, toward her closet full of clothes that I'm sure she's thinking about needing to get packed.

I grab her chin and turn her face to mine so that I can see her. "Why. Are. You. Leaving?"

"I'm sorry," she says, narrowing her eyes at me as she pulls herself out of my grasp. She walks to the closet and pulls out a suitcase. She opens it, laying it on the bed before she returns to the closet and begins pulling out heaps of clothes and then placing them into the suitcase.

"What are you doing?"

"Packing." She continues to throw clothes into the suitcase, not even bothering to fold them.

I move in front of the suitcase as she holds another large pile of clothes in her hands.

"Stop."

"I have to pack," she says, trying to move around me to put the clothes into the suitcase.

I block her. "Stop. The staff can pack for you. You need to talk to me."

She shakes her head. "There is nothing to say."

I frown. This is not how we are going to end. She doesn't get to stop this by just ignoring me and then leaving. That's not how our story ends. Our story ends with great sex and with a twinkle at the thought that, someday, we could run into each other and have great sex again. But that we didn't let our personal lives affect us. That we meant something to each other because what we had was perfect and untouched by the real world.

I pick her up and carry her to the other side of the bed that isn't currently holding a suitcase. I throw her down and pin her to the bed with my body as I lean down and kiss her.

She doesn't kiss me back. She doesn't fight me off either. She does nothing. It's like she isn't even really here. She just stares off into space.

I search her eyes for some clue as to what is going on. I find nothing.

"Who is Gabe?" I ask because I'm desperate. And, even if Gabe is a boyfriend, I need to hear it. I need to know that he is the reason she's rushing home. I need to be angry with someone and not direct it all at her. I don't want to hate her. I need to know why she is thinking about another man instead of me.

She swallows, and finally, I see a little of the fire in her eyes that I'm used to seeing.

"A man who needs me."

I smirk and rub my dick against her thigh. "Right now, no man can need you more than I do."

I expect a smile. A laugh, even. I get neither, just a sad woman with sad eyes.

"If he makes you this sad, why go back to him?"

She swallows. "Because, despite what you know about me, I'm not this person. I don't fuck random men. I don't push people away and forget all of my troubles. That's not who I am. I care deeply about everyone around me. I take care of them even if they don't deserve it. I take care of them even if it hurts me."

I hate him. Whatever he's done to her to make her like this makes me want to hunt him down to the ends of the earth. I want to make him pay for hurting her. I want her to stop feeling like she has to take care of him.

"Stop looking at me like that," she says, her voice soft from beneath me.

"I can't."

She shakes her head. "We don't do this. We don't share personal things with each other. We don't have feelings for each other. We have sex. And it was great while it lasted. You were the distraction I desperately needed this week. You let me be selfish. You let me forget. But, now, our time is up. It's time to return to the real world where we face real problems."

"I need one more fuck."

She closes her eyes rather than looking at me. "We don't get to fuck anymore."

I kiss her again, desperate to get the one more time that we are both owed. She still won't kiss me back. She's already closing herself off to me, and she hasn't even left yet.

"Kiss me, Skye. Let me fuck you. Let me make you forget. One more time."

"No," she says as her eyes open, and she gently pushes me off her body. She swings her legs over the edge of the bed, sitting up. "I need to leave in ten minutes for the airport."

She starts walking to the door, and I follow her. She opens it, standing behind the door, and I know what she is going to ask me to do.

"Good-bye, Brody."

She doesn't kiss me or hug me. She barely even looks at me. I don't have a chance right now to change her mind. I'm not asking for forever, just one more time. But, apparently, that isn't going to happen. We are done.

I pull on some clothes and step out of her suite like she wants because, short of actually kidnapping her or tying her up for real, I don't have any choices left. I hear the door shut behind me, and I feel a stabbing in my body that I wasn't expecting whenever we said good-bye. But maybe it is because this isn't how we were supposed to say good-bye.

I turn and see Bayron standing in the hallway, looking at me with sadness in his eyes as well. I can't stand any more gloom today. And I definitely can't deal with him lecturing me right now about how I broke Skye's heart. If her heart is broken, she did it to herself.

"Would you pass a message along to Skye?" I ask Bayron.

He smiles tightly. "Yes."

7

SKYE

I LEAN my back against the door to remain standing instead of falling to the floor in a puddle like I really want to do. I did the right thing. It was time to say good-bye. My normal life is calling, and Brody does not fit into my normal life. But it still hurts.

Not because I love him. I don't.

Not because I care for him. I do, but I care for a lot of people. It's not what's making me hurt.

Not because I ever imagined any sort of future with Brody. I didn't.

It hurts because this wasn't how we were supposed to end. We were supposed to go out with a bang. Literally. Not with an unexpected good-bye, as I'm being pulled back into a life I don't know how to escape from.

A knock on the door gets my heart racing with far too much hope. I know Brody is standing on the other side of the door, and he's going to try to convince me one last time to fuck him. And I don't have the strength to say no again. Despite not having the time, I don't care. I need to forget. One more time.

I turn around and throw the door open with a smile on my face.

"Bayron," I say, my lips and heart instantly falling.

"He's gone, Miss Skye," Bayron says, reading my thoughts.

"Oh."

"Are you ready for my staff to get you packed up?"

I nod.

He motions to the staff behind him to enter. I step aside to let them pass. I know they will have me packed up in a matter of minutes, and then I'll have nothing left to do but leave.

"He wanted me to give you a message," he says.

I bite my lip, trying to calm down. It's probably just a good-bye. He never gave me a good-bye.

"Do you want to hear it?"

I nod.

"He said that this isn't good-bye. That you aren't finished. He gets one more day. One more time. That was what the agreement was. Seven days. You've fulfilled only six of those days. He said he'll be waiting for you at the airport."

He's going to meet me at the airport. I know it. The grin and life in my cheeks returns.

"Thank you, Bayron. For everything." I lean forward and kiss him on the cheek.

"Be careful, Miss Skye," he says.

"I will," I say, knowing that he means be careful about Brody even though he isn't the one I should be worried about. I put up a barrier between us the second I met him. Brody isn't the problem. Gabe is.

The fact that I'm ending my last day early to run back to Gabe only verifies that he's the problem I don't know how to move on from. He's the one who broke my heart. I never gave Brody the same chance. It's impossible for him to break my heart when I never gave it to him in the first place.

———

I arrive at the airport with excitement and anxiety. My legs haven't been able to stop shaking since I got into the car. I've tried to enjoy the last few minutes of my time in paradise by looking at the beautiful scenery as I am driven to the airport, but nothing holds my attention.

I glance at the clock on the driver's dashboard as he pulls up in front of the airport. I have thirty minutes until my flight. More than enough time to fuck Brody one last time in a restroom before going through security and still making my flight.

I step out of the car and talk to the ticket agent to get my bags checked before I start looking for him.

He's here somewhere; I know it. I pull my phone out of my purse, looking at it before I realize that I don't even have his phone number. I don't even know his last name. I know nothing about him that would allow me to find him.

I could talk to Bayron. He'd give me whatever information he had on Brody if I wanted him to, but I don't. I don't want to know personal details. I just want his body one last time.

I scan the airport lobby, but I don't immediately see him. I know that I can't walk through security. He'll have no chance at finding me there. His flight back home isn't until much later in the day. So, I walk over and take a seat on a bench, and I wait, letting in thoughts of Brody and igniting my deepest desires to have him one last time.

———

My eyes widen when I see him pull the rope out from behind his back. In the last few days with him, I've learned that I love being tied up. I love giving him control over my body. He knows his way around my body better than I do. But even though I've started to trust him these last couple of days, my heart still beats faster and the adrenaline shoots through me whenever he does something even a little bit dangerous.

"Hand," he says. One word, but he commands my soul with it.

I hold out my left hand and he begins tying the rope around my wrist. He looks to my other hand and I hold it out for him as well. He ties my hands together making sure that the rope is tight enough that I can't escape, but not so tight that it will leave a mark.

And then he pulls my arms above my head as he ties my wrists to the headboard. *My arms instinctually pull at the rope testing to see if I can escape or not. I can't.*

I don't understand why I give him so much control. I don't understand why I trust him, especially given my past with men, but I do.

He pulls out another rope and I pant.

He's only ever tied my hands up, so it thrills and terrifies me to find out what it will feel like to completely give up everything to him.

He grabs my ankle and takes his time tying a rope around each leg. Then stretches my legs wide as he attaches them to each of the posts on the foot of the bed.

"Do you trust me?"

"Yes," I breathe.

"Good."

He tosses his shirt over my face, covering my eyes. I wait for him to tie it around my head, but he never does. I can't see him, but it wouldn't take much for me to shake the shirt off my face if I wanted to.

I don't though.

His hands go to my bikini top and he pushes it up off my breasts. Then his fingers hook into the sides of my bikini bottoms, and he slowly pulls them down until I'm naked, completely at his disposal.

I wait for him to kiss me. Stroke me. Spank me. Anything.

He doesn't.

He waits. He's far too patient.

Every second that passes I grow more restless trying to anticipate what he's going to do. He's left me alone before; is that what he's doing again? Leaving me to suffer while he goes and finds new toys?

He hasn't left though. I can't see him, but I can feel him. He's here. I can barely hear him breathing. It's calm and steady, unlike my own that races faster with every second that passes.

"Please," I whisper, needing him so badly that I can't stand it. I pull at the ropes, needing to get my hands on him, but I can't. And he doesn't offer me any relief.

More times passes. It feels like hours to me, even though I know in reality it's only been a few minutes.

Cold. I feel ice cold hit my nipple and I gasp from the unexpected touch. My back arches and my body writhes underneath his mouth.

I feel him use his mouth to move the ice over my other nipple. He swirls it around while my body moves beneath his.

He moves it down my stomach until he lets his slide off over my pussy.

Goosebumps shoot over my body, as I shiver from both the cold and the need for his body.

Again he makes me wait, but much shorter this time before I feel hot drip over my nipples.

"Fuck," I gasp, as the hot mixes with the cold sensation and takes over my body.

I don't know what he's dripping over my body, but it's a feeling I've never felt before. It makes my entire body come alive.

"God damn, I love your body," he says.

I bite my lip as I arch my back again. "I need you."

I can feel him smirk. "Not until you can't stand not to have my dick inside you a second longer, only then."

I struggle against the ropes again. "I can't wait."

His lips touch my neck and I groan.

"Not yet."

His fingers trail down my body far too slowly before he curls his fingers around my pussy and pushes two inside.

"Yes," I moan.

"So wet baby."

He slowly pulls his finger in and out of my pussy and my juices cover his fingers, begging for him.

"I'm ready."

"Not yet," he says again.

He pulls his fingers out and then his tongue replaces his fingers at my entrance. He pushes it inside me before pulling it back out and licking over my clit.

I've never felt anything so intense. I've never needed sex more.

"I'm going to come," I scream, as he licks me again.

"Come."

He moves his tongue faster over me and I can't contain my orgasm. I come over his tongue and lips.

I feel his grin against me, as my body trembles from the intensity of my orgasm.

I'm spent.

I'm exhausted from waiting, and then going through all the emotions I felt before finally coming. I still want his cock, but I'm not sure I can take much more.

"Fuck me," I plead.

He grins. "Not until you come again."

"I can't."

But his tongue darts inside me again and I feel my body give into him, despite my brain saying that I can't take much more. His hands grab my thighs pushing me open, as my body pulls against the ropes holding me down.

It doesn't take me long before I'm coming over his tongue again.

"You taste so good."

"I need your co—"

He doesn't let me finish my sentence. He makes me come again and again. And only when he knows that my body can't take any more, does he finally drive his cock inside me. It's never felt so good to have his cock inside me as it does right now. I've never needed sex as much as I do right now.

My body aches to have Brody one last time. My eyes dart around the airport, but I don't see him. He's making me wait again. I'm fine waiting, but I'm already so turned on that I could come with one kiss from him. I try to think about something else while I wait. And wait. And wait. My thoughts keep going back to Brody though.

I wait until I barely have enough time to go through security, pee, and make my flight. And then I go. I walk through security and then onto my flight. I try not to think of him as I board. I have more important things to focus my attention on and worry about now. But Brody is all I can think about as the cabin door closes and the engines purr to life.

I feel hurt, empty, broken. I feel things I never thought Brody could make me feel. *Why didn't he show up?* That's all I can think about as we push back from the gate. Maybe something happened to him. He was hurt. His car got into an accident. It doesn't make me feel especially better, but it does make me think that he's not that big of an ass. That he did want to fuck me, but he just couldn't get to me for whatever reason.

My phone buzzes in my hands. I haven't switched it to Airplane Mode yet, like I'm supposed to. It's a message from an unknown number.

I bite my lip as I stare at my phone. I know it's Brody. I just don't know if I should open it or not. I hear the engines roar louder, and I know we are about to take off soon and that I won't have a chance to look at the message again until we land.

I click the message to open it, praying that he didn't get into a car accident and is now dying in the hospital while I fly thousands of miles away.

He's not dying.

He's not hurt.

He's not even texting to apologize.

Instead, I get a picture of him with a blonde with fake boobs and a fake smile sitting on his lap on a lounge chair back at the resort. His arms are wrapped around her as he softly kisses her on the cheek.

I read the words that he typed below the picture.

I got a little distracted and couldn't make it. Sorry I'm such a dick.

I delete the image and his number from my phone before I have a chance to do something stupid like texting him back. I reach into my purse and pull out my headphones to put on and try to entertain myself with music or a movie. Even though I know neither will be enough to distract me from Brody.

I thought, the entire flight back, all I would be thinking about was Gabe and how to handle him. Instead, I feel a hatred I've never felt for a man before. And I've felt plenty of hatred for men before. Gabe did a number on me just before I came here.

Brody thinks he's a prick, and he is. That's what I wanted when I came here. An asshole who would make it easy for me to forget about him once I left here. I didn't realize just how much of an asshole he could be. And I made a mistake, thinking it would be easy for me to forget about a dick like Brody after I left. It will be easy to move on from him to another guy when I get back, but I won't be able to forget him. This hatred that I feel will stay with me for far too long after I return home. Brody won't be forgotten, just hated. And I have a feeling that is exactly what he wanted. He isn't the kind of man who would allow me to forget.

8

BRODY

I HEAR a knock on my office door for the hundredth time today. I exhale deeply to keep from doing what I want to do. Telling my assistant to call everyone in the building and demand they all go home so that I can get some real work done. I have a shit-ton of papers to go through and more emails to answer than I could possibly read, and I have some important decisions to make in regard to if we are going to be ready for the launch of our video game that happens in less than three weeks. Because, if we aren't ready, I need to save the company millions of dollars and postpone it now rather than waiting.

"Come in," I snarl at whoever is behind the oak door.

I like my office closed off from the world. The door is solid, the same with the walls. No one can see into my world unless I let them. I don't even have that many windows to look outside. I might be the most important person at the company, but I don't have the nicest office, just the most secluded. But it doesn't prevent me from having to deal with idiots knocking on my door all day.

The door opens, and a young woman steps inside. She's probably in her early twenties. She looks put together but far too eager to be in my office right now. She hasn't been yelled at nearly enough to have the look of despair that everyone else in my office knows well enough to wear on their faces when they enter my office. I'm a controlling fucker who wants things done my way. The proper way. I don't accept mistakes. You get one shot to impress me, and if you don't, you're gone.

The woman standing in front of me is already failing. She thinks she's going to impress me because she looks good in her light-colored skirt and jacket. She's wrong. It takes a lot more than lean legs to get me off.

"Did you forget why you came in here?" I ask, glaring at her for interrupting me and wasting my valuable time. I make far too much money for this company to waste a single second of it not on point.

She smiles, clearly not getting the message I'm sending. "I'm Angela," she says, walking toward me with her hand extended to me.

I look down at her hand, not bothering to shake it.

"What are you doing in my office, Angela?"

She tucks her hand back down to her side as she looks around for a chair to sit in. She won't find one. I don't keep chairs in my office. It invites people to stay and talk. I don't want to talk to people. If we are talking, that means we aren't working hard enough. And, if someone has something to say that is actually useful enough to listen to for longer than five to ten minutes, then that is what meeting rooms are for. Not my office.

"Um...Noah sent me in to meet you."

I rub my neck in annoyance. "And why did Noah want you to meet me?"

She frowns. "Because he said you would like to meet me. I'm his new assistant, and he said that we would be working closely together, so I should introduce myself."

I look at her. Really look at her. She's fresh out of college; that much is obvious. This is probably her first job. She doesn't have a clue what she signed up for when she started working for my company. I give her a month, tops, before she decides I'm too much of an ass to bother working for. It takes tough people to work for me. You have to be able to take getting yelled at and not back down. You have to be willing to fight for what you believe in. She looks like, if I yelled at her, she'd run out of here, crying. Might as well get it over with. Rip off the Band-Aid, as some would say.

"Angela, you seem like a nice girl, but you must not have listened very carefully at orientation if you think that you are ever allowed to talk to me. You are Noah's assistant, not mine. If you have something that you need to tell me, you tell my assistant, Casey. You don't waste my time, trying to talk to me. You don't call me. You don't email me. You don't knock on my door. And you sure as hell don't come into my office for no other reason than to say hello. Got it?"

She bites her juicy red lip, and my mind immediately flashes back to the last woman I saw bite her lip like that.

Skye.

But, even when Skye wasn't wearing red lipstick, like this girl, her lip looked a million times more inviting than this woman's.

"Why haven't you left yet?" I half-yell, half-ask.

She releases her lip. "Sorry, Noah told me you'd most likely yell at me but to stay anyway, that it was good for you. That you would yell at me, but then you'd be nice. That you just needed to vent because you'd had a couple of bad weeks. He said to just wade through your storm of emotions, and then things would be a lot better. That you just needed someone to yell at who could take it, so then you could be nice."

I sigh. I'll deal with Noah later. "Please tell Noah to stop messing with me. It's not helpful. And you would do a lot better at this company if you stopped listening to everything that Noah told you to do."

She smiles, tucking her blonde hair behind her ear. "He said you would say that."

I run my hand through my thick hair, annoyed and frustrated. Noah's wrong if he thinks this is going to get my frustrations out. This is doing the opposite.

She puts her hand on mine. "The company is running well. Just try to relax. I'll see you soon, Brody." She removes her hand, turns, and walks out.

I blink rapidly, trying to figure out what the fuck just happened when another knock rattles against my door, but this time, the person doesn't wait for me to answer. Noah just strides in.

"Hey, boss," he says in his usual chipper self.

"What, Noah?" I want to yell at him for Angela, but that would mean more of my time was wasted.

He grins, folding his arms across his chest while he sits on the edge of my desk. "You fucked up the numbers again," he says.

I frown. "No, I didn't. That's not possible. I checked them three separate times."

He shakes his head and throws some papers on my desk.

I narrow my eyes as I pick up the stack of papers and stare at the numbers. I do the math in my head and can already tell that I'm way off. *Damn it.*

I throw them down in frustration, watching as they scatter everywhere.

Noah smirks and folds his arms across his chest like he's the shit and I'm an idiot. Even though he wouldn't have a job if it wasn't for me busting my balls every damn day for this company.

"Now, will you listen to me?" he asks, but it isn't meant to be a question.

"Why? I fucked up. It won't happen again."

He shakes his head. "Except it's happened almost every day since we got back from the Bahamas. That woman still has your dick obsessed with her."

"So what if she does? I don't use my dick to get work done."

He laughs. "You might as well. Your dick might do a better job than what you are currently doing."

I get up from my desk and walk over to the small window that stares out into Detroit below. I lean against the wall, looking out at the people walking around below.

"You need to do something about this. You need to get her out of your system, so you can focus on what's really important. The launch. We are launching our second video game in less than three weeks. We've done the unthinkable, raising billions of dollars when we have no money ourselves. We don't even pay ourselves enough to live off of. But, if we get this right, then the world will take us seriously, and we can actually start paying ourselves."

I nod. I know he's right. Although I don't care about money. I have a condo my uncle gave to me when he died. And what money I do earn, I spend on fast cars. I don't need anything else to keep me happy. What else could money buy me that I don't already have? I just enjoy creating. Working hard. That's what's in it for me.

"What do you suggest I do about it?"

He grins. "Fuck her."

I narrow my stare at him. "She lives hundreds of miles away from here in Albuquerque. I live in Detroit. It's not exactly easy for me to just go fuck her and then come back to work."

"I think it would be worth the weekend trip. But, if you don't think you can take the time off, I know an assistant who would be more than willing to help you out."

I cringe at that thought. "Really? She's barely twenty."

"So? I'm not telling you to fuck her for her brain or maturity. You haven't fucked anyone since Skye. You need to move on, get out there again."

"Get out of my office, and get back to work," I snap, done with this conversation.

Noah grins and walks out of my office without a word.

I'll decide when I fuck a woman and who she will be. Right now, I don't need the distraction. I'll just increase the difficulty of my workout tonight. That will get whatever this is that I'm feeling out of my system so that I can focus.

———

I open the door to my condo. It's late, as it always is when I get home from work. About a quarter after ten. Sometimes, I wonder why I don't just create an apartment for myself at the office. That way, I don't ever have to leave. I can spend every second being productive.

I walk toward the kitchen, not bothering to flick on the lights. I like it dark. I need to eat, exercise, and pass out. I don't need light for any of it.

I throw the fridge open to pull out the premade meals that I prepare myself once a week, so then I don't have to think about food the rest of the week when I see a shadow move.

I sigh as I pull out my container of food. I walk the three feet to the microwave, pop in the food, and hit the button for it to start.

"What are you doing here?" I ask without turning around. I don't want to look at her. I don't want to talk to her. I don't want her here.

"Noah said you needed some help with relaxing tonight," Angela says, walking up behind me and rubbing my shoulders.

I tense instead of relaxing.

The microwave finishes, and I pull my dinner out and walk over to the bar where there is only one barstool. I take a seat, ignoring her. I begin eating my grilled chicken and steamed vegetables.

She tries to push her body onto my lap, but I don't let her. I just keep eating like I always do by myself.

I'm going to kill Noah. He should know better than to think he can have any control over my life.

"You need to go," I say sternly, still not looking at her.

"I don't think that's what you really want."

I frown and finally look at her. "You have no idea what I want."

She bites her fingernail and looks at me as she cocks her head, like by studying me, she is going to figure out what I want.

"Maybe not, but I know what all men want." She reaches around and pulls on the tie holding her wrap dress closed. The dress falls open, and then she shrugs her shoulders as the dress falls to the floor.

My eyes burn into her black lace bra and thong underwear. She has a gorgeous body. And she's right; I'm a man in need of fucking a woman's brains out. The only reason I'm fighting it at all is that I hate when Noah is right. It will only empower him to pull shit like this again.

"Wait for me in my bedroom, down the hallway to the right."

She smiles.

"And, if you tell Noah about this, you're fired."

9

SKYE

MY HANDS CONTINUE to do compressions over the small puppy's chest. I'm exhausted. I've been trying to save this puppy for three hours now.

Most vets would have given up a long time ago. He was hit by a car, and most of the bones in his body are broken. He has internal bleeding that I know I can't stop. And he's been touch and go since he arrived.

But he's a fighter, and I won't give up on him. So, I keep doing compressions, trying to convince his heart to keep beating.

"Skye," Alicia, my vet technician, says in a stern voice.

I keep pumping my arms over the puppy's small chest.

"Skye, it's time," she says, placing her hand on my shoulder.

I know she's right. That he's already gone. But, for some reason, it's harder for me to give up on the strays than the ones who have an owner. At least the ones with an owner had a good life. They were loved.

This puppy grew up alone. He's barely eight months, and if the car accident hadn't taken his life, starvation most likely would have.

"Time of death: six thirty-three," I say, stopping the compressions.

I stroke his head. This is the hardest part of the job—when I can't save them. This is what I was put on this earth to do, and when I fail, I'm lost.

"You should go home. You weren't even supposed to be on duty today," Alicia says.

I nod. I'll go. I'm too exhausted to be of any use here.

I walk like a zombie to my office to collect my things, and then I start walking the half-mile down the road to the small farmhouse that I call home.

Usually, I like the walk. It gives me time to clear my head before I'm greeted by my herd of animals. But not today. Today, I don't want to think. Today is hard.

My thoughts go back to the beach. To Brody, as they often have these last couple of months since I returned from my vacation. And I feel the familiar feeling of anger take over. It's easy than the pain I feel when I think about the puppy that I couldn't save. A puppy that didn't even have a name.

I open the door to my small farmhouse and am greeted by my four mutt dogs. "Hey, Sherbet, Grumpy, Ernie, and Lady," I say, greeting each dog.

I try to smile, but I just can't today. Even Ernie's infectious grin isn't enough to warm my heart. Not today.

I walk the few feet to the back door and open the door to let them out into the backyard. I might be exhausted, but my day doesn't end when I come home. I have three horses, two cows, six chickens, three pigs, a rooster, four dogs, and three cats that rely on me. So, I follow the dogs out into the yard and get to work. Thankful to have something to keep my mind occupied instead of my lonely thoughts.

The sun is setting fast by the time I'm about finished feeding and giving the animals the attention they need. I start walking back up the field toward the house to make myself something to eat with the dogs fast on my heels, excited that it's time for them to get fed as well.

I sense him before I see him. My body is used to being alert for when I feel danger nearby.

"You're not welcome here," I say, grabbing on to Grumpy and giving the rest of the dogs a look to stay by me.

They all do, sitting carefully next to me as they intently stare at the stranger.

Brody is standing just outside the fence on my property. His face is clean-shaven, and his hair is shorter than the last time I saw him. In a dark suit, he's very out of place here.

"I just want to talk. Can I take you to a late dinner or to get a drink or something?"

"No," I say as I continue to hold on to Grumpy, the only dog I have that isn't fully trained yet. My negative energy transfers through my body to his, the longer I hold him, getting him even more worked up as he fights to try to get to the intruder.

Brody looks down at the dog I'm holding on to. "He friendly?" he asks as he puts his hand on the gate.

"No, he's not friendly. Especially toward men he feels are intruders." I let him jump forward a little bit in my hands as I continue to hold on to him. He growls fiercely, making Brody hesitate.

Brody frowns. "What would it take to get you to talk to me?"

I laugh deviously. "There is nothing you could do to get me to talk to you."

"I hurt you that bad, huh?"

"No, I just don't give a shit about you. You aren't even supposed to be here. You were supposed to be out of my life after the week, remember?"

"I didn't get my last fuck in."

"And whose fault is that?"

"Yours."

I raise an eyebrow. "Seriously? It wasn't my fault. It was yours! You were the one who said you would come to the airport and didn't. It seems you got your last fuck in just fine, just not with me."

He grins. "So, you do care."

"No," I lie.

"You were the one who went running home to Gabe. You were the one who cut our time short." He looks at the dogs. "So, which one is Gabe anyway?"

My eyes darken. He thinks Gabe is one of my animals. Now, it's my turn to hurt him.

"This is Grumpy. That's Ernie, Sherbet, and Lady."

He frowns. "So, Gabe is a cat."

"Tommy, Jordan, and Ruffus."

"A horse?"

"Blondie, Pumpkin, and Sandy."

"The other animals?"

I smile. "Nope."

He runs his hand through his short hair before rubbing his neck. "You aren't going to tell me who Gabe is, are you?"

"Not likely, no. I like that you have too many thoughts going through your head right now as you try to figure it out. And it's driving you crazy."

He smirks. "It's not driving me crazy. Not having your mouth sucking my cock—that is what is driving me crazy. I just want to know who Gabe is, so I know when to duck when he takes a swing at me."

"That's not happening."

"Which part? Because I guarantee that your lips are going to be wrapped around my dick by the end of the night."

I shake my head. "You're still so cocky, aren't you? We are done. I don't want anything to do with you."

"You sure about that? Because your body is telling me differently."

I glare at him. "We are done."

He reaches for the gate and opens it, thinking now is his opportunity to walk inside and catch me off guard. I'm sure he thinks, if he can get close enough where I can smell his cologne again, close enough that I can see his charming dimples, close enough that I can hear his beating heart, then I'll change my mind. I'll just fall back into his arms again, just like we were back on the beach in our fantasy world. That bubble burst the second he sent me the text message with the big-tits woman.

"Don't take another step forward!" I shout.

He doesn't listen. I release Grumpy and release the rest of the dogs with a look. I just wish, for once, they were actually capable of attacking a man when I needed them to. Instead, they run over and attack him all right. Just with kisses and hugs and tail wags.

But it gets the job done. He can't move, and I take the opportunity to run inside. I slam the door shut and lock it tightly behind me as I lean against the door. *Can this day get any worse?*

10

BRODY

God, how I've missed her.

I've missed her sass.

I've missed her wit.

I've missed her charm.

Her smile, body, intelligence, fierceness. Everything. I've missed everything.

Except, now, she hates my guts. I knew sending her that text message would bite me in the ass one day.

I look down at the dogs that are jumping all over me. Slobbering and getting hair all over my suit. I'm not a dog person or an animal person of any kind really. I could be, I guess. But I've never spent any time with them or thought I needed to have an animal in my life. I prefer my alone time in peace rather than having to take care of another living thing.

So, I have no idea how to get them to stop. I slowly back up toward the gate and manage to wiggle out without letting the beasts loose.

I take a deep breath as I walk back to the car I rented and move on to plan B. She clearly isn't happy to see me, but I do know her weaknesses, what she won't turn down.

I open the back door and pull out the bottle of tequila and Chinese takeout. I put on my most charming grin as I walk back to her front door and knock loudly.

I wait, knowing that she's going to be stubborn and not want to open the door. But a few minutes pass, and she slowly relents, coming to the door.

"I brought food and tequila because I'm sure you don't have any food in the house," I say even though I don't know if that's true. I just know that she cares about her animals more than she does herself. That's clear from where I sat in my car, watching her before I got out.

I stare at her more closely, getting a good look at the changes since the last time I saw her months ago. Her hair is pulled back, but it no longer has the blue streaks that ran through her hair before. Her hair is no longer jet-black either; it's more a medium brown. Most of her piercings are no longer covering her face. The tattoos are hidden by her long sleeves underneath her scrubs even though it's the middle of summer.

Her eyes are what give me the most concern though. People change their appearance. Maybe she was going through a rebel phase that she's trying to get past now. But her eyes are expelling a sadness that I've never seen before. Maybe this is the same sadness that she was running from on vacation. Whatever is in her eyes is what she needed me to fuck away and make her forget. Now that I'm gone, the reality of that pain is back.

She opens the door just a little and snatches the food and alcohol out of my hand. Then, she slams the door in my face before I have a chance to push my way inside. Not that I would. I like control, but I would never make her feel unsafe.

I sigh. On to plan C. I walk back to my car and drive the half-mile back to the clinic where my new favorite vet tech, Alicia, is.

"No luck, huh?" she asks when I step back inside.

"Nope, but I have a plan C. And, if that doesn't work, I'll try plan D and so on."

She smiles. "And you want my help?"

I nod.

"I shouldn't help you, but Skye doesn't need to be alone tonight. She could use some company even if it's bad company."

I frown. "I'm not bad company."

"Skye told me what you did in the Bahamas."

"Fine. I'm not the best. But I do know I'm a good distraction, and it seems Skye is in need of a distraction." I bat my eyes at her while saying, "Please."

"If you bring her a sick animal to take care of, she will let you in."

I grin. "That was exactly what I was thinking."

"Hold on," she says, disappearing into the back room and then reappearing with a cardboard box with small holes cut out on the top.

I take the box from her and open the lid. I jump back, dropping the box.

She does a full-belly laugh, grabbing her stomach as she walks over and picks up the box that I just dropped.

"Is this a joke? Did you and Skye plan this to get back at me?" I ask, my voice much higher than usual.

Alicia continues to laugh as she walks the box back over to me. "No, it's not a joke. The snake needs medical attention."

I frown. "I'm not a big fan of snakes."

"I would have never guessed that," she snarks.

"Why can't I bring a puppy or kitten or something that needs her help?"

"One, because most of our puppies and kittens need more medical help than what she can provide at her house. And, two, because I'm still not a huge fan of yours, and I want to make you suffer as much as possible. Consider it my own personal test to see if you are worthy of hanging out with my friend." She holds the box out to me. "Now, do you want to see Skye tonight or not?"

I slowly take the box. I'll just keep the lid on the whole time. I'm not sure if a sick snake is enough to get Skye to let me into her house, but I'll give it a try. If not, I'll come back and find the cutest puppy to take back and try again.

"So, you want to tell me about Gabe?" I ask.

She smirks. "Nope, I'm not touching that conversation. If Skye wants to tell you, she will."

"Thanks," I say, holding up the box a little as I walk toward the door.

"But, if I were you, I wouldn't mention Gabe tonight. She's been through enough tonight, so don't add to her depression."

I nod. *Too late*, I think.

But I'll table the Gabe questions until later. It seems that no one wants to tell me exactly who Gabe is, but I have enough resources that I'm sure I can figure it out if I put some of my guys on it.

I put the box with the snake in the passenger seat next to me, and then I climb in the driver's seat and drive back to Skye's place, keeping my eye on the box the whole time, making sure the snake doesn't slither out. I park the car on the gravel driveway in front of her house, behind an old pickup truck that doesn't look like it has run in ten years at least.

I climb out of the car and walk around to the passenger side. I take the box out, carrying it with both hands as I walk up the gravel driveway to the front of the white farmhouse. It's not very large and much older than any house I've ever been in besides my grandparents'. There are daisies planted outside the red front door. The house is not that big, which surprises me after how much money she spent on vacation. I figured she would have a mansion somewhere. She owns what seems like quite a bit of land, but that still wouldn't cost as much as a nice house would.

I knock on the red door that needs a new coat of paint and wait to see if Skye will open the door or at least respond. I knock again after a few seconds pass. I hear stomping footsteps inside, and finally, she creaks the door open just enough to see me.

"What do you want, Brody?"

I hold up the box. "I have a sick snake that needs your veterinarian skills."

She glares at me as she slowly opens the door. "Well, let's see it," she says, exhaling deeply.

I grin and lift the lid just enough so that she can see inside.

Her gaze darts from inside the box to me. "There isn't a snake in that box."

"Will you just take a look at the snake? I'm not sure if it is sick or not, but I'm concerned."

"I would, but there is no snake in the box."

I throw the lid open and find the box empty. "Shit."

I run back to my rental car and peek into the windows, not daring to open it.

Skye walks slowly over to the car and looks in the window. "Was there ever really a snake, or is this all some stupid hoax where you try to save me from the snake or something?"

"There was really a snake. Alicia helped me out." I hesitantly look over at Skye.

She shakes her head as she tucks a loose strand behind her ear. "Alicia needs to mind her own business."

"She's just looking out for you. She said she was concerned after what happened today."

She looks up at me. "She told you?"

"No, she just told me you had a rough day and to treat you well. That you needed a distraction."

She stares at me for a moment, lost in thought, and then returns her gaze to the car. "There," she says, pointing to the driver's side of the car where I'm standing.

I stare at the snake as it slithers up the side of the seat. I have no idea how we are going to capture it. "Should we call animal control or something?"

She laughs. "You're afraid of the snake, aren't you?"

"No."

"Then, reach in, and grab the snake just behind the base of the head."

I frown. "No, it could kill me if it bites me."

"It's not venomous. And it's sick, so its reflexes are much slower. It shouldn't be a problem at all."

I stare at the snake that seems to be taunting me. There is no way

I'm reaching in and grabbing that snake. I don't care if my masculinity is put into question. Me and snakes don't get along.

Skye rolls her eyes and then throws open the passenger door. She sticks her upper body in, and the next thing I know, she's holding on to the snake and carrying it into her house.

Superwoman. She's fucking superwoman.

I follow after her as she walks into the house, not asking for permission to come in because I don't want to know the answer. As soon as I step inside the small house, I'm greeted again by her four dogs jumping and licking me.

"Down," Skye commands.

All but one listen to her. She gives the last one a stern look, and he eventually stops jumping on me as well.

Skye lays the snake out on the counter and starts examining it while I step cautiously into the kitchen to watch her work. She runs her hands over the snake, like it's a dog or a cat.

"It just has a cold. I'll give her some medications, and she'll be feeling better by tomorrow." She looks at me. "Can you get me the box?"

I frown as I carry the box from the front porch to her. "Don't you think we should put it in something more secure? It already escaped once."

"How did I not realize how much of a pansy you were?" she asks, putting the snake into the box.

I smirk. "Probably because you were too busy getting your brains fucked out to care."

She puts her hands on her hips. "What are you doing here?"

"Isn't it obvious?"

"No, it's not." She walks back to the living room where there is an empty bowl that used to contain her Chinese food and a glass filled with tequila. She takes a seat on the worn-in tan couch. Her dogs climb up next to her, making themselves at home as they curl up with her and each other.

I take a seat on the reclining chair next to the couch, knowing that she isn't going to offer me food or drink. She doesn't want me here, so why would she make it more comfortable for me to be here?

"I want our last fuck."

"You know that's not going to happen. You knew before you came here that I would never give it to you. That, even if you had treated me like a perfect gentleman that last day, I still wouldn't fuck you after you showed up here. I told you, I was only ever interested in one week."

She takes a drink of her tequila, and I watch as it slides down her throat.

"I wanted to make sure you were okay," I say as my eyes burn into hers.

"You don't care about me."

I sigh. "You're right. I only care about you as long as I get to fuck you, but it seems you won't let me fuck you until I pretend to care, so you can see my predicament."

"I'm not talking about Gabe."

"I didn't ask about Gabe. I want to know why you are in so much pain right now. And don't lie to me. I know your body better than anyone. I know that your eyes are usually filled with a little bit of light, but today, they only see the darkness. Your breathing is slow and heavy, like the weight of today is pushing you down, making it hard to move, let alone breathe. Why are you in such pain?"

She stares off into space, giving me no indication if she is going to talk to me or not. "Because bad things happen to creatures that don't deserve it."

I narrow my eyes, not understanding.

"I lost a dog tonight. It was painful. He was just a puppy. He didn't deserve to die, but there was nothing I could do."

She drinks the rest of the tequila. She shakes the glass, listening as the ice rattles around.

"I'm sorry," I say because that's all I can say.

"Life sucks."

I nod and walk back to the kitchen to get the tequila. I grab the bottle and bring it back to her. She takes it from me and pours herself easily three more shots' worth. She's drunk already and getting drunker by the minute.

I don't stop her. She needs the distraction. And, since she won't take me up on my offer to let me fuck away the pain, the alcohol is the only thing that will do.

She keeps talking about how the poor puppy didn't deserve to die. That he didn't deserve the life he was given. But, as sad as it is that she lost the puppy, it's not what she's really sad about. There is still something that she isn't telling me. Something that I'm desperate to know. Because the only way I'll get to fuck her again is if she gets past whatever darkness is currently consuming her.

11

SKYE

I GET a lick on my face, as I almost always do when it's time to get up in the morning. I open my eyes and sit up in bed. I feel like I was hit by a truck, and then that truck backed up and ran me over again.

How much did I drink last night?

I feel my stomach heaving, and I run, making it to the toilet just in time for the alcohol to all start coming back up. Apparently, I drank way too much.

I sit on the cold floor for a minute before I stand and clean my mouth out with water and brush my teeth. I vaguely remember the pain. I remember the tequila. And I remember Brody.

Ugh, why did he have to come back into my life?

He's a giant dick, but he's a dick that I want to ride. And, even though I can't deal with him right now, he's all I'm going to be able to think about until he leaves town. Maybe I can just fuck him once like he wants, and then he will leave.

I doubt it, but maybe the sex will suck, and I'll realize that what we had in the Bahamas was just a fantasy that I played up in my head. It wasn't real.

I take a deep breath and get a whiff of what smells like pancakes. Except it can't be. I don't live with anyone else. I must be dreaming.

I walk out into my living area, and the smell gets stronger. I'm greeted by my dogs and cats, which I give each of them some attention before rounding the corner and continuing into my kitchen.

My stomach flips at the sight of Brody cooking shirtless in my kitchen. Of course, he stayed. And of course, my body doesn't understand that it shouldn't get excited about backstabbers like Brody, no matter how hot they are.

"You know how to cook?" I ask, surprised.

He turns his head as he continues to stand in front of my stove. "I have many talents. Cooking isn't one of them, but I can make a basic meal."

I want to yell at him to get out, but I really want the pancakes. My stomach is aching for some carbs to soak up the alcohol still causing havoc in my stomach.

"Sit down," he commands.

I walk over to my two-seater kitchen table and take a seat. I don't have the strength to argue with him.

He brings me a large glass of water and Advil.

I take the water and drink until the glass is completely empty.

"I made you a Bloody Mary, too. Not sure if you want it though, but it might help to fight the hangover with a little more alcohol."

I stare at the glass; there is no way I can drink it.

"Nope, I'm good," I say, scrunching my nose up at the sight.

He grins, and my heart melts a little at the sight of his dimples.

"The pancakes should help," he says, placing a large plate of pancakes drenched in syrup in front of me.

I dig in without a thank-you. He's the reason I drank too much last night anyway. He provided the alcohol. He amplified my emotions by coming here.

He watches me as I eat while he does dishes at the sink. I continue to eat while discreetly looking around at my house. It's clean. Like really, really clean. The dog and cat hair has been swept off the floor. The counters and end tables are dusted and clean. The clutter of mail I usually leave scattered on the counter is now sitting in an organized pile. The dog toys have been picked up and placed in a basket. And he's not only washed the dishes he created but the dishes from yesterday as well.

I put my fork down as my stomach finally starts to feel better.

"What are you doing?" I ask.

"Dishes."

"No, why did you clean up my house?"

"Because, despite what you think about me, I can be a nice guy if I want to."

"No, you're a dick. You would only ever be a nice guy in order to get something. What do you want?"

He tosses the dish towel he was using to dry the dishes down onto the counter next to the sink.

"I would think it's obvious." His eyes show a desire that takes over his entire body.

I roll my eyes, trying to act like I can easily just forget about him. That nothing he does affects me. Not his stare. Not his muscular body. Not his intense grin. Nothing can touch me.

But he knows my body too well. He knows it's all a lie.

He pulls out the chair across from me and casually sits down, his legs spread and his body leaning back in the chair like he owns it.

Grumpy walks over to Brody and licks him on his arm. Brody gently pets his head.

I frown, staring at my dog that hates everybody. He hates Alicia and everyone else from work. He hates Gabe. He hates strangers. He won't go near them, except to bark. Not Brody, though. Apparently, he's decided, the one person he should hate the most, he actually likes. I'll have to talk to Grumpy later.

"I have a proposition for you," he says.

I take a bite of my pancake so that I can answer him with my mouth full. Maybe, if I'm as disgusting as possible, he won't want anything to do with me. "Let's hear it then."

He watches my mouth as I talk, but it seems to just get him more excited.

"I want to continue our arrangement from before."

"For how long?" I ask before I realize what I'm doing.

He grins and cocks his head from side to side, like this is way easier than he thought it was going to be.

I shouldn't have given him any indication that I was interested in continuing our arrangement. I should have just said no right away. But my big mouth always seems to get me into trouble.

"You tell me. You owe me at least one more day, but I don't think you want to stop at just one more day. I'm good with another day, a week, a year. What do you want, baby?"

I hate how he speaks like he already knows the answer to the question that he is asking. He thinks I'm going to say I want a year. But I won't give him the satisfaction of being right.

"You think you can come here, clean up my house a bit, and make me breakfast, and then all is forgiven, huh?" I grin, taking another bite of my pancake.

"I didn't think I needed forgiveness because you don't give a shit about me."

I narrow my eyes, glaring at him. "You're right. I don't. But I've had enough pricks in my life to know that the only thing to do with them is throw them out with the trash, not make arrangements that only benefit one side."

I get up from the table and walk to my bedroom. I pull out a suitcase and start throwing clothes into it.

I continue to throw clothes into my suitcase, not bothering to look at what I'm throwing in until the suitcase is filled with clothes. I can't think straight. All I can think about is that Brody wants to have sex with me again. And, despite the pain that it will likely cause me, I want to fuck him again, too. But I can't. I walk a few feet to my small bathroom and grab my already-packed toiletry bag from my last trip to LA. I toss it into my suitcase. I have to sit on the suitcase to get it to close.

Then, I look into my closet and find a pair of jeans and a T-shirt. I put them on and pull my hair up into a ponytail. I give myself a quick glance in the mirror and then grab my suitcase. I walk out of the bedroom, carrying my suitcase, hoping that Brody will get the hint and just leave me alone.

"What are you doing?"

I don't look at him. If I look at him again, I'll just start drooling over his shirtless, hard body. I'll start remembering how good it felt to have his strong arms wrapped around me and how good it felt to lick every inch of his chest. I'll start caving, and I can't afford to cave.

"I have a flight to catch. Don't worry about the animals. I have a babysitter coming in a few hours to watch them. But make sure you take the snake back to the clinic."

I walk to the door and throw it open, pulling my suitcase out behind me. The door slams shut behind me. I don't say good-bye to my animals, and I definitely don't say good-bye to Brody. If I spend one more second in the house, I might stay instead of leaving.

I walk to my truck and throw the suitcase in the back. I start it up and drive off. Only when I've driven a few miles away do I allow myself to look into the rearview mirror. He's not behind me as much as I wish on some level that he were. I could really use some distraction even if I can't do his arrangement. It's wrong in more ways than one.

12

BRODY

I DON'T KNOW if she really has a flight to catch or if she just packed and left in an attempt to get rid of me. But it won't work.

I look at the box that hopefully still contains the snake as I grab my shirt and push it back on before I pick up the box and dart out the door behind Skye. I get a glimpse of Skye's pickup truck driving off down the road in the general direction of the airport. I want to jump in my rental and chase after her, ensuring that she's going to the airport. I would if it wasn't for this damn snake.

I throw open the trunk of my car and place the box with the snake in it, keeping it as far away from me as possible. I slam the trunk and hop in the driver's seat. I speed off down the road as fast as I possibly can. When I get there, I carry the box inside and hand it off to the receptionist, not bothering to wait for Alicia to come get it. I make the receptionist verify that the snake is still in the box and not in my car before I leave, but that's all I wait for.

And then I'm back in my car, racing toward the airport, hoping that she didn't lie to me and that I manage to stop her or at least get on the same flight with her.

Thank God for checked bags because that's where I find her waiting in line—to check her bag. I watch her from a distance so that she won't know I'm here. She's oblivious to me as she stands in the line. And it gives me another opportunity to really just watch her. She looks so different from the last time I saw her in the Bahamas. She looked so normal compared to now. Now, she's trying to blend in instead of stand out.

She finishes at the counter, and I immediately go up after her. Luckily, there is a young woman working there. With a little flirting, I get her to tell me exactly where Skye is headed—LA. And there just so happens to be several seats left on the same flight as her, so I buy a ticket. I could try to convince her to stay here and think more about my offer. But I doubt she would consider staying. This way, I get to find out more about her life and what she'll be doing in LA.

The flight attendant calls for boarding, and Skye gets in line while I linger back. She still hasn't noticed me, but I do know that I will be sitting about three rows behind her on the plane. I give her about a fifty-fifty shot whether she will see me or not.

I board the plane and immediately spot her six rows back, fumbling with her phone. I doubt she'll even notice that I'm on the plane, which will give me the entire flight to plan on how I want to reveal to her that I followed her to LA.

As I start walking by her, she looks up. Her eyes widen as she realizes what's happening. She opens her mouth to say something but doesn't get it out before I casually walk past her and take my seat.

I smirk but otherwise don't give her any attention. This is better. Now, she's going to have the entire flight to worry about me.

I put my earbuds in, planning on listening to an audiobook about business strategies to keep my mind occupied. I close my eyes, ignoring the safety briefing and all the other BS that happens before the flight takes off. I've flown enough times to know how everything works. I feel the plane take off at some point while I listen to my book.

"Excuse me," I hear Skye's voice say even through my haze of sleep and the audiobook.

I try to ignore her as she convinces the stranger next to me to swap seats with her. I keep my eyes closed like I don't notice her at all as she finally takes a seat next to me, even after her thigh and hand brush against my leg—whether intentionally or unintentionally. I try to act like I couldn't care less about her when what I really want to do is sneak her into the restroom and fuck her brains out.

"I know you can hear me and that you know I'm here. Stop acting like you can't hear me," Skye says.

"Oh, I didn't realize you were on this plane." I remove one of my earbuds, giving her half of my attention.

"Don't play dumb," she says, reaching for my other earbud and jerking it out of my ear.

"I knew you couldn't get enough of me."

She huffs and rolls her eyes again. She lifts her legs up into her seat, and she wraps her arms around them like she is giving herself one big hug. "Why did you follow me here?"

"I didn't follow you. I live in LA. When you told me you were leaving, I got on the next available flight since there was no longer a reason to stay in Albuquerque."

"Liar. You don't live in LA."

I closely study her. "You looked me up, did you?"

She looks away from me. "No, I didn't."

I laugh. "You totally did."

"No, I didn't," she says empathetically.

"Then, how do you know I don't live in LA?"

"Because you live in Detroit."

I bite my lip to keep my excitement down. She looked me up. She wants me just as badly as I want her. I just have to figure out what the key is to unlocking her hesitation about starting this up again. Because, clearly, the pain I caused her on the last day in paradise isn't the reason.

"Why don't you want to do the arrangement?"

"Because you're an ass."

"I am, but then that's exactly what you wanted. An ass. So, tell me the real reason you won't agree to my arrangement, and I'll leave you alone forever."

"For real? After I tell you the truth, you'll get out of my life and never come back?"

"I promise I'll leave you alone. If that's what you want."

She leans her chair back and closes her eyes like she's going to take a long nap.

"Are you going to tell me or not?"

"I'm going to show you."

———

To my surprise, the rest of the flight is uneventful. We both sleep—or at least pretend to sleep. When we land, we get off the flight, being relatively civil to one another. After we collect our bags, she tells me to get into her car with her.

I do.

The Maserati we climb into isn't a rental. It's a car that she owns but is the complete opposite of her car in Albuquerque. That pickup truck was all about function and getting the job done with no fuss about its appearance. This car is a luxury car with little purpose other than to provide comfort and be flashy to all those who look at it.

"Do you have a split personality or something?" I ask as she drives.

"No."

"Then, explain to me why you have such a fancy car in LA and such a shitty one in Albuquerque."

She glares at me. "My truck isn't shitty."

I raise my eyebrows.

"Just because it isn't what you expect on the outside doesn't mean it isn't worthy on the inside."

"That was deep."

"Just shut up until we get to my condo."

"Is your condo as fancy as this car? Because I have a feeling that your house back in Albuquerque is going to feel run-down compared to your condo here."

She turns a little too fast around the next corner, and I hit my head on the roof of the car.

She smirks. "Like I said, you should probably just stop talking until we get to my condo."

I do but only because, clearly, she won't tell me anything until we get to her condo. Something at her condo holds the key to everything she's been hiding from me. She thinks she's going to be able to get rid of me once we are there, but I don't think there is anything she can show me that will make me want to leave. And all I have to do is get one kiss, and she'll be begging me for more.

Skye parks the car in a fancy parking garage and then makes her way to the elevator. Of course, she presses the button for the top floor. I smirk at her, guessing that her friend paid for this place while Skye pays for her house back home. I just don't know which version she'd rather be, not that it matters. I'd fuck her either way.

The elevators doors open, and she stomps out like she can't get out of there fast enough. I follow, making sure to walk as close as possible behind her to be as obnoxious as I can. She pulls a key out of her purse and unlocks the door, gesturing for me to follow her inside. I do, letting the door close behind me. I watch as a tall man with light-colored hair in a business suit greets her. He wraps her in his arms and firmly kisses her on the lips.

I glare at the man who has my woman wrapped in his arms. My woman's lips pressed against his. A few moments pass before he finally comes up for air. Just enough time for my internal rage to fill every crevice inside me.

"Baby, this is Brody, the man I told you about from my Bahamas vacation. Brody, this is Gabe, my fiancé."

Gabe extends his hand to me. I take it, gripping as firmly as I can.

"It's nice to finally meet you, Brody," Gabe says.

"You, too."

He squeezes Skye one more time with a bright smile on his face, happy to have his fiancée home. She, on the other hand, couldn't seem more uncomfortable in his arms. The only reason she even has a smile on her face is that she can show me that I was wrong. That our relationship is over.

"I hate this, but I have to run. I have a meeting I have to get to. But we should all do dinner tonight," Gabe says, kissing Skye one more time on the lips before giving me a nod and slipping out of the condo.

I'm not sure I believe that the relationship is real. She probably just called an old friend and asked him to pretend to be her fiancé to try to get rid of me. But whatever it is, I'm going to figure it out.

"What the fuck is going on?"

13

SKYE

"That isn't your fiancé," Brody says.

"Are you serious? Gabe is my fiancé. He told you so himself without any probing from me. We kissed. We share this condo together. What more proof do you need?" I say, my voice loud and angry.

I thought he would've stormed out the second he found out I had a fiancé, but apparently, he doesn't believe anything I tell him is true, so I don't even know why I bother trying to explain.

"I need a heck of a lot more proof than that. You didn't even want to kiss him. How can you be engaged to a person and not even want to kiss him?"

"Just because you fucked me for a week in the Bahamas doesn't mean you know me. You have no idea why I reacted the way that I did to Gabe kissing me."

Brody starts walking around the condo, his eyes traveling over everything he can find. He opens doors, sticking his head inside, only to reemerge.

"What are you doing?" I ask, walking behind him.

"I'm looking for proof."

I exhale deeply. "You promised you would leave after I told you the truth about why I wouldn't agree to your arrangement."

"I said I would leave after you told me the truth. I'm not sure you've told me the truth yet."

He walks around our living room, staring at the white and light-gray massive walls that take up almost two stories with a few large pieces of artwork. He raises an eyebrow at me as he walks down the hallway to the bedroom that Gabe and I share, which is also decorated in gray and white.

"Nope, I don't believe you."

I frown. "And why don't you believe me?"

I need him to believe me. I need him to leave. He knows enough. He can't stay and have dinner with us tonight. He'll find out far too much that I don't want him to know.

"Because I haven't found a single picture of you and your fiancé together in this entire condo. Not one single image." He walks to the closet and throws the door open, peeking inside. "Because, despite the fact that you say you live here, there are less than a dozen pieces of clothing of yours in this closet. Because, despite having a fiancé who lives in LA, you still have a home in Albuquerque along with a whole slew of animals, not to mention your veterinarian clinic. You claim to have a fiancé, yet you fuck me on a vacation without him less than six months ago. You claim to have a fiancé, yet you have no ring."

I look down at my bare hand as a tiny bit of hope creeps up inside me. I run into the bathroom and pull out the engagement box out of the top drawer. I open the box and pull out the large square diamond ring, which is easily four carats in size. I place it back on my hand after having not worn it for the past two weeks, and then I race back to the bedroom, holding out my hand to Brody.

"You're wrong. I have a ring."

Brody eyes the large diamond on my finger with suspicion. "How do I know that's not a fake?"

I roll my eyes. "Does it look like a fake?"

He cocks his head from side to side as he stares at it. "How would I know? I'm not a diamond expert."

"It's not a fake. Does it look like Gabe can't afford to buy me a nice diamond?" I hold my hands out to my sides, pointing at all the nice things in the condo that we share together.

"No, I'm sure Gabe could afford to buy you that ring. How do I know it's an engagement ring and not just a ring he bought for a close friend?"

"Really?"

"Fine, it looks like an engagement ring. But, if you're engaged, why weren't you wearing it? Why was it in a box here instead of on your finger in Albuquerque?"

"Because we want to keep our engagement private. Gabe is pretty well known out here, and I want to keep it out of the tabloids as long as we can."

He narrows his eyes. "So, you don't ever wear your ring in public?"

"No."

"When? When did he propose?"

I bite my lip and look away from him. I really don't want to answer him.

He chuckles. "You can't even come up with a quick story of how he proposed."

"He proposed to me the night I got back from the Bahamas. We weren't on the best of terms, which is why I went on vacation. I wanted to get some clarity on what I wanted when I returned. I came home when I found out he'd been in a motorcycle accident. I'd never been so scared in my life. I realized what a mistake I'd made. He got down on one knee and proposed in his hospital room despite being beaten up pretty badly. I said yes and haven't hesitated since."

He just stands there, staring at me, processing.

I sigh.

And then he suddenly starts moving. He walks out of the bedroom while I follow after him, curious if I finally said the thing that will make him leave. He doesn't walk toward the front door though. Instead, he walks into the kitchen, finds the bar, and starts digging through the alcohol. He shakes his head.

525

"What?" I snap.

He pulls out a decanter of whiskey and two glasses pouring us both a glass of alcohol from the decanter. He hands one of the glasses to me, and I take it, happy to have alcohol to finish this conversation. I need the strength to say anything to get him to leave.

"The bastard doesn't even have any tequila. So, you want to explain to me again how this is true love."

I don't answer him. It doesn't matter, and whatever excuse I make for him, it's clear that Brody won't believe me anyway.

Brody opens the door to the balcony and steps outside. I step out as well, happy to get some fresh air.

"Why?"

"Why else do you get married? Love."

"Why did you cheat on him? If you are so in love with him that you said yes the second you came back, why did you sleep with me?" He stares at me as he asks the question, like it's the most important question that he needs to know the answer to. His eyes seem sincere for the first time in a long time.

"Because it wasn't cheating."

I watch Brody's hands drum against the railing, and I want nothing more than for him to take me in his arms and kiss me. I want him to stroke my face. Or even just hold my hand. But it seems that he won't. But he has more self-control than I could've ever imagined while I'm on the edge of doing something very, very stupid.

"Were you on a break? Broken up? Is that why it wasn't techni-cally cheating?"

"It wasn't cheating because we were never together."

Brody reaches out and grabs my hand, jerking me to him. My breathing is fast and heavy, as I'm filled with the weight of what I want him to do but can't let him.

"You're telling me that, after spending a week with me giving you the best sex of your life, you cut that short so that you could go back to marry a man you hadn't even kissed before?"

Pain—that's what I see when I look into Brody's eyes. It can't be pain though because I was nothing but a sex toy to him for the week.

So, it must be something else. It must be that I heard him wrong, or it's jealousy at letting another man take the woman he was just with.

"We had kissed once, but that was it. I didn't think it was going anywhere."

He lets me go and takes a step back. "It must be love then."

My heart aches as he says the words, dripping with the same pain that I myself feel. It doesn't make sense for either of us to be feeling such pain, but it's how I feel.

"So, you'll leave then? I told you the truth. I told you that I wouldn't sleep with you again. And, just as I promised you, you can't stay."

He grins just enough for me to be concerned. "I think I'd like to have that dinner first. It's clear that he's rich, so I'm sure he knows where to get a good meal in town. And I'd like to hear from him a little more about how he got a woman like you to fall so quickly in love. I might need to use the skills myself someday. I'll leave after dinner if that's what you still want."

He says he will leave, but it seems more like a threat. I failed at getting him to leave once. I won't fail again.

14

BRODY

She has a fucking fiancé. A wealthy, powerful, good-looking fiancé. A fiancé who has one of the sickest condos I've ever seen or had the privilege of being inside.

She has this whole other life in Albuquerque, which is completely different than their life here in LA. And I can't make the two lives, the two parts of her, make sense together in my head.

On the one hand, she's such a simple country girl who doesn't care about fancy things or if she fits into society; she only cares about her animals. She cares about doing good in the world, in leaving the world a better place than she found it.

But there's this other side of her. One that enjoys the finer things in life. Expensive vacations, fancy condos, and fast cars. The ring he gave her easily cost more than the wealth of several small countries.

She has two lives. Two worlds. And I don't think I'll be able to fit into either one of them. Because she's in love with the damn fiancé.

Or maybe she's lying. I've definitely seen her give warmer greetings before, and the answers to a lot of my questions didn't make sense. But I can't imagine Skye ever getting married for any reason other than love.

She might have wanted dark, filthy sex with me. The kind that allows for zero attachment, but it was clear the only reason she wanted that was that she was apparently hung up on Gabe.

I adjust my tie and then put on the most expensive jacket that I brought with me. My face is clean-shaven, and I spent time getting a haircut this afternoon to look my absolute best for tonight's dinner. I know that she chose him, but I want her to regret not having one more time with me. And I want Gabe to feel the slightest bit intimidated by me.

I pull out my phone and find the address that Skye texted me for where we are having dinner together tonight, then enter it into my Uber app.

As much as I wanted to spend the entire day with Skye, I knew that it wouldn't be a good decision. I'm not going to ruin her life by turning her into a cheater, and if I stayed a moment longer, that was exactly what would've happened. So, instead, I looked up a nearby hotel that had the nicest suite available, and I booked it. Not that Skye or Gabe will ever know where I'm staying tonight, but I'll know, and my ego is far too sensitive to not stay somewhere nice. Just because I don't typically spend this kind of money doesn't mean that I can't.

I walk out of one of the nicest hotels I've ever stayed in and over to the Uber that's waiting for me. I try not to think about what Gabe will be driving him and Skye to dinner in. Some ridiculous car I'm sure.

What I should really be worried about is how to stop thinking about Skye. Because, tonight, after dinner, I have every intention of walking out of her life forever. It's not that I care about her. I don't. But, man, do I miss her sweet ass. I miss the way her body welcomes me in, like she's been waiting for me forever. I hate how I miss the look in her eye and the sound she makes when she finally comes.

And I have to let go of the dream of ever getting to experience that again with her.

The Uber finally stops in front of the fancy seafood restaurant, and I climb out. I open the door to the restaurant that sits on a pier out over the water all by itself. The kind of restaurant that has white tablecloths at every table, at least three waitstaff per table, and nothing but the best wine on the menu.

"I'm here to meet Skye King and Gabe Cole," I say to the hostess. Names that I figured out after a quick Google search.

She sweetly smiles at me. "Right this way, Mr. Jackson."

My eyes widen a little when she says my name, but I suspect that Gabe also did the same search on me that I did on him. I follow the hostess throughout the whole restaurant to the far corner where Skye is sitting at a table in the corner, overlooking the water. She's wearing a plain gray dress that fits her nicely but isn't overly sexy. It's nothing compared to the dress she wore on the beach the night of our first date. This dress screams business. It seems more appropriate in a boardroom instead of on a date with her fiancé and her ex-lover.

I take a seat at the table, opposite Skye, while her eyes are fixed on me.

"How was your afternoon without me?" I ask.

She cocks her head to the side and pulls her hands together on top of the table. "My afternoon was quite relaxing without you."

"Good. I wouldn't want you getting your feelings mixed up about missing me, not when you have a fiancé who keeps you so completely satisfied."

She doesn't flinch or even blink at my harsh words. "You forget I could never have feelings for a dick like you."

"So, where is your fiancé, Gabe?" I ask, glancing around the room, assuming he went to the restroom or something.

Skye swallows hard and glances out the window. "He's running late. He'll be here soon."

She doesn't have to add to the end of her sentence because it's clear all over her body that she is annoyed with him for being late.

"Can I get you two a drink or an appetizer to start?" the waiter asks.

I motion to Skye, and she answers, "We will have a bottle of your house red wine and the clams to start. Thanks."

I grin as the waiter leaves to go get her bottle of wine.

"Why are you so happy all of a sudden?" she asks.

"No reason, I'm just surprised that you ordered wine. Wine means romance, and since it's not clear if your beau is ever going to show up tonight, I'm shocked that you would be willing to share a bottle of wine with me. It must mean I did something right."

The waiter returns, pouring us each a glass of wine before disappearing again.

"A lot can change in six months. I no longer think of wine as romantic," she says, taking a sip of her wine.

"Some things never change."

"So, when do I get to get rid of you?" she asks.

"I have a flight booked back home for tomorrow. So, as long as you still want me gone, you won't have to see me ever again after tonight."

"Prove it." Her eyes light up with a sparkle and gleam as she teases me to prove myself just like I asked her to prove herself earlier.

I pull out my phone, finding my plane ticket and showing it to her. "See, I have a flight booked for tomorrow. I'm a man of my word. I'll be on that flight as long as I don't discover that you lied to me. Plus, I need to be getting back to work."

"Oh, yeah, you have to get back to the dangerous world of building video games." She snickers. Another fact that I'm sure she learned when she Googled me.

"As opposed to the dangerous world of whatever Gabe does."

She grins. "Security. He risks his life every day to make sure that the richest people in the world stay alive."

"He does not. He hires men to protect his clients."

She shrugs. "Usually, but he also likes the rush of the job, so he often does security protections himself. And him working in this business puts our lives at constant risk."

I'm beginning to see what she might see in him. Because, if I know one thing about Skye, she is a risk-taker. She likes to live life on the edge a little differently than everyone else. Evidently, that's what Gabe can provide her.

Our appetizer arrives and we gobble it down while discussing all the basics that we never got around to discussing in the Bahamas.

Our jobs. Why she became a veterinarian. We talk about families, about how neither of us has siblings and therefore adopted our friends as family. We talk about our favorite music. Hers is surprisingly jazz while mine is rap and hip-hop. We talk about our favorite places in the world. Hers is a small town in Italy while mine, outside of the Bahamas, is France.

We talk for over an hour as we drink our wine and order more appetizers. We talk about everything that you should talk about on a first date. We laugh, we joke, and we tease each other. And I quickly forget that Gabe might be coming. I forget that he even exists. I haven't been on a date with a woman in a long time. At least not one that wasn't just about sex.

"Sorry, I'm late." Gabe's voice rings out behind me, crushing the fantasy that we have created between us.

Skye glares at him as he leans down and kisses her quickly on the cheek before taking his seat next to her.

"Meeting run long again?" Skye asks, cocking her head to one side and giving him a look that means business.

"Yes. Had a meeting with a new client who is interested in my services. Took longer than usual to close the deal, but I did. I always do."

The waiter brings over a third glass and pours Gabe a glass.

"I'm sure the two of you had plenty to talk about while I was gone," Gabe says, looking from Skye to me.

I ignore Gabe studying Skye instead. Her reaction screams pissed. I don't know a lot about love, having never been in love myself, but I suppose you can be pissed off at the person you're desperately in love —but not for too long, or the love begins to fade. It doesn't seem like Gabe is that concerned about Skye's love for him disappearing while her anger is on full display.

He holds up his glass of wine. "I'd like to make a toast to old flings." Gabe drinks from his wine, but neither Skye nor I clink glasses with him or drink our glasses. Gabe smirks as he looks at me. "You didn't like my toast?"

"No, I didn't find it in good taste."

Gabe laughs. "I thought it might break the tension between all of us. You see, I already know about you and Skye in the Bahamas. She told me all about it the night I proposed to her. She didn't want any secrets between us," Gabe says, squeezing Skye into his body.

She pulls away, not happy to have his arms around her.

"Is that why you invited me to dinner then? You wanted to pick a fight with me for fucking your woman when she wasn't even yours."

"No, I wanted Skye to be happy. And I thought we might all be able to be friends now that everything is out in the open."

The waiter returns, breaking through the tension, and we all order our food.

"Excuse me, I need to use the restroom," Skye says, getting up from the table.

I don't know if she really has to go or if she's just trying to get away from having to deal with us.

I lean back in my chair, and Gabe does the same, each of us sizing the other one up.

"For a man who says he doesn't want to pick a fight, it sure seems like you're trying to start one."

"Let me make my intentions clear. I didn't bring you here so that you and I could become friends. I brought you here because I have a proposition for you."

I frown, not liking the sound of that one bit. "What sort of arrangement?"

"I know that you enjoyed fucking my girl in the Bahamas, and I know that you came here in hopes that you'd be able to continue fucking her. But then I threw a wrench in your plan. But I think you can help me with the problem I have. See, I want to marry Skye. I love everything about that woman, but I have needs beyond Skye. I want to have my cake and eat it, too, or so the saying goes."

"I don't understand."

"I want you to fuck Skye once a week. That will allow me to fuck my own women on the side without Skye feeling mistreated. She's a woman who deserves the best, and I plan on giving her the best. But she can also enjoy a little plaything on the side while I enjoy my own playthings."

"What makes you think Skye would agree to a plan like that?"

"She will. She wants you. Skye gets what she needs. I get what I want. And so do you. You can fuck my woman once a week as long as you understand who's in control. I have all the power. I say when this arrangement ends. If I say you don't get to touch her for a year, you don't touch her for a year, got it?"

"Yes."

"Oh, beautiful," Gabe says as Skye walks back toward the table. "That was perfect timing. Mr. Jackson and I have come to an arrangement."

She frowns, looking from Gabe to me with her eyes narrowed. "You have?"

Gabe looks at me. "We have."

"And what is the arrangement?" Skye asks.

I stand up. "That I'm going to kick his ass."

Before Gabe has a chance to react, I dive over the table, knocking him to the floor. I punch him hard in the face—one, two, three times. He basically just laughs in my face. I know that he is more skilled than me and could stop me at any time. But he doesn't. I get off another punch before the waitstaff comes over and starts pulling me off of him.

I stop mainly because I can't be here for another second. I can't let Skye be around him, either.

"What's going on?" Skye asks, pissed off as she looks from Gabe lying on the floor with blood spilling from his lip.

"I'm leaving, and you're coming with me." I hold out my hand to her, begging her to take it, and to my surprise, she does without hesitation.

I thought I came here to end things. I thought I came here to get over the fantasy of fucking her again. I lied. Because I care more than I thought.

15

SKYE

I DON'T KNOW why I took Brody's hand. I don't know why I'm going with him. I should stay with Gabe; that would make things simpler. That would be the right decision, the better choice. But it's not the choice I made.

I don't know what the hell just happened, but I have a sneaking suspicion that Gabe was the one who started it. Right now, I can't stand Gabe, and when I look at Brody, all I feel is disappointment. Both men are idiots who don't deserve me. But, right now, Brody might be the lesser of two evils.

So, I let him lead me out of the restaurant while I keep my eyes on his back, ignoring all the customers who are staring at us, shocked at the scene that we caused. I don't question him when he flags down an Uber, and we climb into the backseat.

It takes a minute for the realization of what's happening to hit me.

The car begins driving away from the restaurant before I find my voice again. "Where are we going?" I ask Brody.

Brody looks at me, and I realize I'm still holding on to his hand, but I don't dare let it go.

"My hotel."

I nod. It's what I expected him to say, but I'm not sure if it's the right answer.

I glance out the window and watch the buildings whiz by as we drive. I have no idea which hotel is Brody's or how long it'll take us to get there, but it's long enough to make me regret my decision.

"Actually, can you take me to my condo first and then drop him off? My condo is just down this street," I ask the driver.

Our driver is an older gentleman. I would guess mid-sixties. "Of course, miss."

"What are you doing?" Brody asks.

I remove my hand from his. "I'm sorry. I can't do whatever you think we're doing. I just need to go home."

Brody runs his hand through his hair, messing up his sculpted locks. "You don't have to go back with me, but you shouldn't go home with him either."

"What happened?" I ask even though I'm afraid I already know. It's going to make me pissed off. And, if I'm pissed off, I won't make smart decisions.

Brody grabs my cheeks, looking at me as he strokes my face. "Gabe is not a good man, Skye."

"What happened?" I ask again. I don't need to be told what Brody thinks of Gabe. I just need the truth.

Brody drops his hands and purses his lips as he tries to find the words to tell me the truth.

"Please."

"He wanted an arrangement where I'd get to fuck you in exchange for him getting to fuck other women. He wanted an open marriage, except it seemed he'd get the much better end of the deal. He's a little cunt, Skye. He's a bitch, a disgusting motherfucker who doesn't deserve another second of your time. Forget about that asshole. He's not worth your time."

I stare out the window while my hand rests on the base of it, fidgeting with the lock button. It hurts, but then I've known for a while what Gabe is.

"Skye?"

I don't answer him. I can barely breathe, let alone speak. I don't know what to do. I don't know how to get out of the horrible situation I've found myself in.

"Skye, what are you thinking?"

I can't. I just can't.

Brody senses that something is wrong. He undoes the seat belt and scoots close to me until his body is pressed against my side. He slowly moves his arms around me, pulling me into a hug. Neither of us speaks as the Uber driver drives toward my condo after Brody tells him the address. He finally stops, and I just sit for a moment in Brody's arms.

"Stay with me tonight. I have a suite, so you can have your own bedroom. I won't talk to you. I won't bother you at all. I will give you some time and distance to figure out what you want."

I nod, still unable to speak. I feel numb, rough. The driver starts driving the five blocks it takes to get to his hotel. He stops outside, and Brody, now deciding to be a perfect gentleman, opens my door and helps me out of the car. He keeps his arms wrapped around me as we walk through the lobby to the elevators. I don't remember the elevator ride, just that it happened along with what I assume was a walk to the door of his hotel room. I somehow make it inside.

"Your room is this way." Brody leads me down a small hallway to the bedroom. He goes over to the bed and pulls down the sheets, leading me over to it and setting me on the edge of the bed. Then, he takes a step back.

"Is there anything I can get you? Food? Drink? Someone to talk to?"

I shake my head.

"Okay. I'll be just down the hallway. If you need me at any time of the night, just come in and wake me."

He turns to walk out.

"Wait."

He does, exhaling as he stops.

He stares at me, and I stare at him.

Then, I stand up and walk over to him. "Thank you."

"Of course." He leans down and sharply kisses me on the forehead. And, in that second, the spell breaks.

I grab his cheeks. I move his lips to mine, and I kiss him. And, damn it, the kiss feels good.

Why did I have to kiss him? Now, there's no going back. There's no way I'm going to be able to stop, and it's just going to make things so much worse. It's not bad enough that I'm about to marry a crazy person, but I have to do it while being hung up with this asshole. My heart and mind are torn between two people, and I'm about to give them both what they want. *But what about what I want?*

I don't know what I want, except that I want Brody to fuck me and make me forget about everything else.

Brody grabs my neck as he kisses my lips over and over. We stumble backward until we're falling on the bed. Arms and legs tangle around each other, but our lips never part. It's almost as if neither one of us takes a second to really breathe and think about what we're doing, so we will stop. So, neither of us will allow that to happen.

Instead, we kiss, we groan, and we tear each other's clothes off. Brody rips his jacket off while I pull his tie over his head. His shirt goes next; buttons fly as it falls in a heap on the floor, showing me his hard, strong chest that I haven't been able to get out of my head since I saw him shirtless again in Albuquerque.

"I knew you wanted me the second you saw my abs again. You're a sucker for hard abs and biceps." He smirks as he flips me over and slowly starts unzipping my dress. "Did you wear this dress for him or me?"

I bite my lip, refusing to answer. If we are going to fuck, we're not going to talk about what's happening. The whole reason for sex is to make me forget, to allow me an escape, not to figure out what I really want.

He spanks me hard on the ass, and I yelp.

"Tell me who you wore the dress for, or I'll spank you again."

My lips curl up a little at that thought. I like this game. He spanks me again, and my whole body jerks at the force. My mouth waters, my nipples harden, and my panties become soaked. I forgot what it felt like to have a man be rough with me in bed. Gabe, for all his rough and controlling in real life, prefers rather vanilla sex.

"Have you had enough?" He kneels behind me, clearly getting turned on himself with every spanking as his hard cock rubs against my ass.

"No."

"Then, I'm going to enjoy punishing you until you tell me who you wore the dress for. Because I think you wore this dress, that hides your body, for me. To keep me away from your sexy body."

He rips the back of the dress in half. I flinch at the sound, knowing now that there's no way to hide what I'm doing from Gabe, not that there was before or that I would have. I'm not a cheater or a liar even if Gabe deserves to be cheated on.

"There's your body. You have been hiding it from me beneath your scrubs and this ridiculous dress but no more."

His lips brush over my ass, lightly kissing each cheek. I gasp as he grabs my legs, spreading me wide, and then his hand comes down, slapping over my cunt.

"You've been a dirty girl who deserves to be punished. Say it."

"I've been a dirty girl who deserves to be punished," I say through gritted teeth as he spanks me again.

I hear him moving his pants down, and I turn my head to get a look at his thick cock, but he grabs my hair and turns me away from him, shoving my face hard into the pillow, so I can't see anything.

"You don't get to look at me, baby. You don't get to be rewarded in any way until you answer me."

"Please."

"Are you ready to answer me?"

I groan.

"I guess that's a no." His cock pushes inside me, spreading me wide, filling me with the pain and pleasure I haven't felt in months.

"Fuck, Skye."

I feel him slip in and out of me as he pounds into my body. He slaps me hard on the ass whenever I try to look at him. And he hardly touches me, except with his dick. He punishes me over and over as he moves in and out, giving me only the tiniest bit of pleasure, driving me mad.

I feel his breath on my neck. "I know you're stubborn, Skye. And we both know how much of a dick I can be. So, answer me. Who did you wear the dress for?"

"You." I glance back at him and see the smirk on his face.

"Good girl." His hand reaches around and starts rubbing my clit as he fucks me, building me in a way that only he knows. He makes it hard for me to breathe or think about anything other than my coming climax.

He brings me close and then stops begging me with his words. "Tell me you're not going back to Gabe. Tell me you're going to break up with him."

My throat is dry, but my body still aches for relief.

"Give me a chance. I know you think I'm nothing but a dick, but I can be so much more. I can behave. I can love you like Gabe never has."

I can't breathe. My heart aches to believe that his words are true, but I've been fooled by too many men before to believe anything that leaves his mouth, especially with his cock still inside me. He doesn't mean a word that he says.

"I won't go back to Gabe. I'll give you a chance," I say, telling my own lie.

He lets me come, and it's the relief and distraction I've been seeking, but it's over far too soon. Moments later, all I can think about are his stupid words and how I wish they were true. I think about the words that I spoke and wish that they were what I was going to do. But, right now, I can't.

16

BRODY

SHE'S GONE. I knew she would be. I knew she was lying last night when she told me that she would leave Gabe, that she would give me a chance. But I still had the tiniest bit of hope that she would still be lying in my arms when I woke up this morning. I hoped that maybe she thought of me as more than just a jerk who had treated her wrong in the past. But, clearly, she thinks I'm just as bad as Gabe—or at least, not much better.

I hear a door open, and my ears perk up. Maybe I was wrong. Maybe she's still here. I jump out of bed, not caring that I'm still naked, and run through my hotel suite, looking for her. I hear a squeal as the maid sees me butt-naked.

"I'm so sorry. No one answered the door when I knocked," she says, hiding her eyes behind her hands.

"It's okay. I'll go back to my bedroom to put some clothes on." I head back to my bedroom, pulling some sweatpants and a T-shirt on.

Damn my stupid heart for feeling anything toward Skye. I wish I could go back to not caring, not feeling anything, but I can't. She might not want to be with me, but I know that she doesn't want to be with Gabe. I don't know what power he has over her. What he's bribing her with or blackmailing her with or what arrangement they might have, but I plan on figuring it out. She might have left, but I'm not going anywhere. I promised I would leave as long as she told me the truth, but she didn't keep up her end of the deal, so I don't have to keep up my end of the deal. I just have to come up with a way to make sure that she's safe. Only then can I leave her alone.

I pick up my phone, and I call Noah's number.

"Hey, asshole. Have you fucked her enough that you can come back to work now?" he answers.

"Have I recently told you that you're fired?"

"Every damn day."

"I need your help."

He sighs. "You must be really desperate if you're calling me, asking for help. I thought you handled everything yourself."

"Well, I'm up against a pro, and you're the only one I can think of with any hacking skills that might be able to give me the information that I need. I need to know everything that you can get me about Gabe Cole. Everything. Understand?"

"If she has a boyfriend, I hate to tell you there's probably not much you can do to win her back, short of just waiting it out."

"Just do it."

It takes Noah an hour, but he got me everything I wanted to know about Gabe and more. Where he grew up. When they first met. And even a strong clue as to why she's still with the bastard. And I'm planning on getting confirmation on that tonight.

I step out of the car and walk into the conference center where the charity event for Love All Animals is taking place. Skye apparently does a lot more than just run her own veterinary clinic. She also owns a foundation that focuses on connecting animals and humans in need of each other. Animals that need a home are given one by people that need a companion. I think it's the reason she puts up with Gabe.

I find my table at the back of the large space, which has a stage at the front with a large screen behind it. I paid over a thousand dollars to attend, but the money was well worth it. One, it goes to a good cause, and two, I get another chance to be near Skye.

I take my seat and ignore the others at the table, who are chatting politely to each other. I'm not here for them. I'm here for Skye.

The lights dim, and a spotlight shines on the stage as I watch Skye walk to the center with a microphone in hand. She seems happy and content. I expect to see Gabe walk up onstage with her, but he doesn't. I scan the room now and find him at a close table, watching her as intensely as I am.

She starts talking, and she commands everyone's attention in the room. Even those who were busy in conversation with others now can't keep their eyes off of her. I expected her to be wearing something professional, a dress similar to what she wore last night, but she's not. She is wearing a skintight black dress that shows off her body, her strong legs, toned arms, and just the right amount of cleavage. She looks gorgeous, and I know she's wearing the dress for me. Because, as much as I knew that she wouldn't stay in my bed this morning, she knew that I wouldn't leave her alone tonight.

"I'd like to tell you a story about the first animal that saved my life. I wish I could tell you the stories of all the animals that have saved my life over the years. Saved me from depression. Saved me from pain and heartache. Gave me hope that the world could seek good. And reminded me that we were all just animals trying to live and to survive, fighting our way through this difficult life.

"But I don't have the time, so instead, I'll share just one story about a mouse named Moe. You see, growing up, I was wild and fierce—both qualities that I loved, but my parents, not so much. My passion for life got me in trouble many times. I skipped school and cheated on tests when I thought I didn't need to learn the material. I drank in high school and smoked marijuana between classes. I drove my car too fast. I did all the things that I know you hope your children will never do."

The crowd chuckles a little, watching her.

"But then I was hanging out with a friend who brought a mouse home to feed his snake. I couldn't stand to watch him feed the mouse to the snake, so I stole the mouse and ran. I brought that mouse home and named him Moe, and he was the best friend I'd ever had for the next year.

"I had a purpose in my life that was greater than me. I cared for the mouse, fed him, and took him to the vet when he was sick. I learned what life was really about. Fighting for others, even the tiny creatures of that we often forget about.

"After that, I found my purpose protecting all animals, all beings that walk the earth.

"Together, we've saved over one hundred thousand lives—animals and humans—and I'd like them to share a few of their stories."

The video starts with story after story of people and animals being connected, saving each other. Animals that were meant for slaughter. Dogs and cats to be euthanized because no one wanted them. Even reptiles, like lizards and snakes, were saved, all given to people who needed help. Some had mental health disorders, and others had physical diseases. Some were vets in need of animal support; others were just troubled youth, needing to find a purpose in their life again.

But, by the time the video ends, there isn't a dry eye in the house. Even I have a few tears in my eyes, even though I watched Skye most of the video.

Then, dinner is served. I bide my time before I go see her. I allow her to make her rounds and talk to everyone that she is supposed to at the event. I let her worry and wonder if I'm really here or not. And only then, when she's standing by herself, do I make my move.

She starts walking toward the restroom, and I follow her, needing a moment alone with her and knowing that this might be the only place that I can get just that. She walks into the restroom, and I step in right behind her.

A woman at the sink gives me a dirty look. "This is the woman's restroom."

"I know. I just need a moment with Skye here. It's an emergency."

Skye pauses when she hears me speak and glances over at the woman. "Could you give us a minute?"

The woman scoffs and walks out the restroom, leaving us alone. I turn behind me and lock the door, so I can have a few minutes alone with her.

She turns around and looks at me. She doesn't seem surprised at all to see me standing there. "If you think you're gonna fuck me in the restroom, then you're crazy."

I chuckle. "Never even crossed my mind." I wink.

She smiles a genuine smile, and my heart sinks.

"You're not with him because you love him, are you?"

She shakes her head.

I put my hands in my pockets to keep my hands off of her. I want to comfort her. Or fuck her in the restroom or do something to get rid of the pain hiding beneath her fake smile.

"I think I know why. It's this foundation right? He has promised to stop funding it if you don't marry him."

She looks at me without blinking. Her eyes grow dark with a fire I haven't seen sparking out of them before. "Are. You. Serious?"

I clench my teeth, trying to understand. "Yes."

She shakes her head. "You men are all the same. No, I'm not marrying him so that he'll keep funding my foundation. I don't give a crap about his money, although it's one item on the long list of things he's tried to threaten me with."

I take a step forward, unable to resist from at least holding her in my arms.

She puts a hand up, and I stop.

"I don't need you to try to fix this. I'm not even sure that it's something that can be fixed and definitely not easily."

"Then, explain to me what's happening. Because I've tried to come up with a legitimate reason you would marry that man or even go back to him after last night, and I can't come up with any. He was the reason you were in pain in the Bahamas. He was the reason you were in pain when I saw you in Albuquerque. He's the reason your hair is tamer, your piercings are gone, and that you would even consider living in a home as fancy as his, which doesn't have an animal in sight. He's the reason for everything bad in your life, so why stay with him?"

She runs her hand through her hair. "Because he owns me."

My mouth drops. "Like, you're his slave? Like, he paid money, and you're now his property?"

She shakes her head. "No, but he might as well have. Gabe Cole is a powerful man who is used to getting whatever he wants in life. He's threatened everyone I love in my life. My best friend, the princess—he threatened her in the back of her SUV. He infiltrated her entire security team. My friend, Alicia—he kidnapped her and then filled her so full of drugs that she couldn't even remember what happened the next day. My grandmother is in a nursing home, and he stopped her oxygen twice. She barely survived. He wants complete control, and he gets that. I've tried to leave him several times before, but every time I do, he threatens someone that I love, and I just can't. Because I think he might actually kill them. Or me. And, now that you're in my life, he'll threaten to kill you. That arrangement game he was playing with you at dinner was just a test to see how much you cared about me. He was just playing with you in order to determine if he could use you as leverage against me. He would never share me."

"Have you gone to the police?"

"Of course. But he is the police. Everyone that I talked to believes his story over mine. I have no options left but to give him what he wants and figure out how to fight to get out of it later."

I can't stand it a second longer. I have to have her in my arms. And, this time, when I move to wrap my arms around her, she doesn't stop me. And I'm thankful that she lets me hold her.

"You need to leave. Go far, far away from here. He knows what happened last night, and he's not happy."

I pull back just enough to look her directly in the eyes. "I'm not leaving you. I'm not going to let him hurt you."

"He won't hurt me."

"Why? It seems like that's all he does."

"Because I agreed to marry him tomorrow."

She looks strong and defiant as she says it, like it is her choice.

Maybe that's what she needs to believe, but it's her choice to save her friends and family from this evil monster. But it's a choice I won't let her make.

I look at her and softly kiss her on the lips, cherishing every moment that I have with her. Who knows when our last one together will be?

"I'm going to save you."

She doesn't argue with me, nor does she agree. Instead, she tightly wraps her arms around me and rests her head in the corner of my chest. She might not trust me, but she should. Because, despite what she might think, I'm not a dick.

17

SKYE

I stare into the mirror, not able to accept the reflection staring back at me. My hair is dark brown and curled without a speck of blue or red or purple or any of the colors my hair usually is to make it seem bright and vibrant. My piercings are all gone. Some of the holes have even healed up. I have a simple white veil on the back of my head, and a simple white dress hugs my body.

I was never the princess. I was never the type of girl who dreamed of the big wedding with the big dress and the fancy decorations. That was never me, but I always thought that it could be a possibility. That maybe, someday, a man would care enough about me that I would want that. But getting forced into marrying a horrible, evil man was never my plan.

He was such a good man when I first met him, but how did someone so amazing turn out to be so horrible?

———

"Your coffee is three fifty," the woman behind the bar says.

I nod and reach into my purse to pull out my wallet, but I don't feel it. I open my purse wide, practically sticking my head inside, searching for the wallet, but it's not there.

"I'm so sorry. It seems I left my wallet somewhere. Let me see if I have some cash at the bottom of my purse." I frantically dig through the purse, trying to find some money to pay the woman. I was just on on a fourteen-hour flight from Monaco to LA after visiting my best friend. I have a six-hour layover until my next flight. There is no way I'm gonna survive without coffee or food or anything.

"Let me pay."

I turn around to look at the man standing behind me. He's one of the most beautiful men I've ever seen. Dark brown eyes, a strong jaw, and muscles for days.

I don't usually accept money from strangers, but I'm desperate, and he is handsome.

"Thank you," I say far too loudly.

He smiles and pays the woman after ordering his own coffee.

"How can I thank you?" I ask as we both walk away from the coffee shop in the LAX airport.

"You can keep me company while I wait for my flight."

I smile. "I'd love to."

———

We talked for hours. We both missed our connecting flight. He offered me a place to stay at his condo, and I accepted. I thought he was going to ask me out that night, but he didn't. He was a gentleman, perfectly nice. Not a glimmer of the monster that I know he is now.

I hear a knock on the door, and I jump.

"Sorry, I didn't mean to startle you. I just wanted let you know that it's time," Samantha, the wedding coordinator for the vineyard where we are getting married, says.

I take a deep breath and work on my fake smile as I stand up, grabbing the flowers out of the vase next to me.

"You look beautiful."

I practice my fake smile again. "Thank you."

"The bridesmaids are all lined up, ready to go down. Gabe wanted to know if you wanted one of the best men to walk you down the aisle or if you wanted to walk down alone."

"Alone." I'm very much alone, so why would I want anything different?

I follow Samantha out of the small dressing room to where the bridesmaids are standing in their cream-colored dresses, each holding a bouquet of red roses, at the doors that lead out to the vineyard. I don't know any of the women, but they all look like perfect models in their dresses. It wouldn't surprise me if there were all women who Gabe used to date or still does.

Samantha walks to the front and starts giving the bridesmaids cues to walk down the aisle. I stand at the back, eyes glossed over, trying to imagine that I'm anywhere but here.

I spent all last night, trying to come up with a plan that ended with me not having to walk down the aisle. But I came up with none. No solution or even an attempt at a solution became obvious. So, that means I'm getting married. I'll figure out a way to undo it later.

Samantha smiles at me, rightly thinking that this is the best day of my life when it's not. It's one of the worst.

"You ready?" she says, her voice chipper.

I nod, and she opens the doors.

I thought that I would smile and put on an act as I walked down the aisle to the man blackmailing me into marrying him. But, in a last-second act of defiance, I don't. I don't smile, not one tiniest bit. I look stern, solemn, like I'm walking down to my funeral instead of my wedding. I walk slowly and deliberately down the grass path lined with beautiful flowers. I don't look at Gabe. Instead, I stare past the people standing at the end of the aisle. I look out to the beautiful vineyard in the distance. I don't even glance around at the seats to see if Brody showed up. I get to the end of the aisle and turn toward Gabe but don't look him in the eye. I continue to look past him, trying my best to pretend I'm not here. The bridesmaid behind me asks if I want her to hold my bouquet for me.

"No," I hiss.

Gabe tries to hold on to my hands. I'll marry him in front of this large crowd of people, none of whom I know, but I'm not going to make it easy for him. I'm not going to hold his hand or smile or show any happiness about it. And I won't give him pretty pictures that he can display all over the newspapers in the morning.

I glare, and he smirks back as the minister begins saying something about love and the beauty that it brings and how much better it makes everyone's lives.

I call bullshit. There is nothing beautiful about love. There was a time when I thought I loved Gabe. We connected on so many things —food, music, movies. Our bodies connected when he wrapped his arms around me, making me feel safe. The way he let me have my independence and respected that I owned my own business and had my own dreams. But it was all a lie. Love isn't real.

"I do," Gabe says, grabbing my hand and placing a ring on it before I have a chance to dissent.

"And do you, Skye, take this man to be your husband?"

"I do." I smile as I take the ring that is wrapped around my thumb and plunge it onto his finger, attempting to cause as much pain as I possibly can as I force the ring over his knuckle.

"I now pronounce you husband and wife. You may kiss the bride."

Gabe grins, but if he thinks I'm going to let him have this epic kiss, he's crazy. He grabs my waist and back and dips me backward, away from the crowd, as his head comes down over me, but he doesn't kiss me.

He stops short and says, "You think you're so smart, defying me, don't you? But, now that you're mine, I will punish you for every act of defiance you commit."

His lips press against mine, and I bite down hard. He pulls back with a smirk. I see the tiniest drop of blood dripping down his chin.

He wipes up the blood with the back of his hand. "I'm really going to enjoy punishing you. Should I start with Alicia or Brody?"

"Leave them alone."

"Behave."

Gabe lifts us back up as the crowd cheers, thinking that we spent the whole time in a passionate kiss together instead of what really happened.

Gave interlocks his fingers with mine, firmly holding me so that there's no way for me to let go.

"Now, smile, or Brody's the first to go."

I smile as Gabe walks me down the aisle. As soon as we get back inside, I jerk my hand away from Gabe's. "Now what? How much longer do we have to do this?"

He wraps his arms around me, pulling me to his body again. "Oh, honey. This never ends. You're mine now. Tonight, we are going to spend the night dancing and drinking in front of my friends and the world, showing them just how much of an awesome couple we can be. Then, tomorrow, we get on a flight to the Bahamas to replace all those stupid memories of your old flame with me. And then, when we come back, all your stuff will be moved into my place. You'll become my full-time wife, at my beck and call whenever I need you. Understand?"

I spit in his face. "Go to hell."

I jerk free just as people start coming into the large building on the property to head into the reception area. All sorts of people I've never met start coming up to me, congratulating me, asking me how we met. Asking if I feel like the luckiest girl in the world to be married to such an amazing, rich man. But they don't really want to hear any of my answers. They just want me to smile and nod and let them talk, so that's what I do. I spend my night talking to strangers, trying to stay as far away from Gabe as I possibly can.

I reach into my cleavage and pull out my cell phone, as I take a glass of champagne from one of the waiters. Maybe if I act like I'm working on my phone, people will start leaving me alone. It works for about five minutes until I see a woman in a dark green dress and low cut neckline walk toward me.

I down my glass of champagne, needing the alcohol to get through whatever conversation is about to happen.

"Congratulations," the woman says to me in a cold voice, so different from how everyone else has congratulated me so far.

"Thanks," I say, averting my eyes elsewhere, hoping she will get the hint and leave me alone.

She eyes me up and down. "I don't understand what Gabe sees in you."

"Excuse me?"

She shakes her head. "Sorry, didn't mean to be so blunt. I'm Tonya, I used to attend college with Gabe. I thought we had a future together, but then he found you."

I sigh. I don't say that too bad she didn't succeed in her mission to keep him. That way I wouldn't be in this mess. I just stay silent.

"I just wanted to say congrats and to treat him well. And if you are ever in the need of some decorating, I'm your woman." She holds out a business card to me and I take it.

I stare at this woman completely confused at what she sees in Gabe. She either doesn't know him well at all or likes the monster inside. Either way, I'm not about to have that conversation with her.

"Thanks, I'm going to get another drink," I say, slipping her business card and my phone back into my cleavage.

Gabe spots me from where he is boasting with his groomsmen. I slip back into the crowd to get another glass of champagne.

I drink glass after glass of champagne, and as the night progresses, I get more and more skilled at staying just out of Gabe's reach. Whenever he tries to talk to me, I push a woman in front of him, and that seems to do the trick in distracting him just long enough for me to slip further away and get lost in another crowd. But, every time he gets closer, I can feel the rage surrounding him, exuding off of him. Gabe isn't into rough sex, but I have a feeling, tonight, he is going to give a whole new meaning to rough sex. But it will be nothing like what Brody and I have done together.

"Skye, the wedding planner had a question about what you wanted to do with the leftover cake," a man who looks oddly familiar asks me. He's in a dark suit, his hair is shaved, and his eyes are bright.

I feel like I should recognize him, yet I can't place him. Maybe I met him earlier today when he helped serve me alcohol or food, although he's not dressed like a waiter.

"Excuse me," I say to the crowd around me. I follow the man out of the reception hall. He keeps walking once we get to the hallway down toward the back of the building.

"Where are we going?"

"Just a little further. Repacking the stuff into the back of the car. She wants to know what address to deliver the leftovers to."

I frown. Surely, Gabe has already thought of all of these things and handled it.

"Who are you?"

He doesn't answer immediately. Instead, he just keeps walking to the back door and pauses when he rests his hand on the door.

He smirks. "I'm here to kidnap you, of course."

I open my mouth to scream as he grabs my hand and pulls me outside. But I'm so broken at the moment that I'm not sure whether I should fight to stay or make it easier for him to kidnap me. I can't imagine anyone worse than Gabe Cole.

He pushes me into the back of an SUV, and my eyes open wide with hope.

"Brody?" I ask even though I know it's him sitting in the seat next to me. I'm still not sure I believe it's real. It must be a dream; there is no way Brody is rescuing me right now.

He grins, flashing me his perfect teeth. "We're here to save you," Brody says.

He wraps his arms around me and firmly kisses me on the lips.

"No, we are here to kidnap her. This plan will never work if Gabe doesn't think we're kidnapping her," the man who brought me out here says from the front seat.

Another man is sitting next to him and begins driving us off.

Brody rolls his eyes at him. "Fine. We are kidnapping you."

"And that means we need to make it look like a kidnapping all the time," the man says.

"Wait, you're Noah," I say, recognizing the man sitting in the passenger seat as one of Brody's friends from the Bahamas.

"Yep, and this is Levi," Noah says.

I smile at both of them. "Thank you for kidnapping me."

"Our pleasure. If you're a friend of Brody's, then you're a friend of ours. He deserves to be happy," Levi says.

My smile falters, but I don't think any of the men notice. Even if they manage to get me out of this mess with Gabe, I'm not sure Brody and I can ever be together. He might not be as bad as Gabe, but he's still a dick at the end of the day. They both even confirmed it to me in the Bahamas.

"Brody, now," Noah says.

"Sorry, but I have to tie you up. There are too many video cameras and cameras from stoplights, and Gabe could see us. We need to make it look like a real kidnapping."

I hold out my hands, and Brody's eyes sear into mine as he ties me up just like he has countless times before. I feel the familiar feelings all over my body, thinking about what is supposed to happen next. He is supposed to kiss me. Spank me. And then fuck me. It's not supposed to just end with a kidnapping.

Brody pushes his ball cap further on his head, trying to hide his face as we go through a stoplight. They are all really concerned that Gabe is monitoring us right now. And, if that's true, then none of us have a chance.

"Stop the car!" I shout.

Levi doesn't even hesitate. He just keeps driving.

"You have to stop the car. You have to let me out. He'll kill all of you for doing this."

Brody grabs my face, forcing me to look at him. He pets the side of my face, trying to calm me down. "He's not going to kill any of us. We have a plan. Just let us follow it."

I take a deep breath in and out.

"Shit," Levi says. The cars jumps forward as he speeds up, running through a red light.

"What the hell, man?" Noah says.

"We are being followed," Levi says.

"How?" Brody asks.

"I don't know. We should have had more time before anyone figured out that Skye was gone. Especially with the woman we got to play Skye. She looks exactly like her from the back; there's no way Gabe would've noticed this fast. Not when we also had one of the hottest women we could find seducing him."

"Do you have your cell phone on you?" Brody asks.

I nod and look down into my cleavage.

Brody reaches in between my breasts and pulls out my cell phone. He rolls down the window and chucks the phone outside.

"Seriously, Brody, you had one job—to make sure she didn't have her cell phone on her," Noah says.

Brody's eyes stare into mine. "I'm sorry."

Brody might be many things, but he's definitely no James Bond. I haven't even been gone five minutes, and Gabe's already on our tail. I don't have much faith that they're going to be able to figure out how to get me out of this safely. So, I'd better start forming my own plan and fast. Or we are all fucked.

18

BRODY

I FUCKED UP. And, now, my mistake might cost us our lives.

We all turn, looking at the SUV chasing after us.

"You need to just let me go. It's the only way to save yourselves," Skye says.

"No way. Not happening," I say.

Shots ring out behind us, and Levi swerves the car as all our hearts jump into our throats. Now, they're shooting at us.

"Levi, Noah, please. Just turn me over to them. Gabe won't hurt me, and you guys will have a chance to go free."

Levi grips the steering wheel hard and glances in the rearview mirror while I give him a death stare, imploring him to keep driving, no matter what.

"We aren't turning you over," Noah says.

Levi nods in agreement.

Skye exhales deeply and then looks at me. "Then, you'd better come up with something fast, or we are all dead."

I pull out my burner phone. He wants one thing. Skye. And I don't think he'd be too happy if she were dead. Or at least, I hope not.

Shots ring out again, and we all duck down like, if we get low enough, somehow, the bullets won't actually pierce our skin.

I reach into the bag at my feet and pull out the small gun inside.

"I don't think shooting back is the answer," Skye says, looking at me with wide eyes.

"Skye's right; these guys are professionals. They will shoot you dead before you even have a chance to get a shot off."

I aim the gun at Skye's had.

"I'm going to make Gabe think that we're going to kill you if he doesn't call his men off."

Skye smiles and grabs the phone out of my hand, handing it to Noah.

"Take a picture, and send it to Gabe," Skye says.

Skye closes her eyes and then opens them, trying to look as terrified as possible while I aim the gun at her head.

"You have to hold the gun closer," Noah says.

I put the gun all the way up to her head, hating how it feels to aim a gun at her, even one that has no bullets in it.

Skye looks at the gun out of the corner of her eye, and she looks terrified, just like she needs to be.

Noah takes the picture but only of my hand and Skye, giving us more time before Gabe realizes it is me who is the kidnapper.

"Message sent. Now, we wait and hope we don't die," Noah says.

I continue holding the gun to her head, hoping the guys behind us will see it and stop.

My heart races as the silence drones on, and we zip down the road, passing car after car. One second passes. Then, another. Then, another.

The phone buzzes in Noah's hand. We all hold our breath as he clicks the button to open the text message.

"He's agreed," Noah says.

We all exhale at the same time.

"They are pulling off the road," Levi says, looking in the rearview mirror.

I toss the gun back into the backpack and grab Skye's head, firmly kissing her on the forehead, thankful that she's still alive. That all of us are. But none of us are naive enough to think that we're safe, long-term.

The phone buzzes again, and Noah clicks the message open.

All of us stare intently at him, waiting for the message.

"He says that he's going to hunt us all down and kill us. But will make it long and torturous if anything happens to Skye. He wants her desperately. We aren't to hurt her. He wants us to return her to him by tomorrow morning, or he will use everything in his power to take us all out."

"Tell him to give us one million dollars and that we define the terms, not him. Tell him we want the money in exchange for her safe return by tomorrow evening," I say.

Noah nods and begins typing the message.

I look at Skye, who has her head cocked to the side, eyes curiously looking at me.

"It will give us enough time to work on plan C."

"Plan C?" Skye asks with a raised eyebrow.

I nod. "It takes a lot of plans, and we will go through as many plans as we need until we are all safe."

"What's plan C then?"

Noah turns around in his seat and hands the phone to Skye. She takes it with her hands still bound together.

"We need to call that rich princess friend of yours to get us a private plane to somewhere anywhere but here," Noah says.

"You can't be serious."

I nod.

She shakes her head. "First, she doesn't just have a private jet on hand at all times to take me wherever I want. Second, Gabe knows about her, he's threatened her and her family before. I'm not going to get her involved, and even if she were to get involved, Gabe would be able to track the plane in a second. If we're trying to be discreet, that's the opposite of helpful."

I rub the nape of my neck hard. "I guess we are on to plan D then."

"Actually..." Skye says, staring at the phone.

She reaches into her bra and pulls out a business card. I can't help but continue to stare at her boobs and wonder how much else she has stored in there.

She begins entering the number on the business card.

"What are you doing?" I ask.

She shakes her head and just shushes me.

"Hello, Tonya. This is Skye."

The other woman must say something, as Skye goes silent.

"You see, I know you don't like me very well. But I made a mistake, and I think you'll want to help me fix that."

A short pause.

"Because you want my husband, and I want an annulment. So, you'll help me by discreetly getting me a private plane out of the country without letting Gabe know where I am, and I'll make sure that he finds his way safely into your bed."

My mouth drops open.

"Done," Skye says, smiling. She moves and lets the phone drop to her hands before she presses End on the phone and hands it to me. "Head to the airport. We have our plane."

"How?"

"I met a woman tonight who was not too happy about me marrying Gabe. She wanted him for herself. She asked me to give her number to Gabe if he ever needed help with redecorating. But I knew it was her saying that she didn't care that we were married, that she would still try to go after him."

"We have our plane," I agree.

I'm not sure I believe that this is gonna work until we pull up at the airport, and there is the plane waiting for us. Still, I don't think it's gonna work, and we all load and carry the guns we bought as we board the plane, expecting Gabe or his men to be sitting on it, ready to ambush us the second we get on. But there is none. Apparently, a woman scorned and in love will do just about anything to have a chance at her ex-lover again.

It's not a huge plane, but it's enough for the four of us.

"Where to?" the pilot asks as he ducks his head into the main cabin of the plane.

"Vancouver," Levi says.

Skye looks at him like he's crazy. But the pilot just nods and heads back to the cockpit.

Skye takes a seat in the back, and I take the seat right next to her. "Seriously? Vancouver? Can't find a place a little further away to head to?"

I look at Levi.

"I have some friends in Vancouver who might be able to help."

I reach over and rub Skye's neck, trying to get her to relax. "I'm going to save you."

She grins. "Sure you are."

We all buckle our seat belts, and the plane takes off shortly afterward. It's only then that I realize her hands are still tied together. When we are safely in the air, I unbuckle my seat belt, and she undoes hers. I motion with her to follow me to the back. She does. We barely draw attention as Levi and Noah talk strategy in front of us.

I'm hoping there's some sort of bedroom or at least a large bathroom in the back of the plane, but there's none. Just a tiny-ass bathroom that's no bigger than a bathroom on a commercial jet. Still, I pull her inside and close the door behind us.

"Finally," she exhales as she throws her tired arms up over my head and around my neck.

Our lips crash together in a passionate kiss that beats all others. I've never needed a woman so much in my life, and it's clear she's never needed me more than now. Our tongues tangle and our breathing becomes one as our kisses dig deeper into each other's smiles. But she is still wearing her wedding dress that she got married to Gabe in.

"I'm sorry I couldn't save you before you had to marry him."

Her lips kiss me again hard. "I don't care. Marriage means nothing to me."

Her voice is sharp, like a woman scorned, not willing to get back into love again.

It's something I'll have to work on later. As desperate as she is for my body, if we survive all this, I'm not sure she'll be as desperate for a relationship with me, as I am with her.

"Fuck me, Brody. Please," she cries into my lips, her entire body begging for me but not being able to do anything about it because her hands are tied and currently locked around my neck.

I lift her dress up and push down the thin white lace panties, finding her tight cunt and pushing two fingers inside. She's soaked and ready for me to enter her in a second, so that's exactly what I do. If there's anything I've learned through this, it's that there is no promise for a tomorrow. Not even another minute or another second.

I push down my pants and pull out a condom, slipping it on just in time as she wraps her legs around me, and I push my cock inside her. I fuck her hard over and over in the tiny bathroom on a plane. Any other time, I would be reveling in the coolness of getting to fuck a woman on a private jet. Any other time, I'd be telling her to be quiet so that my friends wouldn't hear her, and I would get to keep her cries all to myself. Any other time, I would do all those things and more. But not today. Today, I'm just going to fuck her as many times as I can. Because, despite my words of promising her that I can save her, I'm not sure that I can. All I can do is fuck her and take away her pain, however temporarily.

19

SKYE

I SHOULD BE SCARED, but I'm not. Brody has a way to make me feel safe even though he has no idea what he's doing. Even now, there is no way to save me. Not from a crazy man like Gabe. And especially not when we have no skills compared to Gabe.

I feel the light peeking into the room, and I open my eyes. All the boys are sitting around the room on their computers, typing furiously fast. We all stayed in the same hotel room last night so that we could pay with cash and hopefully make it a little bit harder for Gabe to find us. Brody and I slept on the bed. Noah, the couch. And Levi slept on the floor.

"Morning," Brody says, getting up from his computer and walking over to the bed to firmly kiss me on the lips.

The kiss makes my insides warm. I could get used to waking up to kisses like that every morning.

"This is Jeremy and Kate," Brody says, pointing to a man and woman who are also sitting in the room.

They both turn, smile at me, and nod, and then they immediately turn back, typing quickly on the computers.

"They are here to help us hack into all of Gabe's systems. If we can break in and hopefully find some hard evidence of Gabe doing something illegal, we might be able to stop him. Our plan is to turn it over to journalists first, so that then when we turn it over to the police, they won't be able to deny it."

I glance around the room, but all the people are working hard on the computers. I don't know what their credentials are or how good they are with a computer. But I know their skills with a gun and car aren't great. This might actually be where they are capable of doing some damage to Gabe.

Brody eyes me up and down as I wear his T-shirt and boxer shorts. I run my hand down my bedhead, and he takes a deep breath. And then his lips kiss me again like it might be the last time. The rest of the room fades. The people, the typing, the danger. It all escapes us as hold each other.

Noah clears his throat loudly. "You need to be working, Brody. There will be time for making out later. We need all hands on deck."

Brody slowly pulls away from me. "I am working. I'm keeping Skye happy and relaxed."

"Skye is perfectly capable of taking care of herself," Noah says, still typing away on his computer.

Brody sighs and then grabs my hand, pulling me toward the bathroom. He gives me a wink as we enter the bathroom, but just as Brody is about to shut the door, Noah slams his hand hard against the door, preventing it from shutting.

"Seriously? You're not fucking in the bathroom again. You do realize we heard everything on the plane, right?"

My face blushes, but Brody just scowls.

"Get out," Brody says.

"No, you're the best programmer we have. We have a chance at saving Skye, so your ass needs to be behind a computer the rest of the day."

"He's right," Brody says, kissing me hard on the forehead again.

I close my eyes.

And then he walks out of the bathroom and back to a computer.

Noah stands at the door a second longer. "We're going to figure this out. In the meantime, here are some clothes." He reaches behind him and pulls out some jeans and a T-shirt.

"Thanks, really. Brody has some really good friends if you are willing to risk your life to help him."

Noah shrugs. "He would do the same for us."

Noah walks away, and I shut the door. I reluctantly turn the water on in the shower. My heart is torn because I don't know if I want to shower and wash away every remaining scent of Brody in my hair or all over my body. But, on the other hand, I want to wash away every touch from Gabe. But the water will calm me, and I just have to pray that I'll get another moment with Brody even if it is for the last time.

I strip and then step into the steaming hot shower, trying to push both men out of my head and just focus on what I want. I want to be alive. I want to survive to go back to the wonderful life I've created for myself. I love my life, and no man is needed to make me feel better about it.

Still, every time I close my eyes, the darkness of everything that Gabe has done creeps in. And, every time, the only thing I can do to push out those images is replace it with Brody.

I abruptly turn off the water, refusing to close my eyes again. I get dressed in the jeans and T-shirt, but both are too big for me. I applaud the guys for remembering to give me clothes at all. And then I step back out into the hotel room. Everyone continues typing and ignoring me, even Brody this time. He put headphones on to drown out the world, even me.

I walk over to Brody and lightly tap him on the shoulder. "How can I help?"

"By telling me anything and everything you can on Gabe. Tell me some of the worst things you saw that there might be some evidence connected to," Noah answers instead.

"What type of evidence?"

"Threats against you that might have been recorded, threats against other people, money laundering, abuse, anything criminal. Start with the worst, but even something simple that could get him locked away for a few months would be a good start until we can find harder evidence on him."

I sit down on the edge of the bed, trying to think about all the horrible things that I just spent my entire shower trying to push out of my head. "Money laundering, I have no idea about, but I wouldn't put it past him. But I have no idea where to start with that. Abuse? He's never been physically abusive to me, not yet anyway. And threats, he was very careful to never put anything in writing or say anything over the phone or in any public space really beyond the occasional whisper into my ear."

"Tell me anyway. Tell us all the stories you can think of; maybe there's something you're missing."

I close my eyes and let the darkness unfold in my head. It's not that I can't remember all of the horrible things, it's that I've spent the past few months trying to forget.

"The first time I realized that he was a monster was a couple of months after we met. He asked me out. He asked to have me fully and completely. And, if I said no, he threatened the company."

"Tell me the whole story."

————

We would meet up at the LA airport that had become our thing. Every few weeks, I would fly to LA and see him. We'd spend the entire day talking and connecting in the airport. I never left the airport, and he never asked me to. But, each time I flew out, I thought this would be the time that he would ask me on a proper date, this would be the time that we'd become more than just friends.

We have been talking for a while. My flight back is going to leave in less than thirty minutes. We've had another beautiful day of talking and laughing together, but it seems that this time isn't the time either.

Just ask him, my heart said, thumping in my chest.

I should. I don't know why I'm waiting for this man to make the first move when I'm fully capable of doing it myself. The worst he'll say is no or that he already has a girlfriend. I could lose him as a friend, but it's a risk I have to take.

I open my mouth to ask him out when he says, "Would you like to go to dinner with me tonight?"

I grin. "Yes."

I don't care about my flight or anything else I just care about having an awesome day with him.

Gabe leads me out of the airport, somewhere along the way interlinking fingers with mine. And that's all I can focus on—our hands linked together the entire time—as Gabe leads me into the back of the waiting car on the curb. I can't even tell you the name of the car. Just that I'm in one.

I'm blissfully ignorant of everything going on around me until Gabe takes the phone call. He doesn't talk much.

He just says in a stern voice, "Yes, it will be done." Then, he looks at me. "Small detour. I guess you'll get to know more of what I do sooner rather than later."

I smile, happy to learn more about his work. The car stops outside of a hotel. And Gabe helps me out, continuing to hold on to my hand. He opens the door for me to the hotel, and my mouth drops open. It's extravagant with beautiful marble floors and a high ceiling with a large chandelier overhead. Gabe rests his hand on the small of my back as he leads me toward the elevator. The doors open, and we enter. I don't know what kind of work he does that he has to meet someone in a hotel room, but I'm going along with it. That, or it's all a ruse, and he's just trying to get me naked in his bed. I think I like option B better.

He grabs my face and kisses me hard as my heart beats wildly in my chest. His hands go around my body, consuming me. He's definitely going with option B.

The doors open, and he guides me down the hallway to a hotel room where a man is standing. The man hands the key to Gabe, and he swipes it in the lock.

I curiously look at him as he leads me inside the room, firmly holding my hand. When we step inside, I see a man tied to a chair in the corner of the room. I gasp.

"Wait here," he says to me.

I stand frozen, not sure of what the hell's going on.

Gabe walks over to the man, pulls a knife out of his pocket, and slits his throat.

I watch the blood spill from his neck. I watch the light leave his eyes. And I'm terrified. Gabe is a monster.

Gabe drops the knife on the man's lap and wipes the blood that spilled onto his hands off on the man's shirt before walking back to me.

"I want you, and I tend to get what I want. I kill for what I want. You're mine now, Skye, for as long as I want you. For just tonight. Or for much longer."

He tucks a strand of my hair behind my ear. "Unfortunately, I have a flight I have to catch. More work needs to be done, and this mess needs to be cleaned up. And I know you have a trip to the Bahamas. Enjoy yourself. This might be your last week of freedom away from me." He firmly kisses me on the lips again. Then, he takes my hand and escorts me back out of the hotel room.

"George, take Skye to the airport and get her on the next flight back home."

He looks at me. "Not a word to anyone, or I'll kill you like I did to him. And I'll take all your friends and family with you."

———

"I went to the police after that. They didn't believe me; they said it was all some sort of fantasy story. So, instead, I went to the Bahamas for a week and tried to forget. But, when I came back, he proposed and force me to be his. He's a monster. But he is a very careful monster. He kissed me on the elevator, so the cameras would see us, and people would assume that we went to that hotel room to have a quickie. There is no evidence."

Noah puts his hand on my shoulder and then pulls me into a hug that I desperately need right now. He's a good man, although my judgment of men is not the best. If only Brody could be as good as well. Brody's already shown me that he is capable of hurting me.

We hear a loud pop down the hallway, and everyone jumps and

stares at the door. We hear a man yelling at his son, telling him not to slam the door so loudly. It was just a kid, but it was enough to get all of our hearts racing.

Noah gets up and walks over to a bag. He pulls out a gun, handing it to me. I take it from him, getting used to the heavy metal in my hand.

"You know how to use that?" he asks.

"No. Do you?"

"I know the mechanics of how it works and how to make sure that it doesn't go off when you don't want it to. But I've never fired a gun in my life."

"Same."

Noah shows me how the safety works and how to load the gun.

"Make sure it's always on you, just in case."

I nod.

I keep telling him the stories, everything I can think of, while everyone else works. Occasionally, he will go over and transfer what he feels is some important information to the others on the team to look up but after our several hours pass and they find nothing that we can use against Gabe, I start to lose hope that this will work.

Eventually, Brody walks over, and he can see the worry on my face. "We are some of the smartest people in the world when it comes to technology, we'll figure this out. But you have to make me a promise to keep fighting every chance you get. No matter what. Even if you get captured, I will find a way to save you."

"I promise," I say. But I don't think he'll be able to save me. But I can save them.

20

BRODY

DAMN IT. I look at the empty bed as the morning light comes up again.

"She's gone," I say.

Noah nods. "But then we knew she would run if we couldn't save her."

"Time to move on to plan Z."

21

SKYE

IT TOOK everything in me to leave. I snuck out in the middle of the night when everyone was asleep, passed out from exhaustion from working the entire day. But it had to be done. They spent all day searching and found nothing. No evidence to use against Gabe. They can't save me, but I can save them.

So, that's exactly what I'm doing. I stole one of the burner phones and snuck out into the night. I called Gabe and told him I'd give him everything he wanted. I'd come back to him, but he couldn't hurt anybody. He promised, and I have to return to ensure that he keeps that promise. He bought me a commercial flight early in the morning, and I got on it.

But, now, I can't seem to bring myself to get off of it. The whole plane has unloaded, except for me. Still sitting in my seat in the fifth row, I stare at the seatback in front of me. I have to get up. I have to leave. But I know, as soon as I do, my life is over. I'm as good as dead. Right now, I have to worry about saving my friends. Then, I can worry about saving myself. So, I force my body to stand. I force my legs to walk off.

"I'm surprised you had the balls to show up," Gabe says, grabbing my arm the second I depart from the gate.

On the one hand, I'm shocked that he is here instead of sending one of his men. But, on the other hand, Gabe likes to do things that are important to him in person.

"I keep my promises," I say, letting him guide me through the airport and out to his waiting car.

I'm surprised to see that he doesn't have a driver. He tosses me into the passenger seat and then climbs into the driver's seat, speeding off.

"Good girl," he says when I behave.

I look out the window instead of having to look at him. I try to remind myself that I'm doing this for them. Not for him. Not for me. No one else deserves to die for my mistake in judging men.

"Look at me."

I turn my head.

He smirks. "You really will behave now?"

I nod, keeping all the emotion off my face.

"Stop thinking about him. He's nothing. Think of me."

"I am," I say. Even though it's a lie.

I will never stop thinking about Brody. I'll never stop dreaming about him. Gabe can control a lot of things, but he can't control my thoughts or desires.

Gabe parks the car outside of our condo and then says, "Come."

I do, like a dog following a command. He leads me up to our condo. I pray that his damn phone rings with some important client who needs to be killed or secured or whatever the hell it is that he does. It doesn't ring though. We get up to the condo, and he shuts the door behind us, locking it. I know what he's going to want. I'm not sure I can give it to him. I want to protect my friends, but I also won't let him lay a hand on me. Not without a fight.

"Fix me a drink. A scotch," he says.

I walk to the kitchen and pour two glasses of scotch—one for him and one for me. I walk back to him and hand him one. He smirks when he sees the second glass. He clinks our glasses together and then drinks down my entire glass.

"Now, strip for me," he says, his eyes staring into my eyes.

I go to do what he said, but I can't. My hand stops just short of lifting the shirt over my head.

"If you hesitate, I will put all your friends' names in a bowl and pull one out. The name I do dies. And we will repeat that process until you either listen to me or they're all gone. Understand?"

"No."

He hits me hard across the face, knocking me down to the floor. I can't think. Everything hurts. My head is pounding. The dizziness overtakes all of my thoughts. I feel something hard jut into my back.

Gun. I have a gun. I reach into the back of my pants, pull out the gun, and aim it at his heart.

He laughs and rips the gun from my hand before I can react. He tosses it aside like it's nothing before I even had a chance to get a shot off. He grabs my hair and pulls me up.

"You think you're smarter than me, don't you? Better, stronger? But you aren't. You're just a stupid little bitch with a beautiful cunt that I want." He slobbers up my neck and my face when I try to push him off, but he's right. He's much stronger than I am. If he wants something, he'll just take it.

"I'm going to have my way with you over and over again. And then I'm going to do what I said; I'm going to put all your friends' and family's names in and pull one out, and that person will die today. And then I'll keep repeating until they're all gone, and when they're all gone, that's when I'll kill you."

I should be afraid, but instead, it just pisses me off. I kick him as hard as I can in the balls and run. He grabs my ankle, and I fall to the floor before I can take two steps away. I won't let him do this to me or to my friends.

We both look up as the door to the condo is pushed open. Three guys tumble in, all holding guns aimed in our general direction. But they aren't just any men. These are my men. Brody, Noah, and Levi.

I should be relieved to see them here. But I know how bad of a shot they are, and I know that, if they miss once, Gabe will kill them all.

"Run," I plead with them.

Noah looks at me like I'm the saddest thing he's ever seen while Levi and Brody both stay fixed on Gabe.

"Let her go," Brody says.

Gabe laughs. "No, she's mine. But I will enjoy killing the three of you in front of her. It will break her, and then she will be mine completely."

Brody looks down at me for just a second. I know what he's about to do. I cover my head as he shoots. I hear Gabe move behind me, pulling me toward him to use me as a shield as he reaches for his own gun. I grab on to his arm, reaching for the gun behind him with all my might, trying to keep it away from shooting Brody. I hold him off only for a second.

But then dozens of men start pouring into the condo, all with bulletproof vests and helmets. They rush over to Gabe, pulling him to his feet and disarm him.

"Gabe Cole, you are under arrest for attempted murder of Skye, Brody, Noah, Levi, and many, many more."

In complete shock, I watch as they drag Gabe out. I don't believe that this is really happening.

I turn to one of the officers. "Is this really happening? Am I safe now?"

"Yes, he won't be getting out of jail for a very, very long time. You are as safe as you can be."

"Thank you."

Brody comes over and wraps me in his arms. "I told you I would save you," Brody says.

"How? How did you convince the police?"

"I planted a recording device in the gun," Noah says.

"You were able to record our entire conversation?" I ask.

Noah nods.

"We knew you would run if we couldn't find another solution to save us. So, we used it to get the evidence that we couldn't find on our own."

"If you guys wouldn't mind, we would like to question each of you individually. That'll help build our case against Gabe," one of the police officers says.

"Sure," Brody says, slightly pulling away from me. He leans down and firmly kisses me on the forehead. "You're safe now. To live your life however you want."

He walks away, following one of the officers. And Levi does the same, following another officer out. Leaving me and Noah by ourselves in the condo.

"You okay?" Noah asks.

"I will be."

"Good. Will we be seeing more of you around Detroit now?"

I shake my head as I stare at the back of Brody's head. It could be one of the last times I ever see him. "I don't think so."

Noah watches Brody turn the corner out of the condo. "I lied. Just so you know."

"What do you mean?"

"I mean, he's not a prick. He doesn't date countless women and multiple women at the same time. He's hardly dated. And he sure as hell doesn't go around, fucking women willy-nilly. He's a nerd with a big heart. He will love you with everything he has if you let him have that chance. He won't hurt you. He's one of the good guys."

I tuck my hair behind my ear. "He's hurt me before."

Noah narrows his eyes. "You need to ask him about that."

Is it possible that Brody is a good guy? That he won't hurt me?

I run after Brody. "Wait!" I shout.

Brody turns around and gives me a giant smile. I run to him.

"I don't trust men. I know you don't have to guess why. My mind says I should run far away and never let anyone into my life again. But my heart wants something more. My heart thinks you might be a better man than I give you credit for. But I need to know, why did you hurt me in the Bahamas? Why did you text me a picture of you and that woman? Why did you fuck her?"

"Because you needed something to take away the pain. I never had sex with that woman. I just got her to pose with me to make you hate me. It seemed to be what you needed. Just like how you needed rough BDSM-type sex. I've never done anything like that in my life. I had no idea what I was doing. I just Googled and made it up as we went along."

I chuckle.

"I've never owned an animal. I've never wanted kids. I live a completely different life than you. We don't like the same music or the same movies or the same drinks. But I do know one thing. I love you, Skye. I love that we are different. I love that we can grow together and learn to become better people because of each other. I want to learn what it means to love animals. I want to know what it's like to have kids with you. I want to marry you and live happily ever after with you. I want everything with you."

"So, you're not a dick?"

He shakes his head.

"Or an asshole?"

He shakes his head again.

"Or a tool? A prick? A monster?"

"No. I can't promise that I'll never hurt you, but I will do everything that I can to not hurt you if you give me a chance. Will you give me that chance?"

"Yes."

EPILOGUE

BRODY

"WHEN ARE you coming back to Detroit?" Noah asks.

"Not for another three weeks, for the launch of our next video game," I answer into my phone.

"You know if you come back and work here, you could have a nice cushy office."

"And why would I want that? I've never wanted a nice, big cushy office." I glance around my cave in the back of Skye's veterinarian clinic. It's barely bigger than a closet. I'm pretty sure that Skye used to use it as a supplies closet before she let me make it into my office.

"I don't know, so that you would have windows and get to be with the rest of your team."

I laugh. "I hate windows and people. Seeing you every couple of weeks is plenty."

"Fine, fine. Tell Skye I said 'hi' and that she better be coming to the next launch with you."

"She is. She wouldn't miss it."

I end the call and lean back in my chair, taking a deep breath as I glance at the clock. It's six o'clock. Usually, Skye likes working late, and I do too. But it's Friday night, and one of the new vets is coming in early, so we should be able to take off soon. Plus, I have plans in store. I even spent my lunch break setting up for tonight.

I close my laptop and decide to leave it at work, rather than bring it home where I could end up working more. This weekend is all about relaxing together without work.

I look down at Grump, who is lying at my feet. "Ready to go home?"

He wags his tail and I smile, petting him on the head before standing up and walking out of my office to go convince Skye that we should go home and let the vets she hired handle the rest of the cases for today. It will be easier said than done.

I walk down the hallway toward Skye's office with Grump at my heels, following me.

I stop at the door, knocking softly, when I see that she is on the phone.

She smiles when she sees me, and I smile back, leaning against the doorframe while I look at her. She's the most beautiful woman in the world. Especially when she's doing what she loves. Her hair is currently a dark purple. Her piercings are back in her nose and half a dozen on each ear. And she just recently got a new tattoo on her hip that represents the charity that she started. She's back to who she really is, and I love watching her. I thought that after everything that happened she might live in fear, but she doesn't. She's the strongest person I know.

Grump doesn't care that she is on the phone. He walks over to her and paws at her leg until she gives him attention. She pets him lazily on the head while she talks.

I keep my distance, knowing I will have a better chance at getting her to leave if I'm patient. She talks for a few minutes longer and then ends her call.

"I still can't believe how much Grump likes you. I think he might like you even more than I do," Skye says, giving Grump better attention now.

I shrug. "We are just a lot alike. I like my space and being alone. He's the same."

I walk over to her, wrap my hands around her neck, and kiss her firmly, letting her know that she needs to be done working. Now.

She moans a little as I kiss her. And I know if I keep kissing her, and no one comes in to interrupt us, that I can convince her to go home, where I can fuck her. We've tried fucking here before, but it never works. Her desk is too flimsy and if she's here, people are constantly coming to talk to her about a case, since she's the best.

I hear a knock on the door, and I'm about to curse whoever it is that is going to prevent me from being able to take Skye home.

"Sorry to interrupt," Alicia says with a tiny grin. She's not sorry at all.

I glare at her while still holding Skye in my arms, not letting her go for anything.

Skye laughs when she sees my expression. "What's up?"

"Jake is in surgery and could really use your help with a case. He's tried realigning the bone with pins but he just can't get it to work. Do you have a few minutes to help him?"

I roll my eyes. I've lived with Skye now for over eight months. I know that orthopedic cases like this take a lot longer than just a few minutes of her time. They take hours upon hours. If she steps in to help, she won't be home until midnight or later.

"No," I answer for her.

"Excuse me asshole? I can make my own decisions," Skye says, pulling out of my arms.

"I know you can and your answer is no."

Skye folds her arms across her chest and gives me that look like it's going to be a long fight that I'm not going to win. I never win.

But tonight is the one night that I could really use a win. I'm not patient and I have big plans for this weekend.

Skye turns back to Alicia, a woman who I thought was my friend, but definitely isn't. "Of course, I'll help. I'll be right there."

I glare at Alicia, annoyed with her for not sticking with the plan.

Alicia starts bursting out into laughter.

"I'm sorry. Jake isn't in surgery and he doesn't need Skye's help.

But watching your head explode like that was worth the teasing," Alicia says.

I frown. "Seriously? That was a joke?"

She nods.

I roll my eyes and grab Skye's arm. "Can we go home now, before Alicia decides to pull any more pranks on me?"

"Fine, grump," Skye says.

Grump's ears immediately perk up.

She laughs. "Not you," she says to the dog. "You," she says pointing at me. "You are much more of a grump than the dog."

I frown, not sure I like her new nickname for me. One, it's not practical with the dog being named that. And two, I'd much rather her call me an ass or a prick. It's much more dangerous sounding than 'grump.'

"I thought I was an ass?"

She rolls her eyes. "You're that too. But first and foremost, you're a grump."

I chase after her and scoop her up in my arms, tickling her sides as I do to make her laugh, before setting her down slowly and kissing her softly on the lips.

"You're also sweet, and romantic, and handsome, and intelligent. And mine," she says, as she opens her eyes recovering from the kiss.

"Good, now can we go?"

"Yes," she laughs.

I grab her hand and yank her hard, pulling her through the hallways and out of the building. I make sure to walk as fast as I can out of the building, so she doesn't have time to talk to anyone.

She takes her time climbing into the front seat of the pickup truck, that I'm not allowed to drive for some reason, while Grump and I climb into the passenger seat in record time. I give her an annoyed look as she slowly starts up the engine. It doesn't start at first. Instead, it makes a weird clicking sound. We live just down the road from here, but I'm afraid it's going to take hours to get home at this rate.

"Can I buy you a new car yet?"

"No, I don't need a new car. This one works fine. And when I need a new car, I'll be buying it myself."

I sigh. We've had this fight a dozen times. The first video game that we launched is exceeding our expectations and I'm earning a ridiculous salary. Skye makes more than enough money on her vet clinic. She needs a new car, but she won't spend a penny on anything until it actually breaks.

She tries to start the car again and this time it starts up. At least we aren't walking home, although at this rate, it might be faster.

She starts driving again.

"Care to go a little faster?" I ask, as I look down at the ten miles an hour reading on the dash.

She laughs. "In a hurry for something?"

"Yes, in fact."

"And what would that be?"

"I have two things in mind. One, fuck your brains out."

She grins and nods. "Of course. And two?"

"You'll have to wait and see."

She raises an eyebrow, but doesn't question me.

She has barely parked the car when I throw my door open and let Grump out. He, at least, moves quickly. Then I race to her door, throwing it open as well, and pulling her into my arms.

She squeals as I carry her inside.

"You really are in a hurry, aren't you?"

I nod, as I pull her bottom lip into my mouth. "I've struggled to work all day while I was thinking about what I would get to do with you tonight."

Her eyes darken. "What plans did you dream up this time?"

I smirk. "You'll see."

I step inside the house and immediately get swarmed by all of her pets that have somehow multiplied since I moved in. I will never admit it to her, but I do love being around all the animals. But right now they are not a priority. If I put her down, our entire night will be spent giving them attention and I'll never get her back.

She sees the look in my eyes and wraps her arms around my neck

587

as she starts kissing me again. "Fuck me. I want to know what mischievous thing you have in mind."

I kiss her lips, shutting her up, as I head to the bedroom. When I get inside, I kick the door shut keeping our pets out, so that I can have Skye all to myself.

I watch as Skye's eyes widen when she looks around the room at the rose petals around the room and the swing attached to the closet doorframe.

"What's this?"

"A new toy."

"And the rose petals?"

"I thought we could mix a little romance with our dirty sex."

She grins.

I don't wait for her to ask more questions or figure out anything more about what's going on. I grab the hem of her shirt and lift it over her head. She shimmies out of her scrubs and my eyes burn into her black lace panties and bra that she wore beneath her scrubs just for me.

"Like what you see?"

"Love."

She bites her lip and blushes. She does every time that I use the word love. She's about to blush a lot more tonight.

I push her body against the door, where the swing is and kiss down her neck, loving the taste of her skin. She smells like heaven when I kiss her. A mix of sweat, lavender, and sex.

She eyes the swing behind her with a nervous glance. "Have you tested this out to make sure that we don't break my door?"

I bite her bottom lip to shut her up from asking stupid questions. Then I lift her body up, slip each of her legs into the swing, and then tie her hands up at the top so that she can't move.

Her eyes go up to her hands and then down to me.

"Did you want me to test it out first?" I ask, knowing that she really didn't. She loves the thrill and excitement. Of course, I made sure that she wouldn't break the door, but she doesn't need to know that. She's a thrill seeker that lives for this.

I don't let her answer the question. Instead, my lips push aside the lace covering her pussy and I lick her clit, then slide into her already dripping pussy.

Her body clenches around me as her moans fill the room.

"God, I love your pussy."

I watch, as she struggles against the restraints in the swing. I love watching her body spread wide for me.

I take a step back and remove my shirt, loving the look she gives me when she sees my shirtless body. I take my time removing my jeans and boxer briefs. At least, I attempt to move as slowly as I can. Usually, I can be patient; take my time and really savor her. Not tonight.

Tonight, I need to make her mine.

I walk back to her and loop my finger between her panties and skin and rip them to pieces.

"You owe me new panties."

I smirk. "It was worth it," I growl.

I grab her hips, as my cock hardens at just the sight of her naked pussy. My cock rests at her entrance as our lips collide and I push inside her. She feels tight and slick and welcoming. She moans, as I thrust in and out of her.

"Harder," she moans.

I do. She may be tied up and unable to move, but she still has control, even if she doesn't think she does.

I fuck her harder and harder, her body easy to move in the swing. Her eyes roll back in her head, and she bites her lip harder before she screams my name.

I come inside of her, filling her with my cum.

"That was amazing," she says with tired breath.

I grin. "You like that?"

She nods.

"Now help me down."

I hold up one finger as I slip out of her and walk over and pick up my boxer briefs. I slip them and my jeans back on before I walk back to her.

"Down. Now."

I grin and cock my head to one side. "And why would I do that?"

She frowns. "Fuck me again or help me down. You're not leaving me like this."

I sigh and help her remove her legs from the swing, leaving her arms tied.

"And now my arms."

I take a deep breath and then kneel down in front of her.

"What are you doing?" she asks, sounding annoyed.

I reach into my back pocket and pull out a small box. "I'm proposing."

She snickers. "You are not proposing with me still naked and tied up."

"I am too, it's the only way you will let me propose."

She frowns.

"Now...Skye, I love you with everything I have. I've wanted to marry you since the first time I fucked you. I know I've screwed up and that you deserve better, but let me spend eternity making it up to you. Marry me?"

Her eyes widen.

"No."

I sigh. I knew this would be a fight. It's why I proposed with her tied up.

I stand back up. "No? I thought you loved me?"

"I do."

"Then why won't you marry me?"

"Because I don't want to."

"That's not a reason."

"Because technically, I'm still married to Gabe."

I roll my eyes. "He's in prison and you can easily get that annulled. That's not the problem. What's the real reason?"

She sighs. "I don't want to get married, ever."

"Why?"

"Marriage doesn't mean anything. I married Gabe and you saw how well that worked out."

"That's because he coerced you."

"And what are you doing?"

"Asking, very persuasively."

She frowns. "I'm not a normal woman. I don't want normal things. I don't need kids, I'm happy with my pets. I don't need a husband, I'm happy with my partner. Why can't you get that?"

I run my hand through my hair. "I can. You're right. I shouldn't pressure you."

I walk over and place the box on the nightstand and then I start walking to the bedroom door. I open it and start walking out.

"You can't leave me like this!"

"I'll be back when I'm ready to fuck you again." I've left her tied up plenty of times before. It only makes the next round better.

"Wait!"

I stop. Is she going to use her safe word? She hasn't the entire time I've been with her and I've pushed her limits pretty far.

I turn around and walk back into the bedroom, standing in the doorway and loving looking at her standing naked.

"Why is marriage so important to you?"

I think for a moment. "Because it's getting married to you. I love you. I want every experience possible with you. I want the world to know that over all the other assholes in the world, for some reason, you chose me. I want to call you my wife. I want to celebrate you with all of our friends. I want to marry you because I love you."

She sucks in a deep breath, and I think maybe, she might change her mind. Maybe, she'll say yes.

"You're a dick."

I smirk. *Wrong as usual.*

She opens her mouth again and her lips curl up into a grin. "But I love you. I want to spend the rest of my life with you. And if you want to get married then...yes, I'll marry you."

I grin and run back over to her, kissing her firmly on the lips.

"And I'm not saying yes because you tied me up and forced me to talk to you about it."

I laugh and undo the ties on her wrists, releasing her.

She wraps her arms around my neck as she eyes the box on the nightstand. "And if that is a diamond ring, I'm not wearing it."

I shake my head. "Well, open it."

She lets go of my neck and walks over to the box and opens it. She takes the piece of paper out and begins to unfold it.

"What is it?"

"I didn't think you were much of a diamonds person, so this is a picture of a tattoo that I got designed that I figured we could both tattoo on our bodies in lieu of wearing a ring."

She stares down at the picture a tattoo that represents everything she is. Fierce, loving, and strong.

"I love it."

"I love you."

I kiss her again.

"You're still an ass, you know."

I grin. "I know. And tomorrow I'll be a prick, or a romantic, or a jerk, or whatever you want to call me. But I'll always be a man that loves you."

The End

Thank you so much for reading!

If you want to receive updates on when the next book is coming and get a FREE book sign up here: ellamiles.com/freebooks

ORDER SIGNED PAPERBACKS

I love putting my signed paperbacks on SALE!

Check them out by visiting my website:
https://ellamiles.com/signed-paperbacks

ALSO BY ELLA MILES

SINFUL TRUTHS:

Sinful Truth #1

Twisted Vow #2

Reckless Fall #3

Tangled Promise #4

Fallen Love #5

Broken Anchor #6

TRUTH OR LIES:

Taken by Lies #1

Betrayed by Truths #2

Trapped by Lies #3

Stolen by Truths #4

Possessed by Lies #5

Consumed by Truths #6

DIRTY SERIES:

Dirty Beginning

Dirty Obsession

Dirty Addiction

Dirty Revenge

Dirty: The Complete Series

ALIGNED SERIES:

Aligned: Volume 1 (Free Series Starter)

Aligned: Volume 2

Aligned: Volume 3

Aligned: Volume 4

Aligned: The Complete Series Boxset

UNFORGIVABLE SERIES:

Heart of a Thief

Heart of a Liar

Heart of a Prick

Unforgivable: The Complete Series Boxset

MAYBE, DEFINITELY SERIES:

Maybe Yes

Maybe Never

Maybe Always

Definitely Yes

Definitely No

Definitely Forever

STANDALONES:

ABOUT THE AUTHOR

Ella Miles writes steamy romance, including everything from dark suspense romance that will leave you on the edge of your seat to contemporary romance that will leave you laughing out loud or crying. Most importantly, she wants you to feel everything her characters feel as you read.

Ella is currently living her own happily ever after near the Rocky Mountains with her high school sweetheart husband. Her heart is also taken by her goofy five year old black lab who is scared of everything, including her own shadow.

Ella is a USA Today Bestselling Author & Top 50 Bestselling Author.

Stalk Ella at:
www.ellamiles.com
ella@ellamiles.com